W9-BRN-339

"A WINNER. . .
Forceful prose, psychological overtones, and a well-constructed plot."
—Library Journal

"METHODS OF EXECUTION is half-thriller, half-mystery, half–courtroom drama, half–tragic romance. That's four halves, which is about right considering the density of the plot and character packed into this book. You won't find many novels with as complex a story (though perfectly lucid) or as finely chiseled inhabitants. This is not a book that yields its secrets easily."
—Lexington Herald-Leader

The best elements of the classic mystery, a blending of Robert Parker's Spenser and John Grisham's legal storytelling, make this an unbeatable read."
—Elliott Bay Booknotes

"Dense, turbulent, and just sleazy enough for the squeamish."
—Kirkus Reviews

By Fredrick D. Huebner
Published by Fawcett Books:

THE JOSHUA SEQUENCE
THE BLACK ROSE
JUDGMENT BY FIRE
PICTURE POSTCARD
METHODS OF EXECUTION

METHODS
OF
EXECUTION

Fredrick D. Huebner

FAWCETT GOLD MEDAL • NEW YORK

A Fawcett Gold Medal Book
Published by Ballantine Books
Copyright © 1994 by Fredrick D. Huebner

Library of Congress Catalog Card Number: 93-21303

ISBN 0-449-14939-0

This edition published by arrangement with Simon & Schuster, Inc.

Manufactured in the United States

First Ballantine Books Edition: June 1995

10 9 8 7 6 5 4 3 2 1

AUTHOR'S NOTE

This is a work of fiction. In the course of this book, I refer to the King County Prosecutor's Office, the Superior Court of King County, the Washington Court of Appeals, the Washington Supreme Court, the Seattle Police Department, and the King County Police Department. My use of these institutions is intended to convey the veneer of reality, not its substance. The people and events described in this novel are wholly fictional.

My thanks go to Dr. Colleen Morisset, for sharing her psychologist's knowledge of the human condition; to attorney Anne Bremner, for her expertise in the art of criminal law; to Judges William Downing and Robert Lasnik of the King County Superior Court, for sharing some of their experiences in death-penalty cases; to my law partners, especially Bruce Benson, Phil Noble, Jim Frush, and Brad Bagshaw, for friendship, support, and the time to complete this book; to Clyde Taylor, who never gives up; and to Donna Barnes and Jan Anderson, who read my briefs and my books with the same fine critical eye. Any errors of fact, law, procedure, or judgment, are mine, not theirs.

For all that I owe these exceptional people, this book is for my daughter, Katherine, with the hope that she will see a better world than the one her father knows.

Show me a hero. I'll write you a tragedy.

—F. Scott Fitzgerald

JANUARY

CHAPTER 1

The house stood on seven acres of old-growth timber and hay meadow at the end of a gravel road a dozen miles northwest of the town of Quilcene, on the Olympic Peninsula. It was tall and square, with a peaked, shingled roof, rather like an old New England barn. I bought it half-finished, empty for over a year. The original owner had done the hard work: pouring the foundation, raising the frame and closing it in, drilling the well, and installing the septic tank and drain field. He had built well. The frame was honest six-inch post-and-beam, the board siding straight-grain cedar, the double windows framed in clear fir. The federal property manager who sold me the place said he was an honest farmer of the modern sort, growing high-quality marijuana in hidden fields in the Olympic National Forest.

I was laying the subfloor for the sleeping loft, toe-nailing square sheets of thick plywood to the floor joists, when I heard the pounding from the front door. I brushed sawdust from my jeans, scrambled down the ladder, and opened the door. Elizabeth Kleinfeldt stood on the cedar deck, dressed in tights and a thick wool sweater. Her short black hair was tangled from the wind and damp with rain. I stepped aside to let her in. She rushed past me to the tall river-rock fireplace that I was using for heat and stood in front of the fire, hands extended to the warmth of the flames.

"You bastard," she said, half a laugh hiding behind her words. She turned away from the fire to kiss me, her dark eyes alive and merry. "I should have known you'd build a house in

3

the rain forest. My car is stuck fifty yards down your road, in a mud puddle bigger than I am."

"This is the dry side of the Olympics," I replied. "You ought to be over on the coast. They get real rain there. Don't worry about your car. I'll go winch it out for you."

"Leave it there," she commanded with mock severity. "As a warning to others. Have you got anything to drink? I'm freezing."

I went into what would someday be the kitchen and took a bottle of Irish whiskey, a blue-enameled steel coffeepot, and two mugs from a roughed-in set of shelves and brought them to the fireplace. Liz was sitting on an old wooden chair left in the house when I bought it. Her bare, dance-calloused feet were propped on the stone hearth, her leather boots and socks drying in front of the fire. "Limited choices," I said, holding up a bottle of Bushmill's.

She smiled. "It will do, thank you."

I pulled an empty wooden crate over beside her and poured her coffee laced with whiskey. Liz sipped at it and shuddered from the sudden warmth. I felt, as I always did in her presence, the jolt of connection, an emotional electricity that had never quite gone away, even when we were angry or had not seen each other for a long time. I started to say something but then stopped, content for that moment simply to be with her in the fading winter light.

Liz always seemed smaller than I remembered, scarcely five feet tall, as slender at thirty-seven as she had been when dancing with the American Ballet Theatre. She had taken off her heavy wool sweater, and the black leotard she wore displayed the strong, graceful curves of her arms and shoulders. Her large brown eyes were flecked with gold, set in an elegant, angular face. She still danced at six o'clock every morning, her way of keeping something clean and precise and personal for herself.

I had met Liz Kleinfeldt six years before, when she prosecuted an arson-murder case against a friend of mine named Hugh Prokop. Hugh owned a failing marine hardware business. His warehouse burned and his accountant was found dead in the ruins. Hugh was charged when a briefcase stuffed with a quarter million dollars in cash turned up in his office safe. I reluctantly defended him, certain he was not telling me the truth about the source of the money and the cause of the fire. The trial went badly. Hugh's lies exploded in the courtroom, shredding his defense. He killed himself before the verdict. I later learned that he was innocent, but had committed suicide to avoid testifying about a money-laundering and fraud scheme being carried out by his girlfriend, a stockbroker, and the man who owned the brokerage firm she worked for. After many months of painful consideration I understood Hugh's decision, and accepted it. I had never been able to shake the guilt. There should have been some way to discover the truth before Hugh was forced to his terrible choice.

When the case was over, Liz and I became friends, then lovers. Our relationship was a stormy one, between two strong-minded adults. We broke it off a year later when it became clear that our battles over everything from our divergent ambitions to the latest Supreme Court decision were threatening the core of respect we had for each other. We designed a pain-free modern parting, still friends, no regrets. It didn't work out that way, of course. It never does. The fact that we saw each other only two or three times in the first year after we parted was not an accident. After that year the wounds, self-inflicted and otherwise, healed and we cautiously recovered the love and friendship we had nearly destroyed. That gift was tempered by a sense of loss from knowing that we might never find others who completed us the way that we completed each other.

"Aside from the fact that you're pissed at having to come up here," I said, "how the hell are you? I've missed you."

"Tired," she said. She looked it. Even in repose I could see the lines of strain around her eyes. "But the trip up here did me good. Sitting on the ferry drinking coffee and watching the water, driving these back roads with Bach blasting out of the stereo." She yawned and stretched. "I haven't had a day off in weeks."

"That's life at the top," I said sarcastically. Liz had left the prosecutor's office a couple of years before and joined Seattle's newest mega law firm, Lisle, Day & Elgot, as the rising star of their white-collar criminal defense practice, walking proof that crime didn't just pay, it was a growth industry.

She hadn't missed the edge in my voice but said nothing. She finished her coffee and held out her cup. I poured in an inch of whiskey and handed it back. She declined more coffee and stirred the whiskey with a finger, a nervous gesture. I waited. She would not waste too much time on small talk.

"Did you read the stuff I sent you?" she asked anxiously.

"You got it over three weeks ago." She looked away from me, staring into the fire.

"The Polhaus trial transcript? Yes, I read it, and the appellate decisions, and the book of press clippings you sent." I hesitated. "You want my reaction as a former lawyer or as a citizen?"

"Both."

"Robert Polhaus, better known in the press as the Motel Room Killer." I sat back in my chair, trying to remember the basic facts of the case. "A serial killer. Derives sexual gratification from the abuse, humiliation, and death of women. Convicted of strangling two prostitutes, both from escort services. Probably killed a third but the case couldn't be made. They stopped him, thank God, after three victims. The prosecution did a fair job putting together a difficult circumstantial case. The defense strategy of putting him on the stand to explain away the physical evidence was risky and didn't work. That's the lawyer talking. As a citizen I think the son of a bitch should hang." I paused and drank some of my coffee. "My real question is what the hell you're doing with this."

She stiffened, her jaw setting in controlled anger. She did not like what I had said, or the way I had said it. "I've never believed in the death penalty," she began. "I know you do; we've argued about it before. The Death Penalty Defense Group asked me to take a look at this case. Death sentences, statewide, are coming so fast now that they can't keep up."

She put her mug down on the hearth and leaned forward intently. "I had the damnedest feeling when I read the trial transcript. I read it as a prosecutor, put myself in that frame of mind. I kept coming back to one thought: that if it was my case I would have sent it back to the police for more investigation. That something wasn't there."

I shook my head. "Polhaus was made to order for this, Liz. The guy has a history of violence, he's antisocial, hates women, abuses them as part of his sexual pattern. His jacket had what, three rape charges, four assaults? And five convictions. He was a battered child, sexually abused himself. The physical evidence from the crime lab was strong. They found hair from two of the victims in his car. And a semen stain on the bed sheet underneath the third victim that matched his DNA. That's damned near conclusive."

"No, it's not," she replied doggedly. "Look at it another way. There were three victims—Suzanne Parker, Melody

Beasely, and Sharee Klimka." She ticked them off on her fingers. "Polhaus admitted knowing Beasely and Klimka, because they had worked as prostitutes in motels where he worked. But they were the second and third victims. Polhaus wasn't charged in Parker's murder—the first one in the series—because they had no way to tie him to it, no physical evidence or testimony that he was ever in the motel room where she was killed. Yet that murder—the motel room, the prostitute victim, the strangulation with a cloth—was identical. With Beasely's murder, there was no sign of any sexual activity, voluntary or not. And with Klimka, he admitted he'd had sex with her in the room where she was killed. If he had raped her, the semen would have been in her, or on her body. That's the usual pattern." She looked stubborn. "The whole theory of the prosecution was that Polhaus was a serial killer, like Ted Bundy, or the Green River Killer. When you look at the case the first time, it seems to fit that scenario. But it's not quite right. Serial killers usually prey on strangers, not people they know. These killings aren't marked by the killer's psychological progression, the development of an elaborate fantasy, and a ritual to go with it. The killer didn't hide the bodies, or bury them, or try to play games with the police. I know this stuff. I worked in the Sexual Assault Unit for three years. I was the prosecutor's liaison to the Green River Task Force for two years. I've been to the FBI crime lab at Quantico, Virginia, and talked to their psychologists. This case doesn't hang together."

I did not know enough about the studies that had been made of serial murders to argue with her, but I had cross-examined enough shrinks to be deeply skeptical of psychological profiling as a means of solving crimes.

"Did they ever find a murder weapon?" I asked.

"No. George Eakins, the criminalist from the state crime lab, testified that he thought it was probably a man's tie. He found a couple of polyester threads that looked like they could have come from a cheap tie. But they couldn't match them to anything Polhaus had in his room."

"So he threw it away."

"Possibly. But they never found the bludgeon, either. Or whatever the killer used to knock the women out before he strangled them."

"Might have been a sock filled with sand or gravel. I've been hit with one of those and they can do one hell of a lot of damage."

"Again, possible. But it seems like we're doing an awful lot of speculation about a case that's already been proved beyond a reasonable doubt." She frowned and shook her head, as if she were still trying to work through the problem. "The police seized on Polhaus as the killer because he'd worked in two of the motels where the victims were killed. As soon as they ID'd him and did the DNA test, they stopped looking at any other suspects. Polhaus testified that there were two possible witnesses to the third killing, a man standing on the balcony at the China Tapestry Motel, and a woman, dressed like a hooker, running away from the scene. Nobody ever followed that up, looked for those witnesses. They had a case they knew they could sell." She paused, then added, "Serial killings are the hardest kind of murder case to solve. But with this one it was almost too easy, too pat. Almost as if Polhaus fell into the killer's scenario."

"Maybe that's how it smells to you," I said skeptically, "but I don't buy it. Polhaus's story about those witnesses was pretty weak. He didn't mention them in his first statement, didn't bring them up until the trial." I shrugged, then added, "You're reading too much into the fact that they proved the case with circumstantial evidence."

She sighed, frustrated. "I could be. But in a way that's the point. You don't go for the death penalty on just circumstantial evidence."

"Why not? The King County Prosecutor's Office has one of the best reputations in the country for handling death-penalty cases. They've sought the penalty only in extreme cases."

"That's the way it's supposed to work. In death cases, the prosecutor has a duty to make his or her own inquiry in deciding whether to seek the death penalty. Jurors are death-qualified, so their personal sense of morality won't stop them from giving a death sentence. The typical homicide defendant is the worst human being a juror is ever likely to see. The average juror would sentence more killers to death than we ever charge. We won't give the jury a chance to give a death sentence to anyone but the worst of the worst."

"Polhaus qualifies. He murdered three women barely out of their teens. Thank God we've evolved enough so that the legal system no longer just says 'hooker killing' and pleads a case like this out cheap."

She bit her lip, frustrated. "I'm not explaining this right. Polhaus didn't fit the 'right-guy' test. The prosecutor's office will let the jury make the fine moral distinctions a capital case requires—but only if the office is one hundred percent certain that the accused is the right guy. I'm talking beyond reasonable doubt. I mean *no* doubt. They've had horrible cases, multiple victims, and the death penalty wasn't sought because the evidence was circumstantial. Circumstantial evidence is never one hundred percent certain."

"So what went wrong here? Why did they go after the death penalty for Polhaus?"

"Dan Merritt," she said angrily.

"I don't know much about him. I tried one case against him, maybe six years ago. He was just a kid, three or four years out of law school."

"He's the chief of staff for Ed Warren, the county prosecutor. He's one of the reasons I quit. Merritt's only thirty-six. He's political as hell. Ed promoted him to run the office, and run it hard, when Ed went after the vacant U.S. Senate seat two years ago."

"Warren came close that time. Is he going to try again?"

"No. Ed's done with politics. But Merritt's going to run for state attorney general this fall, with Ed's blessing. No one else is running in the democratic primary. Merritt can pick up the nomination cheap. For the past four years, Merritt's been cherry-picking the cases he takes, looking for the ones that will make him look hard as nails on crime, especially sex crimes. He helped push through the new sex-offender statute that provides for preventive detention of sexual offenders if they're deemed dangerous, even if they commit no additional crimes." She shook her head and looked grim. "Polhaus was Merritt's trophy case, his first and only death-penalty conviction. Merritt's got a real shot at getting elected if the conviction stands up. He'll be a handsome new face, hard on crime. That's going to sell."

"That could cut into his liberal support."

"I don't think so, Matthew. Sexual crimes cut across a lot of political lines. It's strong with women voters. We may be liberal on other issues, but on crime we want a lot of policing, and we're not so fussy anymore about how it's done. Think about it. You never have to worry about where you go, how you protect yourself. You're big, you stay in fair shape, nobody is going to hassle you, not even on Second Avenue at two in the morning." She looked away and her voice dropped a little. "There's over a hundred thousand women in this state who have been raped. I was raped seven years ago. You're as good as any man I've met at trying to be empathetic about it, but you can't know what it's like. I live like a paranoid. I don't park in some parking garages because they have rotten security systems. I keep the windows in my house locked at night, even in summer. I take cabs home from the courthouse after dark, rather than walk to my car. Women live with that fear all the time, every day. And Merritt's smart. He's going to exploit it."

She could be right, but it seemed to me that we had gone a long way from the case of Robert Polhaus. I shook my head. "I still think you're reaching when you say Merritt got a death sentence for Polhaus just to polish his résumé."

"Maybe I am," she said doggedly. "Okay. With Polhaus's record, with more investigation, under the charging guidelines they should have charged Murder One, gone for a life sentence." Her voice hardened again with anger. "But Merritt was looking for a case to hang the death penalty on a sex offender, a serial killer. Robert Polhaus was just the right guy at the right time."

CHAPTER 2

The last of the afternoon light was gone. I broke up the coals and laid fresh driftwood on the fire. The blue-green flames from the sea salt in the wood danced in the shadows of the room. Liz stared silently into the fire. In so many ways she was a stronger person than I was, passionate in her work, committed to her beliefs, a better lawyer for risking herself for her clients. I had replaced that kind of commitment with black irony, too content now to stage a performance and stand to one side, telling myself how amusing life was. Or ought to be. But it seemed to me that Liz had gone beyond dedication to mounting a one-horse crusade based on the thinnest of doubts.

"I don't get this," I said, pouring myself another drink. "When you were the head of the Sexual Assault Unit, you were the nastiest prosecutor this state had ever seen. I remember the names they used to call you. The Ayatollah. The head of the Women's Revenge Squad. This guy is no different than the ones you put away. He's the worst kind of shit."

Her mouth suddenly twisted into something very much like grief. She swallowed some of the whiskey in her mug. "It reminds me a little too much of another case," she said softly. "I tried it a year before I met you. Nguyen Tranh."

"I don't remember that one."

"No reason you should. Tranh was a Vietnamese gang banger. He broke into a wealthy Chinese woman's home, on Beacon Hill, with another kid. She was nearly seventy. One of them raped her. When her daughter came home, he raped her, too. When they finished ransacking the place, one of them shot both of them. We busted Tranh and the other boy—they were only seventeen—the next day, trying to fence the stuff from the house. The other kid broke right away. He told us that Tranh was the shooter, had done the rapes. He pleaded out and testified. The forensic skin analysis backed him up. We didn't have DNA tests then and the blood-typing showed that either kid could have been the rapist. I got Tranh the death penalty the day he turned eighteen. The case was appealed four times. All rejected. They hanged him in December."

"I still don't understand. And I don't have much sympathy."

"When Tranh was executed, the lab tech from the state crime lab who worked on the case came to see me. He was hysterical. It took him a while, but he finally came out with it. He said that he'd accidentally switched the lab results. Got the names backward. He figured it out during the trial. He didn't tell anybody. He was afraid he'd lose his job." Her voice suddenly broke. "Oh, God, I couldn't tell anybody this, not even you."

She wept. I took her in my arms and held her awkwardly. She shook with self-anger and grief.

"Tranh wasn't the shooter," she cried hoarsely. "He wasn't the rapist. But he's dead. The other kid gets out of Monroe next year. The lab tech said he never thought they'd really hang him."

"You couldn't have known," I said softly, as the spasms

subsided. I caressed her cheek, felt the wetness there. "Legally he was just as guilty as if he'd been the shooter."

She pushed my hand away. "We couldn't have asked for the death penalty if we'd known. It was my job to know. My much celebrated sense of smell." Her voice was filled with quiet disgust. "I can't let that happen again."

"Lizabeth," I said, taking her hands and slipping into the pet name I had called her when we were lovers, "you don't know that Polhaus is innocent. You don't have a single piece of persuasive evidence. Polhaus's conviction has been reviewed three times. It was a clean trial, no legal error. Even you have to admit that."

She nodded. "But that's not the only way."

"Oh, Christ," I said suddenly. "Now I get it. You're going to attack the death sentence on the basis of actual innocence, aren't you? You know what you have to prove under the *Herrera versus Texas* standard? You've got the burden of proof, and the evidence has to be 'extraordinarily persuasive,' whatever the hell that means. You've got a little over three months before the April 20 execution date. There's no way you can conduct your own investigation and come up with solid new evidence in that amount of time, even if there was something to be found." I shook my head. "And it's so old, Liz. The murders were committed over four years ago. The victims weren't stable, middle-class people. Any witnesses are going to be long gone."

"I know all that," she said, impatient with my doubts. "I've filed a personal-restraint petition in the state court of appeals and moved to stay the execution. Our brief's due in mid-February, and the hearing will be in late March. We'll rehash the legal issues the best we can, probably lose, then appeal up to the state supreme court. I can buy him six months more if we're lucky. In the meantime we keep digging. If something turns up we amend the petition, based on new evidence. Or we could seek clemency, get his sentence dropped to life."

I shook my head, dismayed. "Death-penalty litigation is trench warfare, Liz. The best you can hope for is to stretch this thing out for another year, at most two, before they execute him. And you'll wear this damned case like a hair shirt the entire time." I got up and poured myself a drink, then put it down on the hearth. "I've never seen you like this before. You put your heart into your cases, but you knew how to walk away when you were done, with your sense of self intact.

You're better at that than I was. That's why you're still in the law, and I'm not." I hesitated, then added, "You can't make decisions based on guilt over a mistake. You have your own life to consider. We didn't stay together long enough to think seriously about children, but the time is getting short for both of us."

She looked away. "This is my life. It's what I do. This is what you used to do. Before you quit." She reached up with both hands and pulled me back down beside her. Her eyes searched mine. "You've never told me why you quit the law, Matthew, not really. You've made jokes and dodged and never answered me. You had a good practice, respect, enough money. You're only forty-three. What happened?"

I got up and paced the room. "I got tired of three-day all-nighters," I said at last. "I got tired of too many damned lawyers chasing too few legitimate cases. I got tired of listening to people lie on the stand. I got tired of clients who want a high-class leg breaker, somebody who'll make the other guy hurt, make him bleed, fuck up his life, tie up his property. I got tired of a life that I couldn't share with anyone, not even with you." Even as I spoke I knew the words sounded empty and selfish. But how do you explain a self-hatred that grows in you like a cancer, metastasizes into your bones?

"How will you live?" she asked quietly.

"I'll get by. I've paid my taxes. A rich idiot bought my old house at the top of the market, desperate to have sixty feet of deeded Lake Washington waterfront to moor his boat in. I have a small apartment in the city and this place, both paid for. I grew up on a ranch in Montana, remember? We ate icebox soup and beans for fifteen years."

I picked up my cup and downed the whiskey in one swallow, feeling it hit like a hot wet angry hammer, my body not used to alcohol after the last sober, careful months leading to my decision to leave the law. "It's over for me," I added bitterly. "The whole damn show. I'm a fair carpenter. It's clean work. If the money runs out, I can always do that."

Liz was stunned into silence by the depth of my anger. "I wish I had known how you felt," she said at last. "Because I've boxed myself into a corner on this thing. I've asked for four months to handle this full-time. I can't get it. The firm hates this case. The managing partner, Jack Elgot, is after my scalp. He sees nothing but a filthy sex killer, and all the bad publicity that entails." She shook her head wearily. "But I can't let this go. Not when there's a chance Polhaus will be executed for crimes he didn't commit."

"What do you think I can do?" I asked skeptically.

"Give me sixty days," she said, her voice low, pleading. "Two months. I'll handle the legal side. You take over the investigation. I can't pay you a fee, but the firm can cover your expenses. If you're convinced in sixty days that there's nothing to go on, no new evidence to be found, you can withdraw. But give me that sixty days."

I shook my head. "No. I'm done with the law. Hire a good investigator. Your firm can afford it."

"It wouldn't be the same. I need someone who won't just walk through the paces."

"But why me? Let's be coldly accurate for a moment. I am a burned-out lawyer who did not get rich, did not get famous, did not win all his cases. I lost the most important case I handled in the last six years. To you, as I recall. I did worse than lose. My client killed himself. That wasn't someone else's mistake. That was mine."

She ignored my outburst of self-pity. She poured herself another drink, too much for her small body to absorb. When she spoke again her voice was quiet, scarcely above a whisper. "I hate asking this," she said, head bowed. "I've never asked or needed anything from anyone. But this is the hardest thing I have ever tried to do. I don't know if I can do it alone. I need you with me."

"Not good enough, Liz." The words came out more harshly than I meant them. She stiffened as if she'd been slapped.

"All right," she said coldly. "All right. Because, if you think about it, you need this. Or something like it. Your best quality, Matthew, is that when you get hold of something, you don't quit. Or haven't, until now. I remember the Prokop case. I remember how you couldn't let it go, not even after he killed himself. You saw things that didn't fit, things that no one else saw. You followed your instincts. And you were right." She finished her drink and poured more whiskey in her cup. I saw that she was on the edge of being drunk but made no move to stop her.

"It's sad," she said sarcastically, a bright sharp edge to her voice now. "I've watched you this past year. You turned down the hard cases, dumped your criminal practice, wasted your time grinding out a bunch of contracts and real estate closings. Then you quit. You're hiding up here. What are you so afraid of? What made you lose your nerve?" She waited a moment, then added in a harder voice than I had ever heard her use, "I really hope you haven't fallen apart. I need your obsessiveness, that neurotic quality that drives you. If you find anything that doesn't fit, you'll follow it. I intend to use you for that." She drank again, her words starting to slur now. "Forget about Polhaus for a minute. Think of me, damn it. Me. Because my career and my self-respect are hanging by a thread with this case. Is that a good, selfish reason, the kind even you can understand?"

I stormed out of the house, sunk deep in anger. I stood on the deck and watched the heavy clouds drop from Mount Walker into the Quilcene Valley. The wind picked up and forced the rain into needles that stung my face.

Liz followed me outside. "You're playing Lear," she said, grabbing my arm. "Raging into the storm. There's no one to hear you, Matthew. No one to say, 'Oh, tragic figger of a man.'"

"Lear," I said tightly, turning to face her, "tried his case to a jury consisting of a fool and a madman. I won't do that anymore. Not even for you."

Liz reached up and slapped me as hard as she could. "Damn it. When we fell apart and you left me, you said that if I was ever in trouble you would help me. Well, former lover, I am in trouble. Big time. My client is going to die. I am calling in every marker I have with you. What are you going to do?"

I stared into her angry wounded eyes. Tears mixed with rain on her face. "Feed you," I said coldly. "Beef stew out of a can on a Coleman stove, if you'll eat it. Let you sleep here, so you don't get killed driving drunk on sixty miles of bad road back to the ferry. Pull your car out of the mud tomorrow morning. And try to forget that you ever showed up here."

In the next three days I worked to exhaustion, from six in the morning until well past midnight, driven by anger. I had made my separate peace. I was free of the game, free of taking responsibility for other people's lives, no longer holding the key to the courthouse door. I did not live with the daily fear of not being good enough, smart enough, ruthless enough.

With time the anger faded into painful understanding. I had quit practicing law because I could not resolve for myself the conflict between legal truth and larger truth. I knew that I could not, would not, throw myself into the fight for people like Robert Polhaus, who lacked a conscience, or a soul.

It is not a fine moralistic debating point. The lawyer with such doubts lacks the last ounce of guile, the last inch of steel. That lawyer can get even an innocent man killed.

As I had with Hugh Prokop.

I woke before dawn on the fourth morning after Liz left and drove over the Hood Canal Bridge to the Bainbridge Island Ferry, riding the seven o'clock boat with a mob of sleepy commuters. I stared moodily at the rain falling on the black water, sunk deep in thought. Remembered images drifted through my sleep-starved mind. Liz striding into my house on Saturday mornings in a ragged leotard, gleaming with sweat and laughing from the sheer joy she found in dancing. Liz sitting cross-legged on the floor of my office at three o'clock in the morning, listening patiently as I rehearsed jury arguments. "No, no, back off, you'll scare them," she had corrected, laughing gently, hopping to her feet to push me away. "You're too damned big, you black Irish ox. Slower, softer. *Seduce* them. Christ, it's a good thing you can't dance." And, hardest of all, waking from the wind rattling through the palm-frond roof of a Mexican beach house to find Liz propped up on one elbow, watching me sleep, eyes shining even in the dark.

I would have to put aside my own doubts and fears, somehow borrow Liz's faith. But in those three bitter days I came to understand that I could not let her go out of my life. Not like this.

When the ferry docked I got my car from the auto deck and drove home though the downtown Seattle traffic. And finally, reluctantly, in the late morning quiet of my Capitol Hill apartment, I typed my name and the caption from *In Re Polhaus*, a personal restraint petition, onto a form notice of appearance and mailed it to Liz, for entry before the court.

FEBRUARY

CHAPTER 3

A late-winter norther cleared the skies over the Walla Walla Valley. A thin snow had fallen and dusted the fields of wheat stubble white. To the east and south the dark-forested shoulders of the Blue Mountains rose over the valley. The bright sun was a welcome contrast to Seattle's coat of winter gray. Had our task been different, Liz and I would have filled the rented car with cheerful talk instead of marching through a review of our notes as we drove from the airport to the state penitentiary.

Walla Walla had been founded near the pioneer Whitman Mission, forty miles from the banks of the Columbia River in southeastern Washington, on the path of Lewis and Clark and the Oregon Trail. It is a handsome-enough small town, with generous shade trees on its main streets, a sophisticated small college, Whitman, and one of the more unpleasant American gulags just outside its borders. The Walla Walla prison is the hardest in the state system, a gray stone fortress that houses Washington's only death row.

We stood near the main visitor entrance to the prison, waiting for the escort who would take us across the prison yard to 5 wing, outside the old prison walls, where the thirty-four prisoners on death row lived in two tiers of isolation cells in the prison's Intensive Management Unit. We would not be allowed onto death row itself, but only into an interview room in 5 wing set aside for inmates to meet with their lawyers. Robert Polhaus would be brought down to see us, his hands manacled to a waist belt and his ankles cuffed together by a short length of chain. Once inside the interview room, his hands would be freed but his legs would remain chained together.

Liz took a deep breath and sighed, a white plume in the frigid air. "I'm not hoping for too much from this," she said. "The psychiatrist who examined him last week said that his mental state has deteriorated. He's becoming suspicious of everyone, even his lawyers."

"All we can do is try," I replied. "We need to get a current statement from him, to compare with the statements he gave to the police, and his testimony in court. It's a long shot, but if he gives us any additional information about the murders, it could lead to something that was overlooked."

She nodded. "Here's the guard," she said, turning toward a short, heavy-set man in a khaki uniform who came to us across the yard. The guard was in his mid-forties, with short-cropped black hair and a round pie-pan face. To my surprise he looked friendly and open, almost kindly. In my mind's eye I pictured him sitting in a church pew surrounded by children, singing hymns in a low, off-key voice.

"Good morning," he said politely. "I'm Lieutenant Miller. Have you got your passes? Good. Let me see your state bar IDs for a second." We both wordlessly passed over the white-and-green plastic cards that identified us as licensed lawyers. Miller wrote down our names and ID numbers in a book attached to his clipboard. "Thanks," he added, passing the cards back. "Follow me, please."

He took us at an angle across a corner of the prison yard, then outside the old walls and into the steel-plated doors of 5 wing. A prison is not so much a building as a machine built to control people's movements. On the walk through the gray steel-and-concrete corridors I felt as though we were passing through the valves of an engine, one that exhausted stale air permeated with disinfectant and the harsh raw smell of pine soap.

The interview room was small, no more than twelve by fifteen feet, but it had two barred windows to the outside to let in the low winter sunlight. It felt airy after the claustrophobic corridors. The room contained a battered oak table coated with thick institutional yellow shellac and four brown, mismatched wooden chairs.

Liz removed her heavy blue winter coat, sat down, opened her briefcase, and rooted through the papers inside. She would do the bulk of the questioning. I laid my own briefcase down on the table and paced the room, to her visible irritation. In the days since I had agreed to work on Polhaus's case with her I had found more than a few moments to reconsider my decision and this was one of them.

They brought Polhaus in twenty minutes later. The guard seated him in a chair and removed the handcuffs, taking the cuffs and the waist belt with him. "I'll be in the observation area," he said, pointing to the interior windows on one wall of the room. "If you want something, let me know. You've got about two and a half hours before we have to take Polhaus back to his cell for lunch." He turned and went through the steel door, closing and locking it behind him.

I sat down across the table from Polhaus and studied him for a moment while I fumbled in my coat pockets for the packs of cigarettes I had brought him. Polhaus was now thirty-six years old. He had sandy-brown hair, cropped close to his square head, and a thin mustache of the same color, little more than a dirty smudge above the lips. His hands and feet were quite small and he seemed small-boned, but years of prison weight lifting had built up thick, almost cartoonish slabs of muscle on his arms and chest and neck. He wore a faded orange-red prison jump suit with a dirty white undershirt visible beneath the open collar. His eyes had no depth, blue disks in bloodshot whites. There was a round jagged purple bruise on the cheekbone below his left eye. His face contained no expression other than a flat fuck-you stare.

I put two cigarette packs together and slid them across the table to him. He tore the cellophane and foil wrappings open and put a cigarette in his mouth. "They won't let me have matches outside my cell," he said. His voice was high-pitched, surly, almost childish. I took a gas lighter out of my jacket pocket and lit his cigarette, leaning across the table. He blew smoke out of his nose and the corners of his mouth and waited.

"Robert," Liz said, "this is Matthew Riordan. He's the lawyer I have asked to join me in representing you. As I've told you by telephone, he will be checking into the facts of your case, at least for now. Do you accept him?" She was formal, cold, precise. A slight tremor in her hands revealed the tension she felt at being in the same room with Polhaus.

He shrugged. His empty gaze was fixed on me. "I don't have very many fucking choices, do I? None of you are going to make any difference, anyway."

Liz started to reply but I cut her off. "You've got choices," I said bluntly. "You can work with your lawyers and help them try to help you. Or you can walk over to 6 wing and not walk back." Every Walla Walla inmate knows that 6 wing contains the gallows and the lethal-injection table, the state's Hobson's choice of the methods of execution.

His flat, affected stare was unchanged. "Who the fuck are you?" he said, his voice a reedy monotone.

"Your lawyer. Will you help me, or not? I've got things to do if you're not interested. Drop the tough convict routine. It's not going to impress me or Ms. Kleinfeldt."

He nodded, a lifetime con who knew just how far he could push. His face softened, the hard bony ridges rounding out into a normal expression. "We've been locked down for three days," he explained. "Things are getting kind of wiggy in there." In addition to death row, the IMU housed the prisoners who were the hardest to control, the demented ones who howled in the night. He took another hit off his cigarette and crushed it out in a black plastic ashtray. "What do you want to do today?" he asked.

"We want to start back at the beginning," Liz replied, "and retake your statement as if no one ever had before. Concentrate as hard as you can. It's easy to leave things out because you've been through it so many times before."

"Why?"

"Because Riordan is going to work on the next stage of your appeals. You're down to your personal-restraint petition in state court. As I've told you before, we've had very little success finding any legal defects in your trial, conviction, or prior appeals. What we must do now is search for any new evidence we can find that will support your claim of innocence. It is critical that you cooperate with us. Do you understand?"

"I guess so. Go ahead."

Liz took a legal pad from her briefcase, the pages crowded with her cramped printing, each question carefully numbered. "You were released from the prison at Clallam Bay six months before the motel-room murders occurred. Start from there."

"Well, I got sent into work release in Pioneer Square, doing ship scaling down at Harbor Island," he said listlessly. "There were four or five of us from work release on the job. I stayed in the full four months and I was clean the whole time, no complaints, no violations. When I got done I found a place up on One Hundred Thirty-Eighth and Aurora in North Seattle, a little tourist cabin. I stayed with the scaling job for another two weeks, but the bus ride got to me, and I hated working below decks, no light. So when I got paid off I bought a car, a '68 Camaro. I got a job, security guard, down at the King's Inn on Sixth, north of downtown. I stayed in that job until Christmas, when I got canned." I suppressed a frown at the thought of Polhaus's being hired as a security guard, but the truth was that most private guards have criminal records.

"Let's go back," Liz said. "Suzanne Parker was killed on November 30, 1989, at the JetAir Motel on Pacific Highway South. Where were you that night?"

"I don't know. I tried to figure that out before the trial and I couldn't. It was a Thursday, they told me that. Most Thursday nights I was working."

"The records of the King's Inn show you weren't working that night," Liz said. "What did you do on your nights off?"

"I'd usually lift weights at one of the gyms near my place; most of them would give you two or three free passes if you told them you were thinking about joining. Then I'd hit a bar, maybe the Drift, or Riley's. Someplace close by. I'd drink four or five and go home if there wasn't any action." I made a note on my pad. The Drift On Inn was an old Highway 99 roadhouse dating from the 1930s; Riley's was a restaurant and piano bar in a strip shopping mall nearby. Neither was a hangout for prostitutes. It might be worth checking to see if any of the bartenders remembered Polhaus or his friends, if he had any. An alibi for Parker's murder, the killing he wasn't charged with, would mean nothing legally but might be persuasive.

Liz pressed on, with the same thought in mind. "Did you score that night?"

"Drugs or what?"

"That, or a woman."

"No. If I had, I'd remember. I think I just got drunk. That bastard lawyer I had before, Blanton, said he had an investigator try to check out all the places I'd usually hang out in but he didn't find anybody who saw me." I was not surprised that Polhaus was hostile toward Roy Blanton, his trial attorney. The first thing you find in a prison is that everybody there is innocent, done in by their no-good, lazy lawyer.

"Did you ever meet Suzanne Parker?" Liz asked.

"No. I never knew her."

"She worked for Dreams, the same escort service that Melody Beasely worked for."

He shook his head. "I didn't know that. I never saw her."

"When did you meet Melody Beasely?"

Polhaus shifted his weight in his chair, restless. "I'd been working at the King's for about a week, since the end of September. Jazz—that's the name Melody used—came in with another girl, Fawn. They were gonna do a doubleheader on some guy on the third floor, around midnight. I stopped them, was going to throw them out. This Fawn says, 'Let us do our business and we'll meet you in a couple of hours, show you a good time.' So I hung around and when they were done I copped a blow job from Jazz in one of the empty rooms. Jazz was working the King's fairly regularly, and so I made sure she had no hassles, and she'd ball me to make it even. I'd even give her rides back to her apartment if she was real late and had trouble finding a cab. I got off at six in the morning."

I broke in with a question. "How many other women did you get sex from in return for letting them work at the King's?"

"Five or six. Fawn, Jazz, Shawna, Tana, Sharee. Maybe one or two others."

"Those are all working names?"

"Yeah. I didn't know any of their real names, at the time. Except I guess Sharee used her real name. Sharee Klimka." The third victim.

"What happened on the night Melody Beasely was killed?" Liz asked, returning to her outline. "That was December 22nd, 1989."

He scratched his chin, thinking. "Pretty ordinary. The Friday before Christmas. The motel wasn't very full, maybe half, people from out of town come in to do their shopping. I got on at nine and checked in with the night clerk, a black guy named Wade Smith. I walked the halls and palmed the knobs and got called to put a guy out of the bar. The only thing unusual was that this TV crew was in the hotel. They interviewed Wade and Jaye, the bartender."

"Did you talk to the TV people?"

"No."

"When did you go to the bar?"

"About nine-thirty. A drunk Canuck was hassling Jaye. She had the desk clerk call me on the radio. I put him and his friends out pretty quick, then went back to the room where I could eat, a little closet on the first floor with a desk and the security monitors. I stayed there until after midnight."

"Did anyone see you there? Or see you doing any other work in that time period?"

"No. I mean, I'm not going to knock myself out for six bucks an hour, you know?"

"What did you do?"

"Ate a sandwich, listened to the radio, had a couple pops from a pint."

"Pint of what?"

"Apricot brandy."

"Were you drunk?"

"No. I had maybe two or three pops."

"Did you see Melody Beasely that night?"

"No. I didn't know she was working."

"She was found in room 317. Did you go up there between eleven and one o'clock?"

"I had to walk halls around one; yeah, so I was up on the third floor. I didn't know anybody was in 317."

"I thought you checked with the desk clerk when you got in," I said.

"I did, but I didn't look at the register after that."

"There wasn't anybody registered in that room," I said, "according to the King's Inn records. So how did she get in?"

"I don't know. She could have tipped somebody. Housekeeping, I don't know."

"Housekeeping shuts down between ten at night and five in the morning," I continued. "So how did she get in there? And why would she want to go into a vacant room? The john usually has to have a room number for a callback before the service will send somebody out."

"I don't know," he repeated, his voice uneasy. I glanced at Liz. She pressed her lips together in frustration. When Polhaus had taken the stand at his trial, the prosecution had pounded home on cross-examination the fact that Melody Beasely had been found dead in an unregistered room, with Polhaus, the desk clerk, and the night manager the only three people who had access to room keys or pass keys. The night manager and the desk clerk both denied giving Melody Beasely a key when called as rebuttal witnesses. It was the kind of small but telling fact that jurors grab hold of in deliberations.

"The couple who identified you as being on the third floor," Liz said, beginning again. "When did you see them?"

"It had to be earlier, before I went to the bar to toss out the drunk. I didn't see anybody when I walked around at one A.M. The place was quiet. I did another tour at three, still nothing shaking. I got off at six, went home."

"When did you talk to the cops?"

"Around nine in the morning. The manager called me up and told me to come back in. I went back and talked to them and later I signed a statement."

"That was false, right? Your statement?"

"Well, yeah. I told them I didn't know her and hadn't seen her that night, didn't know anybody was in the room. If I'd told them I knew her I'd have been canned. The rest of it was true."

"Were there any other prostitutes working the motel that night?" Liz asked.

"Not that I saw. Oh, hang on. The bartender, Jaye, told me there was a couple of hookers working the lounge around ten-thirty, eleven, but she booted them." I made a note on my pad. That was a fact, however insignificant, that hadn't come out before.

"Did you see anybody else that night, around the third floor?"

Polhaus shook his head.

"Did you see anyone who looked out of the ordinary, dazed, upset, in a hurry, anything?"

"No. It was real slow for a Friday night. Ten or fifteen people in the bar, watching the hockey game; four or five people in the halls, nothing."

"Who else did you see in the hall?"

"Just the couple up on third, the ones that testified against me, and one other couple, a real Mr. and Mrs. Hick, on second, before ten-thirty. Nobody after that."

"Why do you call them hicks?"

"They looked like farmers. He was wearing a cap with some name on it. She was big as a house."

"Nobody else?"

"No."

Liz stopped, searching for new questions, better answers. I drew a circle on my pad and put a slash through it, the mathematical symbol for nothingness. Polhaus's trial lawyer, Roy Blanton, had put a floor plan of the King's Inn into evidence at the trial, showing the three doors to the hotel that were not observable from the front desk, the garage attendant's station, or Polhaus's security desk. It was possible that someone else could have gotten into the motel unobserved. But the law is very clear: a possibility does nothing to create reasonable doubt.

CHAPTER 4

The interview room grew tighter and hotter in the afternoon as Polhaus filled it with smoke from an endless stream of cigarettes. Liz varied the subjects of her questions, trying to keep Polhaus alert and on edge. I struggled to match her intensity, drinking cup after cup of the black acid the guards called coffee.

Polhaus was fired from the King's Inn that day after Beasely's murder, when Greer, the night manager, found out that he had been drinking on his shift. He went to work at the China Tapestry on Christmas Eve as a fill-in for a vacationing night clerk, not telling the owners of the motel of his criminal record.

"When was the first time you had sex with a prostitute at the China Tapestry?" Liz asked.

"About a week after I started. This Fawn, who I knew worked out of the Dreams agency, was at a pay phone on Aurora when I spotted her. I went over and told her where I was working, and that it could be just as cool as it was at the King's if she wanted. She took me up on it that night and came back the next day, said that she and Sharee and one other girl were going to be having a party for a couple of guys they knew, regulars, off the books from the agency, on New Year's Eve. She wanted to use a couple of rooms, offered to pay me a hundred bucks under the table and give me my choice of the girls the next day. We were looking pretty empty, so I went with it. They paid one of the housekeepers to clean the rooms and Sharee came by my place on New Year's Day to pay off."

"Is that when Sharee Klimka got into your car?" Liz asked.

"Yeah, she came in a cab. Her car was broke down, so I gave her a ride to a house up on the north side."

"Did anyone see you there?"

"I don't think so. I let her off in the driveway."

"Could you find the house again if you had to?"

He shrugged, nearly worn out from the questioning. "Probably not. I think she said the house belonged to her cousin, something like that. It was up near Richmond Beach Road, a side street off there, on the hill above the Sound. It was a nice place," he added. He spoke with the bitterness of a child, face pressed to a glass shop window. Polhaus had never had a decent home and never would.

"What other prostitutes did you get sex from at the China Tapestry?"

"Just Fawn and Sharee."

"When was the next time you saw Sharee Klimka?"

"On the night of the fifth. The night she got killed. She said she had a date with one of her regulars, one of her off-the-book clients. She wanted to use a vacant room, if I had one. I don't think she wanted him at her place."

"Do you know why?" I asked, cutting in.

He shrugged. "No. Not really. I think Sharee was worried that the guy was getting weird. She'd just moved and didn't want him to know where she lived."

"What time did she get to the motel?"

"Around nine-thirty."

"How did she get to there?"

"By cab. I guess she figured she would just check in at the next place down the strip if I didn't have anything."

"What did she pay you?"

"Twenty bucks, enough for the maid, and said I could have an hour with her."

"You had sex with her?"

"Like I said at trial."

"Did you use a condom?"

"Yeah, but it broke as I was taking it off." I made a check mark on my list, striking that point. It had occurred to me, as it had to Liz, that if Polhaus had been set up, someone could have smeared the semen from the used condom on the bed sheet to implicate him.

"What did you do about the front desk?" Liz asked.

"Turned on the 'No Vacancy' sign and locked the door. I

didn't figure Mr. Chin, the owner, would be back that night; he'd already worked the day shift himself."

"What time did you leave her room?"

"Couldn't have been later than eleven. When I got back to the office I switched the 'Vacancy' sign back on and turned on the TV. The news had just started."

"Did Klimka call anybody from the motel?" I asked. I hadn't seen any telephone records listed in the trial exhibits.

"Not from her room," Polhaus said. "But there was a pay phone up on the second floor, right by it. She could have."

"Did you see anyone coming in after you got back to the office?" Liz asked.

"No. Not until about midnight, when this couple from Portland checked in. I put them in a room down the other way, on the first floor. Sharee was in the main wing, on the second."

"Did you leave the manager's office when you checked them in?"

"No. Wait, I got up to get their license-plate number, they couldn't remember it but their car was right outside. I didn't see anybody else, though."

"Did you leave the manager's office after that?"

"No. Not until close to one."

"What happened then?"

"I don't know. I heard something but couldn't make out what it was. I'd dozed off watching TV at the desk there. I went outside to smoke. And I saw this woman running, just a flash, as I was coming out the door."

"Which way was she running?" I asked.

"Toward Aurora," he said, naming the main arterial street in front of the motel. "At kind of an angle, like she was cutting across the parking lot."

"What did you do?"

"I said, like, 'Hey!'—shouted something at her—but she was gone."

"Why did you shout at her?" I asked.

"Because of the way she was dressed. Like a street hooker, you know, tight elastic pants and a shiny jacket. It was cold that night, rain off and on, and I didn't expect to see anybody working the street that late. I thought for a second she might have rolled somebody in the motel, you know, and the last thing I wanted was to have a guest call the cops. Mr. Chin got very uptight whenever the cops came around. I looked back at the motel, to see if anybody else was chasing her. I didn't see anybody at first, then I saw the guy on the second-story land-ing, in the back wing, looking out at the street."

"This is the man you testified about at your trial?" Liz asked.

"Yeah. I couldn't make him out too well. The lights are on the outside wall, behind where he was standing, so I couldn't see his face."

I stopped Liz and asked Polhaus to draw a map of the motel showing the location of the man he had seen. Polhaus took my pencil and a sheet of yellow legal paper and thought for a min-ute, the tip of his tongue pushed to the side of his mouth like a small boy solving a math problem. I watched as he made a couple of false starts, then turned the paper over. I knew from the trial transcript that Polhaus had dropped out of high school at fourteen, when he was sentenced to the work farm, but his trouble in putting together a simple sketch of the motel and parking lot made me wonder if he was developmentally dis-abled in some way.

Polhaus produced a diagram on the third try, taking a bird's-eye view, sketching the motel as a crude block L, the separate office building as a small box, and the parking lot as an irreg-ular shape fronting on Aurora Avenue. "The man was there," he said, pointing to an X he had placed near the crook of the L, on the leg of the motel that paralleled Aurora. "He was maybe twenty yards, call it four rooms, away from the inside corner where the two wings meet." Polhaus made a thick black dot on the other wing about halfway down. "That's the room Sharee was in."

"Let's get back to the man," Liz said. "How tall was he?"

"I don't know. He looked pretty big. And I think he might have been bald, because the outline of his head looked round, you know, like he didn't have much hair." He thought a little more and added, "Or his hair could have been slicked down. I just don't know."

"What else can you tell us about him?"

"Nothing. Roy Blanton figured that he was in room 224, 'cause that room paid cash and checked in before I came to work. He must have left before I got off. I don't know what car he was driving."

"Did he look like he was watching the woman running? Did he say anything or call out to her?"

He thought. "More like having a smoke or something."

"What happened then?"

"Well, I looked back down Aurora, looking for the hooker, but she was gone. Like she'd cut down one of the side streets, maybe."

"How tall was the woman who ran away?"

"I couldn't tell. She wasn't real little. Medium-sized. She had that red hair. But you know about that. That's the only thing I could say about her at trial: she had that long red hair."

"What happened then?"

"Well, I walked around the parking lot for a minute, you know, to see if anybody else was around, in case the hooker I saw had rolled a guest. But the man was gone. I didn't see anybody else, and it was real quiet. So I went back to the office."

"Did you go by Sharee Klimka's room?"

"No. I figured she was gone by then. When the maid came on at five in the morning I told her to clean up the room Sharee was in, 212, and gave her some money for it."

"That's when the maid found the body?"

"Yeah, around six, maybe an hour after she started working. I went in there and saw Sharee and called the cops."

I leaned back in my chair and thought. Polhaus letting the maid discover the body was the one fact that suggested he might not be the killer. Polhaus had been arrested fifteen times. He might be stupid, but he couldn't have been stupid enough to think that the cops wouldn't smell the convict on him and eventually check his record. Not twice, not after the King's Inn. It also did not fit the standard criminal profile for serial sexual murder. Disposal of the victim's body is usually a part of the killer's ritual conduct. I made a note on my pad, but knew that it was too flimsy, too ambiguous, to do any good on a motion to hear new evidence.

Liz handed him his statement, signed on the morning after Klimka's murder. "Is there anything you told the police that isn't in your statement?" she asked.

Polhaus read the statement slowly, his lips moving as he struggled with the words. He scratched his nose with his thumb, a lit cigarette cocked between the fingers of the same hand. "No, this is it," he said finally. "I left out the stuff about the woman running and the guy on the balcony because I didn't connect it, you know, to Sharee being killed."

We knew. The omissions in Polhaus's statement had all but convicted him when Daniel Merritt read it to the jury during closing argument.

Liz stopped her questioning, trying to think of something else to ask. Polhaus had given us nothing new or inconsistent with the prosecution's theory of the case, no crevice big enough to work open and see where it led. Liz checked her pad again, flipping back through the pages, reviewing the carefully numbered list of questions written in her small printed hand. When she put the pad down and looked up again, the expression on her face was coldly angry.

"Tell me something, Bobby," she began quietly. "I've been through your sheet. Several times. Robbery, burglary, a couple of assaults, and the manslaughter. Tell me about the assaults, Bobby. They're all against women. Why is that?"

Polhaus was silent, retreating behind the blank fuck-you stare he had worn when he entered the room.

"The women, Bobby; tell me about them."

"I don't know what the fuck you're talking about." He fished angrily in the cigarette pack, then fumbled with my lighter as he tried to get the cigarette lit.

"Let's take a case in point. Julie Swanson, nineteen years old; you met her in a bar down in Chehalis, in 1982. You offered to give her a ride home. When you got there you hit her five or six times, hard enough to break her cheekbone and two of her ribs. Then you raped her. The P.A. in Lewis County didn't want to try the case because Swanson had a reputation for liking strange men and you got to plead to second assault, did two years. Why'd you hit her?"

Polhaus said nothing. He stared at Liz, then broke the eye contact and looked down at the table.

"Then let's take Lois Summers, twenty-four; she was a heroin addict, you picked her up when she was hooking on Pacific Avenue in Tacoma. That was four months after you got out of the work farm in 1975, you were only eighteen, you remember. You took her down by the docks. You hit her so hard that her arm broke when she tried to block one of your blows. Then you raped her in your car. That's the one you got lucky on. She OD'd before trial and you walked. Why'd you do it, Bobby?"

Polhaus was silent.

There was an angry taunt in Liz Kleinfeldt's voice when she spoke again. "Tell me the truth, Bobby, goddamn you, tell me the truth. You like to hurt women, don't you? You like to hurt them, rape them, it's the hurting you really like, that's what gets you hard, isn't it?" She slammed her leather-covered pad on the table. Polhaus seemed to cringe. "That's why you do it, isn't it?" she shouted.

Polhaus looked up from the table. There was a dark hard light of something very much like hatred in his eyes. "Yeah," he said finally. "Yeah." He got up and hobbled to the door, his legs still bound by the short chain. He hollered angrily for the guards and waited while they cuffed his hands to the waist chain and let him out of the interview room. When Polhaus was gone I looked at Liz. She was staring across the table at Polhaus's empty chair. I was puzzled by the questions she had asked, fearful of the toll that representing a rapist like Polhaus was taking on her. In the first year after she was raped, Liz had continued as the head of the prosecutor's sex crimes unit, taking a full trial load herself, no matter how horrific the facts of the cases. What looked like steel resolve to the world had been, I knew, a form of denial that had taken a part of Liz's soul, even after she transferred to the less-taxing appeals unit and entered therapy.

"What the hell was that all about?" I finally asked. "We know he's a violent rapist. We're not going to be able to make him smell any better in court."

Liz shook her head. "You're missing the point." She took a deep breath to control her visible disgust with Polhaus before she spoke again.

"He's a hitter, Matthew," she said at last. "A hurter. He was quite capable of killing those women. But the three murdered women have no signs of gratuitous violence. None. 'Soft tissue ligature of the neck, probably caused by strangulation with a piece of cloth,' " she quoted. "That's what the medical examiner found. No struggle, no tissue under the nails, no clumps of pulled-out hair gripped in the hands. No signs of rape, no vaginal tearing." She paused as she slowly gathered up her notes and documents, placed them carefully into her briefcase and snapped it shut. "Something's not right here," she said softly. "Something isn't right."

CHAPTER 5

We missed our scheduled return flight and it was past eight o'clock when we finally got back to Seattle, to the soft rain of a winter night. Liz was exhausted by the long interrogation. I could see the dark circles beneath her eyes in the harsh airport lights. When I suggested that we have a quiet dinner before I drove her home, she shook her head, no.

"I've got to go back to work," she explained. "I have a couple of cases that are hanging fire and I need to see how they're going. Will you drop me at the office?"

"Sure. There's a few papers in your files that I'd like to look at. I'll make copies, if that's all right."

"Of course." She lapsed into a discouraged silence that lasted the rest of the way into the city.

Lisle, Day & Elgot's offices were on the top four floors of a new fifty-story, vaguely post-modern building on the Fifth Avenue side of the downtown financial district. Lisle, Day had been formed by the merger of three Seattle, Portland, and Los Angeles law firms. The Seattle office was the firm's headquarters, and no expense had been spared in the creation of instant tradition, from Honduras mahogany paneling and marble floors to low, rounded chairs and couches upholstered in rich hunter-green wool. I followed Liz down a long outside corridor lined with leather-bound legal reporters. Half the offices were still lighted, filled by ambitious lawyers working twelve-to-fourteen-hour days. As we turned a corner toward Liz's office we heard a dry, Southern-accented voice call out Liz's name.

"Shit," Liz mouthed silently, as she turned back toward the corner office.

"Yes, Jack?" she asked.

Jack Elgot, the firm's managing partner, stood in the doorway of his corner office. A slender man under six feet tall, still athletic in his early fifties. His gray hair was cut short in front but curled to his collar. His face was small, fine-featured, and shrewd. Elgot wore a navy-blue cardigan with a heavy shawl collar over his white shirt and red silk tie. Black reading glasses dangled from a string around his neck. He carried a thick legal brief loosely in one hand.

"Well," Elgot drawled, "how was the state pen?" His voice had a slight sardonic edge.

"Cold," Liz replied.

"Did you get anything useful out of, what's his name, Polhaus?"

"Not much," she admitted. "But we still have a lot of work to do on that case before we give it up."

"I see. I thought you might like to know that the feds pulled Marty Harwood into the grand jury today." I knew from the newspapers that Martin Harwood was a prominent real estate developer facing federal mail- and wire fraud charges for falsifying laboratory analysis reports to hide the fact that the site of his proposed Kent Valley shopping mall was contaminated with toxic wastes from an old electrical plant.

"Oh, no," Liz said, genuinely upset. "Mike Sharp, the assistant U.S. attorney, swore to me that Harwood wouldn't be called until tomorrow, at the earliest. Who went down with him?"

"I had to send Morrie Dickerman; he's the only other lawyer who knows the case."

"But Morrie is a real estate lawyer, Jack. He doesn't know what to do with a grand-jury target."

"I'm perfectly aware of that, Elizabeth," Elgot replied. "And I suspect that both Morrie and Mr. Harwood know that, too. I'm afraid both of them looked pretty pale when they got back this afternoon. Mr. Harwood, in particular, seemed to miss your comforting presence."

Liz was silent, running her hands through her short black hair, a sign of frustration I knew too well. "I'll see Martin in the morning, Jack," she said. "I prepared him thoroughly, and I'm sure he did fine."

"I do hope so. By the way, I've scheduled a meeting of your pro bono committee tomorrow afternoon to review the progress on the Polhaus case. I'll be there, of course."

"Of course," Liz said tonelessly. She turned and headed back to her office. I started to follow her, but Jack Elgot called me back.

"A moment, Mr. Riordan. If you don't mind?" he asked politely.

"Of course not," I replied.

"Well, come on in then."

I followed him into his office. It was larger than some apartments I had lived in, furnished with a striking mixture of modern and antique furniture. Elgot casually tossed the brief he had been reading on the slab of Carrara marble that served him as a desk and opened the glass-fronted doors of a nineteenth-century cherry-wood bookcase. "Drink?" he asked. "It's about that time of an evening. I'm partial to bourbon myself."

"That would be fine," I replied. "Just neat, thank you."

"Good man. No sense spoiling good bourbon with water or other adulterants." He poured two shots into crystal old-fashioned glasses, then turned and handed one to me. I took it and sat down on one of a group of low upholstered chairs. Elgot sat down on the sofa, facing me. "Cheers," he said. I sipped at my drink and waited, wondering how long the polite fencing would go on.

It turned out to be not long. "I was frankly surprised when Elizabeth told me that she had associated you on this case of hers," he said bluntly. "I fail to see what you can add that our firm can't manage on its own. We have some very fine young lawyers, from top law schools, who are eager to work on a high-profile case like a death-penalty appeal."

"I'm sure that's true," I said dryly, "but hooker killings are not a subject taught at most law schools."

"You bring a special expertise to the subject?" There was heavy sarcasm in his voice now.

"Some," I said evenly. "Elizabeth is the real expert. She spent seven years in the prosecutor's office, prosecuting violent crimes, especially crimes against women."

"And what do you bring to this party?"

"I've been a lawyer for eighteen years," I said, as evenly as I could. "I was an Organized Crime Strike Force investigator and prosecutor in the Ford and Carter administrations. I spent three years at Winthrop, Walters in New York, where I tried the Commodity Exchange fraud cases. I've been in Seattle for over ten years, with half my practice in criminal defense. Best of all, I'm not costing you a damned thing."

Elgot smiled briefly, like a cross-examiner who got stuck with an answer he didn't like. "But what on earth can you do?" he persisted. "The fact record stands as it was at trial. Any attack now will have to be on legal grounds."

"Normally, that's true. But Liz is concerned that there are no winning legal grounds to challenge Polhaus's conviction or sentence. My assignment is to try to find a basis for seeking a new evidentiary hearing."

He sounded doubtful. "To get a new hearing you have to have evidence that wasn't introduced at trial and couldn't have been discovered through reasonable diligence."

"Also true. It is a very long shot. But Liz believes that there was something missing in the original investigation of this case. She is going largely on instinct at this point. Her instincts are usually good."

"My God. You're going to be out there interviewing hookers and police officers and every potential witness you can think of, just on a hunch." He shook his head in disbelief, then very slowly put his glass down on the coffee table in front of him. He leaned forward and rested his hands on his thighs, staring at me intently. "Well, let me be very clear and specific, Mr. Riordan. I know that you are Elizabeth's former, or maybe current, lover. That makes me wonder a little bit. So I've asked about you. I'm not at all happy with what I hear. I'm told that you are a hot dog with a taste for strange cases, that you get too personally involved. I'm told that you had to give up your practice because you couldn't make a go of it. And I'm telling you that if you involve this firm in ugly or unethical behavior, you will never work again, not even charity work like you're getting from us now."

I was silent. I could feel the red flush of anger on my face as I carefully placed my glass on the table. "Is there anything else?" I asked softly, getting to my feet.

"No," he said scornfully.

"When this is over," I said, my voice still quiet, "you and I will have another discussion on this subject."

He paled slightly. "What the hell does that mean?" he asked, flustered.

I said nothing as I turned my back on him and walked away.

* * *

It was after midnight when the buzzer sounded in my apartment. I put down my book, a fine biography of Dwight Eisenhower by Stephen Ambrose. History soothes a troubled and angry mind. It demonstrates that mistakes, bad judgments, and unbridled arrogance are a normal part of the human condition.

I answered the intercom. It was Liz. "Can I come up? I heard what happened with Jack."

I buzzed her in the front door and waited for her in the hallway. She trudged up the stairs to the top floor, weighted down with a large briefcase and a small workout bag.

"I'm sorry," she said as she reached my door. "Jack had no right to talk to you like that. I'm embarrassed to say that I'm grateful you didn't insult him. Or slug him. He deserved both."

"It's all right," I said, ushering her inside and closing the door. "There was some truth in what he said. Perhaps more than I would like to admit. But be careful with him, Liz. Elgot takes no prisoners. And he lives for that law firm of yours."

Liz dropped her bags in the front hallway. "I know," she replied. She walked into the living room, her natural curiosity about my new apartment getting the better of her. She surveyed the room, with its wall of books, sparse furniture, and small tile fireplace. A large post-expressionist Thayer oil, a gift from the artist, hung above the mantel. French doors opened to a narrow balcony overlooking Volunteer Park. Liz smiled. "Very simple. Well organized. Good natural light. A nice screw-you touch, hanging a quarter-million-dollar painting in a plain wooden frame. Very Riordan."

I laughed. "Such as it is. Or I am."

She tried to laugh but her exhaustion got the better of her. Tears welled up in the corners of her eyes. She put her arms around me and buried her face in my chest. "May I stay here tonight?" she asked plaintively. "Please. Just to sleep. I am so tired."

"Of course," I replied, but I felt the memory of our once-bitter parting twinge like an old wound. "We've tried this before, Lizabeth," I added gently.

"Maybe we've both grown up," she murmured.

Before we finally fell asleep, exhausted from making love, I remember walking to the window of the bedroom and staring out at the rain falling gently into the courtyard. I felt the warmth of Liz's hand against my back. "No, darling, you've got to sleep," she murmured. They were words she had spoken a long time ago, but when she said them that night it was as if she had never been gone.

CHAPTER 6

I spent the next morning, after Liz left for her office, reading the box of documents produced by the prosecutor's office to Polhaus's defense lawyer, Roy Blanton, in discovery prior to trial. In a criminal case the prosecution must turn over any evidence it has which may be helpful to the defense. The so-called *Brady* disclosure is named after a United States Supreme Court case, *Brady v. Maryland*, which created the obligation as a matter of constitutional due process. As near as I could tell, the *Brady* documents were mostly useless, a collection of police interviews with the victims' friends and other prostitutes, follow-up reports, warrants and search inventories, and lab analyses. I skimmed through the entire box, trying to get a feel for how the investigation had been conducted, then carefully read through the more important documents, hoping to pick up any inconsistencies in the facts. It was clear to me, after my initial reading, that the police had fastened on Polhaus as their only real suspect and concentrated on building a case against him.

By one o'clock I was brain-weary. I had nearly twenty pages of numbered notes, a fair case of writer's cramp, and only a couple of ideas. I needed more background in the prostitution side of the case, in order to understand the sometimes cryptic references to escort agencies and confidential sources.

A driving winter storm lashed rain against the apartment windows. I put on rubber-soled boots, took an old Burberry trench coat from the front-hall closet, and went down the stairs to the basement garage to pick up my car and head downtown, in search of Terry Lasker.

Lasker was the star columnist for the Seattle *Tribune*. I had met him a decade before, when he was the paper's courthouse reporter. Since then Lasker had acquired a Pulitzer Prize for investigative reporting, and a three-times-weekly column, the best read in the city. Lasker wrote with a fine cynical eye for the shallowness of city politics, and with an open heart for the working poor and homeless struggling to survive the rising rents and social scorn in Seattle's economic boom. On the side he crafted true-crime books with the style and sensitivity of a novelist. He handled the money and the local fame with an understated grace that left him with few enemies, and possibly the best news sources in the city.

The receptionist at the Tribune Building on Fairview Avenue said that Lasker was out working. With Lasker, that meant he could be anywhere from Sitka, Alaska, to Key West, but if he was in town he would probably show up sometime in the afternoon at Firenze, a coffee bar and café on Bell Street in the Denny Regrade. I splashed through the wet streets and settled in at the bar with a sandwich, a bottle of Ballard Bitter, and the morning edition of the *Tribune*.

Lasker showed up just over an hour later, a tall, rail-thin man in his late forties, with long gray hair combed straight back over his head and rimless glasses spotted with rain. He caught my eye and smiled as he stood in the front of the café, shaking water from his umbrella and raincoat. He hung them up on a brass coatrack and came over to the bar and shook my hand.

"Riordan," he said, smiling, "good to see you." He wiped his glasses dry with a napkin. "Twenty years in this town and I still hate the rain. I told the managing editor this morning I needed to do a week's worth of features. From Cabo San Lucas." He turned to the woman tending the bar. "Jean, a double cappuccino for me, please. Matthew, you want some coffee?"

I nodded and ordered a regular coffee with steamed milk. Lasker had given up drinking a couple of years before, when a five-star hangover caused him to miss the opening statements in a trial he was writing a book about. He'd substituted caffeine for alcohol ever since. I once watched him nod off to sleep during a fund-raising dinner after consuming two black triple espressos.

When the coffee arrived we moved over to a marble-topped cast-iron café table in a corner of the smoking section. Lasker lit a filtered Camel and leaned back in his chair until his back touched the exposed brick wall that was hung with Italian watercolors of street scenes and cafés. His perpetual sardonic smile was stitched on his face.

"So how is retirement?" he asked. "As a former workaholic, I imagine you're finding the going kind of rough."

"As it happens, I'm working again," I replied.

"On the house you're building?"

"No. Liz Kleinfeldt asked me to help her on a case she is handling. A death-penalty appeal for a convict named Robert Polhaus."

"The Motel Room Killer," he said, nodding. "Why on earth is Liz mixed up in that? She's in private practice now, I thought."

"She is. It's a pro bono case. She wants me to take a look at the original investigation. She's not convinced that Polhaus was guilty."

He shook his head. "I didn't cover that trial, I was tied up with the column. But I read the coverage, to see if there was a book in it, and it didn't seem to me like there was much room for doubt."

"I'm not very hopeful, to tell you the truth. But I agreed to work it for a couple of months and see whether there might be anything that was overlooked."

"That's a tough one. You're thinking I can help. How?"

"All three murdered women worked as escorts, two of them with the Dreams escort service. I need some background in that business: who's running it, how it's being run, what the cops were doing. You did a series on escort agencies about three or four months before the murders took place."

"Man, that's over four years ago." He drained his coffee cup and took a meditative drag on his cigarette before crushing it out. "The escort business is like any other prostitution business. It's illegal and the cops do their best to shut it down. The typical arrangement is that the women work as independent contractors for the escort-agency owner. They charge a base fee, fifty or sixty dollars, that goes to the owner of the service. The women then charge additional fees for sex, a hundred dollars and up, depending on what the john wants. Some of them have their own books of customers, some of them specialize, say in bondage or S and M or some kind of fantasy. The

agency owners are usually men, not always, there's one or two
women-owned and -run services in the area. The johns are
middle-class or better, mostly white, although there is a big demand from Asian businessmen who come to town from cul-
tures where prostitution is considered no big deal."

"What kind of money do the owners make?"

He smiled. "Thinking of investing? They make a fair
amount. A good-sized service like Dreams probably brings in
three to four hundred thousand a year above the table, more
when you count the skimming. The guy who owns Dreams,
Larry Poole, is a sexual entrepreneur. In addition to the escort
agency, he owns a string of nude dancing clubs, also named
Dreams, from Federal Way up to Bellingham, and distributes
porn videos and magazines in Washington, Idaho, and Montana."

"That's interesting. Porn distribution is usually a mob activity, at least in San Francisco and L.A."

"It probably is, although Poole doesn't look like Marlon
Brando. He's a relatively young guy, late thirties, drives a Benz
with a telephone, good suits, looks like a successful real estate
broker. Or lawyer. He wouldn't let me interview him on the
record but I caught up with him at his health club one day and
we had a chat over a couple of raspberry sodas." Lasker made
a face, probably at the memory of the raspberry soda. "I found
myself almost liking him. He was so refreshingly and completely venal. A yuppie dabbling in crime. The Seattle police
and the county both have pretty extensive intelligence files
about him. They knew what he was doing then. From what
I've heard, he's still in the business. They've never put a case
together on him. There are rumors that a couple of women
who worked for him at one time or another have disappeared,
supposedly gone on to work in other cities, but nobody ever
heard from them again. And—do you remember the shooting
in Magnolia, a big house on Perkins Lane, down by the water?
A guy named Porter. The word was that Porter was a competitor in videocassette distribution in Portland and was going to
move into the Seattle market. I asked him about it. Poole
smiled and said he didn't know anything, his competitors *never*
bothered him. He put just the right amount of emphasis on
'never.' "

"What about the other agencies?"

"They're all smaller than Dreams. It's a relatively easy business to get into; anybody with a phone, a computer, and credit-

card access can get into it, provided they can recruit the women. Getting the talent is the hardest part of the business."

"If Poole is the most prominent, why hasn't he been busted?"

"That's a pretty good question. He's careful, like most of them. Everything is done on computer, and the records get wiped out if the cops arrive. When I did that series I went on a raid, a different agency operating out of an office building in lower Queen Anne. The receptionist had a big magnet in the lower drawer of her desk and she laid it on her computer's external hard drive as the cops came in the door. Bye-bye evidence." He paused for a movement to think. "But Poole has had absolutely no problems. They've tried to sting him, using policewomen as decoys. They've never gotten close. The decoys are just politely turned down for employment."

"Did Poole get some warning from inside one of the local vice squads?"

"I thought about that when I was doing the series. Didn't have any evidence, couldn't run with the story."

I paused, trying to come up with another question. I was still thinking when Lasker asked, "Did the cops locate the dead girls' john books?"

"I didn't see any listed that way in the trial exhibits or in the Brady material turned over in discovery."

"Take another look. They might be listed on a search inventory as an address book, maybe a calendar. If you don't find any, then something's screwy. All three victims probably had private clients. The first thing the homicide people do is try to find out who the clients were; they're the prime suspects in any hooker killing."

"Good point," I said. "I'll check it. Thanks."

"Not at all. When you get to the right place in the case, let me talk to Liz about doing a column on her. She's good-looking, we'll run a photo with it."

"I'll tell her," I said, smiling as I rose to go. "But I don't think she'll want to do it. She's pretty snake-bit when it comes to the press."

"I'll be nice. I'd better get to work. I'm running tomorrow and I still don't know what in hell I'm going to write about. The column is a monster that's constantly hungry. I suppose I can feed it the city council, if I get real desperate." He smiled and ordered another coffee as I stood to go. I got my coat and turned back to say good-bye, but he had a pad out and was already writing, feeding the beast.

CHAPTER 7

I hadn't worked out for a couple of days and my back was clenched like a fist. I spent an hour on the YMCA's running track and in the weight room, then swam a mile before collapsing in the sauna. On my way to the showers I stopped in front of a locker-room mirror. There was no cure for the long bony face and hawkish nose, broken and badly set after a football game twenty-five years ago, but I noted with grim satisfaction that two months of hard labor, no alcohol, and long morning runs at the Quilcene house had finally eliminated the roll of fat above my hips that I had gotten as a present for my thirty-fifth birthday.

I phoned my message service from the Y and found a call from Vincent Ahlberg, a Seattle police captain and the long-time skipper of the SPD's Homicide Unit. Ahlberg was widely considered the second-most-powerful copper in the SPD, an independent power who had survived four chiefs and three mayors in the homicide job. I had known Ahlberg for almost ten years and both liked and trusted him, a rare-enough situation between lawyer and cop. Despite our natural affinity—repressed Scandinavian, repressed Irish Catholic—we were not friends. I had never eaten with him at his home or spent social time with him on his off-hours. Part of Ahlberg's untouchable political standing came from his reputation for straight dealing. He considered personal friendships with lawyers who were potential opponents too close to the line.

When I returned the call he was still in his office, even

though it was well after six. He sounded tired when he came on the line.

"Riordan? I've got a couple things to chat with you about. When can we meet?"

"Anytime," I replied. "In fact, I'm two blocks away right now."

"Good. Come on up, then." He rang off before I could agree, the habit of command.

I found him in his den on the fourth floor of the Public Safety Building, his door open to the half-empty squad room. When I rapped on the doorframe he looked up from the paperwork on his desk and motioned me in. I hung my raincoat on a hook and dropped into a chair. Ahlberg was not tall but even in his fifties had the build of a logger, broad-shouldered and barrel-chested. I knew he controlled his weight with roadwork, handball, and an hour every other morning on Lake Union in a single-scull. Ahlberg sat very straight and still while he worked. I waited as he carefully marked his place in the report he was reading and stacked the papers neatly to one side, the movement of his thick, blunt hands sure and efficient.

"I'm going off duty," he said, taking the gold cuff links from his starched white shirt and rolling the sleeves up on his forearms. "Care for a drink?"

"Where do you want to go?"

"Here," he said, pulling a bottle of Famous Grouse from his bottom desk drawer and producing two glasses. "Rank has some prerogatives." He poured and passed one glass across his desk; I lifted it and said "To prerogatives," before taking a sip.

He allowed a small smile to pass across his long, squared-off face. "I haven't seen you for a while. I understand you gave up your practice."

"True. I shut down January first."

"Mind if I ask why?"

"No. But I'm not very good at explaining it. I simply didn't want to practice law anymore."

He frowned and took a sip from his glass. "I'm sorry to hear that. I never knew you to do anything too dishonest."

"High praise, indeed," I replied. "Like Saint Anselm, the Breton: 'a lawyer and not a thief, and the people were amazed.' "

"Somehow I don't think you're sainthood material," he said dryly. "I also hear that you're working for Liz Kleinfeldt on the Polhaus case."

"You hear correctly. The courthouse telegraph must still be up and running."

"If you've quit, why are you taking on a stone loser like that?"

I thought about trying to explain but quickly rejected it. Ahlberg was not a man who dealt in grays; his cop's world was Manichaean, white or black, guilty or not. "Liz asked me to. I couldn't say no. You know why." Ahlberg was one of the few people around the courthouse who knew that we had been lovers. "She thinks that there is something wrong with the way Polhaus got convicted, but hasn't put it together yet."

Ahlberg stopped his drink halfway to his mouth, then carefully put it down on the glass top of his desk. There was genuine surprise in his pale, almost colorless eyes. "You're kidding."

"No. You worked with Liz when she was in the prosecutor's office. She does not kid. She's not always right, but she has good reasons for what she does."

He shook his head. "Liz was as good a prosecutor as I ever saw, but she's in left field on this one. We had a solid circumstantial case and Polhaus fits the profile for a serial killer. We were lucky we stopped him after only three victims. Some of them we never find. Like Green River. What's bothering her, anyway?"

"Several things. The profile, for starters." Liz had insisted that I read the FBI psychological literature on serial murders.

"Polhaus isn't a roamer," I began, referring to the serial killers' pattern of driving endlessly around and between cities, sometimes hundreds of miles apart, seeking victims. "The victims' bodies weren't transported and they weren't hidden or buried. All three victims were found in the motel rooms, a much more public place. There wasn't any message in the placement of the bodies, no fantasy play being acted out. The women were just found lying on the beds."

"Nonsense." There was no heat in his voice. Ahlberg considered himself, with good reason, an expert, self-taught criminalist and would debate the subject for hours. "You're focusing on superficial traits, not core psychological characteristics. Polhaus fits the serial-killer profile. He was sexually abused as a child, developed a deep-rooted hatred of women. He's been getting off on inflicting pain for a long time. That's plain from his criminal record, if nothing else. The victims were 'messaged': they were placed on the beds, after being killed on the floor of the rooms. I don't know what particular significance that had for Polhaus, but to me it suggests some kind of reference back to the abuse he received as a child. I checked the social workers' records on him to try and find some specifics, but they didn't keep detailed records twenty-five years ago." Ahlberg rubbed his face as if fighting fatigue. He had probably been on duty for more than twelve hours. "There was a progression in the way Polhaus did the killings. The first one, Parker, the one we couldn't get enough to prosecute on, was pretty rough. The crime scene was a mess—lots of evidence of a struggle, and it looked like he took off fast, high on the adrenaline. With Beasely and Klimka he took his time. He was learning how to build a scenario, a fantasy, and stretch out the pleasure."

I reached for my glass and swallowed the rest of the Scotch. It tasted sour.

Ahlberg said, "You lawyers never like to be reminded about your clients."

"No," I said sharply, "we don't. But that doesn't mean we won't do our jobs. What about a murder kit? You never found that."

"No, but we could identify it from traces found in the rooms. We found a couple of pieces of fine gravel, the kind the city uses for street repair, on the rug at the King's Inn. That suggests a sock or leather pouch, filled with gravel, was used to stun the victims. The ligature could have been any kind of cloth. As to his being a roamer, the pattern was tighter than most, about twenty-five miles south to north, but it's not outside the range. Bundy started like that." He sipped at his drink, then added, "This isn't really a science, you know. It's based on what the FBI psychologists have observed over the past fifteen years. Besides, you haven't even mentioned the most important factor."

"What's that?"

"The killings stopped. We arrested Polhaus, and the killings stopped."

I was silent. The termination of a series of criminal acts is not legally admissible proof of guilt, but I tended to agree with Arthur Conan Doyle about the strange thing the dog did in the night.

"So what else is bothering Liz?" he asked, lighting one of his small Cuban cigars. The chief of police had banned smok-

ing in the Public Safety Building two years before, but no one
had the balls to tell Ahlberg about it.

"Liz and I have both been through the transcript and the police reports. You never looked at any other suspects. I can understand why, since you had Polhaus in hand. But this is a
death case, Vince."

"I know. I was surprised when Merritt filed for the death
penalty in a circumstantial-evidence case and more surprised
when he got it. But there was a lot of public pressure and he
went with it."

"What kind of pressure?"

"What you'd expect. The publicity over another serial murder. Women's Rights. Ten years ago a hooker killing would get
buried. Now it's considered violence against women, and that
triggers a lot of public interest. I'm not saying it's wrong to
look at it that way, but when we get pressure groups trying to
tell us how to do our jobs, it doesn't help anybody. We investigate a homicide the same way no matter who the victim is."

Not always, I thought sourly, but I had the sense to keep my
mouth shut. "How bad was the pressure on this one?"

He shrugged. "The papers had the mayor going, and shit
flows downhill. Merritt was in here every damned day, too."
He looked sour at the memory. "It doesn't bother my people;
I insulate them from that. But Merritt has been running for attorney general since he was ten years old. And Task Force
Tommy is always running scared." Task Force Tommy Knut-
son was the then-new Seattle police chief at the time of the
motel-room murders, a former Internal Affairs captain on the
Chicago police who made his name during the Greylord police
and judicial bribery scandals. He was widely thought of as a
consummate police bureaucrat, widely disliked in the ranks. He
got the nickname because he appointed a task force to solve
every problem. I had heard from a bemused city council aide
several months before that there were now twenty-seven task
forces within the SPD.

Ahlberg finished his drink. He would not have a second one
as a matter of discipline. Not in the office. "So tell me what
you think should have been followed up," he said.

"There's a couple of weak points," I replied. "First, the man
on the balcony and the running woman that Polhaus testified to
were never found. Nobody looked for the victims' john books
or questioned their customers."

"Nobody heard Polhaus's story about the man and the running woman until he testified at trial. We went back out to check on it but we didn't have much time, and couldn't come up with anything. If the man on the balcony existed, he must have been registered under a phony name. We found three phonies on the motel's register, but couldn't find the people. As to the john books, I don't think we found any. We only had the second and third murders in the city. County handled the first one, the Parker woman."

"Yeah, but the medical examiner's office spotted the similarity in the cause of death right after the second girl was killed. I'd still expect to see a lot of county reports on Parker in your files. Parker documents should have been turned over even though Polhaus was only charged with the Beasely and Klimka killings. Besides, you had a county man working with you on the motel-room killings. I've forgotten his name."

"Ray Leach. Task Force Tommy insisted we set up a joint task force with the county, and Leach was right for the job—six months in county homicide and five years in county vice before that."

"The detective from your shop who worked on the motel-room murders, this Nancy Karras, how is she?"

His normally expressionless face brightened. "Karras is very good," he said. "She was a Portland PD vice detective for a couple of years before her marriage broke up and she moved up here. On SPD she worked burglary and juvenile, as well as vice. I brought her in to homicide after she worked with us on a child-abuse death. She's a damned good interrogator, good with witnesses, especially kids and women." His eyes narrowed in shrewd appraisal. "You'd like her," he added. "She's a lot like you."

"Why's that?"

"She's dogged about her work. Compulsive. Doesn't quit, doesn't talk too much."

"Thanks," I said dryly. "I think. That's the second time I've been called neurotic or compulsive lately."

He chuckled. I got back to the main point. "There was one follow-up report, I think by Leach, that indicated that the Parker woman's apartment had been searched and a couple of people questioned about her. The list of items taken in the search includes an address book, but there's no follow-up on anyone being questioned who was named in the book. It's two reports, actually, a county report from December 15, I think, and then a joint report on an SPD form dated December 28, when the two murders were being looked at together." I had been carrying some of the files in my briefcase and had looked at them at the YMCA after talking to Terry Lasker.

"Let me check," Ahlberg replied. "I've still got the files up here, they haven't been sent to storage." He left his office and went to a bank of file cabinets in the squad room. He returned holding a couple of three-inch-thick files. He sat down and scanned the two reports, then looked up and said, "So what's your point?"

"No point, maybe. I'd just like to see the women's john books. There's a reference to Parker's book; it's not been produced in any of the discovery, and it's not mentioned again."

Ahlberg shrugged. "You're assuming that this address book was the john book. Maybe it wasn't, and Leach and Karras went on to other leads."

"Maybe."

Ahlberg was silent. He reread the December 15 county report. He was still reading when a very thin, red-haired detective named Wechsler stuck his head in Ahlberg's door and said, "Skipper? Can I see you for a minute? I need your take on something."

Ahlberg stood up, distracted. "Sure, Tom." He turned back to me and said, "I'll be back in ten minutes or so. You want to wait?"

"Okay."

While Ahlberg was gone I took the two files from his desk and read the reports over again, wanting to make sure that I had correctly remembered the sequence of the reports and their findings. Ahlberg had read them before; they had occasional notes or questions penned in his squared-off schoolboy's printing. I turned to the December 15 report, reading Ahlberg's notations along with the text. On the second page an arrow had been drawn from a reference to the questioning of a friend of Suzanne Parker's who was also a prostitute. The arrow led to a series of numbers that had been written in the margin: 5-8656. I quickly read the rest of the report but found no other references to the numbers. By the time Ahlberg returned I had replaced the files on his desk.

"This is going to take some time, I think. Sorry. We'll talk more later if you want."

"That's okay. Is there anything else you wanted to see me about?"

"No. I just was curious why you were on this case with Liz Kleinfeldt."

"Listen, now that I think of it I'd like to talk to the two investigators sometime soon. Off the record. I just want to know what they covered and what they didn't, things like this address book. I haven't got the time or the money to do your detectives' job over again."

He hesitated. "Let me think about it. It's not procedure, but maybe I'll bend a rule. I know you haven't got too much time."

"Call me. Thanks for the drink."

I left the Public Safety Building and splashed my way up Fourth Avenue toward my car. I gave brief thought to stopping at one of the downtown watering holes for another drink and some dinner, but my curiosity about the number Vince Ahlberg had written on the margin of the report got the better of me and I drove straight home. I dumped my raincoat on the living-room sofa and headed into the small maid's bedroom of the apartment that served me as a study. I pulled the city and King County telephone directories from the bookshelf and sat down at my desk. The King County government telephone prefix was 995. I turned to the King County Police Department listings and ran through the numbers. I found 8656 in the middle of the directory. It was the number for the sheriff's Internal Investigation Unit, the group charged with investigating wrongdoing within the department.

I sat straight back in my chair and bit my lip. I shouldn't have been surprised. The criminal justice system is called an adversary system for good reason. The cops keep their business, especially their dirty business, their own. But for the first time in the ten years I had known him, Vince Ahlberg had held out on me.

CHAPTER 8

In the morning I went to Liz's office to review the first draft of the petition brief with two young Lisle, Day associate attorneys, Wayne Porras and Gretel Anderson. They had done the research and prepared the first draft. Porras was a short, fat man in his mid-twenties with a helmet of styled black hair and horn-rimmed glasses perched halfway down his bulbous nose. Porras's blue suit was new but already rumpled, as though his tailor had struggled long and hard and finally said the hell with it. Anderson was slender and athletic, with a firm, intense manner that belied her blond-princess looks and designer dress. Both were red-eyed and yawning from several long nights of library drudgery. We closeted ourselves in a windowless conference room near the firm's library and read through the draft together, honing the statement of facts, always the most crucial part of any brief, searching for the right words to emphasize the circumstantial nature of the evidence against Polhaus and the plausibility of his defense. At eleven o'clock we broke for Porras and Anderson to return client phone calls, and I wandered down the corridor to Liz's office, wanting to pass on what had happened with Lasker and Ahlberg the day before.

Liz was in her chair, elbows propped on the desktop, hands kneading her temples, shouting into a telephone speaker.

"That's your problem, Howard. You can take it or go to trial. You have a shitty case and I'm not going to be held for ransom. And Howard—stop whining." She speared the "off" button and turned to me.

"How much do you carpenters make an hour?" she asked testily.

"Eight or nine bucks, starting out."

She swallowed two aspirin with water from a carafe on her desk. "I should have taken a job from you. How'd you do with Ahlberg?"

"So-so. Nothing he said. I asked him about the victims' john books, if they'd found any. Suzanne Parker's address book, possibly her john book, was listed in a search inventory but wasn't turned over in discovery. Ahlberg started reading the references to the address book but he got called away. I looked at his copy of the report. Ahlberg had written the telephone extension number for the King County Police Internal Investigation Unit in the margin. There was an arrow to a name of a witness, probably a hooker, and the name was circled."

"Was she one of the prostitutes Polhaus listed, that he'd extorted sex from?"

"No. Her name was Jacqueline Rogers. I think she was a friend of Beasely's and she had to know Parker, since the report she was mentioned in predated Beasely's death. I'm going to try to find Rogers, but I'll talk to the cops first."

Liz nodded, distracted. "IIU?" she asked, using the acronym for Internal Investigation Unit. "Why?"

"I don't know. Have you got a gossip relationship with anybody in the King County force who would have a line into IIU?"

"I don't think so, but I'll try. Give me the witness's name on a piece of paper so I don't forget."

"I will. If Rogers gave a statement to IIU, would that show up anywhere?"

"Not in a public file. Not even in the prosecutor's case file. Ordinarily Ahlberg, in SPD, wouldn't hear anything about a King County IIU matter. But he's got his sources, too."

She frowned. "I think we should talk to Roy Blanton again, ask him if there's any other discovery he thinks he got stiffed on. I'll call to set it up. Five o'clock okay?"

"Sure. In the meantime the galley slaves will be downstairs, going over the case law on ineffective assistance of counsel."

"Tell them to order lunch," Liz sighed, "and I'll be in with my whip. How're they doing so far?"

"They're bright kids, Liz. It's going to be a good brief. But I'm not promising it's going to be a winner."

"Me neither." She picked up another case file, then dropped it and drummed her fingers on the desktop. "Damn them. What did they hold back?"

* * *

At ten minutes after five we stood in the elaborate art deco lobby of the Smith Tower, a 1920s terra-cotta skyscraper at the edge of Pioneer Square, waiting for one of the brass-cage elevators, the last in Seattle with human elevator operators, to take us to Blanton's office on the twenty-sixth floor.

The elevator doors opened into Blanton's lobby, a small expanse of parquet floor covered with a threadbare oriental rug. There were a couple of old leather benches pushed back against the walls, with 1940s-vintage chrome ashtrays mounted on smoking stands beside them. The lobby adjoined a library lined with the yellow buckram-bound volumes of Washington State and federal case law. A heavy oak library table flanked by four banker's chairs stood in the center of the room. Law books and case files spilled off the table onto the floor. Wooden doors darkened by layers of old varnish closed off the lawyers' private offices. By modern standards Roy Blanton's chambers were a shabby mess, but I liked them. They looked the way law offices used to look before lawyers discovered interior designers.

Blanton's secretary was gone for the day. Liz knocked on the door to his private office and got no response.

"Roy?" she called out, knocking again and trying the door. It was locked. Liz turned back to me and shrugged.

We were on our way out when a tall young woman with curly black hair, dressed in jeans and a turtleneck sweater, came out of one of the other offices, lugging a pile of West Federal Reporters under her arm. She wore thick rimless glasses and no makeup. There were ink smudges on her forehead and nose.

"Roy's not here," she said. "I'm Sarah Goldman, the law clerk. Was he supposed to meet you?"

"Yes," Liz replied, barely suppressing her irritation. "We had a five o'clock appointment."

"Roy must have spaced it," Goldman said unruffled. "If I were you, I'd try the Seven Hundred. That's Roy's usual hangout. Sorry, but I've gotta get back to this brief." She dumped her load of books on the library table and went back to her office, closing the door behind her.

"Come on," I said to Liz, "at least we can have a drink."

The 700 was a bar and restaurant five blocks north of the Smith Tower at the base of the new FedWest Bank Building. The 700 had been designed to look like a men's club bar from the 1940s, with wood-paneled walls, an enamel-and-chrome bar, and deep red leather booths. It even had a hatcheck and a cigar stand. The nostalgia was so effective that the 700 drew a mostly male stockbroker-and-lawyer crowd in their forties and fifties.

When we reached the bar I saw Blanton holding court with some of the other regulars. He was an oversized shambling bear of a man in his late fifties, dressed in a brown suit that bagged from too many wearings without a pressing. His face had thickened with age and weight. His thinning hair was stained a peculiar brown-gray, probably from Grecian Formula. He had his hand wrapped around a double something on the rocks, a lit cigarette protruding from his fingers. He seemed to be in the middle of a story, gesturing and pointing with his free hand. Liz didn't wait for him to finish. She cut into the crowd at the bar and stood in front of him, impatiently.

"Roy," she said when he paused for breath, "we had an appointment to talk to you about the Polhaus case."

He looked down at her, slightly puzzled, then seemed to remember who Liz was.

"Hell, that's right," he replied. "Kleinfeldt and Riordan, whoever he is. Sorry about that. Let me buy you a drink. Max," he called to the bartender, "another one for me, and get these two whatever." We both ordered club soda. Blanton looked at us scornfully.

"How's Bobby Polhaus doing?" he asked, when we were seated in a booth.

"He doesn't much like death row," Liz replied dryly. "But for now he's surviving."

"You've got to file your brief pretty soon, don't you?"

"Yes, it's due in a few more days," Liz answered. "The reason we wanted to see you, Roy, is that I'm not optimistic about getting a reversal. We're going to try all the usual legal grounds, but I don't think they'll work in this case. We need to go over the facts of the case with you and review the discovery. Matthew Riordan, here, is investigating the case, starting from scratch, trying to determine if there was any evidence overlooked in the trial that could justify a new evidentiary hearing. On grounds of actual innocence."

Blanton looked at Liz with feigned amazement, as if he were mugging for a camera. "Liz, have you gone soft in the head since you left the prosecutor's office? We looked at everything we could. Dick Bartke, my investigator, logged over three hundred hours on that case."

"Most of that went into locating witnesses for the penalty phase of the trial," I cut in. "I thought you did a thorough job with that. What we're looking at is the guilt question."

Blanton shook his head and lit another cigarette. "I still don't follow."

"You got stiffed in discovery. The victims' john books weren't produced, or weren't found. Your investigator never located the other witnesses to the Klimka murder. The man on the balcony and the woman running away from the scene."

Blanton snorted, puffing out little clouds of smoke. "Riordan," he said, "I don't know anything about you, but it's pretty clear you don't know that much about Bobby Polhaus. That crap about the other witnesses didn't come out until the second time I interviewed him. And I interviewed him real carefully, if you get my drift. I said, 'Now, Bob, are you sure there wasn't anyone else around? Think hard.' And it was only after I asked him that question four or five times that he came up with his story about the man on the balcony and the running woman. It was the only thing we had, it threw in something new for the jury to think about, and it didn't conflict with his explanation for why he knew the dead girls. So I ran with it. But if you're asking me deep down—do I believe it?—the answer is hell, no, I don't."

"Did you have it checked out?"

"Sure I did. Dick Bartke took a look at the registrations at the motel and came up with a couple of phony names, cash payers, that were there that night. He interviewed other people staying there, in nearby rooms, and they didn't see anything. He checked out the license numbers on the registration cards and tried to match them up with the people staying there, but only about half the cards had license numbers written down, and we couldn't find any plate numbers that didn't match up with the known people staying there. The only thing we ever got was that the day desk clerk, who worked the shift before Polhaus, checked in a man around six who paid cash. That desk clerk was the owner's nephew or something, a kid just a couple of months off the boat from Hong Kong who didn't speak much English and thought all the round-eyes look alike. The description we got from him was pure shit, could have fit anybody. There was something funny about that description, now that I think of it. The kid said that the guy he checked in looked familiar to him, like he'd seen him at the motel before. But he still couldn't give Bartke a description that could be used for an identi-kit sketch."

"Is Bartke still around? I'd like to talk to him."

"Sure. His office is up in Ballard. Give him a call. He's probably still got most of his notes on the case."

Blanton stopped talking long enough to drain his glass and motion for another drink. "Where the hell are you going with this, anyway? You've got to attack this thing on the law, go after the sentence. Polhaus did those hookers. His background showed tremendous hostility toward women. I had two different psychiatrists examine Polhaus and couldn't get a decent opinion out of either of them. Even though I was paying them."

"That's just the point," Liz replied. "Polhaus would have beaten the victims, raped them. There wasn't any gratuitous violence in these deaths. They were just knocked unconscious and strangled."

"You're assuming way too much, Kleinfeldt." The alcohol was getting to him and his *s*'s and *d*'s had turned to slush. "You can't know how a killer is going to turn out, or why, especially a sex killer like Polhaus."

Liz shook her head in disagreement. "You didn't sound this way two months ago, Roy, when you talked me into taking this case on."

Blanton shot her a withering look. "I've been fighting in these trenches for thirty years. I don't ask my clients whether they're innocent; I give them a defense whether I think they are or not. You should be doing the same."

"I intend to," Liz replied. Her voice was brittle. "That's one reason I'm going to argue ineffective assistance of counsel."

Blanton's mouth dropped open in surprise. "What?" he asked thickly.

"You heard me. Why in hell didn't you follow up in discovery? Question the other johns? Why didn't you object to the DNA evidence? DNA testing is being challenged in four or five courts right now. The DNA identification from the semen stain was the only evidence that put Polhaus in the room where Klimka was killed. If you had kept it out, the state's circumstantial case would have been so weak that the jury might not have convicted. Even if they had, they'd never have gone for the death penalty. I'm probably not going to be able to raise the issue now because the court will say that you've waived it."

An angry red flush appeared on Blanton's face. He grabbed for his drink and downed it in two swallows. When he finally spoke, his voice was low, his eyes mean.

"I am the best fucking criminal lawyer in this town," he said. "No court is going to overturn a conviction saying I was incompetent. I let that DNA ID come in because the chances of keeping it out were zero. I didn't want a lot of testimony in front of the jury about how conclusive DNA testing is. The only story I had to work with was that Polhaus was banging these girls and we had to admit that he had sex with Klimka. My strategy took all the sting out of the DNA evidence, explained it away. And if you can't see that, you're too dumb to be handling this case."

He started to get up from the booth, his eyes now glassy with alcohol. Before he could leave, Liz said, "Wait. There's one other thing I have to know. Why didn't you put on any of the other prostitutes Polhaus extorted sex from? They at least could have corroborated part of his story."

Blanton suddenly laughed. "Go talk to 'em," he taunted. "We talked to one, the girl who called herself Shawna, or Tana, or something like that. Then you'll know why I never put them on."

He turned to go. I stood up and grabbed his arm. "Tell us what you know, Blanton. We don't have the time or the money to redo the work you've done. You may not like what we're doing, but you've got an obligation to the client to help us."

Blanton peeled my fingers from his arm. He smiled, but his smile was a taunt. "The girl we talked to was pretty specific about what Bobby Polhaus liked to do," he said. "He liked to tie them up in bed. With rope, with pieces of cloth, with strips of leather. Tied them tight enough to hurt them. This girl we talked to said he liked it. Sounds familiar, doesn't it?" The angry smile flashed one more time before he turned and walked away.

CHAPTER 9

Much to my surprise, Vince Ahlberg agreed to a meeting with the two detectives who had investigated the motel-room murders. On the next morning, a Friday, we met in one of the stuffy conference rooms in the SPD Homicide Section on the fourth floor of the Public Safety Building. The two detectives, Nancy Karras of SPD and Ray Leach of King County Homicide, were seated pensively at the conference table when I arrived. Karras was a trim woman in her mid-thirties, attractive in the athletic Pacific Northwest style, with straight brown hair that fell to her shoulders and dark eyes. She dressed casually but well, a beige linen blouse over matching slacks, with a wide leather belt cinching the blouse at her waist. Despite her careful makeup and grooming she looked spare and restrained, a matter of attitude as much as appearance. Only her hands betrayed the fact that she worked a physical job. They were chapped and reddened, nails chipped and repainted, a bandage on the left hand. When Karras saw me looking at her she folded her hands in her lap, out of sight beneath the table.

Sergeant Raymond Leach was an altogether more typical old-style copper, a once well-built six-footer in his mid-forties now running to fat that gathered around his waist. He had a round face that even the charitable would have called ugly; bright, close-centered eyes under heavy brows and a rubbery reddened nose. His graying black hair was carefully styled and unnaturally thick in front, the sign of a hairpiece or weave, a pretty good one. Leach wore a white short-sleeved dress shirt with brown slacks and black rubber-soled shoes, a yellow-and-brown striped tie, and a brown herringbone sport coat. As

I sat down I saw Leach pop a thick piece of Nicorette smoking substitute gum in his mouth and chew vigorously. I smiled as I shook his hand.

"It took me years to quit," I told him. "Good luck with it."

His wide fleshy face split into a smile. "Yeah," he said. "Well, it's been thirty-one days, twelve hours, and about thirty minutes. Not that I think about it."

"Right," Ahlberg said, clearing his throat. "Okay, here's the deal. Riordan here is one of the new lawyers for Robert Polhaus. He wants to ask a couple of questions about the investigation that led to Polhaus's arrest. This is strictly informal, but Riordan is not much more honest than the average lawyer, so be careful what you say. Okay, ask your questions."

"Thanks, Vince. I've read the investigative and follow-up reports that the prosecutor's office turned over in discovery. I just want to get some things cleared up so that we are not going over ground that you covered. First, even though Polhaus wasn't charged with it, the first victim appears to have been Suzanne Parker, who was killed on November 30th, down near the airport, in county jurisdiction. Sergeant Leach, you were the investigating officer, right?"

"Yeah," Leach replied. "We got the call from the manager at the JetAir Motel when I came on duty, the morning after it happened. When we got there we found the Parker woman on the bed, nude. We could tell right away that she had been hit, there was a bleeding bruise on her right temple. I secured the scene and had the crime-lab technicians and the medical examiner's people handle the body. We determined at the scene that she had been strangled from the pinpoint hemorrhages in her eyes and on her gums. No sign of whatever she'd been strangled with or of a blunt instrument; the killer had taken them with him. We did a pretty extensive survey of the motel and the surrounding area and came up with nothing. Nobody saw the Parker woman enter the motel. She was probably there to meet a john, but we never identified anyone."

"When did you identify the escort service she worked for?"

"Within a day or two. I'd seen her before, when I was on county vice. The airport area was our biggest prostitution zone, still is. I checked with a couple guys who knew her and they confirmed that she was working out of the Dreams agency. We went up there to question the agency people, but you know how that goes."

"No, I really don't."

"Well, the only thing they would say was that she had worked for them but she wasn't working the night of her murder. I'm sure she was, but they wiped the data out of their computer, because if we'd found the john and he talked, we could bust the agency for promoting prostitution. We got a search warrant for their offices, but that never works. Everything was cleaned up before we got there."

"How did they know you were coming?"

"Huh? Oh, I get it. I assume they heard about the girl's death and cleaned up before we could get the warrant served. It takes two or three days for the warrant, you know."

"I see. I also saw that Parker's apartment was searched. Did you get anything useful?"

"Yes and no. We were still nowhere on the case when Melody Beasely got whacked, and the medical examiner noticed the similarity in the cause of death and called both SPD and county to coordinate. We looked at the stuff we got from Parker to compare with Beasely, but the only common link we found was that both of them worked out of Dreams."

"What happened with that lead?"

He shrugged. "When the task force got put together, a few days after the Beasely woman was killed, I questioned Lawrence Poole, the guy who owns the Dreams agency, and got the same runaround I did before. We were hot to know if Parker and Beasely had been screwing the same guy when each of them was killed, but we never found that out from Dreams. We had a big fight with Dreams and their lawyers about getting the records. They kept saying they didn't have anything. We also questioned everybody who worked at Dreams and dispatched the women, but we never got anything."

"Did you compare the names listed in Parker's john book to a list of Beasely's regular clients?"

"I didn't know Parker had a john book."

"Sure you did," I said, my voice mild. "It was listed on the return of the warrant for the search of Parker's apartment." I rooted in my briefcase and brought out the warrant return and inventory, signed by Ray Leach. "See here on page two? 'Address book.' "

Leach read the list carefully, then looked up, puzzled. "That's what it says," he said, "but I don't remember this address book being a john book."

"Do you remember checking it out? I know it was over four years ago, that's hard to remember."

"I don't," Leach said slowly. "I wonder if I made any notes."

"Would they be in the discovery turned over to Polhaus's defense lawyers?"

"Probably not on Parker. If I remember right, the judge ordered us to turn over our reports on the Parker case to Polhaus's lawyer, but it was up to him to tell us if he wanted anything more specific, and we never got another request. And we wouldn't turn over rough notes without going to court on it. That's policy with the county and with the prosecutor's office."

Rough notes are taken by an officer during a search, witness interview, or other action. They are usually reduced to typewritten reports the same day and often destroyed. "Did you keep your rough notes?" I asked, just to be sure.

"No. I threw them out after he was convicted."

I decided to stay focused on the john book. "Do you know if the Parker john book—or address book—is still in the files somewhere?"

He shook his head. "If we had it, it would be in our evidence lock-up, but it might have been released to the next of kin by now, since it wasn't used at trial or made an exhibit." He paused. "Funny. I really don't remember this." He stood up. "Be back in five. Too much goddamned coffee this morning." He left the room quickly.

I turned to Nancy Karras. "I understand that your first involvement was after Beasely was killed. Is that correct?"

"Yes." She nodded without warmth. I saw that she had arranged her notebook and two pens and two pencils on the table in front of her with military precision. "We received the call the morning after the murder, reporting that a motel housekeeper had found the body, just like county had with Parker. We secured the body and the scene. I had two patrol officers join me and my former regular partner, Jim Madding. We surveyed all the guests in the motel. We did not want to lose any potential witnesses. That took the better part of the first morning."

"Did you identify Polhaus as a suspect immediately?"

"No. An out-of-town couple had seen him near the room where the body was found. We didn't think much of that at first, since he was a security guard, and would be expected to be in the area. My primary thought was to locate the john. Detective Leach checked with county vice and ascertained that Beasely was working out of the Dreams agency. He served a warrant on them, which also came up empty."

"Did you search Beasely's home?"

"Yes. She was sharing an apartment with another woman, a Jacqueline Rogers, also a prostitute. We did not locate an address book or a customer list for either of them."

I made a notation on my pad. Jacqueline Rogers was the name that had been circled on Ahlberg's copy of one of the follow-up reports, listed as a friend of Suzanne Parker. She had ties to both Parker and Beasely. Until I knew more, I didn't want to ask a lot of direct questions about Rogers.

"How soon after the murder was that?" I continued.

"Probably several days. The report was turned over in discovery; you can check the dates."

"What did Rogers have to say, if anything?"

"I can't recall exactly. It's in the report. I do recall that she did not know whether Beasely was working that night or not. Rogers was not very cooperative. She and Beasely had had a disagreement of some sort and were not talking to each other."

"Did you follow that up?"

"Yes. The Rogers woman had an alibi. She was working as a nude dancer on the night Beasely was killed."

"Polhaus said there was a TV crew in the King's Inn on the night of the Beasely murder. Did you look at the tape they shot?"

"I did, yes." She rubbed her hands together nervously. "Polhaus wasn't in it. There was nothing out of the ordinary. It was some kind of feature. For Mark Starrett's show."

"Were the tapes kept?"

"No. They were meaningless. I just looked at them and returned them."

Ray Leach returned and I sat for a moment trying to frame my next question. Nancy Karras remained silent. She had answered each question without visible emotion, but I sensed some tension behind the blank expression. I didn't think she was holding back anything. It was more like the strain of an overschooled witness, trying to make each statement with an unnatural precision. And it was entirely possible that she was just uncomfortable being questioned. Most people are.

"What about the third victim, Sharee Klimka?" I asked. "Was a john book ever located for her?"

"What're you trying to drive at here, Riordan?" Ray Leach asked, jumping back into the conversation. "You trying to make it look like the victims' customers did them in?"

"I'm not trying to do anything, Sergeant. I just read the reports and wondered if anything had been done to locate these victims' customers and see if any of them had a screw loose."

"We did some of that, sure," Leach replied. "Only we couldn't find anything. We never did get a list of customers for Klimka, did we, Detective?" Leach was referring to Nancy Karras. I was mildly surprised that each referred to the other by title, not first name. It seemed likely that their working relationship was not a happy one.

"No, we did not," Karras replied, answering Leach.

"Could you determine whether she was working on the night she was killed?"

"We were fairly certain she was," Karras said. "We found a handbag containing a credit-card imprinter, a larger bag with a change of clothes, and various paraphernalia."

"I'm sorry, I don't understand."

Karras's pinched, narrow face colored. "Leather straps. A pair of handcuffs. A blindfold. Paraphernalia associated with bondage as sexual play."

I could feel my own face redden. You can take the boy out of Montana but not the Montana out of the boy.

"Was there ever any follow-up to see if you could locate the two witnesses Polhaus claimed to have seen on the night Klimka was killed? I'm referring to the man on the motel balcony and the woman running from the scene."

"If they ever existed," Karras replied. "Polhaus left them out of his first, noncustodial statement that he gave us on the morning after the murder. We didn't become aware of them until trial. I had to stay with the prosecution team in court, but Sergeant Leach did try to find them."

"Yeah," Leach added, "I had five guys on it for two days. We never turned up anybody. By then it was next to impossible. We had no place to start. We tried our street contacts, figuring the running woman was another hooker, but came up empty. That's not surprising, most of the street girls don't have any kind of permanent address. Their pimps move them from motel to motel, city to city. We contacted everybody staying in the China Tapestry who gave their real name, which at that place doesn't happen too often. Nothing." He bared his nicotine-yellow teeth in what he used for a smile.

I turned back to Karras. "Did you ever identify the john that Klimka was supposed to meet at the motel that night?"

"No."

"How hard did you look?"

Karras stiffened. "We contacted the escort service she worked out of," she replied. "The owner insisted that Klimka was not working on the night of her death. The interview report is in the discovery materials. The owner's name was DiGregorio."

"Did you believe him?"

"Her. Sergeant Leach questioned her. I was on a few days' personal leave. But I reviewed his report, and saw no reason not to believe her."

"Despite the fact Leach had heard the exact same thing from the Dreams agency that employed the other two women?"

"Hey, look," Leach cut in, "after Klimka was killed we knew Polhaus had to be the prime suspect. It couldn't have been a coincidence, him working in two of the three motels where the girls got killed. After Detective Karras saw Polhaus at the China Tapestry, we pulled his record and tied him in. Christ, we even got his semen from the bed where the Klimka woman was found. What more do you need?"

I was debating the merits of answering hypothetical questions when the door to the conference room was slammed open by a red-faced, furious Daniel Merritt.

"Ahlberg," he said, barely controlling the anger in his voice, "what in hell is going on here? You're meeting with defense counsel in an active case without a lawyer from my office? Without even telling me, for Chrissake?"

Merritt stood in the doorway breathing heavily. He looked younger than thirty-six, with the combination of styled dark-brown hair and hard blue eyes that television cameras found so appealing. He was a short man, only about five-six or so, but with a broad-shouldered athletic grace that made him seem bigger than he really was. The courthouse rap on Merritt was that he was technically very skilled, but projected his arrogance so often, even in court, that he had offended juries and some of the King County bench. His biggest weakness was his tendency to overextend himself. He carried a full trial load on top of the administrative duties of chief of staff and sometimes didn't fully prepare his cases.

Ahlberg flicked him a look of relaxed disdain. "Calm down, Daniel," he said. "This is informal. All Riordan wants to do is ask a couple of questions about the investigation; what was done, what wasn't done. The request was not unreasonable and I granted it."

"Maybe you forget, Captain, who is in charge of a case once it has been referred to the prosecutor's office."

Ahlberg's eyes narrowed. "I've not forgotten anything, Daniel. Why don't you go back to work, write a press release or something? We're just about done here, anyway."

Merritt bristled. "Like hell I will. Riordan," he said, turning to me, "I can't believe you're doing this. Haven't you heard of the Rules of Professional Conduct? I'm going to file a bar complaint about this."

"Go ahead and file," I replied, trying to keep my temper in check. It had been years since I had been in court with Daniel Merritt. The case had been relatively minor, an assault beef in which I had defended the owner of a concrete-cutting firm who'd gotten into a fight with a subcontractor. The subcontractor hadn't told Merritt that he had taken the first swing at my client, with a shovel. The Auburn cops failed to turn up the electrician working late on the project who saw the fight. Merritt had to dismiss the charges and took the whole thing personally. I was not surprised that he remembered me. It was possible I had rubbed his nose in it.

"Look, Daniel, you know what kind of time pressure we're under," I added. "If we're going to give our client decent representation we have to get on top of the facts quickly. Besides, the RPCs don't apply here. You're not counsel for the SPD, and you're not counsel for the state in this case any longer. So why don't you stop trying to fuck us over?"

Merritt finally lost control of his temper. His face turned bright scarlet and he stuttered when he tried to speak. When he had calmed down he said, "You can tell it to the Disciplinary Board. This interview is terminated."

"Before you make that kind of rash decision, Daniel," I said, "maybe you'd better take a look at your own performance. When you were asked for discovery in the Polhaus case, you kept quite a few things out. Like Suzanne Parker's john book. I'm sure the defense would have liked to know the names of all her customers, especially since you linked the Parker case in the press to the Beasely and Klimka murders, yet you couldn't prove a connection when you got to trial."

Merritt took the bait. "Bullshit. We turned over everything we had to, and you know it."

"Then why wasn't Parker's john book turned over? I've got a list of every document and every piece of physical evidence you produced, and I know it wasn't there. We could be talking about a *Brady* violation here. Maybe that's why you're so pissed."

"That's crap," he said quickly, but the color was beginning to drain out of his face. A serious *Brady* issue, even one uncovered this late, would give us a chance to stall Polhaus's execution, possibly even get the case reopened. Merritt saw it coming and decided to back off. "I'll tell you what," he said. "If you want the goddamned book so bad, you can have a copy of it. It won't get you anywhere."

"We accept your offer, Counsel. Suppose you send it up to Lisle, Day's office this afternoon. The original, not a copy. I want to examine it."

"Fine." He turned back to Ahlberg. "Get him out of here, Captain. I don't want you or your people talking to him again." He swept out of the room, slamming the door shut behind him.

Ahlberg stared at the closed door. "I almost hope he gets elected attorney general," he said. "At least it would get him out of King County." He sighed and turned back to me. "Is there anything else you wanted to go over?"

"Not right now. I think we'd better quit, if only to save your officers some political grief. Thank you all for your time."

I repacked my briefcase while Karras and Leach filed out of the room. Ahlberg hesitated for a moment in the doorway.

"I still don't get it," he said. "I'm not a lawyer but I know you can't get a murder conviction reversed just by poking some holes in my detectives' investigation. What are you after, anyway?"

"Let me ask you a question," I replied. "Why does your copy of one of Leach's follow-up reports have the phone number for the King County IIU written on it?"

Ahlberg's face darkened with anger. "Were you rummaging through my files when I left you alone in my office the other day?" he demanded.

"No. I checked your copy of the report because I'd left mine in the car and I wanted to be sure I had my facts right when we talked. Why in hell was IIU involved in this case?"

"They weren't. Between you and me, I'd heard Leach was a turkey. He'd had some trouble and I wanted to know what it was before I took him on. It was nothing. A hooker complained he'd been rough with her back when he was working in the Vice Unit. They opened a file, but the hooker dropped the complaint."

"If it was nothing," I said, "then why did Leach go running out of here to call Merritt when I started pushing him about Parker's john book?"

"He probably did the right thing. You set this meeting up on the pretext you needed background and then you start cross-examining my people."

"That's not an answer, Vince. What the hell is going on here? I asked a few basic background questions and Leach and Merritt panicked. Why?"

"Out," he said, hooking a thumb at the door. "I know what you're trying to pull. You're going to blacken my cops any way you can to get his conviction reversed."

"If I have to. But you're halfway admitting that the tar's already there."

He shook his head and stalked out of the conference room. I packed up and followed him out. I wasn't surprised that Ahlberg would get territorial when I started probing his cops' work. His natural instinct was to back up his officers, even one who was dumped on him, like Raymond Leach. Leach looked to be a county Mountie of the old school, a survivor of the mid-1980s reforms that weeded out some of the corrupt and hopelessly dumb coppers who used to police the county with a nightstick for the poor and a blind eye for the connected. Leach's call to Merritt showed some advanced survival skills. I turned the problem over in my mind on the walk up Fourth Avenue to the towers of the financial district and Lisle, Day's offices. I still didn't have an answer when I got there and Liz said it was time to go back to work on the brief.

At ten-thirty that Friday night I gave the last section of our rewritten brief to a word processor in Liz's office and returned to the small conference room that we had turned into a war room. The table was covered with stacks of West's Case Law Reporters, empty coffee cups, sandwich wrappers, and piles of notes and rejected drafts. Liz was curled into one of the leather chairs, her eyes closed. I sat down in the chair next to her and finished the cold dregs of my coffee. When she didn't stir I put a gentle hand on her arm. She came awake slowly and smiled at me.

"What happened to Porras and Anderson?" I asked. The two

junior lawyers had volunteered to stay the night if we needed them.

"I sent them home. They can check the case citations tomorrow, which gives us Monday morning for a final reading."

"How do you feel?"

"We've done the best job we can with what we've got. I think the constitutional challenge to the death-penalty statute, the use of parole status as an aggravating factor, is pretty strong. It should be enough to get us a stay of the execution date, for a couple of months, maybe. I just wish we had something on these john books. The court's not going to give us an evidentiary hearing unless we come up with something."

I reached out and took her hand. "That's not what I meant, Lizabeth."

"Oh." She smiled wearily. "I feel okay, I guess."

"Want to get something to eat?"

"I don't want to go out. I'm a mess." She looked at her watch and sighed. "It's too late, anyway."

"It's still raining. Why don't we go up to my apartment? I'll order some Chinese takeout and light a fire."

Liz hesitated. "I don't ... what are we slipping back to, Matthew? Are we going to be lovers again? I don't know if I'm ready for that. The other night ... that might have been a mistake."

I shook my head. "If it was, that's something we'll find out soon enough. I couldn't have guessed how much it meant to have you back in my life, Lizabeth. And all I'm asking is that we take it one day at a time. If you're willing."

She thought about it for a long time. "I'm willing," she said.

As I turned off Prospect into the alley leading to my garage the car behind me slowed and pulled into the entrance to Volunteer Park. I paused in the mouth of the alley and waited for the car to turn around and head back down the hill to Broadway. When it didn't return I pulled ahead into the garage, saying nothing. I waited in my living room until Liz had gone into the kitchen to telephone a Chinese restaurant before opening the French doors to the terrace. The same car was parked across the street, facing west, lights off. It was a dark-colored mid-sized American sedan, a standard rental or government car. From above I could not determine its make or see its license plates. I felt a brief cold touch of fear. What the hell had we stumbled into?

I heard the car's engine grind into life. The car pulled away, lights still off. I stepped back quickly into the apartment and closed the doors. It had been a very long day and I decided not to tell Liz until the next morning that we had been followed home from her office.

CHAPTER 10

Saturday dawned with another barrage of wind and rain. The late-winter storms were lined up in the Gulf of Alaska like artillery rounds waiting to be dropped on the city. Liz left for her office reluctantly. Both of us wanted nothing more than a quiet day of coffee and books, with a fire to chase the damp chill from my apartment. But she had to catch up on her regular caseload and to keep tapping her sources about Leach's IIU file. I had a grimmer task—to go back through the crime-scene photographs and to look at the motel rooms where the murders had taken place.

Any investigation worthy of the name is something more than the dry accumulation of facts on paper. When I was trying cases, even civil cases, I made a point of going to the place where the accident or assault or robbery happened, the homes and workplaces of the people involved, the cafés where they ate breakfast, the taverns they hung out in every night. I was looking for something more than inconsistencies, like the witness who swears he saw the accident from his bedroom window, and when you go to his house you find that it is two blocks away and screened by thick trees. I was searching, in some nonscientific, mystic way, for psychological insights that would help me understand the all-too-fallible human beings involved. I had no idea what I might learn from seeing the motel rooms, but I had to find out.

The JetAir Motel was on the Pacific Highway South, in the sprawling, nasty gore of motels, neon-lit taverns, car-rental agencies and third-rate office buildings that had grown up around the Sea-Tac Airport. The motel dated from the 1960s, a two-story box with the doors to the rooms on the back side, away from the highway. The motel sign, a stylized 707, was rusty and the neon tubes were broken. The bored, middle-aging desk clerk had beer on his breath at eight-thirty in the morning and listened to scarcely half my explanation before handing me the room key and turning his back to watch some over-muscled bleached-blond wrestlers on cable. I didn't even have to bribe him.

I splashed through the rain to the main building. The room where Parker had been murdered was on the first floor, the number 9 inscribed in dulled brass on a cheap plywood door. The inside of the room was no better: lime-green shag carpet, darker-green bedspread, two ripped brown vinyl chairs beside a chest of drawers with peeling veneer. The bathroom had a moldy tub/shower combination and a persistent drip from leaking pipes. The room had not been rented in several days and stank of disinfectant and stale smoke.

I took out the Parker crime-scene photos, gritting my teeth as I always did at the first sight of the body. Most of my time as a federal prosecutor had been served on the organized-crime task forces, but I did my first two years in the Washington, D.C., United States Attorney's office, working my way up from street misdemeanors to a second-chair role on homicide cases. I had never developed a thickened skin for the photographs. The victims were always too young, too battered, often young women destroyed by men they had trusted, even loved.

I compared the photos with the room, moving to place myself where the photographer had stood when each photo was taken. The furniture in the room had not been changed. Parker's large shoulder bag was on the floor, apparently kicked over in a struggle. Tissues and bottles and tubes were strewn on the floor. Her clothes were piled in a jumble on one of the chairs. The body had been found on top of the bedspread, as if lying on a bier. I lay down on the bed and tried to mimic the position of Parker's body, face-up, hands folded over her pubis. The natural position would have been more open, with the hands falling to the sides. One point to Ahlberg: Parker's body had been placed that way by the murderer. I shrugged off the chill dampness of the room and left, trying hard not to draw conclusions too soon.

Room 317 of the King's Inn north of downtown Seattle had two single beds, each with a headboard, a nightstand between the beds, a single dresser-desk combination bearing a television, and a round table with four green vinyl chairs. Melody Beasely's body had been found on the bed farthest from the door, near a large window that overlooked an alley and a run-down brick apartment building. I took the crime-scene photos and again walked through the photographer's paces. Beasely's body had been found in the same position as Parker's, face-up, on top of the bedspread. Her purse and shoulder bag were intact beside the bed, her clothes stacked on one of the dressers, neatly folded. I paused for a moment and listened to the sounds of the motel. The King's Inn, unlike the JetAir or the China Tapestry, had inside hallways, making it more difficult to get in or out of a room without being seen by a passing maid or guest. The neatly folded clothes suggested that the killer felt comfortable he would not be discovered and took the time to straighten up before leaving.

Room 212 of the China Tapestry Motel had been decorated with a heavy hand. Blood-red carpeting, matching bedspread; black-lacquered headboard, chairs, and dresser; off-white walls; cheap oriental prints of dragons and mountain scenes mounted in black plastic frames screwed into the Sheetrock. The light was bad. The room had small windows and heavy draperies. Even with the draperies pulled open I had to turn on the room lights to see. Klimka's body was found in roughly the same position as the others, but the bedcovers were pulled down and to one side.

I sat down on the bed and looked at the photos of all three rooms. It looked as if Ahlberg's scenario for the murders was correct: Polhaus was a developing serial killer who struggled with the first victim and ran, then learned to kill and relish the act of killing, arranging details more suggestively each time. I leafed through the photos a second time with the nagging sense that I had missed something important. Eventually I found it. All three motels had ice machines. Ice buckets, multiple ashtrays, and extra glasses were spotted around the rooms. Presumably all three women drank. Polhaus did, heavily, and he chain-smoked. It was only at the third motel, the China Tapestry, that there were dirty glasses and used ashtrays in the backdrop of the pictures. The police had not gotten Polhaus's prints from the glasses because they were too smeared to be readable, a fact the prosecution explained away by implying that Polhaus wiped them, even though Klimka was the only victim Polhaus admitted seeing before the murder. The condition of the rooms seemed to support his story. If he killed all three of them, why would he drink, smoke, and have sex with one victim, and not the others? It made no sense.

I was still puzzling over the photos when a maid knocked on the door to tell me that the motel was filling up and needed me out. I left quickly, sure that these rooms were not places that I wanted to sleep in. Or die in.

I was fumbling for my keys in the parking lot when an unmarked SPD Dodge Aries pulled up beside me. Nancy Karras cracked the window open and said, "What on earth are you doing here, Mr. Riordan?"

"Trying to understand what happened when Sharee Klimka was killed. Why are you here?"

"I saw you from the street. On my way home from my errands." Karras waved at two bags of groceries and a pile of dry cleaning in the back seat. She got out of her car and stretched. A light rain was still falling and she pulled her trench-coat collar up around her neck to ward off the chill. Her hair was pulled back into a short ponytail. She wore no makeup and looked almost relaxed compared with the grim professional I had interviewed the day before.

Karras gave me a tentative half-smile and said, "I'm sorry things blew up yesterday. I don't mind answering your questions. I know you've got a job to do and you're under a lot of time pressure fighting the execution date. But surely you don't doubt that Polhaus killed these women. Off the record."

"Off the record. Not a reasonable doubt. Not yet. But that stunt Leach pulled, calling Merritt in to bust up the meeting, has me wondering."

"That's Leach," Karras said heavily.

"Meaning?"

She shrugged. "He's a scorecard cop. Take the file and get it closed, beat the defense lawyer in court, move on to the next one. I don't think he's hiding anything from you. To him you're just the enemy."

"Maybe. Did you know he had an IIU file?"

"Not back then. It wouldn't have made any difference to

me. Every cop who works vice gets one sooner or later. I've got one, too, if you're checking. From a couple of years ago. A forty-year-old accountant who was chicken-hawking a teenage boy on Second Avenue. He took a swing at me, and I popped him. His lawyer filed an excessive-force complaint, trying to confuse the issue a little." She smiled ruefully and shook her head.

I looked at her a moment. "I might be imagining things, but I got the feeling yesterday that there's something about this case that still bothers you. Am I wrong?"

"No." She looked back at the China Tapestry, the dingy brick and peeling paint, the sagging balconies, hard by the busy arterial road with its endless drone of traffic. "I am still troubled by it. But not because of Polhaus. It's his victims. They were so young—the oldest was just twenty. They'd been hooking for years. They'd been thrown out by their families, thrown out of school, just plain thrown away. Disposable people. And dying in places like this."

"Ahlberg said you've worked juvenile and vice. You must have seen this kind of story before."

Suppressed anger glinted in her dark eyes. "It never gets easier. Not for me. This is what sexual exploitation looks like, Riordan. It looks like cheap motels and strutting pimps and children in body bags. You know about your client's record? The rapes? The beatings?"

I nodded. "I know. But he can only be convicted for what he's done. Not for what he is."

"Maybe that should change." She took another look back at the motel and shook a little. "I'm getting cold. And wet. You're not going to find anything to help Polhaus here."

She started to go back to her car. "Will you answer a couple more questions?" I asked.

She turned back. "Why?"

"Because I think you're an honest cop."

"Go ahead."

"Did Leach bury the Parker woman's john book? Did he have some reason for not wanting to question her customers?"

"Jesus Christ," she said, exasperated. "The answer's no. Not as far as I know. Everything we had pointed to Polhaus." She took a step closer and stared at me for a moment, anger building again in her eyes. "Your client," she said distinctly, "is a serial killer. He can't or won't be reformed or cured. He preyed on prostitutes because they were the most vulnerable, exploitable women he could find. I'm glad we stopped him. And I find it more than a little obscene that you want to put him back on the street so he can kill again." Karras was cold, bitter, and precise.

"That's not what this is about, Detective. You know that."

She wasn't listening. She turned to the street, distracted by something caught out of the corner of her eye. I looked past her and saw a car stopped across the road in the far right-hand lane. The driver honked. A black teenage girl, maybe sixteen, tottered out to the car on high heels from the doorway where she had been standing. She stuck her head in the door, negotiated quickly, got in. The car pulled away.

Karras took out a pen to write down the license-plate number. "That child could be dead in the next twenty minutes. The odds are she will die in the next three years. At least I know that Polhaus isn't driving that car. That there is one less monster on the street. And that, Mr. Riordan, is what this is all about."

CHAPTER 11

Jennifer DiGregorio, the owner and manager of the escort service that employed Sharee Klimka at the time of her death, had an office in the lower level of a glass-and-concrete office park off Interstate 405 in Bothell. I parked behind a screen of tall pines and knocked on the door of a small basement office marked with the name "Bobbie Jean Services, Inc." The woman who answered the locked door was small, dark, intense, and wary. She admitted to being Jennifer DiGregorio but to nothing else. When I explained what I wanted she took me inside a fairly tasteful two-office suite, with low rounded chairs and sofas covered in gray fabric and desks finished in red-toned mahogany. Most of the desks had personal computers and telephone consoles. The prints on the walls were vaguely abstract, the sort of mass-market imitation art you can rent with office furniture.

DiGregorio caught me eyeing the decor as we walked to her office.

"Something wrong?" she asked.

"For a sex business, it's disappointing," I said.

Her look wavered between amusement and alarm. "We're not in the sex business, Mr. Riordan. We're in the introduction business. We bring together adults for conversation and business entertainment. What they do after that is up to them and none of our business." She sounded rehearsed. It was a speech she had made before.

"Look," I said, "if you want to keep the necessary legal fig leaf in place, that's fine. We can talk hypothetically, I can start out every question with the word 'assume,' or we can cut the nonsense and get down to business. I've got no interest in talking to the cops about you. All I want is some background information on Sharee Klimka. She was working here when she got killed."

DiGregorio didn't answer. She wore black stirrup tights and a matching top that showed off her busty, slightly stocky shape. Gold loops dangled from her ears. She sat down behind her desk and took a glass ashtray and a gold pack of Benson & Hedges out of a desk drawer and lit one. She leaned back in her chair and said, "That happened a long time ago. What do you want to know?"

"On the night Sharee Klimka was killed, was she working out of your agency?"

"No. She wasn't scheduled for anything that night. We had somebody call and ask for her, not by name but by type—a tall skinny blond lady—and we tried to reach her about taking the date. She didn't answer the phone or the pager."

"Do you know what time that was?"

"No. It could have been anywhere between nine o'clock at night to three in the morning."

"Would you have any record of it?"

"Not anymore. We purge everything but revenue data after three months."

"Then how can you remember calling her?" I was pushing again and the tone of my voice made DiGregorio defensive.

"I put it in my police statement," she replied. "It sticks in my mind for that reason."

"Did Klimka talk to you about Robert Polhaus, or about a motel desk clerk who was extorting sex from her?"

"No. I didn't know anything about it. I'm not a den mother, and the women who work here don't confide in me unless they have a problem they can't handle."

"Did Klimka have any friends here, anyone she would confide in, anything like that?"

"Not really. Or, I should say, not that I know of. She would talk to me, talk to others—normal stuff, nothing special."

"Was she gay?"

"What difference does that make?"

"If she was, I'd want to talk to her lover, and ask the same questions."

"She wasn't gay. A couple of women here wanted to know if she was interested, but she wasn't."

"Did she have a boyfriend? Or a family?"

"She had boyfriends, off and on, none serious. As I recall she did not have a regular man when she was killed. Like many women in this business, she'd been burned by men who wanted to live off her earnings. I don't know where her family was. Out on the Olympic Peninsula, I think, one of the timber towns. She didn't talk about her family."

"I thought she had a relative somewhere in the north end. A cousin or something."

DiGregorio shrugged, a surprisingly elegant, almost catlike gesture. "It's possible, but I don't remember her mentioning anyone."

"How long had she been working for you before she was killed?"

"Not long. Maybe three, four months."

"Did she have any specialties?"

"What?" Her eyes darkened with anger.

I closed my eyes and rubbed the bridge of my nose. The day had been dark and long and I hadn't enough wit left to run a proper witness interview. "Let's not fence. Did she dress up like Little Bo Peep, or a cheerleader, or do doubleheaders?"

DiGregorio shot me another dark look. "Are you serious?"

"Extremely. I am not shopping and I am not a police plant. Her body was found with bondage gear. Was it hers?"

She pushed a nervous hand through her short spiky black hair. "Sharee did some scenes. Nothing really serious."

"What kind of scenes?"

"The leather stuff, you know? No pain, just the image. She looked very good in it, all that thick blond hair and black leather."

"So it was her stuff, found with her body."

"Yes. I mean, probably. I didn't look at it."

I paused for a minute to think. If Polhaus really was innocent, we had to start thinking about alternate suspects. A regular customer of all three women who was into leather goods might not be a bad start. A fetish gone haywire might explain the common pattern of strangulation among all three victims.

"Who were her customers? For S and M or bondage?"

Her mouth took on a stubborn set. "I'm not giving you any names."

"But she had a list?"

"The agency had a list. We had two or three women who did some fantasy stuff. Sharee was one of them. We always sent them out in pairs, to make sure nobody got hurt."

"Did Sharee Klimka have a private john book?"

"Not that I ever saw. We don't want the women here working their own private clients. We can't get help to them if they need it if we don't know where they are."

I paused for a moment and thought. There was no chance that DiGregorio would give me any information that could lead me to Klimka's customers. If I pushed she would stop talking completely. I decided to get what I could. "Do you know where Klimka was working before she came here?" I asked.

"Yes. At Dreams."

"Why'd she leave?"

She looked suddenly angry. "Do you know Larry Poole?"

"I know of him. Some people say he's dangerous."

"Well, some people are right for once. Poole's a sadistic creep. Most of the men who run agencies have enough sense to leave the women alone. Poole doesn't. He treats them like they're his personal harem. Sometimes he hurts them."

"Is that what happened to Sharee Klimka?"

"It's the reason she came here. Poole took her up for a couple of weeks. He hit her. When she split from him, he broke into her place and raped her. She didn't report it. He finally lost interest in her, and she got out. She's lucky it wasn't worse."

"What is worse than a rape?"

She shrugged. "He might not have stopped as quickly as he did."

"Meaning he might have killed her?"

She stopped herself. "You're trying to put words in my mouth. How could I know something like that?" Her voice was cautious. She was saying too much, and she knew it.

I paused, trying to figure out my next question. While I was thinking she lit another cigarette and blew smoke at the ceiling. I finally said, "Look, you sound like you care about the people who work for you. That means you've got a good ear for what goes on in your business. You'd have to, to keep your people safe. What else can you tell me about Poole? Anything."

She looked at me warily. "And this goes no farther?"

"You know I can't promise that. I need to use whatever you tell me. But the information will get used without your name attached, unless you know something that relates to Sharee Klimka's murder."

She thought that over. "I don't think I do," she finally said. "But I don't understand. Sharee's killer was caught and convicted. Why start over now?"

"The woman I work for is a very smart former prosecutor. Sure, she's representing Polhaus, and it's her job to get his conviction overturned. But she took the case because she doubts Polhaus was guilty. She's trying to get the facts, one way or another."

DiGregorio shrugged. "I already told you what I know about Poole. Over the past six years, since he got into the business, there were three or four women who worked for him, and then disappeared. Supposedly they just left town, up to Alaska or down to L.A. Nothing came of it. Poole is connected with a pretty good crowd, lawyers and doctors and the occasional politician or two, hanging out in the best places in Seattle and in Bellevue. He collects friends in high places."

"That's not very specific," I replied. "Who are his friends? And how does he get them?"

"I don't know their names. But he's said to throw some parties for them, at his expense. He provides them with women. Sometimes they pay, sometimes they don't."

"Where are these parties? At his house, a hotel, what?"

"I don't know." She snubbed out her cigarette. "A couple of the women who work here now used to work for him. I suppose they could tell you more."

"I'll need their names."

She looked doubtful, caught between what seemed like a pretty clear hatred of Poole and her personal interest in keeping her business from the police. "I shouldn't have told you that. I've got your word they won't be hassled?"

"Yes."

"Okay. Call me next week, Monday or Tuesday. You'll have to talk to them here. Otherwise they won't tell you anything."

I nodded. "Thanks."

She stood up to dismiss me. "Anything else?"

"Yes, there is."

She sat down reluctantly. "What?" she demanded.

"Tell me about Sharee Klimka. The kind of person she was."

"Oh, God, I don't know," she said, exasperated. "You want to know what she was like? She was nineteen when she was murdered. She was on the streets at seventeen and the only thing that kept her from getting killed there was her looks and a good body. She got off the streets and into the safer part of the business. She didn't use anything except alcohol and some occasional cocaine. She learned to make her tricks use condoms and she got tested and she didn't have AIDS. She had an apartment full of toy stuffed animals and she liked to go down to Mexico a couple of times a year and pretend that she was a rich girl, lie in the sun and talk about cars and boys and the kind of house she was going to have someday. She was so damned dumb." Her voice caught and she heard herself and she stopped. "And that's it," she added. Her voice grew cold. "That's all I know."

"Except that you had a crush on her."

She looked up at me, her black eyes flashing anger. "You're a real bastard, you know that?"

"Positively. But we are on the same side here. If Polhaus killed her, he's on death row and he'll eventually hang for it. If he didn't, I'm the only guy who's trying to find out who did kill her. If you think of anything else, give me a call." I handed her a card with my name and home telephone number. "Anything at all."

I went to my car and waited. I had half a notion that DiGregorio might go somewhere, talk to someone about the questions I had asked her. If she did she would do it in person, not over a phone that could be tapped. I sat for an hour watching the door to her office through a gap in the trees surrounding the low white concrete office park. Nothing happened. Eventually a couple of other women entered the office. I waited another hour, just to be sure, and finally decided that DiGregorio had told me something that resembled the truth, especially about Sharee Klimka. From the evidence photographs I knew only that Klimka had been young and vacantly pretty in a blond, coarse sort of way. Now I could see in my mind's eye the half-grown woman who had been hard enough to ply her trade and soft enough to like stuffed toys and the earnest attentions of Mexican boys on the beach.

Halfway down the interstate to Bellevue I pulled off at a gas station and called Liz at home. When she answered her voice sounded distant, nearly smothered by the overpowering strains of Beethoven's *Ninth* in the background.

"How are you?" she asked after she'd turned the stereo down.

"Covered in slime, sort of," I replied. "I've been to the death scenes, ran into Karras, and spent most of the afternoon trying to pry information out of an escort-service owner. Look, you want to have dinner, see a movie, go to bed? In any order you like."

She sighed. "I . . . that's probably not such a good idea. We've been having things happen pretty fast between us."

My hand tightened on the phone but I kept my voice soft. "Lizabeth, that's not what you said last night."

"I didn't say we'd start living together again," she snapped.

I felt a vein throb in my forehead. "That's not what I'm asking. I have had a shit day working your case and—"

"So I got you down from your mountain and now I owe you?" she demanded, her voice rising.

It was starting to be a script I could have written from memory. "Damn it, you're . . . no, you're right. My mistake."

"Matthew, I'm sor——" I missed the rest. I put the phone back down on the cradle. I got in my car and took the freeway south to I-90, back into Seattle, looking for any reasonably friendly saloon that would take me in.

The Pink Door is a high-ceilinged Italian joint carved out of a warehouse space at the north end of the Pike Place Market. It has marble-topped tables, low lights, and warm, yellow-painted walls. It has more than passable lasagna and a friendly bartender who talks to anyone who shows up alone. It almost always has its collective tongue firmly planted in its cheek.

When I got there it was only seven-thirty and the bar was

about half full. I found a stool at the end of the bar and had a vodka martini and a half bottle of red wine with an antipasto plate, followed by lasagna and salad. I dawdled over coffee, trying to look charming, and gave the venture up as hopeless soon after. The night belonged to the happily coupled and to students from the University and the local colleges, all dressed in arty, head-to-toe black. I paid the check, thanked the bartender, and walked out through the dining room to the stairs leading to Post Alley. As I went up the stairs I saw Vince Ahlberg and Nancy Karras at a corner table. They were huddled over a wine list, their heads together. It was not a staff meeting and it was not my place to intrude. I walked by them without slowing, unnoticed, and went home with one more uncomfortable fact to sleep on.

CHAPTER 12

I had left messages for television reporter Mark Starrett since Friday, hoping to see the videotape his crew had shot at the King's Inn on the night Melody Beasely was murdered. I wasn't looking for anything in particular, just trying to get every possible piece of information that related to the case. He finally returned my call late on Sunday afternoon as I was dozing over the scattered remains of coffee, bagels, and the three Sunday newspapers—Seattle, New York, and Los Angeles—that I subscribe to.

"Sorry I haven't been able to get back to you," he said. "What's this all about?"

I quickly explained who I was and what I wanted. There was a long pause on the telephone while Starrett thought.

"You're supposed to get a subpoena," he said at last. "But

I'm willing to show it to you if you want. We've still got a file copy of the show. I don't think there's anything on the tape that's relevant to Beasely's murder. It was a fluff piece. The title was *Working Stiffs at Christmas*. Something like that. I'm at the station now, getting ready to anchor the evening news. If you want to watch it, why don't you come down?"

"Great. I'll be there in half an hour."

KSTO, Starrett's television station, was off Fifth Avenue at the foot of Queen Anne Hill. I got there a little after five and waited in the dimly lit lobby, watching the network news feed from New York. Starrett finally showed up at five-thirty, an exasperated look on his face.

"Sorry to keep you waiting," he said, signing me in at the security desk. "Ted Offenbacher is out with the flu and nobody's written the copy for the six o'clock news, so I'm on a dead run. But I'm curious. Do you really think you'll find anything?"

I shook my head. "Probably not. I know you're busy. All I need is to be put into a room where I can play the tape. I won't bother you."

"I'll get one of the station interns to set you up. Please stick around until I get done with the news. I may want to do something on the show about this case of yours. Sounds interesting." He phoned from the reception desk, then led me down a long corridor to the rear of the studio, past the news and talk-show sets, into an editing room. I waited while the intern, named Joyce, switched on the video equipment and pushed the casette into the player. "You wanted the December 24, 1989 show, *Working Stiffs*, right?" she asked.

"I guess so." I watched as the credits rolled and a voice-over announced that I was looking at "Puget Sound's Number-One-Rated Video Magazine." Starrett appeared in front of a brilliantly lit Christmas tree in Westlake Plaza. A choir sang carols in the background. "Tonight on Christmas Eve," he was saying, "*The Starrett Report* looks at the lives of the working stiffs around this city that worked long hours this holiday season to make your days and nights brighter. We begin at the King's Inn Motor Hotel in Seattle, filled with holiday shoppers and guests."

"This is it," I said. "Thanks."

"I'll be back in twenty minutes to see if you need anything else," she replied, and left.

I settled in to watch the tape. The show began in the motel

coffee shop, where tired middle-aging waitresses worked the dinner shift. The footage and the interviews were cleverly mixed, catching just the right tone of dignity in a job well done despite aching feet, testy customers, and the meanest short-order cook west of Montana. The tape cut to brief interviews with the motel desk clerk, several maids, and finally the bartender, the woman Polhaus had called Jaye. She was tall and lean, her face hardened beyond her years. "You've got to keep them happy," she said, "even when they've had too much and it's time to cut them off." The camera shifted to a table of drunken salesmen sitting beneath a big-screen television showing a hockey game. They pounded their glasses on the table, demanding another round. The bartender tried to jolly them out of what was clearly going to be the one drink too many. When one of them got up and tried to dance with her she wormed her way out of his grasp and reached the telephone behind the bar. There was a camera cut. Polhaus appeared in the next frame, getting an arm lock on the unruly drunk and sending the group out the door. Starrett reappeared and briefly talked to the drunks as they stood outside on the street. There was a dead space in the tape, apparently for a commercial. The next segment dealt with two salesclerks in the women's clothing section of The Bon Marché department store as they guided a couple of befuddled husbands through the onerous chore of buying Christmas presents for their wives.

I listened to the rest of the show with half an ear, disappointed. I took out my notes to question Starrett about his exact movements on the night Beasely was killed, ready to pass the next hour until Starrett would be free.

The show ended with the closing credits superimposed over Starrett's sign-off shot, a handsome, sunny, summertime view of the downtown Seattle skyline from the deck of one of the Bainbridge Island ferries. The tape blanked to white electronic snow. I got up to switch it off. Suddenly the screen filled with another view of the King's Inn bar. Jaye served a lone customer at the bar, then walked to a rear corner table where two women had just sat down. The women were dressed in short cocktail dresses with plunging backlines, the amount of skin jarringly out of place in the shoddy motel bar. Jaye huddled briefly with them, her voice too low to be picked up by the portable mike. She straightened up and gestured toward the street door of the bar. The women pushed their hands out in a placating gesture, then got to their feet. They slammed their chairs angrily against the table as they left. There were another four or five minutes of quick disjointed camera cuts and short scenes set in other parts of what looked like the same motel, from the car park to the basement laundry. I watched the tape carefully, eventually realizing that I was looking at some of the rejected, cut footage shot for the same show. The segment at the King's Inn ran about ten minutes; the camera crew must have originally shot three to four hours of film.

I rewound the tape to the show's end, then played the outtakes back again at one-half speed, rubbing my eyes to ease the slow-motion distortion. At half speed it took about eight minutes to replay the scene in the bar of the King's Inn. I remembered what Polhaus had told us in Walla Walla: that Jaye had thrown two hookers out of the bar after he had been called to toss out the Canadian salesmen. The tape seemed to confirm Polhaus's story.

I backed up the tape. When the two women stood up to go, I stopped it and stared.

One of the women had long red hair. The other woman, younger and thinner, had darker skin and black hair.

Polhaus testified that the woman he had seen running from the China Tapestry Motel had long red hair.

I sat back in my chair and tried not to get my hopes up. The lighting was filled with shadows; I couldn't make out the faces of the women. At a guess there were ten prostitutes, or more, in the city who had red hair. The odds were far too long that the same woman could have been present when both Melody Beasely and Sharee Klimka had been killed. And yet it was, maybe, the slightest confirmation that Polhaus had told the truth at his trial.

I was still sitting, watching the frozen tape, when the intern came back. "Everything all right?" she asked.

"How hard would it be to get this tape duplicated?"

"Not hard. We have high-speed equipment. I could do it in five minutes. The tape quality might suffer a little."

"Be sure to copy the entire tape. How much does it cost?"

"Thirty-five dollars. But I need to get permission."

I wrote out a check and handed it to her. "I'm sure Mark will okay it. He's coming back as soon as the show is over. And could you do something else for me? This tape has some footage on the end that looks like it was left over from the original shooting. Could you check and see if there is any other leftover footage shot on the same night, December 22, 1989, at the King's Inn?"

She grumbled a little at the extra work but returned half an hour later with a videotape cassette. "Here's your copy. I looked but couldn't find any other footage. We reuse the tapes or erase them, so that's not too surprising. Somebody must have made the file copy for the show on one of the original cassettes." She handed me the second cassette. "I recorded it on VHS so you could play it back. We use three-quarter-inch here in the studio."

"Thanks," I said. Starrett came back into the room as she was leaving. He wore a suit jacket and tie over a pair of blue jeans. His face had the unnatural, orangish tan of on-camera makeup.

"Find anything?" He asked.

"I'm not sure. Let me show you something." I put the original tape back in the player and put it on fast forward to the end of the show.

"What time were you at the King's Inn, filming?" I asked.

"From seven until ten-thirty or so. We shot in the coffee shop first, then the lobby, laundry, housekeeping, and finally the bar."

The tape reached the point where the raw footage shot in the bar started. "What's this stuff?" I asked, pointing to the screen.

"Unused tape," he replied. "I liked the bartender, a real lady of the 'It's not the years, it's the mileage' type. And we had some action when those drunk salesmen got pitched out." He watched the tape closely. "I remember this. We went back into the bar a second time, so I could ask the bartender some more questions. We were still set up when the bartender asked those two women to leave, so I had my cameraman film it."

I stopped the tape as the women were getting up from the table. "There. See that one with the red hair?"

"Yes."

"Did you get a look at her from the front?"

"Briefly. Nothing sticks in my mind about her, though. I remember the hair. I think she was older than the other woman. That's about it."

"Did you see her again that night? Talk to her on the street, anything?"

"No. I didn't get a good look at the other one either. They left pretty quick and I decided not to chase them down and talk to them. The piece was supposed to be light, the motel was cooperating, and I didn't want to embarrass them by showing the hookers in their bar. Is it important?"

"I don't know. The redheaded woman fits the description of somebody Polhaus described, a possible witness, that we can't find. The other woman, the smaller one, could be Melody Beasely, the woman murdered that night at the King's Inn."

He chewed his lip, thinking. "The redhead was a witness to the murder at the Kings' Inn? I don't remember that."

"No. Polhaus testified at trial that after the third murder at the China Tapestry, he'd seen a woman, dressed like a prostitute, running away from the scene. The only thing he could remember about her was that she had long red hair."

"Did you have our intern check for other footage?" Starrett asked.

I nodded. "She said it had all been reused."

"She's probably right, but I'll look again."

"Thanks. A couple more questions. When the cops looked at this, did they see the raw footage?"

He frowned. "I don't know. Probably. They were here in late December or early January, so we still had all of the raw footage. Anything else?"

"Did you see Polhaus anyplace else in the motel, other than in the bar when he tossed out that group of drunks?"

"No."

"Did you see anyone else who looked out of place, wandering around the motel, anything like that?"

He shook his head. "The motel was pretty empty, because it was the Friday before the Christmas weekend. The only thing that sticks in my mind is that scene in the bar with the drunks. It was like a Raymond Carver short story, those guys away from home, getting tanked in a crummy motel bar right before Christmas. The motel wasn't too happy with us for using it." He looked at his watch. "If that's everything you need, I'm heading home. Let me walk you out."

As I followed him out of the editing room, the frozen image of the woman with the red hair remained on the screen, a flickering electronic ghost without a face or a name.

CHAPTER 13

"Damn."

Liz played the final scene from the King's Inn bar several times, freezing the image of the red-haired woman on the screen. "This is hopeless," she said. Her initial excitement had soured into frustration. "We can't get any kind of ID from this. And Starrett is sure he can't identify this woman? Well, at least she does exist. That's something."

"Or nothing." I paused to get more coffee as a clerk delivered Liz's office mail. When she was gone I shut the door to block out the Monday-morning hustle of the busy office. "I can't tell if the other woman is Melody Beasely. The tape doesn't prove that Polhaus was telling the truth about what he saw at the China Tapestry. It probably isn't even the same woman. If it was, she may be another victim. I'll check the homicide records and talk with Dick Bartke, Roy Blanton's investigator. And I'll look for the bartender who was working at the King's Inn." I sighed and made a series of notes on my legal pad. I was going to be living out of my car for a while. "Did you get anything on that IIU investigation concerning Leach?" I asked.

"Some," she replied, sitting back down behind her desk. "I spent a couple of hours on it yesterday afternoon, calling people I worked with in the prosecutor's office. Most said they knew nothing about it. But I did find one guy who'd worked on some IIU cases. At first he denied everything and I got a little bitchy with him."

"Meaning you called him a gutless worm, or some other term of endearment?"

Liz smiled nastily. "Something like that. I'm entitled, I used to date him."

"Hazardous duty."

Liz's smile grew forced. She put her hands flat on the desktop. "You want to have this out now or later?"

"Now would be good, except you've got a sentencing argument at ten-thirty. I'm not sure we could get done that fast."

"No, we probably couldn't." She swept a hand through her hair, frustrated. "Look, let me just tell you a couple things, about what I was thinking. A mess of things. Guilt for dragging you into this case before you were ready. Feeling like I was repaying you with sex. And—this case. Being around Polhaus, the kind of creep who raped me. The pimps, the hookers, the escort services, this tape. The whole thing just makes me want to stay in a bathtub for days."

I reached across her desk and touched her hand. "Don't shut me out, Lizabeth. That's all I ask. I know the timing is terrible." I took a deep breath, then added, "I'd like to try to make things work this time. If I have to wait until this shitty case is over, I will."

She nodded, straining to smile. "So tell me what your friend said about the IIU file," I said to break the silence.

"He finally said very precisely that the rules prevented him from talking about the case. He didn't say the attorney-client privilege, he said the office rules. It didn't make any sense to me until I had a chance to think about it."

"Meaning?"

"He was referring to the prosecutor's office rules against disclosing information about an ongoing investigation. That's what he was trying to tell me. When he left six months ago, the file on Leach was still considered open. After four years! Leach has got to be dirty."

"But we don't know if Leach's IIU file has anything to do with this case," I said, thinking out loud. "Be careful," I added. "If Merritt puts as much importance on Polhaus's conviction as you think he does, and he finds out we're trying to get our hands on a copy of an open IIU file, he might just write up an obstruction charge. With our names on it."

She snorted. "He wouldn't dare. If it affects this case it should have been disclosed before Polhaus went on trial. By the way, Merritt called me this morning. They can't find the Parker john book. He promised we'll get it soon, though."

"Don't count on it." I went over my list and said, "I think

I need more background on the victims. Maybe interview the families, check the court records, try to figure out some way to identify their customers. And see where it gets us. Okay?"

"Okay. But hit the court records and the police photo bank to see if you can find that redheaded hooker. She may be all we've got."

"If she exists. If she's alive."

"She's around. I can feel it."

"I'd like a little more evidence than that." I thought for a minute, then added, "Want to hear a crazy idea?"

"Why not?" she asked grimly. "We've hit the bottom."

"Terry Lasker says that Poole used to tape the women who went to work for him. In some kind of compromising way to screen out police decoys. And the escort-service owner I talked to says that the escorts who do the rough scenes work in pairs."

"This is mildly ugly stuff for a Monday morning, but where are you going with it?"

"I don't know. If the woman in the bar was with Melody Beasely, maybe she was working with her. Out of Dreams, the escort service owned by Larry Poole. Maybe he taped her, maybe he knows her real identity. He's still around."

Liz frowned, thinking. "There's no way he'd cooperate. He'd be admitting to a series of criminal acts. If we subpoenaed him he'd burn his tapes and files."

I shrugged. "I said it was crazy."

She gave me a crooked smile. "I didn't say we shouldn't try it. Damn! I just can't get out of my head that the same woman might have witnessed two different murders. And that *nobody* knows who she is."

I spent the rest of the day on the telephone at my apartment, listening to the winter rain drum on the windows, calling the victims' families, swallowing their hostility, pleading for a chance to interview them. I tried to explain that they had a stake in the fairness of the process that would either take Robert Polhaus's life or spare it. It did no good. I was shouted down by Suzanne Parker's father, an Issaquah insurance salesman who ended the call by telling me that I would rot in hell. Parker's mother, long divorced from her husband, responded with numbed alcoholic pain and the telephone number of her lawyer. The lawyer politely suggested that my chances of ques-

tioning Parker's mother were about the same as my swimming
the length of Puget Sound with a piano on my back.

Sharee Klimka's parents, a disabled logger and his wife
from the hardscrabble timber country near the Olympic Peninsula town of Forks, were even less help. They had not seen
Sharee for two years before her murder. Even her body had
been identified by others. They knew nothing of her life or the
circumstances of her death. At first I thought them cold, but
quickly understood that Sharee's death was beyond their ability
to cope. With six other children to feed and clothe on disability
pay, they had written Sharee off long ago like a miscarried
pregnancy, a vague, painful memory.

Clarissa Beasely, Melody Beasely's grandmother, was listed
in the telephone directory as living on Twenty-sixth Avenue,
off Cherry, in the heart of Seattle's mostly African-American
and Asian Central District. As I tried her number for the third
time late on Monday afternoon, I half hoped she would not answer. She did and listened patiently as I recited who I was and
what I wanted. When I was finished she said in a low quiet
voice that she would be home until eight o'clock and would
talk to me if I cared to come over.

The house was a turn-of-the-century two-story with square
lines and wide eaves, a style locally known as Seattle Box.
The entry was recessed under the second story to create a
deep, rectangular front porch. This block of Twenty-sixth had
been spared the worst ravages of urban renewal. The old
houses looked warm in the light from the old cast-iron street
lamps, framed by firs and maples. A few had been renovated
and stood out proudly in new coats of cream and blue and yellow paint. Most had steel bars across the first-floor windows
and doors, a precaution against the Crips, who sold crack cocaine out of abandoned storefronts on Union Street, a few
blocks away.

Clarissa Beasely was in her late fifties, a stocky gray-haired
woman dressed in a burgundy skirted suit. She spoke with a
trace of what might have been a Jamaican accent. I accepted
her offer of coffee and looked around as she left for the
kitchen. The living room had bare polished wood floors that
smelled of lemon oil. The furniture was comfortably worn. The
walls and the mantel above the tile fireplace were covered with
photographs of family, including a proud-looking middle-aged
black man in a Marine top sergeant's dress blues. There were
other photographs, of Clarissa Beasely with the mayor, several

city and county council members, and the pastor and elders of
the politically powerful Mount Zion Baptist Church.

I was still looking at the photographs when she returned.
"That's Melody, near the center of the mantel there," she said,
placing a small china coffeepot and two cups on the cocktail
table. I looked and found a photograph of Melody at about
twelve, a pretty child with a wide, gap-toothed smile, freckles
on her light-brown skin, and green eyes. I tried not to think
about the bruised, distended face of the older Melody I had
seen in the morgue photos.

I turned back to face her grandmother. "I appreciate your
taking the time to see me," I began.

"Or to see you at all," she said tartly. "I worked as a secretary in the prosecutor's office for ten years, before going to
work for the city attorney six years ago. I can imagine that the
victims' families have said some unkind things to you."

"I don't blame them. I know that I was asking them, and
you, to relive some of your pain."

She sat down in a brocade wing chair and poured coffee for
me, then herself. "Pain is a relative thing, Mr. Riordan," she
said quietly. "It passes, the edges dull over time, it can be lived
with. Justice is something else. You said on the telephone that
the man who was convicted of killing Melody might be innocent. That troubles me, and it's why I agreed to see you. I
would like to be sure that justice is done in this case, if they
are going to put that man to death."

I nodded. "What can you tell me about your granddaugh-
ter?" I asked.

"Not that much, I'm afraid. My daughter Susanna, Melody's
mother, lived a difficult life. She never married Melody's father. My husband and I raised Melody, off and on, while her
mother was following her singing career. Susanna was killed in
a car accident when Melody was fifteen." Her voice grew bitter. "Melody's father was long gone, dead from heroin. He was
white, and his family wanted nothing to do with the child. That
hurt Melody terribly. She dropped out of school and used
drugs and alcohol. We placed Melody in treatment several
times, but nothing really helped. My husband died just as she
turned seventeen. It was a hard time for me and I couldn't
cope with Melody's problems any longer. She left me and
moved out. When I learned she was involved in prostitution I
tried to help her. After she was arrested I contacted a friend
who worked in a prostitution prevention program to help her.

Judge Tyner, who I knew from the prosecutor's office, arranged a special sentencing so that Melody could enter the program, get counseling." She sighed. "It did not help. Nothing did."

"Tell me about the prostitution prevention program. I hadn't heard of it before."

"It started four or five years ago. The city, the county, and some private groups contribute to it. They work out of an office on First Avenue near the market. They try to divert young girls and boys, street kids, out of prostitution. If they can't get them out of prostitution, they supply condoms and AIDS-prevention information." She spoke with the same matter-of-fact style she might have used for a committee report.

"Do you know any of the people there?"

"Yes, I can give you the name of the director." She rose from her chair and left the room, returning a few minutes later with a piece of note stationery in her hand. "The director's name is Karen Sasser," she said. "I can call her and ask her to talk to you. She is a friend, goes to the same church as I do."

"Thank you." I opened my briefcase. "I have a tape I'd like you to look at," I said. "It was made the night Melody died, at the King's Inn. I need to know if you can identify her."

"I'll try," she said, looking puzzled. She put the tape into a VCR on her television cart. "I wonder why the police detective didn't show me this when she questioned me after Melody's death?"

"The police may not have known about this tape when they talked to you." I took the remote control and found the rough footage shot in the King's Inn bar. "There. See the woman at the table? Could that be Melody?"

Clarissa Beasely played it back and forth several times. Each time she played the tape she seemed to grow tenser, smaller, her calm dispassionate manner dissolving as she watched the screen. "It's Melody," she said at last. Her voice grew husky and she cleared her throat. "I can tell from the way she's sitting, her shoulders kind of hunched together like that. She would do that as a child when she wasn't feeling sure of herself. Kind of drew herself in." Mrs. Beasely frowned. "Who is this other woman at the table?"

"I don't know. I was hoping you could tell me. She may have been working with Melody."

Clarissa Beasely took the tape from her VCR and gave it back to me, holding it loosely in her fingers, as though it were edged with razors. "I don't know anything about what Melody was doing, who she was working with."

I took a deep breath, feeling the old woman's anguish wash over me. I wondered if she would forgive what I was going to say next.

"She was working out of an escort service called Dreams at the time of her death. The owner's name is Larry Poole. Melody may have been working directly with him, providing special sexual services to a group of wealthy men. Did she ever talk to you about that?"

A sudden overwhelming sadness creased Clarissa Beasely's face. Her body twisted and shook as she collapsed to the floor, sobbing. I quickly helped her back to the sofa and sat beside her, holding her as she wept.

When she spoke again I could barely hear her agonized whisper. "We are never supposed to judge," she said slowly. "But I judged Melody. Harshly. I can't tell you who she worked with because I wouldn't talk to her for the last six months before she died. I drove her away! And she died because of it."

I tried to find comforting words and failed. All I could do was stay where I was, holding Clarissa Beasely, telling her over and over that she would be all right, those stupid words we need to hear the most when we know they are not true. When she finally recovered a little I said, "What happened to Melody's effects? Did the police return any of them to you after the trial?"

"Why, yes," she replied. "They told me they had searched her apartment and taken her things. I asked for them. Two big boxes. Mostly clothes. I gave them away, the proper things, to the church. She had other . . . outfits, that she wore for the men, and I threw them away."

"Did you keep anything?"

"A few things. Why?"

"I'd like to see whatever is left."

"I don't see how they could help you," she replied. "It's just her personal things—purses, pictures, sketches she had drawn herself, a few records things, like her checkbook."

"I'd like to see them. It may be nothing, but it could help."

She stood up, stiffly, painfully. "I have them upstairs. Please come with me."

I followed her up a narrow open staircase to the second floor. The air grew musty, the smell of unused rooms.

"I don't come upstairs much," she said, as if reading my mind. "I have an arthritic hip, and the house is far too big for me alone. I should get an apartment. But we were so proud of this house. We bought it when my husband returned from Korea." Her voice grew warmer with memory. "It was a lovely neighborhood then. We raised our children here, and when I feel alone at night, I can hear my children's laughter come right out of the walls."

She led me to a small corner bedroom, still furnished with a narrow child's bed and a white-painted dresser. "This was Melody's room," she said. "Everything you want is in the box on the closet shelf."

I opened the closet and took down a cardboard moving box about two feet square and put it on the bed. Conscious of Mrs. Beasely's eyes on me, I went through it carefully, gently placing things on the bed as I made a mental catalog of the contents.

A makeup case, full of brushes and tubes and jars of cosmetics. A panda bear. A few framed 8-by-10 photographs, professionally taken head shots and publicity stills, of a black woman in her twenties and thirties, undoubtedly Melody's mother. A pair of expensive leather aerobics shoes. A sewing kit. A Walkman portable cassette player, with cassettes. Several purses, one empty, one filled with junk, combs and tissues and, embarrassingly, condoms and a tube of K-Y jelly. A fake-fancy mirror-and-brush set. A couple of paperback horrors by Stephen King and John Saul. A clutch purse, better quality than the others, good Italian leather. I opened it. It had a wallet containing a checkbook and a credit-card holder inside. I opened the wallet's zippered inside pockets. They were empty, but I could feel something stiff inside. I found a hidden pocket behind the plastic credit-card slides. It held a small address and date book, no bigger than two by four inches, and only about a quarter-inch thick. It was for 1989, the last year of Melody's life. Names and dates and telephone numbers were scrawled on its pages in a wide, looping hand.

I turned and looked at Clarissa Beasely. "Has anyone else seen this book, or asked you about it?"

"I don't think so," she replied. "I didn't know it was there. The police never said anything about it. Neither did that girl who came by."

"What girl?"

"A white girl. She said her name was Jackie, and that she

shared Melody's apartment. She said that when the police came to the apartment, after Melody was dead, they took some things of hers, too. She wanted them back. She was missing some clothes, I think she said. By then I'd gotten rid of most of Melody's clothes and couldn't really help her. She looked through this box and took a couple of things, combs and makeup and such, but she left the rest of it alone."

"And she didn't say anything about this book?"

"No, sir. Now that I think about it, she did seem to be looking for something specific. She went through these things carefully. But she didn't find that little book."

"I would like to take this, if I could," I said. "At least long enough to copy it. It could be important. I think the police missed it when they searched Melody's things before the trial."

Clarissa Beasely's face twisted again in momentary pain as she understood what the little book held. "It's the names of the men, isn't it?" she said in a slow whisper. "The men who bought her."

"Yes. I think so."

She drew herself up, straight and rigid. "Take it," she said at last. "Keep it, if it means anything."

I shook my head. "I'll return it when we're done. May I take Melody's driver's license and other papers? They could help me track down where she was living, try to locate some of her friends."

"Of course," she said. Her voice was toneless, as though she was trying to reconstruct the emotional shell that protected her. "I'm afraid I must get on to my church meeting now." It was still well before eight o'clock, the time she had mentioned earlier, but I knew she wanted me to go.

I gave her a card and said, "Please call me if you can think of anything else about Melody that you know, anything at all. Her friends, names she mentioned to you, anything."

She nodded. I followed her down the stairs. Her walk was slow and painful. She rested on each stair and gripped the railing hard. I turned back to her at the front door.

"I'm sorry," I said.

She shook her head and closed the door. I paused on the front porch to put on my raincoat. As I walked back down the street to my car I remembered something that a friend of mine had said to me on the night his first child was born. I had asked him how he felt. He started to say that he was very happy but then he stopped. "I feel terrified," he finally said.

"My son wraps up the future into a very small package. What if I go wrong? Or he does?"

I had no children and did not really understand my friend. But as I left Clarissa Beasely to her empty house I began to see why he was so afraid.

CHAPTER 14

I left Melody Beasely's address book with Wayne Porras at Liz's office the next morning, instructing him to have a paralegal prepare a typed list of the names and addresses in the book. Beasely had often written only initials, not full names. Cross-checking the telephone numbers for names and addresses in a reverse directory would be a long, time-consuming chore. I drove north over the Ship Canal Bridge to the Ballard district. I had breakfast there with Dick Bartke, Roy Blanton's investigator, at a fishermen's hangout called the Vasa Grill in one of the brown brick storefronts on Ballard Avenue.

Bartke was a cheerful little fox of a man, less than five and a half feet tall, with sharp features and a sharper wit. Over salmon cakes and eggs he outlined the work he had done on the Polhaus case and handed me a neat package of files. "Give it a read," he said, finishing his eggs and cutting up a hot cinnamon roll with his knife and fork. "There's not a damn thing that will help. We wanted to confirm Polhaus's story about the girls he was getting sex from. Roy planned to call them as witnesses. Polhaus didn't know their real names, only the working names, Fawn and Tana and Shawna and so on, so it was a real bitch trying to track them down. The first one I found was Marilyn Winter, the one who called herself Tana. She told us about the bondage and rough stuff that Polhaus liked to do.

Roy got worried then and told me to stop looking for the others. We didn't want to lead the cops to them."

"Where's this Tana now?"

"Beats the hell out of me. These girls move a lot, city to city, living in motels. I do a lot of skip tracing. The kids involved in prostitution are harder than hell to find."

"What about the man on the balcony, and the running woman at the China Tapestry? Did you get anywhere with that?"

"Nothing. You know how hard it is to track people who stay at a motel like that, weeks later? Impossible. Must have spent fifty hours on it. Didn't find a single witness. The cops got no place either."

"Did you try any of the other motels where the killings occurred, ask the clerks or the maintenance people if they'd seen anybody who matched Polhaus's description of the man and woman?"

"No," he said slowly, "no, I didn't. Do you think these people could have been involved in the other murders?"

"I don't know. I saw a tape that a TV crew shot at the King's Inn on the night Beasely was murdered. There was a hooker in the hotel bar who looked like the woman Polhaus described, with long red hair. She was with Beasely about three hours before she was murdered. I heard that these women sometimes worked with other women when they thought a customer was dangerous. I think this red-haired woman was working with them, or watching out for them. That's why she was at the China Tapestry."

"You haven't got a prayer without a description," Bartke replied. "Not after all this time."

I got ready to leave. "Just between you and me," I asked, as I handed the waitress a twenty-dollar bill to cover the check, "what's your opinion on the case?"

He stared at me for a moment, a toothpick dangling between his lips. He took the pick out of his mouth and stabbed the table with it.

"I think Polhaus killed all of them," he finally said. "I really do."

The King County court records showed that all three murdered women started working as juvenile prostitutes. Suzanne Parker had been arrested twice while working the cocktail lounges in airport-area hotels, apparently before she began working for the Dreams Escort Service. She also had a cocaine-possession conviction and had served ninety days work-farm time. Sharee Klimka had no adult convictions, not surprising in light of what Jennifer DiGregorio had told me, that Klimka got off the streets before her eighteenth birthday, and had no arrests once she had started working for escort services. Melody Beasely had two juvenile convictions for prostitution—street walking in the Jackson Street area of Chinatown and on Aurora Avenue North, both about a year before her death. She also had a conviction for lewd conduct while working as a dancer at one of the Dreams topless clubs down in Federal Way. All three women were referred to the prostitution prevention program by the courts. I copied the arrest reports and the judgments, returned the files to the clerks, and headed down to the elevators in search of coffee and a place to spread out my notes and think.

It was five minutes to twelve and the elevators were jammed with the lunchtime rush. I squeezed onto a down car and waited for the doors to close. A commanding voice said, "Hold, please," and I grabbed at the closing doors. As I did Judge Sean Tyner stepped into the car. His nod of thanks turned into a thin smile of recognition.

"Good day, Riordan," he said. "Casual today?"

I glanced down at my jeans and black turtleneck sweater. "Just doing research, Your Honor," I replied. I squirmed in the crowded elevator to get my briefcase out of his way. Sean Tyner was the chief judge of the state court of appeals for the Seattle Division. A big-boned, ex-university-crew star, at forty-two Tyner was still hard as a board, a bruising competitor in the lawyer's touch-football league I used to play in.

"You're slumming, Your Honor," I added. "It's a long way from these dirty hallways to those fancy chambers of yours at appeals."

"And you're supposed to be retired. If you really have quit practicing, you ought to call me Sean. I prefer to be on a first-name basis with the man who broke my collarbone last year."

"A clean tackle."

"In touch football?" He laughed, a sharp braying sound that set my teeth on edge. Tyner was from a moneyed family. He'd been a hard-driving prosecutor, appointed the state's youngest superior court judge at thirty-three, then jumped to the court of appeals three years before. He was an intelligent judge, impatient and tough on the lawyers in his court. He had a bright, tough personal charisma and rumored political ambitions. I had no particular reason to like or dislike him, just a general sense of unease when I was in the same room with him.

The elevator doors opened and we stepped into the gray marble lobby on the Third Avenue side of the courthouse. "What brings you down here?" I asked, still trying to be polite. After all, I had broken his collarbone.

"Teaching. At the judicial college in Reno next month. Judge Hofstedtler and I are teaching evidence and courtroom skills. Been working with him on the new textbook all morning. How about you?"

"A death-penalty case. Liz Kleinfeldt asked me to help out. It's in your division, so I shouldn't say any more."

"Polhaus?"

"That's it."

"I'm not on it, and won't be. I think I sentenced one of the victims on a prostitution charge when I was a trial judge. That's not a conflict, but I'm careful about that stuff. So I took myself off, for good." He paused, then added, "Funny, I knew Kleinfeldt took the case, but didn't know you were on it. How's it going?"

"Too soon to tell. Actually, I came across your name in doing some research on it in the court records. Can we talk about it?"

He frowned, thinking. "I suppose so. You want to ask me something about a sentencing, I suppose. I think that's all right. I guess that's what I had in mind when I recused myself." He looked at his watch. "I'm short of time today. I was going to get a deli sandwich and take it back to Gerry's chambers. He's out giving a speech to a Rotary luncheon. We can talk there, if you want."

Twenty minutes later we were sitting at the conference table in Hofstedtler's chambers. Tyner opened a ham sandwich to layer on some mustard. I did the same with a tongue on rye and handed him the sentencing reports.

"All three of the victims passed through juvenile when you were on the bench. The one girl, Beasely, got a special pass from you despite a felony rap, into counseling rather than the work farm."

"True." He chewed at his sandwich and swallowed some nonalcoholic beer to chase it down. "Did you talk to Beasely's grandmother, Clarissa? My secretary at the prosecutor's office, years ago. Great lady. She came and pleaded and I went soft

on the kid. I only wish it'd helped. God, that was hard on
Clarissa. I don't think I remember the others. You know, I
think I was the only judge willing to sit at Twelfth and Alder
in those years. The rest of the bench would rather spend a year
hearing an asbestos case than sit at juve."

I understood. The juvenile facility at Twelfth and Alder was
a snakepit of overloaded dockets, underpaid social workers,
and the kind of boys and girls who would make Father
Flanagan say "The hell with it." In the last five years one
judge had been shot on the bench by a fourteen-year-old gang
member, another assaulted and badly beaten leaving the building.

"What about this program you sent them to?"

"Prostitution prevention program, in the Public Market. It's
semiprivate, gets a lot of grant money. They do good work.
Gets the kids off the street, into structured living, gets them
jobs, drug treatment, keeps them away from the pimps. The
county council won't fund it directly because it gives abortion
referrals. The chickenshits. Don't tell anyone, but I've given
them a fair chunk of family dough. Somebody's got to do this
work, and they've got guts."

"How common is a sentence there?"

"As common as I could make it. Having the kids spend
sixty days in detention isn't going to help them."

"Does it work?"

He frowned. "Pretty well. They don't rescue as many as
we'd like. Maybe forty percent that go through the program
stay off the streets for at least one year. That's compared to a
ninety-percent failure rate from the youth facility. Where're
you going with this, anyway?"

"Nowhere, probably. I'm looking at the common patterns
among the three women Polhaus was convicted of killing.
They all went through this program. They all ended up working for an escort service. The same one, actually. A place
called Dreams."

"Never heard of it," he said firmly. He finished his sandwich
and swallowed the last of the beer. "I hate to cut this off, but
I've got to get back to court for the one-thirty calendar. Humor
my sporting interest for a second, since I'm going to be on the
other side of the Chinese wall from the judges hearing your restraint petition. Do you really think you've got a chance on
this Polhaus case? Off the record. Just like a touch-football-
league chat."

I hesitated. Anyone gullible enough to think judges don't talk to each other about their cases is a good sales prospect for bridges and time-share condominiums. Talking to Tyner was a backdoor way of talking to the court, but overselling what we had would be as bad as admitting that we were nowhere. "Off the record. Liz is the true believer. She's had doubts about Polhaus's guilt from the beginning. I've got a lot more questions than I should about a death case."

"Sounds like a tough one," he replied. "Sorry I can't be more help, but I just don't remember any of these kids. Some days I had fifty hearings on the Hill. They all just blur together now. Gotta run." He wadded his sandwich wrappings into a ball and tried a backhand shot into the wastebasket.

Naturally, he made it.

CHAPTER 15

The Seattle Prostitution Prevention Program had a warren of second-floor walk-up offices above the last remaining peep show on First Avenue, across from the Pike Place Public Market. Until the early 1980s, First Avenue was Seattle's controlled vice zone, where generations of sailors dropped a month's pay on port call. The neighborhood was seedy, relatively safe and defiantly bohemian. The successful restoration of the Market started a real estate boom in the area. The owners of new, upscale shops and apartment buildings pushed the old-fashioned sex merchants and corner taverns out of the area. But the gentrification was uneven. Landlords on the fringes of the market had emptied their old buildings to sell them for redevelopment. When the real estate market dropped, the buildings stayed empty. Homeless children, as young as nine years old, squatted in the abandoned buildings and sold themselves on the streets. The crack and heroin dealers followed them there. The district grew more vicious, more predatory. Now, late in the day, with the tourists gone for the winter and the office workers headed home in the rain, BMWs and Toyotas idled on the side streets, occupied by predators waiting to pick up children of both sexes.

The small waiting room had dirty brown walls covered with posters for AIDS prevention and drug treatment. There were five beat-up plastic chairs and a gray linoleum floor scarred by hundreds of cigarettes. The air was clotted with stale smoke and the wood-rot smells of an old building.

Five minutes later I was standing in the office door of Karen Sasser, a short, scarecrow-thin woman of about forty, with black hair pulled back into a ponytail, brown eyes, and the pale, almost translucent skin that comes from living indoors too much in a damp climate. She wore no makeup and was dressed in jeans and a sweatshirt with a caricature of Gertrude Stein on the front. Sasser had a telephone cradled between her shoulder and her ear. With one hand she kneaded her forehead, trying to get rid of a headache; with the other she tapped ashes from her cigarette into a large Cinzano ashtray half-filled with stubs.

"Uh-huh," she said, impatient. A blue vein pulsed at her temple. "Where's she going to be arraigned? Shoreline District Court? All right. Get her on the night calendar tomorrow and I can be up there myself. What time? Fine, eight o'clock." She spoke with a Louisiana, come-from-poverty accent, the kind that, if you close your eyes, you can't tell if the speaker is black or white. She put down the phone and took a deep drag off her cigarette before stubbing it out. She pursed her lips and blew smoke away from me. "You're Riordan?"

"That's right." I put my state bar card and my driver's license on her desk. She looked closely at both of them and tossed them back to me. I picked up a pile of file folders from a plastic side chair, put them on the edge of her desk, and sat down.

"Tell me again what you want to know," she sighed.

"I want to know about three prostitutes you tried to help who were murdered in late 1989 and early 1990. Their names were Suzanne Parker, Melody Beasely, and Sharee Klimka. I'm trying to find out who killed these three women. I'd like to know anything you can tell me about them. Friends, people they worked with as prostitutes, pimps, anyone they might confide in, the names of repeat customers. Anything at all."

Sasser looked at me with doubt plain on her face. "I don't get it," she said. "The killer was convicted. He had a funny name. He's on death row."

"Robert Polhaus is on death row. The woman I am working for, Elizabeth Kleinfeldt, has doubts about the conviction."

"You're working for Kleinfeldt on this?"

"Yes. If you know her, maybe you should call her."

She shrugged. "I've got no reason to doubt you. I knew Kleinfeldt when she was a prosecutor, and she's a good woman. I followed the trial of what's-his-name—Polhaus. I think Liz may have slipped a gear. He smelled guilty to me. Doesn't matter. I've got a phone message here somewhere from Clarissa Beasely. She called and said I should answer your questions about Melody. So I can do that much, I guess." Sasser got up and went to the hallway, then returned with a file folder and two Styrofoam cups of coffee. She handed one cup to me and sat back down. I sipped carefully at the cup and made a face. Even the cops made better coffee.

Karen Sasser allowed herself a quick grin. "Good?"

"Awful. Is that Melody Beasely's file?"

"Yassah. And no, I'm not going to let you copy it. We operate as a treatment and referral facility. We refer these kids out for drug treatment, regular medical help, mental health treatment. Their files are privileged, just like your medical records."

"She's dead. Death terminates the privilege."

"Not quite. Not here, anyway. You come in with a signed, notarized release from Clarissa Beasely, I'll let you have the file if our lawyer likes it. Otherwise no. But ask me some questions and I'll tell you some answers."

"Did Melody Beasely report any friends, pimps, clients, people she worked for, that kind of thing?"

She glanced at the file. "I see just one name here, a roommate, Jacqueline Rogers. Other than that she wasn't very talkative. That's not uncommon when they get sent here from the courts."

"I've got that name. Is there anything about who she was working with, or where?"

"No. Just the police reports. She was streetwalking at the time. You've probably known that."

"What did you do for her?"

"Basic intervention. Got her off the streets into a room of her own. Medical care—she had clap. AIDS test was negative. Mental health care."

"Who with?"

"Let me see ... oh. Dr. Bolger."

"Why did you say that?"

"Say what?"

"You paused before you gave me the name of her therapist, like it had some special meaning to you."

"I didn't mean anything," she said, slightly annoyed. "You haven't heard of Martin Bolger?"

"No."

"He was a professor of psychology at the university. He helped start this program eight years ago. He raised us some money, volunteered his time to treat the kids at night. Marty was the finest man I ever knew."

"Was? He's dead?"

She nodded. "Suicide. Over four years ago now." I heard deep sadness in Karen Sasser's voice. "He was prone to depression but he couldn't handle the side effects of antidepressants. He used to work himself to exhaustion fighting it. I guess he just couldn't do that anymore."

"Are Dr. Bolger's patient files here, or someplace else?"

"Oh, some are here. He might have kept his original treatment notes at his clinic, at University Hospital. You're not going to get our copy without Clarissa Beasely's permission or a court order."

"I understand that. Will you tell me what they say?"

She shook her head. "I don't want Marty's ghost haunting me. He was a real bear for doctor-patient confidentiality." She fell silent and read through the file, the typed pages of treatment notes. I saw tears forming in her eyes as she continued to read. When she was done she looked up with an almost defiant expression on her plain face.

"You gotta develop a taste for irony in this business," she began. "I won't tell you what Marty's notes say. But he thought he could put Melody back together and get her out of prostitution. He had hope." She closed the file and put it on the desktop.

"What happened to Beasely? After she left here?"

"She went back to the life, almost right away. With one of the escort agencies. I tried to get her back and couldn't. It's so damned hard. They get short of money, they don't like their job, usually something menial, or they start using drugs again. The escort services and the street pimps come sniffing after them. And they're back in it." Her voice was flat. She looked worn out.

"Did you keep track of Beasely after she left?"

"Not much. I can't afford to. We've only got the resources to give kids one shot."

"Her grandmother identified her on a videotape that was shot by a TV crew in the motel where she was killed, maybe a couple of hours before her death. There was another woman with her, possibly a prostitute. She had long red hair."

"Were they working together? Doubleheader or something?"

"Possibly. I've got the tape with me. Do you have time to look at it?"

She grinned. "You think a VCR would last five minutes in this office? I don't know who this woman could be, but I'll try it at home tonight."

I gave her the tape and went back to my list of questions. "When were Parker and Klimka here?"

"About the same time as Melody."

"Did Dr. Bolger also treat them?"

"I'll have to look. My guess is he did. Marty handled most of the kids early on, did a lot of the intake screening. Most of the kids do need psychological treatment."

"All three of these women went to work at Dreams, the escort service run by Larry Poole. Any idea why?"

"It runs in streaks. That bastard Poole's gone untouched for years. He starts them out as dancers in the clubs and then works them back in to hooking."

"Do you know Judge Tyner? He sent all three women here."

"Yeah, I know Sean. He's a white suburban liberal who thinks he should be President." She grinned sourly. "I shouldn't say that. Sean's been a supporter. He was one of the few judges who stuck it out at Twelfth and Alder, sent a lot of kids our way. He's no longer directly concerned with these kinds of cases, since he's on the court of appeals now, but he's given us money." She thought for a minute. "There's a guy out of juve who worked with one of the victims in your case, a social worker. Ted Ricks. He could fill you in on how the courts refer people to us."

Sasser lit another cigarette and waited, pensively, while I looked at my notes. She had too much to do and I was taking too much of her time.

"Just a couple more questions, please. When did Bolger kill himself?"

"January 6, 1990."

"Right after the last of the motel-room murders?"

"Yeah." She stopped with her cigarette halfway to her mouth, thinking.

"You talked to Bolger about the killings didn't you?"

She nodded. "I almost wish I hadn't. Marty was so down. His depression had been getting worse for months, and the killings really made it bad for him. He called in a couple of times that last month to cancel therapy sessions, something he'd never done before. He was obsessed by the killings, really upset. He'd done some consulting work for the Green River Task Force, back in the mid-eighties, and ended up treating a lot of cops who had worked on it for stress. He thought these murders might involve another serial killer. And that they'd never be able to find him."

I nodded. I was beginning to understand that despair. Children dumped outside the system—prostitutes, drug abusers, petty thieves—were perfect victims, unseen, unheard, dumped like so much toxic waste.

"I think it just sent Marty over the edge, since he'd treated the kids, knew them, liked them," Sasser was saying. "God, we were so scared, all of us."

"Did he talk to the cops about it?"

"Marty told me that the police asked for his records on the victims. He said they'd gotten consents."

"Which cop? Raymond Leach or Nancy Karras?"

She shrugged. "I don't know. Marty handled it. I think he would have told me if it was Nancy, though."

"Why? Do you know her?"

"We both knew her. She worked juvenile and vice. We saw a lot of her for a while, working with kids here. We both thought she was a good cop, a caring one. Sometimes we'd see each other at parties, or have a drink after work, things like that. After a while I didn't see Nancy anymore. She'd got burned out on juvenile. This is tough work, you know. You scrape kids out of abandoned buildings when they're near dead from crack and spend months working with them. And then half the time they call you a motherfucker as they walk out. Nancy came around a couple of times after Marty died. I don't think she was too happy to be back in the pit."

"Why?"

Sasser looked away, uncomfortable. "I shouldn't say this, but when Nancy was on vice she roughed up a john one night. He was picking up a fourteen-year-old girl Nancy'd spent a lot of time working with. She nightsticked him, damn near broke his balls. Hit the girl, too. The john decided not to press charges because Nancy's lawyer threatened him with a public hearing. He didn't want to get in the paper, and it blew over. But Marty told her she had to get out of doing this work. That's when she transferred to homicide."

"Karras mentioned something like that to me," I replied. "But she said the guy was chicken-hawking a teenage boy."

Sasser scratched her forehead. She looked puzzled. "No, I think I got the facts right. Why are you asking about this? Nancy's a friend of mine, sort of, anyway."

"Did you talk to her about the motel-room murders? Not in an interview, just having a drink or something."

"No. I tried to bring it up after Marty died, but they had Polhaus and she didn't want to talk about it. Marty meant a lot to both of us, and the whole thing was just too much."

She looked at her watch. "Anything else? You're the most persistent man I've met in a while, but I'm not sure I know what you're looking for."

"Me neither. I just keep asking questions until I find something that makes sense. I'm not doing so well with this."

Sasser smiled, open and warm, for the first time since I'd walked in. I caught a glimpse of the kind of brown-eyed Southern girl that rock and roll was invented for. Her New Orleans accent thickened. "I've got to go, my friend. Two more calls tonight and then I can go drink red wine and eat fried oysters with a nice lapsed Mormon man. Hell of a way for a Baptist girl to behave."

"I'm going to be back," I said, "with a release from Clarissa Beasely; and for the others, if I can get the parents of Klimka and Parker to agree to let me see the files." I stood to go. "Thanks for your time."

Sasser tapped the file folder with Beasely's name on it. She took a book off her shelf and handed it to me. It was called *Until Morning Comes*, and was written by Martin Bolger. His picture was on the back, a blunt-faced man with a big nose who looked more like a stevedore than a shrink. I looked at Karen Sasser, puzzled.

"Read it," she said, "if you're going to be spending any time working around these kids. It's based on Martin's experi-

ences treating adolescents. I still read it. When I need some
more hope." She was about to add something when her phone
rang again and she picked it up. "Uh-huh," she said impatiently.

CHAPTER 16

I crossed First Avenue to the Public Market, turning up the
collar of my coat against the chill of the rising wind and rain.
The market was still open and the bright lights and colors
warmed me as I searched for a telephone. I found a booth on
the ramp to the lower market and called Liz. When she finally
came to the phone, her voice sounded drawn and tired.

"What's up?" she said hurriedly. Her voice was thick from
a new head cold.

"This doesn't sound like a good time for me to come up and
talk," I replied.

"I don't have good times. Not this week, anyway. I checked
my calendar and nobody scheduled any for me. I've got plenty
of the other stuff."

"What's the problem?"

"The same thing I . . . shit, you haven't been in today. You
haven't heard."

"Heard what?"

"We got screwed by the court of appeals. Blown out. They
ruled on the basis of our brief that the petition was frivolous—
'stale claims, heard and rejected, brought solely for purposes of
delay.' That's a quote. They refused to stay the execution date.
We're going to have to go the supremes now."

"Jesus Christ. Who signed the opinion?"

"McMurphy, acting as chief judge. Tyner recused himself, a one-liner, no explanation."

"I think I know why. Tyner had all three victims in front of him when he was sitting on the juvenile bench, in superior court. He said he remembered one of them."

"You talked to him?"

"He said it was okay."

She was silent except for muffled heavy breathing. "What are you getting at?"

"Nothing, so far as I can tell. I talked to Melody Beasely's grandmother and then to the prostitution prevention program. Beasely was given probation on a lewd-conduct conviction to go through the program. Tyner sent all three of them through this program when he was on the superior court juvenile bench. I'm looking for all the common characteristics I can find between the three women. They all seem to have left this program and gone back to hooking for the Dreams escort agency. Two of them, Parker and Beasely, knew somebody named Jacqueline Rogers. I want to check Rogers out."

She sounded doubtful. "You might just be chasing coincidences. And I can't believe Sean Tyner had anything to do with this. You know what a clean reputation he's got."

"I know. Karen Sasser said she knew you. What do you know about her, and this program?"

"It's a good program. Karen has an ear for what happens on the street, dozens of contacts. She does everything but mother those kids. Sometimes I think she saves the ones she does just by sheer force of will. Karen is one of those rare people who's driven to make something out of all the disappointed lives she comes in contact with. Maybe it comes from her own past."

"I don't follow."

"Karen was a prostitute in New Orleans at fifteen. When she was twenty-two she did prison time for stabbing a man in a fight over a dime bag of heroin. She kicked heroin in prison, finished school, became a social worker. It's a pretty good story, one she doesn't hide." She sighed. "I meant to talk to Karen about this case, just to see what she'd heard on the street. I'm glad you interviewed her, but I'm not sure it leads anywhere. We've got to have witnesses. I want you to find the redheaded woman and the man on the balcony. Have you looked into that yet?"

"Yes and no. I talked to Blanton's investigator out in Ballard. He assumed, like I did, that the woman was a hooker and the man a john who registered at the motel under a false name. I'm going to try and talk Ahlberg into letting me look at the mug shots of every woman arrested for prostitution in King County for the last five years, but who do I match them to? It's hopeless without a good picture or at least a description."

"Well, try. We're running out of options now. We need some evidence."

"I know."

"Is there anything you need from me?"

"A couple of things. Did Merritt send Parker's john book up to your office to be examined?"

"No. I'll call him and chew him out. I'm beginning to think he's buried it intentionally. What else?"

"I dropped off Melody Beasely's address book early yesterday morning. The names of her johns are all by initials, but I have one of your clerks running the telephone numbers through the reverse directory, to get the names and addresses. Speed that up. Have the names compared to Parker's book if we get it tomorrow. If there are any unlisted numbers, have them put them on a separate list for me. I'll take care of that."

"Do I want to know how?"

"No. My way is faster than a subpoena and I don't want anybody given notice. Finally, I want one of your associates to draw up some consent forms so that I can get Beasely's, Klimka's, and Suzanne Parker's treatment records from the prostitution prevention program. The broadest possible language on the consents. The relatives, except for Beasely, live out of the city. If they draft the forms and get them to me, I'll go see the families and get them signed."

"No," Liz replied. Her cold-muffled voice was impatient. "Let me worry about the records. I'll have the two associates who worked on the briefs go out and get the consent forms signed. It's about time for them to learn that there are real people and real tragedy in the world. And there might be some other things we want. Let me think about it."

"I'll need one more thing. The victims were treated by the same therapist, Martin Bolger, through Sasser's program. He killed himself shortly after the killings stopped. I'd like to see the police reports."

She didn't answer right away. "What are you getting at?"

"Maybe nothing. But Sasser said he was obsessing about the murders, that he thought a serial killer was at work. I'd like to know what he was doing, why he killed himself. Maybe there's a note or something."

Another pause. "Okay. I'll get them."

"Good. Where do we stand on the IIU complaint against Leach?"

"Nothing so far, but I've got a couple more people to talk to."

"Okay." I hesitated, wanting Liz to spend the night, not wanting to ask. "See you in the morning. And, Liz?

"We may be at a dead end. I am nowhere. Absolutely nowhere. If the worst happens, it isn't your fault."

"I know," she said quietly. "But we're not done yet."

Two hours later I was standing in the living room of an elderly apartment manager in a dingy stucco building called the Pineview Arms hard by Interstate 5 in the Northgate area of North Seattle.

The old man was white-haired and ruddy-cheeked, a look good enough for a role in a Frank Capra movie. He scratched his whiskery jaw as he thumbed through a loose-leaf book of leases.

"Here it is," he said finally. "Apartment 303. Thought you was talking about them. Lease was under the name of Rogers, just like you said. Moved out years ago."

I leaned toward the notebook. He pulled it back. "Why'd you say you wanted this girl's new address?"

"I told you. We think she was a witness to a traffic accident. My client got hurt pretty bad, and we need a witness to prove the other guy was at fault."

A light gleamed in his eyes. "Then it ought to be worth something."

I sighed. So much for Frank Capra. "Fifty for the address and anything else you've got on her. Not negotiable."

He looked unhappy. "Well . . . all right."

I took a fifty-dollar bill out of my wallet and wondered how I was going to put a bribe on my expense request. The old man reached for the money and I pulled it back. "The book first, friend."

He passed it over. I looked at the lease and the damage-deposit receipt. Rogers had moved to a trailer court in Snohomish County, just north of the county line, about six months after the murders. It was better than nothing. I copied the address down and gave the book back to the old man.

"What can you tell me about her?"

"Not much. She and the other girl, the black one, used to have some parties. Nothing I couldn't handle. In and out at all hours. But that went with their business, I guess."

"What business was that?"

"They were dancers. At some of these stripper places." The greedy light came back into his eyes. "I saw 'em a time or two. Pretty good." He cackled appreciatively.

I ignored him. "What about the other girl, the black one?"

"Never saw her around that much. She was a pretty thing, and nice, too. Always had a smile for me."

"Did she have any regular visitors, anything like that?"

He looked suspicious. "What's this got to do with your accident?"

"Just background." I had enough. I gave him the fifty dollars and left.

The trailer court was on Highway 99, south of the Edmonds exit. The road was badly lit, the street numbers confusing. I missed it on the first pass, then found a small weathered sign that said "Seattle Heights Trailer Court" in faded white paint. The park was old; this ugly patch of arterial highway, body shops, cheap apartments and fast-food stands hadn't been called "Seattle Heights" since the end of the Korean War.

I followed a narrow gravel drive through a fence gate and down into a flat-bottomed gully. The trailers were cheaply made of aluminum or sheet steel, with flaking paint and cracked windows. The trees had overgrown the place, hiding it from the road but blocking the light. My car slid through a couple of mud puddles the length of swimming pools and I wondered if it ever dried out down here, even in the summer. The numbers on the trailers were small and black. I couldn't make them out from the car. I parked and walked on.

I found Rogers's trailer in the back, near the chain-link fence that surrounded the court. For one dizzy moment I wondered whether the fence was intended to keep people in, or out.

The woman who answered the door after my third pounding knock wore a pink fake-satin dressing gown and a pissed-off expression.

"What the hell do you want?" she snarled.

"My name is Riordan," I said, handing her an old business card. "I'm a lawyer. Are you Jacqueline Rogers?" She had dark hair and a pouchy, resentful face that did not look much like the booking photo of Rogers I had seen, but in the dark I couldn't be sure.

She took the card and tossed it back at me. "No," she said. "She doesn't live here anymore." She started to close the trailer's thin metal door.

"Listen to me," I said, blocking the door open with my boot. Size 13 feet are good for some things. "All I want to do is talk to Jacqueline Rogers. She may have been a witness to an auto accident. She could help a badly hurt guy get the money he has coming to him."

The woman perked up at the sound of money. "I know where she works," she said. "Come back later."

"Is she working now?"

"Yeah."

"Then tell me where she works and I'll get out of here."

"Why don't I just call the cops and tell them you're trespassing?" she said, her voice rising.

There was a loud male voice from somewhere in the trailer. "Hey, honey. Can we get back to business here? I can't stay all night."

The woman looked at me, frustration growing in her eyes. The rain was starting to trickle inside my collar. My feet were soaked and I had mud splashed up to my knees. I laughed at her, and myself. She wasn't going to call the cops, not with me in the doorway and a hundred-dollar trick in the bedroom. She pouted. I laughed again. She gave up.

"She works at Dreams, okay? The new club, near Scribner Lake Road. She'll be there until closing, three A.M." The tin door slammed shut.

I left and drove north on 99. The rain was coming harder now. Sheets of water splashed across my windshield, smearing the colors of the roadside neon lights. I had been working for nearly twenty hours and was curiously pleased with myself. It was a night for fool's errands, and I was qualified for the work.

CHAPTER 17

At Terry Lasker's suggestion I had gone to the *Tribune*'s clipping archive and read every story they had run about Larry Poole and his various operations. Most of the articles had concerned zoning fights over the siting of his nude dance clubs. In past years the sex businesses in Seattle and its suburbs had been pretty much hole-in-the-wall operations, located in rundown industrial areas. Poole put his clubs into commercial districts with better traffic along the main arterials. He dressed them up, defending them as legitimate, Las Vegas style, entertainments. The club he had built from an old grocery store near the Scribner Lake Road intersection had a new facade with the name "Dreams" spelled out in brilliant neon lights, but the parking lot and front door were behind the building. Poole might have been passing his places off as Disneyland with sex, but he was smart enough to know that most of his customers didn't want to be seen from the street.

I paid ten dollars to a tuxedoed thief at the door and walked in. The music was loud, grinding heavy metal. Smoke rose in clouds from the half-filled tables. Dancers worked on three separate stages, each kicking and writhing with no particular attention to the beat of the music. Other women worked the tables, offering table dances for twenty dollars to flash a breast or grind in the john's lap. I found a table in a corner, bought a five-dollar diet soda, and waited uneasily for my eyes to adjust to the harsh mix of darkness and colored strobe lights. Everything was slick and new but there was an edge to the place. The separation of fools and money is nasty work.

115

The first dancer who approached me was a tall willowy black woman in a leotard that was mostly string. I motioned her to sit down next to me. "I'm looking for Jacqueline Rogers," I said over the din of the music. "She working tonight?"

She shrugged. "I'm better," she said.

"I don't doubt that, but she's the one I need to talk to."

Her eyes were cautious. "Cop?" she asked.

"No. She's a friend." I handed her a ten. "Find her, okay?"

She shrugged again and took the money. She walked over to the nearest stage and said something into the ear of the woman who was putting on a bra as she stepped off the stage. The woman came over to my table and sat down.

Jacqueline Rogers wore a short silk robe that made her look thinner than she really was. Her face was handsome, dark-eyed and olive-skinned, with thick, curling black hair. She was maybe twenty-five, older than most of the women working in the club. She was sweating from the hot stage lights and her perfume was cloying, heavy, and sweet. She looked at me with brief scorn, hooker for john. She thrust out her heavy breasts, pushed them against me. I felt brief arousal, followed by momentary anger, more at myself than at her. She caught my eyes and backed away.

"What's on your mind?" she said nervously, lighting a cigarette and dropping the match carelessly on the floor. "Did you go through the agency?"

"Not exactly. My name is Riordan. I'm a lawyer. I need to ask you a couple of questions."

"This isn't the best place," she said warily. "And it's my prime working time."

I said nothing. I took two fifty-dollar bills out of my wallet and smoothed them on the table. When she saw General Grant she slid the bills off the table and made them disappear. "Order me a drink," she directed. "Then we can talk without being hassled."

I flagged a waitress down and bought her a drink. "You knew Suzanne Parker, right?"

She paused. "I knew her. Is this about her murder?"

"Yes. How did you know her?"

"We were friends. She worked in the Federal Way Club, where I started. I crashed at her place once for a couple of nights, when my old man beat me up and threw me out of the house." She slid a perfume vial, an inch and half long and about a third of an inch in diameter, from her bra. She un-

screwed the cap, held the vial to her nose and snorted flake cocaine. She offered it to me. I shook my head, annoyed. If she
got coked up too badly she'd be worse than useless.

"When's the last time you talked to Suzanne Parker?"

"The day she got killed. I told the cops she didn't say anything to me other than 'Hi, how are ya.' "

"I know that. What did she really say?"

"She wanted to know if I would work a scene with her."

"What kind of scene?"

"Leather work. You know. Straps and cuffs. She wanted me
there, a doubleheader, so it wouldn't get rough."

"Did she say who the john was?"

"No. She said it was somebody she knew of, she thought it
would be cool, but she didn't want to take chances. I guess she
was wrong."

"Did you call her or did she call you?"

"She called me. Late in the afternoon, maybe five-thirty, six
o'clock. I worked at the club in the afternoon, talked to her on
the phone before I went home."

"Did the john come through the Dreams agency?"

"I don't know. She didn't say."

"Did Parker have her own book of johns?"

"Yeah, Suze had some regulars, guys she'd meet at the club
or something. She kept them private so she didn't have to kick
back any money to the service."

"Did Dreams make you kick back part of the fee the john
paid you directly?"

She looked at me as if I were some kind of child. "You
think they're in business to make sure we get laid a lot?"

I ignored her sarcasm. "Did Parker ever say anything about
Robert Polhaus to you?"

"No, but I know he was the guy they busted for killing Jazz.
Jazz knew him good. She'd ball him and he'd let her work the
places he was a guard at."

"You shared an apartment with Jazz. What did she tell you
about Polhaus?"

"That he was weird. That he liked to tie her up."

"Anything else?"

She nodded. "That she was afraid of him."

"Did you ever have sex with Polhaus so you could work out
of the motels where he worked?"

"No. I thought he was a creep."

"The detective who talked to you about Parker was Ray Leach, right?"

"Yeah." She bit the word off.

"You're angry. Why?"

"The bastard belted me around one night. He was on county vice then. He picked me up outside the Federal Way Club and wanted me to ball him. He was drunk. He said he'd bust me for hooking there. I told him to fuck off. And that's when he popped me. I filed a complaint on him. Police brutality. They took it seriously, too. A woman came out to interview me, said she worked for a part of the cops that investigated cops. But then people here said to drop it. So I had to."

"People here?"

"At Dreams."

I was getting into a dangerous area, one where she would soon stop talking, but I wanted to get what I could before she decided to back off. "Let's go back to Melody Beasely for a minute. Were you sharing an apartment with her when she got killed?"

She swallowed her fake champagne and shook her head at the same time. "I think we'd split up by then." She looked around cautiously and then hit the vial of coke a second time.

"Jazz had her own john book, didn't she?"

"I don't know." She spoke too quickly, even through the coke. The problem with cocaine is that it only makes you think you're smart. Coke talk is even stupider than drunk talk.

"Yeah, you do know. You were still living with Melody when she was killed. You told her grandmother that the cops had taken some of your things when they searched the apartment you shared. You lied to her grandmother to get to Melody's things, because you were looking for her john book. Why?"

She tried to cover her surprise but did it badly. "I don't know what you're talking about," she said thickly.

"Of course you do. Who sent you for the book?"

"I've got to go," she said suddenly. "I'll be back."

She wasn't, of course. I waited for the inevitable response. It came about five minutes later. One of the club bouncers came to the table. He was dark haired, sepia skinned, with the broad, open face of a Samoan. He wore a soiled white dinner jacket that bunched clumsily over his twenty-inch neck.

"Mr. Riordan?" he said politely. "The owner would like to see you."

"Really," I replied. I looked past him to a second bouncer standing halfway between the corner where I was seated and the door. The Samoan followed my glance and looked back at me with a half-smile. "Did you play nose guard?" I asked cheerfully. "Or linebacker?"

He ignored the question. "The owner says you're upsetting one of our dancers."

"I'm impressed. A three syllable word." He took a step forward and I put a hand up as I got to my feet. "Don't get hostile, pal, I'm too old to take on you and Bubba over there." I gestured toward the other bouncer, a short blond bodybuilder with a dense, mean expression on his blocky, squared-off face.

"His name ain't Bubba," he said, smiling again. "But I'll tell him you called him that."

He led me to an office doorway near the bar, behind the disc jockey's booth, knocked once, and opened the door.

The office was cramped and spartan, empty but for a couple of file cabinets and a gray steel desk. A thin man, medium height, with styled, curly black hair, sat on the edge of the desk. He wore black jeans over black tooled cowboy boots and denim shirt. He had a good silver-and-turquoise ring on one hand, a steel Rolex on the other wrist. Nothing too flashy, nothing too overstated, slightly tan from a week at Cabo or perhaps Maui. He could have been a banker or broker but for the wiry strength that he projected. In a serious one-on-one with the bodybuilder on the dance floor I would have taken Poole. And given points.

He looked up from the computer printout he was studying and smiled. "Hang on just a second, Riordan, while I finish. I don't want to lose the numbers in my head." He went back to reviewing the printout. I sat down in a cheap plastic chair and waited. I was nervous and shifted my weight, trying to get comfortable. I hadn't smoked, even under stress, for quite a while but I wanted a cigarette just then. I bit the inside of my lip and waited.

The man at the desk made a couple of notations on the printout with a red felt pen and dropped it on the desk beside him. He looked up at me and smiled with easy, genuine grace.

"The problem with a cash business is that everybody who works for you robs you blind. I don't mind if they keep it in bounds; I just figure it into their compensation package. But if you're not careful, the IRS will come around and say that you've been skimming it." He sighed. "Not that I need to tell my troubles to a lawyer. Not yet, anyway. I'm Lawrence Poole, of course," he added, extending his hand.

I half-rose from my chair and shook his extended hand. I began to understand why Terry Lasker had been fascinated with him. Poole was the antithesis of the popular conception of a man in the vice rackets—calm, obviously intelligent, even charming. "I think I'm supposed to ask why you want to see me," I said dryly.

"On the contrary. I thought that as long as you were here, you and I could talk. I know that you are representing Robert Polhaus, trying to overturn his death sentence. I know that you have been asking questions about me and my business interests. That's not an unreasonable course for you to take, as you've discovered that all three of Polhaus's victims worked for my companies at one time or another. But surely"—he spread his hands, a gesture for understanding—"you can see that I would be concerned. I deal with police harassment every day. Having someone else investigating me could lead to misunderstandings, legal expense for me, and exposure I don't really need."

I stared. The man belonged in a Fortune 500 company. I would buy the stock. "Where did you get your MBA?" I asked, half joking.

He laughed, showing perfect white teeth. "Chicago," he replied. I had to laugh in turn. I wouldn't have been surprised if he was telling the truth.

"Look," he said, "why don't you ask me your questions? Then you can stop wasting money bribing my dancers."

"Did you know Parker, Beasely, and Klimka?"

"Only slightly. I don't manage operations directly, haven't for years. I monitor cash flows, pay the bills, do strategic planning for expansion. I knew of them, they danced in my clubs, worked as escorts. I had no personal relationship with any of them."

According to Jennifer DiGregorio, he had opened with one fairly major lie but it was not one I was in a position to press. "The police subpoenaed your escort service records," I said. "Which, of course, ceased to exist sometime prior to the subpoena getting served. But tell me. Were any of the three victims working out of your agency on the nights they were murdered?"

"I see where you're going with that," he said. "Good strategy. Try to find some fellow they had in common. An alternate suspect if you get Polhaus a new trial on some technicality. They weren't working for me when they got killed. I protect my employees, Mr. Riordan—that's why I've got those men outside—and I tried to find out who the customer was after every one of those girls were killed. We never did. That's why I try to keep the women from having outside clients. I can't protect them."

"And it cuts into the net."

He looked at me sharply, then let the comment pass. "And it cuts into the net. But not as much as having a homicide investigation take my business apart, piece by piece. I cooperated with the homicide investigators, quietly, and told them what they wanted to know."

I almost believed him. It was logical. Poole was, if anything, a disciple of the logic of money. "That would have been Sergeant Leach, with the county."

"I think so, yes. I don't really remember the name. The officer chain-smoked in my office during the entire interview."

"That's Leach," I replied. "He's quit, though."

"Good for him," he said primly. "What else?"

"Did you hear anything at all—street rumor, reports from your people, gossip—about these killings while they were going on?"

He frowned. "Not really. I paid close attention to what I did hear. People were, by and large, afraid. The talk was about whether the Green River Killer was killing again, or if some other maniac was targeting escorts. We tightened up the screening of customers, refused services to people we didn't know, even if they were vouched for. We told the dancers not to pick up any stray men from the clubs, which of course we do anyway."

"Of course." His careful, over-precise little speeches were beginning to frustrate me. Lawyers like to believe that any witness can be tripped up, caught in a contradiction or pressured into telling the truth. It doesn't happen. In real life you can crack maybe one liar in ten. You hope that the jury knows what a good liar looks like. Poole was very good indeed.

"I'm curious about Leach," I told him, trying to raise the stakes a little. "Had you known him for a long time prior to his interviewing you about these killings?"

Poole was impassive, his narrow, fine features composed. "I'd seen him one or two times before," he said cautiously. "Dealing with the vice people is a cost of doing business."

"Is that why you had Jacqueline Rogers withdraw her police-brutality complaint against him? Because it would raise the cost of doing business?"

"I'm not sure I follow you."

"Yes, you do. Rogers knows you well enough to come straight in here when I started asking her difficult questions. She told me that you had her withdraw the complaint." Which was not quite what she said.

"I don't recall that. What are you trying to suggest?"

"That you've had Leach in your pocket for some time now. I'm just following your logic. If I were running your businesses, I'd want as many tame, friendly cops as I could get."

"I don't buy the cops, Riordan. I hire damned good lawyers and let them make the cops' lives miserable. It's cheaper in the long run." He checked his watch. "I'm late for dinner. I'd ask you to join me but I already have a date. Though I doubt she's as good a conversationalist as you are." The smile returned but it was hard work for him now.

I rose to go. "Just one more question," I said. "Why did you send Rogers out to find Beasely's john book? The trial was over by then. What did you want it for?"

He shrugged. "I'm mystified again," he replied.

It was finally my turn to smile. "Then don't worry about it. You see, I've already got it. Thanks for your time."

I finally got home at one in the morning, feeling bathed in slime. Poole's club didn't sell sex, it sold a pornographic facsimile of sex, the ancient male harem fantasy: the man surrounded by available women, needing only to wave a hand to be serviced. It was a harmless enough dream until you saw the flip side of it, the women bleeding in emergency rooms at three o'clock in the morning, battered and raped. One didn't cause the other. They just fed off the same fantasy. It made the pulling below the belt I had felt in Poole's joint a little more difficult to live with.

I showered and made tea instead of the whiskey that I wanted, remembering what Karen Sasser had said about Bolger's turning over the victims' treatment records to the police. I burrowed into the box of police reports, determined to find the damned records and check them off my list. I started by looking for a reference to the subpoena served on Bolger. An hour later I had the files spread across the floor of my apartment and I was on my hands and knees, carefully check-

ing each file folder and document against the discovery index.
It took me most of the night. The subpoena didn't exist.

CHAPTER 18

When I got to the Lisle, Day offices early the next morning,
Liz was already at work, curled in a corner of her office sofa,
dictating. She looked up from a pile of letters, crumpled Klee-
nex, and bottles of cold syrup. "I'm glad you're here. We need
to talk."

"What's the problem?"

"This." She stood up and moved to her desk, reached under
a stack of file folders and pulled out a typed list of names.
"These are the names and addresses of the people listed in
Melody Beasely's john book. Both for the appointments listed
on particular days and for the address book pages in the back.
There's nothing listed on the night she was killed."

"I knew that," I replied. "I looked at the page for December
twenty-second as soon as I'd found it. What about the others?"

"Thirty names you've never heard of," she said. "And about
seven or eight that you have."

"What does that mean?"

"Here." She showed me the highlighted names. "State Sen-
ator Alan McGill. Dave Kroger, the chief financial officer of
Minpro, the computer software company. They're our client.
Wade Millner, the jeweler. He's president of the Chamber of
Commerce this year. A client. Ted Akita, owner of Japonique,
the restaurant. Client. And here's a kick, three of them, actu-
ally. Your friend Terry Lasker, the *Tribune* columnist. Judge
Sean Tyner. And Sergeant Ray Leach, county homicide."

"What do these letters mean?" I asked, pointing to a column paralleling the names.

"Something the paralegal spotted. It's apparently what they like, the kind of sex they want, the fantasy they want. I can guess at a couple things. Not that I want to. It makes me feel like a window peep."

"Jesus. Melody Beasely had some unusual friends." I took the list and skimmed it. "And some rich ones. Here's a couple names you missed. Kevin Marchibroda, the dean of the personal injury defense bar. And Rob McCoy, who runs Pacific Public Relations, everybody's favorite mouthpiece in a crisis." I kept reading. None of the other names meant anything. I saw the name of Martin Bolger, the psychologist who had treated Melody Beasely, but that didn't surprise me. The dates when his name appeared corresponded to the time when she had been going through therapy in the prostitution prevention program.

"The important one is Leach," I said, dropping the list back on her desk. "This is evidence he had prior contacts with Beasely he never reported. It might just support a discovery motion for his IIU file." I hesitated. "Tyner and Lasker I can't figure out. I've known them both for years."

"Not that well, I hope," Liz said dryly. "We've got a problem. Jack Elgot took a copy of the list from my office last night. We've already talked about it this morning."

"I'm sure he's thrilled."

"Was he ever. He wants this case dropped, now."

"That's not quite right," Jack Elgot said, his soft drawling voice drifting in from the hallway. "What I really want is for this case to be handled responsibly. And that means using some discretion and common sense before Riordan here goes off to accuse a sitting court of appeals judge and half the firm's clients of being involved in these murders."

"Good morning, Jack," I said.

"Good morning," he replied stiffly, fingering the half-lens reading glasses that hung from a chain around his neck. He closed Liz's door and leaned on the frame. "Now, people, what the hell are we going to do about this?"

"I don't see any problem," I replied. "We interview the people we need to talk to. When the time comes, we submit the john book to the court under seal."

He frowned, not liking my answer. He took a china cup

from the coffee set on the mahogany credenza behind Liz's desk and poured a cup of coffee from her silver pot.

"You don't see a problem," he said slowly. "My God, isn't that just perfect."

"We've got to follow up, Jack. I'm going to try to limit the number of people on this list I question, not because you're worried about getting snubbed at the Rainier Club, but because we have limited time and I don't want to cost somebody a marriage."

"How are you going to cut the list down?"

"By cross-checking it with the list from Parker's john book," I said. "Liz, did we get it?"

"No," she said. "Merritt called me late last night, at home. Totally pissed. It seems nobody can find that little book. It was checked into the courthouse evidence room. Now it's gone."

I swore vehemently. "That's the only explanation? Just gone?"

"That's all they're saying."

"Then we have to interview these people," I said. "Beasely's john book is the only piece of new evidence we've got. If we can link Leach to the other victims, or tie some of Beasely's customers to them, we've got a chance at a new hearing."

"No." He was abrupt and final.

I flared up. "Then go to hell."

He backed up like a small dog ready to fight. "Ed Warren called me last Friday about your little stunt in interviewing the cops without a prosecutor present. He's furious."

"Tough. He's never going to push it. Not when his office has lost a key piece of evidence in a serial murder case. Evidence that they never followed up on and failed to produce at trial."

He bit his lip, thinking. I looked at Liz. She was still curled up on the sofa. She seemed to be in physical pain. Her career was hanging by a thread, and she knew it.

"Jack," she said quietly, "we have to. You saw the court of appeals opinion. They threw out every legal issue we could raise. Now we have just one piece of new evidence. I know you don't like this. But Polhaus is our client. We have massive malpractice exposure if we don't check this out." She hesitated. "And there's one other thing," she added, her voice harder but still quiet. "If you try to shut this investigation down, I will pull the case from the office, go out on my own, and do it anyway."

He thought for another thirty seconds, his coffee cup forgotten in his hands. "Goddamn you," he said softly. "Both of you. You've got me by the short hairs, and you know it." He drank coffee and made a face. "It's cold," he said. "I'll have them send some fresh. Don't fuck this up."

When he was gone I got up and closed Liz's door. "That took a lot of guts."

Her smile was tentative. "What's a career?" she asked sarcastically. "I'll be teaching dance to the kids in my neighborhood yet." She tossed the list on her desk and pushed up the sleeves of her white silk dress, as though getting down to work. "Let's go through everything. What have we got?"

"Not much." I opened a cabinet on Liz's wall that contained a white drawing board. I wrote the names of the three victims across the center of the board and drew lines connecting each. "Three victims. All three get sent to the prostitution program by the court." I added Sean Tyner's name to the board and drew a dotted line to all three victims. "All get treated by Martin Bolger." I did the same with Bolger's name. "Bolger gets extremely upset and depressed while the murders are going on, kills himself soon after." I added a question mark by his name. "All three women drop out of the program and go to work at the same escort service, Dreams, run by Larry Poole." I added Dreams and Poole's name. "Poole knows Leach and does him a favor, gets a woman named Jacqueline Rogers to drop her brutality complaint against him. Rogers knew Parker and roomed with Beasely," I said, adding Rogers's names to their columns. "Dreams never produces any business records about the victims. Parker's john book disappears. Leach had access to it. Rogers tries to recover Beasely's book, but misses it. And Karen Sasser told me last night that she thinks Bolger gave his treatment records on the victims to Leach in response to a subpoena. But there isn't any subpoena, or any treatment records, in the discovery file. Again, Leach had access but the documents are missing."

"You've left something out," Liz said. "The red-haired woman at the two motels. Karen Sasser dropped the tape by this morning. She said she didn't recognize her."

I added the red-haired woman to the chart and drew lines and question marks connecting her to Beasely, Klimka, and Poole. The chart looked like a wiring diagram. I stepped back. Liz put a hand on my shoulder and shook her head. "What a mess," she sighed.

I looked at the chart again. "Maybe not. It's the customers' names, Liz. Somebody is trying to keep the names of the victims' customers quiet. It has to be Larry Poole. He's the only one who could manipulate the events like this."

"Why would Poole be trying to protect a customer?"

"I keep going back to something that this DiGregorio woman said. Poole has a lot of wealthy, powerful customers, who became his friends. They're his cover, his warning system if the cops get too close. Suppose one of those customers killed these women, and Poole found out. Is he going to cover for them? Hell, yes. He has to. The homicide investigation alone would shut him down, just because of the publicity." I grunted in frustration. "But we can't touch him. Anything we do—subpoena, deposition, whatever—he just smiles and says no. And that's the end of it."

Liz looked at me curiously. "Are you starting to believe my hunch?" she asked.

"That Polhaus didn't kill these women? Maybe. So far, just maybe."

She smiled. "Then go after these guys. But," she added, looking worried again, "do it carefully. I don't want to teach dance that bad."

I nodded. "Do what you can to find out more about the IIU report on Raymond Leach. If they've really tied him to Poole, we just might have enough to get this case reopened."

I fought rush-hour traffic across the Evergreen Point Bridge east to Interstate 405 and north to Bothell. Rush hour used to be from seven to nine in the morning; now there was permanent gridlock that strangled the entire Metro area. I got to the office of Bobbie Jean Services a little after eleven, nerves raw, supply of profanity exhausted.

Jennifer DiGregorio had, as promised, arranged interviews with three other women who worked out of Dreams with Sharee Klimka. I talked to each of them separately, trying to draw them out. Most of my questions had to do with Larry Poole and the bondage clients that Sharee Klimka worked.

When I finished it was about one o'clock and Jennifer DiGregorio waited for me in her office, smoking. I fought back the urge to bum a cigarette from her and sat down in one of her chairs with a sigh.

"Well?" she demanded.

"I'm even less likely than I was before to want to be hand-cuffed to the bedposts," I replied.

That drew a half-smile. "That's your hang-up, Riordan," she replied. "What else?"

"I've wasted my time. Nobody wants to talk about Larry Poole. Nobody admits to working a bondage scene with Klimka. Nobody ever worked a private party for Poole. None of them knows a redheaded prostitute who might have worked with Beasely and Klimka."

"I guess I'm not surprised. The women who worked for Poole are still afraid of him."

"I'm concerned about one other thing. I saw Larry Poole last night. He knew that I had been asking questions about him. I'm sort of wondering how that happened."

"I don't know what you're talking about."

"I think you had a worry attack. I think you called him up and told him to watch out for me. I think you told these women I just talked to to keep their mouths shut."

She started angrily from her chair. "You think I'm crazy enough to dump on Poole and then tell him what I did?"

"I don't know. I'm dealing with some kind of netherworld here. You've got these rules, spelling out what you'll tell me, what you won't. I'm trying to figure out how little of what you tell me is true and how much is garbage."

"I don't know why in hell I'm talking to you at all."

"You're doing it because you want to know who killed Sharee Klimka. That's a good reason."

"Your client killed Sharee Klimka."

"I'm beginning to doubt that. There's too many leads that weren't followed up before he was convicted. And Poole fits into this somehow."

"If he does, I don't know how."

"I don't buy that. I think maybe the one thing you were telling the truth about, before you stopped yourself, was Lawrence Poole. You hate his guts and you suspect that he was involved in some way. So help me this much. You told me you wouldn't give me any names. I've got a list of names from one of the other dead women. My guess is that some of the names were on Sharee Klimka's list, too. The special list, the one you have for the boys who like to do the tying up or to be tied. You don't have to give me any names. Just nod when I hit the right ones."

She shook her head, hands gripping the edge of the desk. "No."

"Goddamn it, I'm not going to take you or them to the cops." I took a copy of the list of names from Melody Beasely's john book and handed it to her. "Look at the list," I said. "Then call me. Or I'll be back with a subpoena and if you try to destroy files on me I will have you in court for the rest of the year. Budget about thirty grand for your lawyers' bills. Give it some thought."

CHAPTER 19

The traffic was no better returning to the city. It was late afternoon by the time I reached the Tribune Building and found a parking place in a lot off Fairview Avenue. The seemingly endless late-winter rains had broken and the trees in Denny Park looked ready to bud into new life with the sun. It had become a fine day and I wished the way I felt had changed with it.

The city room of the *Tribune* was about half full with reporters getting stories written for the early edition the next day. I walked past the mass of reporters' desks, jammed together and buried under telephones, reference books and stacks of files, hearing the dry click of computer keys as I headed for Lasker's office at the northwest corner of the floor. For once Lasker was there, going over the copy of his column with one of the paper's city editors.

"For Chrissakes, Terry," the editor said, rubbing her neck as though she were afflicted with youthful arthritis, "you can't say that the president of the city council has his lights on, but that nobody's home."

"You weren't at the housing hearings, Sheila," Terry replied. "I know a guy who's half-blasted before lunchtime on a working day. From personal experience. And that of my friends. One of whom just walked in here."

Lasker's editor looked up and gave me a bleak look. "Who the hell are you?" she asked.

"A friend of Terry's. Why don't you just print that the hearings were extremely relaxed? The right people will get the message."

Lasker shot her a smile. "I could live with that," he said, laughing. "Go with that. Let 'em wonder what I really mean." The editor surrendered and walked out, leaving me with a look that said I ought to have a knife sticking four inches into my back.

"Never let a columnist have a no-cut contract," he said jovially. "So what can I do for you, Riordan? You don't look particularly thrilled with this break in the rains."

"I'm not." I sat down in one of the metal chairs opposite his desk. "This is a list of the customers we found in Melody Beasely's john book." I handed it across the desk. He took it carefully.

"You're giving me this on the record?" he asked, surprised. He took the sheaf of typed pages, set it on his desk, and ran a hand through his slicked-back hair.

"Look at the third page. Then tell me if you want this on the record."

He did. When he had found his name he looked up. "I see your point," he said carefully.

"I'm not sure you do," I replied. "In fact, I don't know whether to be surprised or just real pissed off."

He nodded. "You're thinking I held out on you."

"I'm thinking that I've been your friend for ten years. I'm thinking that when you asked me for stuff I didn't hold out on you."

"Unless it was in the interests of a client. Then you set a record for the most 'no comments' in a single interview."

"That's different."

"Not all that different. What do you want me to say? That back then I was newly divorced, that my head was a mess, and I wanted a nice uncomplicated lay?"

"That would be a start."

"Well, that much is the truth." He took a white plastic coffee carafe from the table behind him and poured himself a cup. "I met her at a party during the NBA play-offs that year. She was there with a player I knew. I'll be blunt. She turned me on. And I saw her two or three times."

"With the whips and the chains and the black leather?"

He looked shocked. "Hell, no. I'm not that complicated."

"Well, some of her clients were."

"She told me that. I wasn't interested, personally."

"What else did she tell you?"

"That she was working for Poole, which I knew. She knew some of the places he liked to hang out. That's how I found him, at his athletic club."

"What else?"

"That Poole liked to go with the women who worked for him. That his tastes were a little strange."

"Did she say that he was abusive? That he liked to hurt them?"

"No. She never said that."

I paused. "I have to ask," I said. "Where were you on the night she was killed?"

He stared at me with his mouth hanging open, then closed it. "You're joking," he finally said.

"Not for a minute."

"I don't know. Give me the date again."

"December 22, 1989."

He rummaged in his desk drawer and came up with his pocket diary for that year. He flipped through it. "At City Club," he said, tossing the diary on his desk. "Dinner for politicos, lawyers, and other lowlife. Including one named Riordan. Dinner ran late, as I recall. Didn't get out until midnight." He put the diary away. "You've got a fucking nerve," he added.

I pressed a hand to my forehead. I had forgotten. "Let it pass," I said. "I'm stupid today."

"Wouldn't dream of it," he said sarcastically. "And while we've got all the cards out on the table, maybe you'd like to answer some questions. Like why you're pressing me on this."

"Because you held out on me. You should have told me you knew her."

"Why? You know the kind of stuff I write, and you know I've never stuck it to anybody about their sexuality—gay, straight, or otherwise. And I've had a hell of a lot of chances."

"You aren't investigating three murders for a client who is going to hang in six weeks," I replied angrily.

"Oh, God." He rolled his eyes. "Spare me this self-righteous crap. I should have told you. Fine, I agree with you. But I am just another middle-aging guy who feels it and has the odd secret to keep. Are you that different? We used to hang out together a lot, in our drinking days. I knew you when you were in your promiscuous phase, after you and Liz broke up. A smile and a laugh and drinks and dinner in a nice quiet restaurant, and lots of friendly slap and tickle. Knowing full well you'd never see them again after coffee the next morning."

I shook my head. "Nice try," I said sarcastically. "The issues are a little different."

"Are they? What makes your neurosis different from mine?"

"I didn't pay them for sex."

"Didn't you? There's all kinds of coin in the world. Flattery. Promises. Flowers. Hope."

It was possible he was right and I didn't like the possibility. I bit my lip and calmed down enough to say, "I came here for information. Is there anything else you know about Melody Beasely, anything at all, that could relate to her murder?"

"No." His voice was cold.

"I've been told that Larry Poole used to throw some parties. For important guys—police, money, government or the media. Men he could use. Did you ever go to a party like that? Or hear about them?"

He thought. "I heard a couple of rumors. But not anything that Melody ever said to me. And nothing I could ever confirm."

"What about the tapes? You said before that you heard a rumor that Poole taped the women who worked for him to keep out any police decoys. Is that something you got from Beasely?"

He nodded, his face coloring in embarrassment. "Melody said she had to have sex with Poole, that every woman who worked for him had to. And that later she'd found out she was taped."

"Jesus Christ." I had a sour feeling in my gut, as if I'd been watching a friend having sex through a bedroom window. "I'm sorry about this," I added.

He looked away, trying to recapture the shreds of his dignity. "That makes two of us. Give me a few days to let the raw spots go away. In the meantime I'll ask a couple of the police-beat guys whether they've heard anything about these parties that Poole throws. I'll call you and buy you a coffee if I get anything."

"Thanks."

"You're welcome. Now get out of here. I've got work to do." He gave me the list back, but not before reading it. "Sean Tyner," he mused. "That self-righteous hypocrite. Now, doesn't that make three of us."

"What do you mean, three?"

"You must not know Tyner as well as you think. Sean the mighty oarsman also fancies himself Sean the mighty cocksman. There was a dust-up about him and a student at Seaside School some years back. He used to teach some seminars or something there. One of your less genteel lawyer colleagues was pissed at Tyner about a decision and wanted me to play the story in my column. I threw that bastard out so hard, he bounced."

"Then why tell me about this now?"

"Christ, I don't know," he said tiredly, looking out his window again. "It's Dirt Day. Go ask Tyner why he's on this list."

Sean Tyner hung his courtroom robes carefully in a nineteenth-century mahogany armoire and sat down behind an English banker's desk, gesturing to a low leather chair. It was five o'clock, after the last of the three oral arguments he'd heard that afternoon. Pale western sunlight had worked its way through six blocks of downtown office towers between the waterfront and Tyner's windows, as though responding faithfully to a court order. The light played on a trophy wall filled with plaques, commendations, and old crew medals, each carefully framed.

"What's this all about?" he asked, filling a brier pipe with tobacco, then laying it aside. "You told my clerk it was personal."

"It is. We located the john book belonging to Melody Beasely, one of the three motel-room victims. Your name is in it, Sean. I have to ask you why."

"Christ, Jack Elgot called this morning and said I might be having this ludicrous conversation." He shook his head. "When you say 'john book' I assume you mean some kind of address book. I must have sent three dozen underage prostitutes, male and female, through the prostitution prevention program when I was on the juvenile bench. I didn't stop with the sentencing. I worked with that program, giving the kids talks, letting them know the system cared about them. I told them they could call me if they wanted to talk. Obviously this girl wrote my name and phone number down. I don't remember her calling me, though."

"I see." His explanation was reasonable, if unusual. Most judges take pains to avoid any kind of out-of-court contact with people who have appeared in front of them.

"Of course," he added, "I did catch some shit for it. But I've never been a judicial eunuch. I wanted to help these kids. So sometimes I was father figure and social worker, along with judge."

I went on. "Judge, all of the motel-room victims failed the program. They went to work for the Dreams escort service. Did you—"

"Never heard of it," he said abruptly.

"You've said that before. What I was asking was whether any kind of follow-up had been done that you were involved in, trying to get them back in the program."

"Not like that. I had no contacts after they were out of the program. Always a structured setting." He leaned forward. "What the hell are you after? Is this just because the court threw out your personal restraint petition the other day?"

"Of course not. We're trying to get Polhaus a new evidentiary hearing. The victims' customers were never properly investigated. And someone has gone to a great deal of trouble to cover those names up."

"And you think I—Jesus. What are you going to do, smear everybody whose name might be connected with this case? You son of a bitch."

"Judge, that's not what I'm doing, and you know it. You know I have to ask everyone—"

"Bullshit. I've seen some pretty cheap tactics in court, Riordan, but you're setting some kind of record."

I stiffened. "Damn it, I represent a death-row client. I have to follow every possible lead. You say you played Mr. Rogers to these kids, fine. I go on to the next name. But there's a connection here somewhere, Sean. All three victims worked for Dreams. The owner is Lawrence Poole. He may have a tame King County vice cop working for him. The same cop investigated the motel-room murders. Evidence is missing. It stinks."

He shook his head. "This is insane. I think I've given you enough time."

I stalked out of his office with clenched teeth. I shouldn't have been angry with Tyner. I knew I was going to get the same reaction from every man listed in Beasely's john book. But Tyner had taken pains to tell me nothing at all.

I spent what was left of the day chasing the ghost of the red-headed woman I had seen on Mark Starrett's videotape. Vince Ahlberg reluctantly let me spend the dinner hour in his office, reviewing the past four year's combined city-county homicide reports and missing-person reports. None of them seemed to fit.

At seven o'clock I went to the King's Inn and interviewed the night clerk who had testified at Polhaus's trial. He had nothing to add to his court testimony, and couldn't recall ever seeing the red-haired woman, adding stuffily that the motel had better security now. The bartender, Jaye Bruner, was long gone, moved on to other jobs. I followed her trail from hotel to cocktail lounge to tavern until I finally caught up with her at half past midnight, working behind the bar at the Sea-Tac Airport Holiday Inn.

Jaye Bruner was a tall, lanky woman who moved easily and laughed well with the knot of salesmen clustered at the far end of the Formica-and-Naugahyde bar on the top floor of the hotel. I slid onto a stool, wincing slightly as the muscles in my lower back complained. I hadn't worked out and had spent most of the day in my car.

She drifted over to take my order. I took out a ten-dollar bill and ordered a bourbon rocks, a stronger drink than I needed but one that would blow some of the day's futility away. When she returned with my drink I pushed the change back at her.

"I don't suppose the management here lets you have a drink while you're working," I said.

"You've got that right," she replied in a flat California-Okie drawl.

"Well, have one when you're off, then."

She left the change on the bar and gave me a flat appraising stare. I returned it. She was somewhere around forty. Her dark-blond hair was long and pulled back into a twist. Her skin had the weathered look of someone who grew up in a desert climate.

"Thanks," she finally said, picking up the change. "But I've got to warn you, I don't provide advice to the lovelorn. Or the horny."

"That's not what I'm after. Your name's Jaye Bruner, and you worked at the King's Inn, downtown, until about fifteen months ago, right?"

"That's me."

"My name's Riordan. I'm a lawyer." I handed her an old business card. She put it down on the bar and looked up, puzzled.

"Do you remember a night, a couple of days before Christmas 1989, when a TV crew came out to the King's Inn? They shot some tape in the bar and talked to you."

"Sure. The same night the hooker got killed in the motel. I remember."

"Good. I looked at the footage the TV crew shot in the bar. There was a part they didn't use, where you went up to two women sitting at a table and asked them to leave. Do you remember that?"

She looked away, trying to remember. "Vaguely. I had to call security for a table of drunks I cut off. That was mid-shift, maybe nine-thirty. Then—you're right. A couple of hookers came in around ten to work the bar, empty as it was."

"How did you know they were hooking?"

She shrugged. "I've tended bar from L.A. up to Anchorage, in between husbands. I just know. They didn't openly hustle anybody and I'd have let them alone except the TV crew was still there. I was afraid the manager might come in and blow his stack about the bad PR. The drunks they filmed were bad enough."

"Do you remember what the women looked like?"

She shook her head. "Not after all this time. I see hundreds of faces a month tending bar. I'd go crazy if I remembered all of them."

"One of the women I'm interested in had long red hair. Does that help?"

"Nope. Maybe if I had a picture."

"I've got some of the TV footage. It's not good, but I'd like you to take a look at it. Can we set up a time for you to come to the office?"

"Do you have the tape with you? I've got a VCR here in the bar, if you can wait until closing." She looked at my glass. "Want another drink?"

I hesitated before ordering a second round. I had ended too many nights this way, staring at the bottom of a glass and at my own pale reflection in a barroom mirror. "All right," I said. "Coffee too, on the side."

She brought the drinks and I waited until past one-thirty, when the bar finally thinned out. Jaye Bruner returned and took the VHS cassette. I waited as she played the tape on the bar's TV set. She replayed the footage of the two women several times, staring intently at the images on the screen.

"It's no good," she said at last. "I remember doing this, remember that night. But I just can't put a face on that woman. The bar at the King's was so dark. I'm sorry." She rewound the tape and handed the cassette back to me.

"Did you ever see the red-haired woman around the bar at the King's any other time?" I asked.

"Not that I remember. But I might have seen the other one."

"The one with dark hair?"

"That's right."

"Was she black or white?"

She thought. "Possibly black, but a real light complexion. I can't recall her face, but the woman I'm thinking of was young and thin, with styled black hair like that." She played the tape again. "See? It's kind of punky, moussed up. That's what I remember. Is this real important?"

"I don't know," I said, frustrated. "The woman with black hair was almost certainly Melody Beasely, the murder victim." I opened my briefcase and rooted around for a picture of Beasely. I found two: a high school portrait and a morgue photo showing Beasely's bruised face in death.

I gave them to Jaye. She blanched at the morgue photo but looked at it carefully, and finally nodded.

"After you threw them out," I continued, "Beasely got back into the motel somehow. Did you tell anybody else, the desk clerk, Polhaus, the night manager, that you'd pitched them and not to let them back in?"

"No. I just handled the situation. It wasn't a big deal." She handed me back the photos. "I mean, at the time."

By the time I got home it was nearly 3 A.M., too late to call Liz even if I had something more than bad guesses and uncertain witnesses to tell her about. In the past week she had been uncertain about our relationship, putting me off with a mixture of promises and pleas for understanding. I told myself not to push too hard, too soon. But when I heard her voice from my answering machine it was hard not to get my hopes up.

"I may have something, babe," she said from the tape. "Leach and what IIU was really after him for. If it pans out we could be done with this stinking case. It's a real get-out-of-jail-free card. It's got to be checked, but I think I can confirm it. I'll call you in the morning. Champagne for breakfast and all day in bed if it looks good. Let's hope so, my love." The tape clicked once and then stopped.

I called Liz's home number and got no answer. I played her message again, vaguely worried at where she might be. I stripped out of my tired, smoke-drenched clothes and told myself to relax. The case had broken open. Liz had just switched off her phone for her most peaceful sleep in a long time. After all, her voice had sounded bright for the first time in weeks.

CHAPTER 20

At five-thirty in the morning I was standing under a hot shower trying to shock myself into consciousness after less than two hours sleep. My throat was raw with Liz's gift of a new cold, my mouth sour from the whiskey of the night before. I heard an insistent pounding. Eventually I realized that the pounding came from the door to my apartment and not my head. I shut off the water, grabbed a towel and a shower robe and went to the door, expecting to see Liz.

I pulled the chain and the locks and opened the door. Vincent Ahlberg stood in the doorway. He was dressed for duty, his trademark black trench coat over a chalk-striped blue suit, red foulard tie, heavy, bench-made English shoes buffed to a dull gloss. His face was grim and tired, as though he had worked most of the night and was paying the price for it.

"It's Liz," he said quietly. "She's dead."

* * *

Freeway Park is an urban forest on a two-acre concrete lid built over Interstate 5, next to the Washington Convention Center, east of the downtown financial district. The parking garage is cut into the side of First Hill, below the park. Ahlberg pulled his unmarked cruiser into a green space at the center of the park in the cold blue hour before dawn. An elevator descended to the garage from a concrete bunker in the trees.

Liz's silver BMW coupe was parked on the fourth level. A crime scene crew was working in a circle about thirty feet in diameter around the car, taking sweepings and samples of anything that might constitute fiber, cloth, or even mud that could be traced to the killer. Later they would expand the circle to cover all routes to the exits.

"I had the elevator swept first," Ahlberg explained, "so we could use it to get in and out."

My response was numbed, clinical. "What about the first-level entrances and exits?"

"We've closed the garage, but a couple of people came in to park before the body was found. They may have screwed up any evidence there."

I was distracted by the sharp rasp of metal on concrete. Twenty yards away the ME's crew was loading a covered gurney into a county medical examiner's wagon. I started to run toward the gurney. Ahlberg caught me halfway there.

"Don't!" he said sharply. "Let us do our jobs." The ambulance crew froze with the gurney half-loaded into the back of the ambulance. Liz's body was painfully small under the drape. I shuddered and turned away. A dry heaving nausea suddenly dropped me to my knees.

"I'm all right," I said hoarsely, pushing Ahlberg's arm away as I got to my feet. "All right."

Nancy Karras came up to Ahlberg. "We've completed the base circle," she reported. "We're going to spread out now." Karras turned to look at me, puzzled by my presence.

"They were old friends," Ahlberg said shortly. "Be downtown in half an hour so we can work this up."

She nodded and turned back to the crime scene. A minute or so later she went off to her car and returned with a Styrofoam cup of black coffee for me.

"I'm sorry," she said softly.

I nodded my thanks and turned back to Ahlberg. "Can I

look at the car?" I asked, struggling to keep my voice from breaking.

He turned to Karras. "Is it okay?"

"I think so. The photographers are done and the car has been vacuumed and checked for prints. But don't touch anything. We might need a second pass."

I walked to the car with my eyes on the cement floor, careful not to step on anything. Ahlberg followed a pace behind.

The driver's door was open. The sheepskin cover of the driver's seat was stained black with Liz's blood. I fought back the urge to scream.

"We think she had just gotten into the car," Ahlberg said tightly. "The killer must have jerked the door open before she had a chance to lock it. She was probably trying to get her purse out to give him money when she was shot. He couldn't have been over a foot away. There were flash burns on her coat." He turned away from the car and walked thirty yards away from the crime-scene area, then took a small cigar from the leather case in his jacket pocket.

"I hate this damned garage," he said, lighting the cigar and carefully pocketing the wooden match. "It's six blocks from the nearest crack house on First Hill. It's open twenty-four hours but the security goes home at nine. They might as well put a sign up in the crack houses: 'Come get the lawyers working late, they have money and won't fight.' We've had six muggings in here this year already. Now this." He spat out a piece of tobacco leaf, as if for emphasis.

"I don't get it," I said numbly. "Why would Liz park in here? She's got monthly parking in Pacific Center, where her office is." I pointed back to the car and the blue parking sticker on the lower left side of the windshield.

"I saw that too. The Pacific's garage is about a third the size they need, always full. We'll talk to her secretary, get her schedule from yesterday, figure out why she was here." He looked at his watch. "Come on. I'm going to get together with Karras and Tom Wechsler. I'm assigning them both to this, full time."

We took the elevator back to the park, and to the waking day, in silence.

CHAPTER 21

I finished a fourth cup of coffee, black.

"I'll take her office staff," Tom Wechsler was saying to Nancy Karras. She nodded and started writing out task lists. Wechsler uncoiled his lanky frame from the chair he was sitting in and took a cigarette from the pack Ahlberg kept for him in his desk. He handed the pack over to me and I shook one loose and lit it, my first cigarette in years. My throat burned from the smoke.

"Are you ready to be asked some questions?" Ahlberg said, looking at me.

I nodded dumbly, barely aware of where I was.

"What was your relationship with Liz?" he asked.

"We were . . . friends. We'd been lovers, years ago. You knew about that. We broke up and it took a long time to work things out. In January she sent me the transcript of the Polhaus trial and asked me to help her work on the appeal. I'd quit practicing law, told her I didn't want to do it. She insisted. She was having a lot of trouble with her firm and she wanted somebody she could trust not to stab her in the back if the case went sour." I paused and swallowed bile. "We were spending a lot of time together. Some of the old feelings were starting to surface. A couple of weeks ago we started having sex again. I don't know whether we would have gone back to being lovers, gotten married, whatever. I wanted her back. Now——" I stopped suddenly. The cold stone weight of suppressed grief rose and I pushed it rudely away.

"Was she seeing anybody else?" Karras asked.

I shrugged. "Not recently. In the past year she mentioned

people from time to time. A lawyer in the U.S. Attorney's office, Tim Bolan, I think. And a fellow named Stein, last fall, anyway. I had lunch with them. He worked for the Symphony, doing promotion or something like that. The business end. I don't think she was serious about anybody. She'd been working like hell, trying to make partner at her law firm." I paused, then added, "I don't know where I stood either, to tell you the truth." Karras sat with a chair pulled up to the corner of Ahlberg's desk, making notes on what I was saying in neat tiny print.

"Did you talk to her yesterday?" Ahlberg asked.

"We met in the morning, part of the time with Jack Elgot, her firm's managing partner. We went over the Polhaus case. There's only six weeks until his execution. I spent the rest of the day tracking witnesses. I found the last one after midnight, a woman bartender who'd worked at the King's Inn when the motel-room murders took place. She's working at the Airport Holiday Inn now. I got home around three in the morning. There was a message on my service from Liz. She had called around eight. I called her back, got no answer. I just thought she was asleep."

"What did she say in the message?" Karras, again.

"I'm not sure I can tell you the content," I replied. "She was working on the Polhaus case, had something to tell me."

"For Chrissake, stop playing games," Ahlberg said roughly.

"I'm not," I explained. "I want to tell you. But it's Liz's attorney-work product in a live case. I need a stipulation from the state that what I tell you won't be used against Polhaus and won't be a waiver of the privilege."

Karras sighed. Ahlberg said, "Get Dan Merritt down here and get him to stipulate." She turned to the phone.

"That won't work," I said. "The state attorney general is counsel of record. Tell Merritt to contact them. If he brings a fax stipulation over from the AG's office I'll sign it, and tell you what she said."

It took half an hour. I went outside and breathed the wet morning air as clouds moved in from the west and rain began to fall. When Merritt finally arrived, he was brusquely self-important.

"Ahlberg," he said impatiently, "What is this non-waiver crap? I could've done this over the phone."

Ahlberg rose from behind his desk with as plain a fury as I have ever seen on his face. "Daniel," he said, his voice hard,

"I have a witness here who's acting properly, as an attorney, under a good deal of personal distress. You'd better have that damned stipulation from the attorney general in writing or I will punt you back across the street to the courthouse."

Merritt looked at Ahlberg, looked at me, and made the right decision. "I've got it," he said quietly. He turned to me. "And I apologize. I'd forgotten that you and Liz were friends. I really am sorry."

I put out a hand. "Forget it. Let me look at the stipulation." It was correct and I signed it. "Send me a copy, care of Lisle, Day, for the file." He nodded.

"I'm going to try this one personally," Merritt said grimly. "Liz was the best. I know how much she meant to my office."

I gave him the benefit of the doubt. I knew that trying the murder of a former prosecutor with Liz's reputation would look good to the voters. But I said nothing.

"Let's have it," Ahlberg said. "What was Liz working on?"

"Liz," I said carefully, "was trying to find out why the county sheriff's Internal Investigation Unit was involved in the Polhaus case. She knew this much: There still is an open investigation into Raymond Leach. Liz apparently found another source, she didn't say who, yesterday. She got something new. She said that if it checked out, Polhaus's conviction would get reversed."

Merritt was stunned. "What the hell are you talking about?"

"Leach withholding, probably destroying, probative evidence. Leach steering the investigation to Polhaus to protect somebody else. And that IIU knew it and didn't disclose it when Polhaus was on trial. She said it was a get-out-of-jail-free card. That's the only thing she could have meant."

"You son of a bitch," Merritt said, his voice low. "You son of a bitch. Liz isn't cold and you're trying to use her death to support some crazy theory of yours and get that killer off."

I took a deep breath and looked at Merritt. His dark, handsome face was twisted with scorn. I turned back to Ahlberg.

"If you want to question me further," I said, as quietly as I could, "get him out of here. Or I'll break every fucking bone in his body. I mean it."

Merritt stiffened. We stood two feet apart, ready to rip into each other with one more word.

"Daniel," Ahlberg said carefully, "let me question this witness, for now. You'll be fully informed. But your presence is making my job difficult. And, to be perfectly frank, if he decides to bust you into little pieces I'm inclined to let him. He will, believe me. Are we clear on this?"

Merritt looked steadily at Ahlberg, then at me, his face bright red. He turned suddenly and left without another word.

When he was gone Ahlberg said, "Now cut the crap. What are you talking about?"

"Somebody didn't give you everything on that IIU report, Vince," I replied. "Jacqueline Rogers withdrew her complaint, but the file was left open. IIU was investigating whether Leach was on the pad, working with Poole, even during the motel-room investigation. All three victims worked for Poole's escort service. Poole is touchy as hell about the links between the victims and his service, about Leach, and about the women's john books, their lists of customers. He had Rogers withdraw her complaint."

"What are you saying? That Poole and Leach were tied into the motel-room murders? That we ought to be looking at Poole and Leach as suspects in this homicide?"

"Yes. Leach has a career on the line. He lied to you during the Polhaus case about his contacts with Poole, and stole the victims' john books to keep the names of their customers from being discovered. Poole has a business turning something like a half million dollars a year in profit on the surface, and a lot more below. His operations are exclusively in the county's jurisdiction. I talked to him and I talked to the girl that filed the brutality complaint against Leach. Poole got her to withdraw it. Leach was supposed to be working on Poole's operations when he was in county vice. Yet Poole's never had a bust, Vince, not one. Poole knows what's at stake. Get a pattern of convictions on him for promoting prostitution, you could bust up his operations, confiscate his assets under the state racketeering statute."

Ahlberg shook his head, a fresh cigar clamped between his teeth. "You're spinning something, Matthew. You haven't got a hard link between Poole and the murders of the three prostitutes. I know that's where you're going. But you're not even close. With Polhaus we had means, opportunity, and a hell of a lot of physical evidence."

"All circumstantial. Liz didn't think it was enough. Neither do I."

He must have seen the look on my face. He came around the desk and put a hand on my shoulder. "Look, we've barely started this. Let us do the groundwork. I'll be back to you if anything breaks. Even if we've got nothing, I'll call you and get you back in here to nail down the details of her movements for us."

I broke away and shook his hand off. "Vince, I'm not getting through. Poole and Leach were involved in the motel murders. They had a motive to kill Liz. When she left that message for me she was trying to confirm what Leach had done to your investigation. You've got to bring Leach and Poole in. Sweat them. At least do that much."

He was still thinking when Nancy Karras said, "I'm sorry, Matthew. I truly am. But Ms. Kleinfeldt was killed in a robbery. All the evidence points to that. I don't know the basis for these charges you're making about withheld evidence." Her voice tightened. "I know I withheld nothing. Leach couldn't have steered this investigation, because I was running it, and I found enough evidence to have Polhaus charged and convicted." She started to pick up her notepad from Ahlberg's desk, then added in a gentle voice, "I know you'd like things to be different, to give Ms. Kleinfeldt's death some meaning. I do understand that. But you must deal with the reality of this, in order to help us." She turned to Wechsler. "We'd better get started on the people at Kleinfeldt's firm. They should be able to tie down her schedule." Wechsler followed her out of Ahlberg's office with a shrug of his thin shoulders.

I turned back to Ahlberg. "Listen to me," I said urgently, grabbing his shoulders. "Liz was five feet three inches tall. One hundred four pounds. She was scared to death of parking garages with no security. You remember why? *Seven years ago she was raped in one.* She would never have gone to Freeway Park. She'd have gone to Two Union Square, or Puget Sound Plaza, if her garage was full. If she had to walk to her car late at night she would have called a security guard to go with her. And the timing's not right. When she called me, around eight, she was on her way somewhere trying to confirm the information she'd gotten. Even if she had parked in Freeway Park she would have been out of there hours before eleven o'clock. Somebody forced her there. Or lured her there. Somebody who had information she wanted about this case." I swallowed something bitter and balled my hands into fists. "I'm going to go talk to that bastard Leach."

"Don't!" he commanded. "Karras is right. You're superimposing whatever you and Liz were checking into for Polhaus on top of this case. I'll have somebody get a formal statement from you tomorrow. Get some sleep, if you can. You'll think more clearly."

I knew he was trying to do the right thing but my grief and anger burned like phosphorus. "You can't," I said bitterly, "be objective about advice from a cop you're sleeping with, Vince."

The slap of his open hand nearly took my head off. I rocked back on my heels and tasted blood and sour bile.

"You can't," I repeated. I turned and stalked out of Ahlberg's office, raising my handkerchief to touch up the blood from my mouth as I hit the street.

The days blurred. Waking hours were burdened by memory. Sleep, when it came, was uneasy, sweat-soaked, racked by dreams.

The memorial service was held on Sunday. The mourners splashed through the gray rain-soaked streets of lower Capitol Hill around the Temple de Hirsch Sinai, huddled together under umbrellas and raising the collars of their coats against the wind. They filled the benches under the temple dome and listened as the King County presiding judge, David MacGregor, spoke of Liz's life and work, celebrating her courage and grace. Susan Bedell, the head of the Women's Bar Association, recalled the crisis of conscience that had led Liz to abandon her career as a prosecutor in protest against the death penalty. Unlike most public funerals, there was a sense of shock, of stillness and decency. No one worked the crowd or cut deals or tried to get a leg up on the next election.

I sat near the back, alone. Jack Elgot had spotted me before the service started and stiffly invited me to sit with the delegation from Elizabeth's law firm. I declined, not out of dislike for Elgot, but from the desire to be alone with my thoughts. I watched Elizabeth's father, a retired San Francisco surgeon, and her mother, a poet. They were seated on the dais with Ed Warren, the county prosecutor for whom Liz had worked, and a row of judges and elected officials. Their grief was plain. The death of the child before the parent is particularly cruel. Yet they held themselves with the strength and dignity the day demanded.

I had met them only once, years before. They had the kindness to invite me to the private service. Later that night, in a Queen Anne Hill living room, a small circle of family and friends, lawyers and doctors and dancers and writers—seven Jews, two blacks, six WASPs, and one Irishman—said Kaddish for their honored, and beloved, dead.

MARCH

CHAPTER 22

The unmarked cruiser was waiting for me at dawn when I returned from three laps around Volunteer Park. I saw it from the hill overlooking Prospect Street, parked around the corner from my apartment. I took the towel from around my neck and wiped the sweat off and looked again. I couldn't make out the driver.

I still had not given a formal statement to the police investigating Liz's murder but I couldn't imagine Ahlberg sending a car up to my house to haul me down. He had been angry, but not that angry. I thought it might be Raymond Leach, looking to cut out a piece of my heart because of the statements I made to Ahlberg after Liz was killed. That was okay. I wanted him to try it. I walked cautiously down the hill, surging with adrenaline.

When I reached the street the driver's door opened and Nancy Karras slid out of the car. She stood by the side of the car and waited as I approached. She wore khaki slacks and a heavy wool sweater against the morning chill. The sun had just risen and the fog still hung thick in the meadows of the park.

"Good morning," she said. Her voice was polite, almost shy.

I nodded, trying to calm myself down. "You're on duty awfully early, aren't you, Detective? It isn't even seven o'clock."

"I thought I would stop and see you before logging in, if you don't mind."

"There's coffee on upstairs," I said abruptly. "Come on."

I led her into my building and up the stairs to the top floor. I picked up the morning papers from the hallway floor and opened the door to my apartment. "The living room is straight ahead. The coffee's in a white carafe on the kitchen counter. I'm afraid it's got milk in it; I take it that way. There are cups and boxes of tea in the cabinet, if you'd rather have that. Help yourself. I'm going to clean up. I'll be with you shortly."

I took a quick shower and put on jeans and turtleneck, still vaguely irritated at Karras's sudden appearance at my home. It was four days since Liz had been killed. If Ahlberg wanted a statement from me he should take it downtown, with a stenographer, and give me a chance to review it. Karras was here on her own to tell me off.

I got myself a cup of coffee from the kitchen and returned to the living room. Karras was standing in front of the library wall, a mug of herbal tea in hand, inspecting the titles of the books. I wasn't wearing shoes and she had not heard me return. When I spoke she visibly started.

"That's about half of them," I said. "I had to put a lot of books into storage until the house I'm building gets finished."

"Sorry," she said, embarrassed. "Force of habit. I'm a reader, too. I like to look at collections other people have put together."

"No problem. Please sit down, Detective." I sat down on a teakwood-and-black-leather Eames chair, facing her as she seated herself on the sofa. Her expression was composed but a little on edge. Her witness-interview face. I waited for her to begin.

"I thought we should talk," she said. "So far we haven't gotten along very well."

"That goes with your job. And mine."

"I also wanted to tell you how sorry I was about Ms. Kleinfeldt. It's very hard losing a friend like that. I know."

I made a face. "You're fencing with me, Detective. What is this about?"

She shifted a little on the couch. "I wanted to follow up on the statements you made in Captain Ahlberg's office after Ms. Kleinfeldt was killed."

"What I said about the case, or about you?"

"Both," she said calmly. "Look, Mr. Riordan, my private life is none of your business." She swept a hand through her straight brown hair and looked at me directly. "But if you think it's influencing the steps we take in finding out who killed Ms. Kleinfeldt, you're quite wrong. I'm not sleeping with Captain Ahlberg. We're friends. We might become more than that if and when I'm no longer directly assigned to him, but until then we are both adults and we both know the rules. And follow them."

I studied her for a moment. She was a handsome woman in a precise, neat sort of way. Her eyes were her best feature. They were large and dark brown, and they hinted at emotional depths that only time and closeness would reveal. I found myself wanting to like her, despite my anger with the way she and Ahlberg were handling the investigation. "I apologize," I said at last. "I was distraught."

"I understand. How are you holding up?"

"Well enough," I lied. "If we're going to work together I'd like to know something about you."

She shrugged, rubbing her hands together compulsively as she had before. "Not much to tell. I'm thirty-five. The only daughter of a county sheriff down on the Oregon coast. I've been a cop for thirteen years, seven in Portland, six here. I had a divorce, a bad one, there. That's why I left." She stopped abruptly. "None of which is relevant."

"Then tell me what's going on."

"It's not good," she replied grimly. "No witnesses, no leads, no weapon, no physical evidence that means anything. The credit cards have not been fenced. I checked with the card companies and there was no activity on them since the day before the murder. We've pieced together Ms. Kleinfeldt's schedule on the day of her death. She took a half-hour deposition at four o'clock, but didn't return to her office until seven. She left again at eight-fifteen. She made three phone calls, two on other cases, and the call she left on your answering service."

"Liz told me that she was trying to confirm what she'd learned about the IIU investigation. Do you know where she might have gone, who she might have talked to?"

"No. No idea."

"So the facts are still consistent with your theory. That Liz was killed by some street punk who doesn't have smarts to fence her credit cards properly."

"True. But I'm troubled by some things."

"Like?"

"Like the Parker john book. You brought it up when we met with you two weeks ago, and Merritt promised to get it for you. I was surprised when you asked about it. Leach never told us he had it. It still hasn't turned up. And I checked with the county prosecutor's office. There has been a serious internal investigation into Sergeant Leach's conduct. It started with a brutality complaint, from a topless dancer that he arrested, just as you said. When Captain Ahlberg asked the sheriff about it, he was told that it was bogus and to forget it. I raised hell and the sheriff's IIU people finally admitted that Leach's file was open until about six months ago. I've looked at the file. They were investigating the links between Leach and Lawrence Poole. They didn't find enough to make a case, but the suspicions were one of the reasons Leach was transferred out of vice, into homicide."

My face fell. "There has to be more than that involved. We guessed that much. Liz wouldn't have been excited unless there was something new, something important."

"I'm sorry. That's all there was." She shook her head, disturbed. "That little is still way too much. When I was working on the motel-room murders I did not know any of this. I saw the coincidence, with two out of the three victims working out of the Dreams agency, and the third had worked there in the past. We made the usual effort to get the list of customers the women were seeing. I should say Leach made the usual effort. Ahlberg assigned that project to him because of his vice background."

"And now you're wondering just how hard he tried."

She nodded. "Nobody thought Leach might be dirty. And after the third murder, we had Polhaus. I'm not saying Polhaus isn't guilty. I know he is. The evidence is just too overwhelming. But there may have been something else going on involving Poole, something I didn't see."

"So where does that take you?"

"To the point of trying to determine whether Ms. Kleinfeldt's murder might be related."

I took my coffee cup from the leather footstool in front of me and got up to go to the kitchen. "Detective, you just bought yourself another cup of tea, if you want one."

When I returned from the kitchen with two fresh cups, she had a pad out and was taking notes. "I'd like to follow up on the investigation you've done. Why did Ms. Kleinfeldt take on this case and bring you into it? The evidence against Polhaus is so convincing."

"It was a gut reaction for her," I replied. "Liz was a rare person, a dedicated prosecutor, but morally opposed to the death penalty. When she got into it she developed doubts about the investigation."

"What were they?"

"At first, simply a sense that the investigation had focused on Polhaus to the exclusion of all other suspects. Liz told me that if she had been the prosecutor she would have sent the file back for more investigation. She felt that Merritt was wrong to seek the death penalty in a purely circumstantial case. She thought the two potential witnesses that Polhaus testified about, the woman running away from the motel and the man standing on the balcony, should have been found."

"I don't think they ever existed."

"I thought that too. Now I'm not so sure."

"Why?"

"I looked at the tape Mark Starrett, the television news reporter, shot at the King's Inn on the night Melody Beasely was murdered."

She shrugged. "I saw the program, as I told you. We interviewed Starrett and his cameraman, they said they didn't see Polhaus except when he cleared a couple of people out of the bar. Other witnesses confirmed that, and it didn't give Polhaus an alibi, because the murder was several hours later."

"Then you didn't see all of it. Starrett's file copy of the tape was re-recorded on a cassette containing the rough footage the cameraman shot. Starrett's camera crew went back in the bar about an hour later, around eleven. The bartender, Jaye Bruner, ejected two women she thought were hooking from the bar. Starrett didn't use that part in the final show. One of the women had long red hair. The other woman was Melody Beasely. The tape was shot about two hours before Beasely was murdered."

She leaned forward, suddenly intense. "Did they get a clear picture of the women's faces?"

"No. Beasely's grandmother was able to identify her, but neither the bartender nor Starrett remembers what the redhead looked like."

She thought for a moment, then shook her head. "Then I don't think it helps you. We did try to find the woman Polhaus described, because the prosecutors wanted to call her in rebuttal. I went through the bookings on prostitutes for the last two years prior to the murders, looking at booking photos. I didn't find anyone who came close to matching the woman's description."

"The woman could have had no record in King County. Liz and I both knew it was shaky, but it seemed to corroborate a part of Polhaus's story that everyone, even his own lawyer, assumed he made up. The woman could have been working with Beasely, and might have worked out of the Dreams agency."

She frowned and made a notation on her pad. "I don't know how we can trace this red-haired woman any further than you already have, but I'll look at Starrett's tape again, and all the booking photos since the killings. I'll get a list of all the women that vice knows that have worked out of Dreams or been associated with Lawrence Poole for the last five years." She dropped her pad on the table in front of her and picked up her teacup. "What else did you get?"

"Melody Beasely's john book. I don't think you ever found it."

"No, we didn't." She made another note. "Who was in there?"

"Some pretty prominent people. I'll send you the list. Beasely's ex-roommate, Jacqueline Rogers, went to Clarissa Beasely's house after Beasely was killed, looking for that book. Poole denied sending her for it, but I don't believe him."

"Why?"

"Poole is a very strange man. He's slick, businesslike, organized, cautious. He collects important men who use the escort service. That's his protection. He doesn't want their names exposed as clients of the murdered women."

"When did you get this?"

"In the three days before Liz was murdered."

"And you think there's a connection."

I nodded. "About ten days ago, the day after I talked to you and Leach, Liz and I were followed here from her office." I saw the polite, skeptical look on her face. "I know what you're thinking. Maybe the driver was just lost. Nothing else happened in the next week, so I dismissed it. But now I wonder."

I could feel the walls of my apartment close in as they had so often since Liz had been murdered. I got up and opened the French doors to the narrow balcony and stepped outside. I looked down at the street where the car had been parked, the driver watching my apartment. It seemed to have happened so long ago. "The ironic thing," I said, still facing the street, "is that we actually didn't know what we were doing. We had no facts, no theory. I was just wandering around asking any questions I could think of."

Karras had gotten up from the sofa and joined me on the balcony, a gentle hand on my arm, saying nothing. I turned to her and said, "So I have to know, Nancy. I have to know if some stupid blundering thing I did got Liz killed."

CHAPTER 23

Jack Elgot scheduled a meeting to pick up the pieces on the Polhaus case for one o'clock the same day. I got to his office ten minutes early, tired and oddly shaken. The brief warmth from my talk with Nancy Karras was gone.

Wayne Porras and Gretel Anderson, the young associate lawyers who had worked on the briefs, were already present, seated on the navy-blue sofa in Elgot's office. They fiddled nervously with the coffee service on the Queen Anne coffee table in front of them. We made a few attempts at conversation, then lapsed into a desultory silence, watching the clock.

Elgot walked in precisely on the hour, shedding his suit coat in favor of a gray cardigan. He took a file from his desk, perched his reading glasses on his nose, and paused to read his notes. He had not spoken a word in greeting.

"It goes without saying," he began, "that Elizabeth's loss will create a tremendous void, not just for this case, but for the firm. We will have to carry on as she would have wanted."

"I agree," I said, cutting in. "We have five weeks left until Polhaus is executed. There is no assurance that the state supreme court will stay the execution date to hear our appeal. It's vital that you assign another senior attorney to this case. Mr. Porras and Ms. Anderson have done a tremendous job, but the additional investigation, briefing, and argument call for experience. If you have no one to spare, I would be willing to take that on if I can have these lawyers to help."

"It is my intention to re-assign this case," Elgot said, a waspish frown on his face. "We have about two weeks to file a brief under the existing schedule. We'll ask for an extension and stay because of Elizabeth's death."

"That's cutting it awfully close," I said, frowning. "But the key thing is to put our resources into questioning Beasely's customers. Given the possible link between this case and Elizabeth's murder, we will have to cooperate with the police on that, consistent with maintaining the work product and attorney-client privileges. It's going to be touchy."

Elgot slowly removed his glasses. "What on earth are you talking about? The police said that Elizabeth was killed by a mugger. It's got nothing to do with this case."

"They're not so sure now," I replied. "They are looking at the possibility the cases may be linked. I spoke with the investigating detective this morning. She intends to pursue the issue."

"I see," he said coldly. "On what conceivable basis?"

I took him through the links between the three motel-room murder victims and Poole's escort service, the probable tie between Poole and Raymond Leach, the loss of the Parker john book, and Liz's last, cryptic message that she had uncovered misconduct that would mandate a reversal of Polhaus's conviction. When I had finished Elgot sat for a moment, tapping a gold pencil on the file in front of him.

He finally said, "What do you suggest we do next?"

"Two things. First, we have to identify the person Liz talked to, and find out exactly what evidence was withheld during the original trial. I'm going to check Liz's notes, see if she made any reference to the identity of her sources. Her statement that the case could be over tells us that the withheld evidence is much more important than we originally thought. Second, as I said, Beasely's customers."

"Have you been able to determine whether any of Beasely's clients were also clients of the other women?"

"No. Not yet. Parker's john book is missing, probably destroyed. No one's found a list of johns for the third victim, Klimka. I've been trying to force the owner of the escort service that Klimka was working for at the time she was killed to turn over a customer list so that we can cross-check. We should subpoena her records and take her deposition if she won't cooperate."

Elgot frowned at the file in his lap and looked up at me. "I've decided to take this case on myself," he said. "It's been some years since I practiced criminal law, but at this appellate stage I think I can hold my own. I'm sure you'll understand,

Mr. Riordan, that every senior lawyer needs to have the flexibility to staff the case as he or she sees fit. I want you to know that we are grateful for the work you've done, and we appreciate that you left retirement to assist Elizabeth when she asked for your help." He opened the file in front of him and removed two documents. "I've had Mr. Porras review your expense records and prepare a bill for court approval, as well as a notice of withdrawal. In addition, as a token of the firm's gratitude, we've cut a check for your time. I hope a hundred and fifty an hour is all right. I think you'll find the papers in order, and we'll present them to the court for you." He held them across the table between our facing chairs.

I leafed through the withdrawal papers. I could feel my face redden with anger. "I'm grateful for the offer of a fee," I said dryly. "And I do appreciate your willingness to carry on without me. But I think I have to see this case through. I owe Liz that much." I dropped the papers and the check on the table.

"Perhaps I haven't been clear," Elgot said, his face still a mask of cold courtesy. "I have decided to terminate you as our co-counsel."

"No. You were very clear. I'm refusing to go. I was not associated by your firm. I was hired directly by the client. Check the wording of the court order approving my retention. The only person who can discharge me is Polhaus. When and if I hear from him, and if I'm assured that his decision is based on all the facts, then I'll reconsider the matter."

Elgot's voice was frigid and precise, all trace of a drawl gone. "You don't have the right to refuse."

"I have every goddamned right!" I shouted, smashing a fist down on the low table. "Don't you understand? Liz was killed because of something she learned. Or something I blundered into. We have to pursue it." I stopped and breathed deeply, struggling with my temper.

Elgot remained in his chair. He calmly took the withdrawal papers from the table and replaced them in his file. "That outburst," he said calmly, "is the best reason yet for getting you off this case. I'll not have you out there using this firm to harass people because you've conjured up some ridiculous conspiracy. Turn over all your notes and work papers, including any evidence or documents you've checked out from the firm, immediately. Don't attempt to communicate with my client, Mr. Polhaus. And as of now you're not to set foot in our offices again."

I stood up. "You're going to have to go to court, Jack. I'm not going to let you bury this case because you think it's bad for business." I turned to go, then stopped and turned back. "You bloodless son of a bitch," I added.

CHAPTER 24

The phone was ringing when I walked into my apartment. I caught it on the last ring and switched off the message service.

"Matthew? You there?"

"Yes. Who's this?"

"Terry. I'm glad I caught you. I may have something for you. But you need to get down here now. Can you do that?"

"To the paper?"

"Right. God-awful about Liz. Do the cops have any leads?"

"Nothing."

"Do you think her death connects to the Polhaus case?"

I hesitated. "Off the record?"

"Sure."

"I think it connects. She was killed just a few hours after she left a message for me saying she'd found new evidence."

"What kind of evidence?"

"It has to do with an IIU investigation into Raymond Leach, the county homicide cop on the motel-room murders. Liz didn't tell me who her source was. Her law firm's fired me from the case and won't give me access to her notes."

"Can they do that?"

"Not without a fight."

He hesitated. "Well, come on down here. What I've got may or may not help." He hung up.

The city room of the *Tribune* was quiet. The night final edition had just gone out. The reporters were cleaning up their desks and heading out for late lunches and the gym. In fitness-obsessed Seattle, not even reporters drank anymore.

Terry Lasker had two people in his office, a man and a woman. The man was in his mid-twenties, sandy-haired and slightly overweight, dressed in a reporter's notion of fashion: faded blue dress shirt, corduroy jeans, and running shoes. The woman was a bit older, perhaps thirty, painfully thin, with dark-blond hair. She wore an inexpensive blue business suit and black pumps. She fidgeted nervously.

"Matthew," he said as I came in, "this is Carolyn Ritter. The lazy reporter sitting on the window ledge is Bobby Ward."

I shook hands with both of them and cleared a pile of books from the remaining visitor's chair in Lasker's small office before sitting down. Lasker said, "Carolyn called Bobby, who's a friend of her family from their home town, to ask for some help. When Bobby heard her story he came to me, and I thought you should hear it." He turned to the woman. "Carolyn, Matthew is a lawyer and an old friend. He is working on a case that might be related to your problem. I trust him, and I think you can. But it's up to you whether you want to tell him about it."

She looked at me with wary gray eyes that were red-rimmed from lack of sleep, or possibly tears. Care and fatigue had roughened her once delicate features and aged her beyond her years.

"I'm representing a man named Robert Polhaus," I said. "He's been convicted of killing three young women. I'm working on his appeal. I think he may not have committed the murders. All of the victims were young and involved in prostitution."

"I don't know how you can help," she said warily. "I'm looking for someone."

"Tell me the story, and we'll see. If there's no connection, I won't repeat anything you tell me to anyone else."

She nodded. "It's my sister. Andrea Jacoby. She's been missing for over four years now."

"Tell me what happened."

"She's much younger than I am. She's only twenty-two. She grew up kind of wild, and her father didn't much try to help her. He and my mother were divorced a long time ago." She stopped, aware that she was getting away from the main point. "I'm sorry," she added.

"Don't be," I replied. "I'm interested in anything you have to tell me, and that includes all the background you want to put in."

"Well, Andrea ran away from home a couple of times. Five years ago she left for good. She was only seventeen. She came up here to Seattle, and I think she was on the streets for a while. She wouldn't talk about it, even to me, and I'm the one in the family she was probably closest to. About three months after she left she started working at a topless bar. She had more money. Later on she got an apartment, nice clothes, even a car. She came home for a couple of days and patched things up with our mother, some, anyway. When she went back to Seattle she'd call me every couple of weeks, just to talk. Eventually she told me that she was working for an escort service called Dreams."

"Where do you live?" I asked.

"Chehalis. Outside of it, actually, a little town called Winlock, about ten miles away."

"Is that where Andrea lived before she left home?"

"Yes, in my mother's house. I live there now."

Lasker was impatient with my background questions. "Go on," he urged. "Tell him when your sister disappeared."

"She called me at home on a Wednesday night, actually about three o'clock in the morning on Thursday, the sixth of January, 1990. I have the date right because I wrote down a note. She sounded terribly frightened. 'I have to get out of here,' she kept saying. I asked her why but she wouldn't tell me. I told her to come home, but she said that wouldn't do her any good, it wasn't far enough away. She wanted me to send her some money, but I couldn't, I just didn't have it. I'm a legal assistant, in a small law office. I don't make very much. I have to support my son, and help my mother out, too. I wanted to help her, but I was just stone broke."

The significance of the date slowly sank in. Sharee Klimka had been killed just before midnight on January 5. If this woman was right, Andrea Jacoby had called her sister in a panic about three hours later.

"What happened after she called you?"

"Nothing. She disappeared. Her landlord called and told me to come get her stuff. I asked a friend who's on the Lewis County sheriff's force to check with the Seattle police. They called and I filed a missing-persons report but nothing ever turned up."

"Why are you coming up here now to look for her? It's

been four years. That's probably too long to find her." I tried to keep my voice gentle but she heard it as an accusation.

"I know. It makes me sound terrible. I just . . . between my job and my son and helping take care of my mother, there wasn't any more that I could do."

"You misunderstand," I said. "I'm not accusing you of anything. I was asking if something has changed, something that makes you think she might be found now."

"A schoolteacher at home fishes up in Alaska in the summers. He flew up to Anchorage last month to meet with his partner about buying a new boat. They were drinking in a dive bar and Mike, the teacher, thought he saw Andy with some guy. He went over and said hi to her, but she told him he'd made a mistake, she wasn't who he thought."

"He could have been wrong, if he hadn't seen her in years. Especially in a dark bar with a few drinks in him."

"He's sure it was her. He said Andy started to say hello to him, then acted like she didn't know him."

"Why did you come here, to the paper?" Terry asked.

"I've got to find her. My mother's dying. She wants to make up with Andy, say good-bye. I've been telling her for the last couple years that Andy is all right, that I get a call every few weeks, that she's traveling. I'm running out of stories to make up. I came to the paper because I know you keep files of clippings. I thought maybe Bobby would let me look at them, because he's an old friend. I wanted to see if I could find anything about Andrea, you know, arrests. Or, if Mike was wrong . . . to see if she was dead."

Lasker turned to Ward, the young reporter. "Bobby," he said, "go through the clippings morgue. Run the girl's name and also check on the Jane Doe homicide stories statewide for 1990 and 1991. Check any Alaska stories, too. And search the King, Pierce, and Snohomish County police records." Ward slid off the windowsill and headed out to the *Tribune*'s library. Lasker turned back to Carolyn Ritter.

"I want you to be very specific, as specific as you can, about what your sister said to you when she called you. Can you do that?"

"God," she said, "I was sound asleep. It was something like, 'Carol, it's Andy. I'm in bad trouble and I've got to get out of Seattle. I'm broke. Can you send me any money?' I was hardly awake and said something like 'What is it, honey? What happened?' She said, 'I saw something and I think they're going to come after me. I have to get out of here, get far away. Please, please, send me some money.' And then I said I didn't have any but I'd sell my car and send her the money, and she said that would take too long, she had to leave right away. I told her to come home and she said she couldn't. And that's all."

"Have you tried a skip-tracing service, a private detective, anything like that?" I asked.

"No. I will, though. I talked to Bill Houle, the lawyer I work for. He said he'll lend me the money to hire somebody. But I haven't yet."

"Have you got a picture of your sister that we could use?"

She nodded. "This is a high school junior-year picture. It's the best I have." She handed me a wallet-size photo. It showed a young woman not as attractive as her sister; her heavily made-up features were harsh underneath a heavy brow. She had long brown hair that fell in loose waves away from her face.

I passed the picture across the desk to Lasker. He looked at it and shrugged. I said, "Women in prostitution use working names, Carolyn. Do you know what your sister called herself?"

She nodded. "Fawn."

"Son of a bitch," I said.

"What's the matter?" Ritter asked.

"I'm sorry. It may be nothing. An investigator who worked on the trial of the man I represent, Robert Polhaus, was trying to find a woman named Fawn when Polhaus was on trial. They thought she might be a witness. He couldn't find her. He just assumed she'd moved on somewhere," I added hastily, seeing the sudden fear on Carolyn Ritter's face.

"I don't know what anybody can do," she said. "I can't go to Alaska myself, not and take care of my mother."

I thought for a long minute. "I've got just one idea," I said. "It could be a waste of time." I borrowed Terry Lasker's phone and called the prostitution prevention program office and asked for Karen Sasser. The gruff voice of the off-duty cop who worked as their receptionist said that she was out but would be back after seven o'clock. I looked at my watch. It was just past five. Two hours to kill. I looked at Carolyn Ritter.

"When was the last time you ate something?"

She was startled, then smiled for the first time. "This morning, I think. With my son."

"Is his dad taking care of him?"

"No. I'm divorced. My boss's wife is picking him up from

school and giving him dinner. She'll keep him tonight if I get home late."

"Good. There's someone I want you to talk to but she won't be back for a couple of hours. I haven't eaten all day, either. Terry, you coming?"

Lasker shook his head, still writing notes in a long, thin reporter's notebook. "I'm dining with the Humane Society tonight," he said regretfully. "Lost dogs and such. Hopefully not on the menu. But I promised."

"Okay. I'll try to catch up with you tomorrow."

"Sure."

I took Carolyn Ritter to a small bistro in a Denny Regrade storefront on Second Avenue. I was hungry for the first time in days. They had just opened. The full dinner menu would not be ready until six-thirty, but the bartender seated us, brought a bottle of Oregon Merlot, lit the candles on the table, and promised pepper steaks and warm salads inside half an hour.

Carolyn Ritter opened the menu and blanched. "I doubt if I can pay for my half of this," she said grimly.

"Forget it. You're saving me from eating alone."

Over the next hour I coaxed her into talking about herself and her life. I learned that she was twenty-eight and the mother of a six-year-old son. Her ex-husband had a fishing boat in Alaska but seldom made the court-ordered support payments. She liked her work in a small-town law practice and hoped to attend night law school at the University of Puget Sound in Tacoma. I admired her courage and her ability to fight for a better future despite her careworn present. It seemed as though she had not talked about herself and her dreams for a very long time. As I listened to her stream of words I thought I could feel myself beginning to come to life again.

Karen Sasser was working the telephone when we arrived, trying to track down a sixteen-year-old boy who had split from the Orion halfway house.

"Uh-uh," she said, dropping the telephone receiver onto its cradle and turning to face us across her cluttered metal desk. "I heard about Liz Kleinfeldt," she said to me, abruptly but not unkindly. "I was back east, in Chicago, trying to snag some foundation money, or I would have gone to the service. You know her a long time?"

I nodded.

"I'm sorry," she said. "Good woman. Who's this?"

I introduced Carolyn Ritter to her, told her what had happened, and passed the picture of Andrea Jacoby across her desk. She took the picture without enthusiasm.

"Yeah, I knew her," she said. "She came in once, on her own, almost. The VD clinic at the Public Health Hospital sent her over. I tried to talk her into staying. That was years ago. Where is she now?"

There was something in her voice that did not ring true. The no-bullshit quality was gone.

"I was hoping you could tell us," I said dryly.

A mixture of defiance and embarrassment passed across her face. "What does that mean?"

"What it sounds like, Karen. Think. The girl called you while the motel-room murders were going on. She was desperate to get out of town because she thought someone was trying to kill her. I think she'd try everybody she could think of. If she'd been here before, that includes you."

She looked down. "If this gets out, my ass is in serious trouble."

"Nobody here wants that. The girl's mother is dying. We want to get them back together. If you can find her, I want to talk to her about the murders. That's all."

She paused to think and took a cigarette from one of two crumpled packs on her desk, straightened it, and tamped it on the table. I leaned across her desk and lit it with the gas lighter I still carried from the time when I had smoked.

"A gentleman," she said wryly, burlesquing her accent like a bad actress playing Tennessee Williams. She blew smoke toward the open window. The night sounds of First Avenue drifted in, the shouts of teenagers from the corner of Pike, stray bits of drunken conversation, the muted grinding of traffic, a siren in the distance. "Okay, I saw her. She came to my apartment—I live a couple blocks away, in the Market—at five o'clock on a Thursday morning and said she had to get out of town, that she might be killed. I tried to stop her, get her in here, but we can't protect people if there is serious shit on their heads. So I called up Alaska Airlines and charged a ticket for her, and gave her fifty dollars to tide her over. She had friends in Anchorage and I knew she'd find work there, even if it had to be hooking. At least it was a long way from here."

"Why'd you do it?" I asked.

"She had me convinced she was in trouble. She was working out of Dreams and you've probably heard what Poole can be like, the son of a bitch. I thought she'd crossed him and at least I was going to save her from a beating. Or worse."

"Did she say what the problem was?"

"Only that she'd seen something she shouldn't have, and people were going to be after her. I know it sounds weak. At first I thought she was just scamming me to get coke money. But I know terror, I see it in these kids. And in her, it was real."

"Do you know where she is now?"

A crease of concern appeared on Sasser's plain face. "No. Not that I expected to. She said she'd pay me back, but . . ." She let the words fall away. She did not have to explain that a cokehead whore was not a good prospect for repaying a debt. Or for living very long.

Carolyn Ritter's hopes fell, hard. "Oh, no," she said plaintively.

"Look," Sasser said, "I can try. I'll leave word with Social Services up there, tell them to look for her. They're like we are, they have good contacts out on the streets. If she's working up there, they can find her."

"No cops," I said. "If she's run once, she'll run again."

"No." Karen Sasser crushed out her cigarette. Her dark eyes looked out from deep hollows, her skin stretched taut over bone. She turned to Carolyn Ritter. "I hope I did right by your sister," she said wearily. "Sitting in here, you know, it's just so damned hard to tell."

CHAPTER 25

Harry Glickerman was one of life's optimists, a mathematics graduate from the University of Washington who made a living writing computer software for the telephone company. Harry was a quiet, unassuming man who dreamed of the higher realms of statistical theory, applied to roulette. He was coming closer, he said, to a system that would get him the one big score and the endless lazy days on the Costa del Sol he was sure would follow. Over my years of practicing law I had made investments in his system, asking only for certain telephone company records in return. The standard investment was five hundred dollars in small used bills. I had called him to make an investment the day after Liz was killed. On the morning after my blowup with Jack Elgot he delivered a printout containing every call made to or from Liz's home and the Lisle, Day offices in the three weeks before her murder.

I spent half a day collating the telephone numbers, looking for calls to the county prosecutor's and sheriff's offices, then matching the calls from Liz's home to the home telephone numbers of every deputy in the prosecutor's office. By three o'clock I had a list of one former and three current prosecutors Liz had called. There were three calls to the home telephone of a woman named Sharon Scovill and one call to the prosecutor's office at two-fifteen on the afternoon of the day Liz was killed.

Scovill's name was familiar, though I couldn't remember why. After half an hour of pacing around the apartment I finally had it: Scovill had once been a deputy under Liz's supervision in the Sexual Assault Unit. She was gay. She had been outed by a radical gay newspaper in the middle of a bitterly disputed multiple-rape trial, along with her lover, the King County police sergeant who had investigated the case. The defense seized on the story to contend that the case against the defendant, a black male social worker, was fabricated out of racist and sexist motives. The judge declared a mistrial amid the ensuing media circus. Scovill was demoted and transferred to the Civil Division over Liz's vehement objections. The Civil Division handles IIU matters until they are referred for prosecution.

It had to be right. I put a call through to Scovill.

"This is Matthew Riordan," I said abruptly, when she came on the line. "I was working with Liz Kleinfeldt. I know you were Liz's source on the IIU investigation into Sergeant Leach. You're going to talk to me. I'll be there in about fifteen minutes."

There was a long silence. "Not here," she pleaded. "Wait." She covered the telephone with her hand while she spoke to someone. When she came back on the line she said, "I can't talk to you now."

"It had better be damned soon. Or I'm going to take up residence in your office and stay there until you do talk to me."

"Please. I've got to be in court. And my job is hanging by a thread. Do you know where the Washington Rowing Club dock is?"

"No."

"It's in Fremont, on the north side of the ship canal, in the Burke Industrial Center. East of the Fremont Bridge. There's a health club in the first main building, on the southeast corner. The dock is across the parking lot from there. I'll meet you at six o'clock."

I put a call through to Nancy Karras.

"I've found the source who gave Liz the real story on Leach's IIU file," I said. "I'm only going to hear it once and I'm going to need a witness. Do you want to be there?"

"Of course. When?"

I gave her the time and place and added, "I'm trusting you on this, you know."

"I know. I'll be there."

At ten minutes to six Karras and I were standing on the ramp leading down to the rowing club dock on the ship canal. The steel arch of the Aurora Bridge soared a hundred feet above us. Across the canal there was a cluster of houseboats and single-masted sailboats moored near Wilson Marina. As dusk fell I watched the lights come on in the houses studded on the north side of Queen Anne Hill. The wind was rising, the sky pregnant again with spring storms.

I didn't hear Scovill approach until she spoke. "Riordan?" she asked. I turned quickly and saw a stocky, blunt-faced woman dressed in athletic tights and a heavy rowing sweater. A wool cap covered her hair. "I thought you'd come alone," she said, her voice tight. "Who the hell is she?"

"Never mind. I've got to know everything. When and where you talked to Liz, what you said, everything you knew about the IIU investigation."

"You've got to promise that you won't leak what I tell you. I'll lose my job for sure if Dan Merritt finds out I've talked to you."

"I won't make any promises. You have no choice but to talk to me. And you know it."

She stared at me under the dock lights, her eyes bitter. "IIU has been working on Leach for years. The investigation started with a complaint that he'd roughed up a prostitute who turned him down for sex."

"I know that," I said. "What else?"

"When the complaint got dropped, IIU decided not to close the file. They thought Leach had pressured the woman. They found a couple of other vice officers willing to say they'd seen Sergeant Leach together with Lawrence Poole, who runs an escort service. Leach wasn't well liked and a couple of his own people decided to stick the knife in him. IIU kept looking but they couldn't get enough evidence to file charges. They got the sheriff to transfer Leach out of vice and left the file open. When Leach was assigned to the motel-room murders they decided to keep an eye on him."

"And they didn't tell Ahlberg he had a potentially dirty cop on his hands, with ties to the owner of the service where the murdered women worked? Jesus Christ."

She nodded grimly. "IIU tends to get high-handed. They back-checked his work on the Polhaus case because of his connection to Poole. They found a couple of evidence tickets that were logged in, but the items were missing. When Liz got in touch with me about this, she asked specifically about the prostitutes' john books. I checked the evidence tags myself. And I confirmed that Parker's book was missing."

"What else was missing?"

"A couple of scraps of paper that were found in Sharee Klimka's purse at the motel where she was killed. Notes, or something."

"Names? Telephone numbers?"

She shrugged. "Maybe. The evidence log didn't say."

"When did you tell Liz this?"

"Just before . . . the afternoon of the day she was killed. She'd been after me for a week. I owed her, you know. She saved my job. She was the only one who stuck up for me when . . . when the media came after me."

"Go on."

"That's it."

"Where and when did you see her on the day of her death?", Karras asked, speaking up for the first time.

Scovill nodded. "I met her at five-thirty in the locker room at a women's gym I belong to down in Pioneer Square. Liz bought a temporary pass and took the locker next to mine. We talked for about ten or fifteen minutes, then she left. I didn't see her after that. When she was killed . . . God, I didn't know what to do. I knew I'd be fired if I gave the police a statement. I thought about it all weekend. I just couldn't do it. Not after everything that's happened to me." She looked down at the dock.

It was a pretty story, with just enough remorse, carefully designed to save Scovill's job if word leaked out that she'd talked to us. There had to be more. I grabbed Scovill by the arm and snapped her around. "Now tell me the rest. I want everything."

"What are you talking about?" Her eyes filled with fear.

"Liz left a telephone message for me after she talked to you. She said Polhaus's conviction would have to be reversed because of some kind of police misconduct. What you've told me doesn't come close. It doesn't help Polhaus's defense. Now what the hell did you really tell her?"

"Let go of me! There isn't any more! I told you everything I told her."

I gripped her arm harder, stepped so close that my face was inches from hers. "Bullshit," I said. My voice was angry, taunting. "You've had time to think it through. You know Polhaus's conviction was Merritt's prize, the one he thinks will carry him to the attorney general's chair. You know that if you tell me what really happened he'll blow you out of your job, and with your history you'll never work as a lawyer again in this city. You're trying to play it safe. It won't work. I'll go public on you. One phone call to Merritt, one phone call to the sheriff, and you're done for. Don't think I won't burn you. I will." I let her go, shoving her away.

A look of endless, weary dismay filled her features. "It never stops," she said slowly. "Nobody will leave me alone to do my job. That's all I want to do, damn it. My job." She broke down and wept, chest heaving.

"Too bad," I said sarcastically. "You probably were a pretty decent lawyer." I started toward my car.

"You pig," she hissed. "You bastard pig."

I turned in a rage and slapped Scovill with an open left hand, hard enough to send her sprawling on the dock.

"Riordan!" Karras shouted, seizing my arms as I went after Scovill. "Stop. You're not doing any good."

"The hell I'm not. She's holding back. She talks or I ruin her."

"Wait," Scovill said brokenly, still on her knees. "Wait." Karras helped her to her feet. I stared at her impassively.

"There was a witness," she said. Pain clouded her eyes. "A witness to the third murder. A woman, a hooker. Leach found her. He got rid of her so she couldn't testify."

"He killed her," I said slowly. "Or fingered her to be killed."

"Maybe. It wasn't clear."

"Where did they get this?"

"It came from a snitch, a junkie prostitute who died a couple of weeks later from an overdose. IIU knew it could fuck up Polhaus's trial, and they buried it."

"Whose snitch was she?"

"I don't know. They closed the file six months ago. When I went back to check it for Liz, everything about the missing witness had been removed."

"Did Merritt know?" I demanded.

"I'm not sure. I don't think he knew about the snitch. But he knew Leach had a file."

"Could you have been followed to your meeting with Liz?"

"I don't think so. I left work early, got in my car, drove down south of the Kingdome and waited in a parking lot to make sure I was clean."

"Did you tell anyone else what you told Liz?"

"No one. I'm not crazy, you know."

"Then how did the killer know what Liz had found out? He murdered her five hours later. Unless you panicked and killed her yourself."

Scovill was silent. She had envisioned a lot of bad scenarios, but not one that had her becoming a murder suspect.

I pressed her. "What about the cop you live with? Your lover. Did you tell her?"

She didn't answer. She straightened up, summoning what was left of her strength, her face dark with hatred. When she spoke again her voice was low and the words came through teeth that were clenched together. "No." Then she hit me with a balled fist on the side of my face.

I stepped back and stared at her, shocked for the moment out of my anger. Scovill stood under the dock lights, the anger draining out of her, shoulders slumped in defeat. She knew that if I confirmed what Leach had done, the prosecutor's office would eventually get the word and her career would be over. "We won't name you," I said. "We'll figure out another way." I paused, wanting to say more—that I was sorry, that I was half crazy with grief for Liz—but it wouldn't do any good. When I left, sick at heart from what I had done, Scovill was still standing on the dock, staring emptily at the dark water.

"You cannot do this. You cannot go on like this," Nancy Karras said urgently. We stood on the deck of her apartment staring out at the Shilshole Bay Marina. A cold harsh wind blew up from the water. I was drinking Bacardi rum, the only liquor she had.

"They fucked you over," I said bitterly. "You, Ahlberg, Polhaus, the court system. To save a dirty cop who might just be a murderer. To make sure Merritt got his conviction. Doesn't that mean anything to you?"

"Of course it does," she said quietly. "And I am going to find out what happened. But even if the IIU file hadn't been destroyed you wouldn't have proof that Polhaus didn't commit the murders. Maybe Leach is just protecting the john who went to meet Klimka at the China Tapestry."

"I don't buy that, Nancy. You don't either. This thing goes too deep. They've taken too many risks."

"We can pursue it."

"With what? You heard what Scovill said. IIU destroyed parts of its own file on Leach to protect Polhaus's conviction. Scovill doesn't have personal knowledge, only hearsay. Nobody else is going to come forward. You're never going to get the prosecutor's office to look at this. Not with Merritt in charge. The courts will say it's all inadmissible."

She touched my arm. "Let's go back inside." I followed her into the small colorless living room, precisely furnished with a low, pale-gray rectangular couch and chair, white-lacquered bookcases, and a small jungle of ferns. There were large photographs framed in steel on the white walls, silver-toned black-and-white pictures of empty alleys and doorways, essays in the play of light on form. I walked over to the wet bar in her dining room and poured another glass of rum before sitting down on the edge of a chair. Karras sat down on the sofa facing me. She had taken off her heavy sweater and her shoes and I was suddenly conscious for the first time of the soft swell of her breasts and the graceful lines of her strong neck and shoulders. I looked away, embarrassed by the rush of sexual attraction. I had been living too long with no sleep, ragged and manic, everything too bright, too vivid, too harsh to bear.

"Listen to me," she said quietly. "You have the look of a

cop about to go wrong. You have to back away from this before you hurt someone."

"Something you know about from experience," I replied.

"What are you talking about?"

"The john you nightsticked. You told me he was trying to pick up a boy and he hit you. That's not the way it happened, though, was it? It was a young girl you'd worked with, cared about, and you went a little crazy and hit him. You hit the girl, too. Or did it happen twice?"

She started angrily, then caught herself. "All right," she said. "I did it and I'm not proud of it. I do know what I'm talking about. I backed away from it, got out of vice. You have to do the same thing. Get out of this case."

"No."

Karras said nothing. She took my free hand. "Your hands are shaking."

"It's the cold."

"How much are you drinking?"

"Not enough."

"Don't joke. Are you drinking to get to sleep at night?" Her face was somber, worried.

I nodded. "Does it show?"

"Your face is puffy. You missed a place shaving this morning. And your hands aren't cold."

"All right," I said shortly. "I hear you." I swallowed the rest of the rum in my glass. "Karen Sasser told me that you got help. From Martin Bolger. Did you investigate his suicide?"

"What?" she exclaimed.

"Karen Sasser said you knew him, that he helped you. I was wondering what you knew about the suicide. Bolger died one day after Sharee Klimka did. He hanged himself in a motel not far from the China Tapestry, just over the line in Snohomish County. If he killed himself. A hanging suicide can be faked."

A sudden bleak emptiness drained her face of expression. "Martin was a friend to a lot of people," she said softly, looking away. "Someone who would listen when you needed to talk. It was almost like he couldn't part with what you told him, no matter how bad it was, he took it into himself. I don't think anyone killed him, Matthew. He'd suffered from depression for years. He knew it, he'd tried all the drugs, and nothing worked for him. He'd just had too much pain, a victim of the people he tried to help. And half the time they hated him for helping. That's how it always is." She paused, then added, "No. He killed himself. I'm sure of it."

"But why the timing? Why the day after Klimka was murdered? Because he was her therapist?"

"I didn't know he knew her."

"I thought you did. I thought you subpoenaed his treatment files on the motel-room victims. He treated all of them through the prostitution prevention program."

"No. I didn't get his files."

"Leach must have. And buried them, like he destroyed the john books. But why?"

"I don't know." The bleak emptiness I had seen before returned to her face. Her eyes were dark and weary. "I'm sorry, Matthew, but I'm going to ask you to go. I'm just so tired. Please don't press yourself so hard on this. You're far too emotionally involved and you're going to hurt someone badly. Most likely yourself."

I should have listened. But my mind was already far away. "Can I borrow your phone? There's a call I need to make."

"Of course. In my study. Down the main hall on your left. The light is just inside the door."

I found her study and turned on the lights. Instead of a desk it contained a long wooden worktable with tools for matting and framing photographs. Open shelves on the far wall were filled with cameras and equipment. There were more of Karras's photographs on the walls, matted but unframed. They were vastly different from the quiet, elegiac studies in light and form that graced her living room. These were black and white portraits of street kids, male and female prostitutes, some of other cops. They were etched with raw pain and a dark sense of the grotesque.

I looked at them slowly, one at a time: a blond call girl in a torn, blood-splattered evening dress, her face battered almost beyond recognition. A skinny teenage street chicken, strutting like James Dean out of a downtown alley, a parody of tough in cycle chain leathers. A woman street cop, shot and bleeding from the shoulder, grimacing in pain as the paramedics pulled her into a sitting position.

I was still staring into the sneering, almost demonic, face of a fourteen-year-old girl drawing on a cigarette when Nancy Karras touched my arm. She had loosened her hair and changed into a Chinese silk robe the color of a pale winter sunrise. She looked open, vulnerable for the first time. Her hands worked convulsively. "This is how I know where the edge is, Matthew. Now, please stop before you hurt someone."

CHAPTER 26

"This is the Bartke house." The voice that answered was young and small and very serious. I could hear other children playing in the background, the raucous play that comes when bedtime is very near. I smiled, grateful for the small reminder that there were still people alive and well and not living in the dark cave I had found myself in.

"Dick," I said when he got on the phone, "How much would it take to get you to drop everything and go to Anchorage tomorrow?"

"Three thousand bucks," he replied. "That's for the ticket and five days' time, minimum. What's this about?"

"I want you to find one of the prostitutes Polhaus knew. One that you couldn't find before. Her name's Andrea Jacoby. She called herself Fawn." I quickly explained why Karen Sasser thought she might be in Alaska. "Swing by my place tonight and I'll give you a check. By morning I'll have some names of her friends that you can start with."

"What do I tell her if I find her?"

"Tell her that her mother's dying. That you've been hired by her sister, Carolyn Ritter, to find her and ask her to come home. I'll give you another five hundred for her ticket. Leave me out of it, for now, and don't mention the motel-room murders. Do what you have to in order to sell it, but get her on a plane."

"What's she know that's so important?" he asked.

"I'm just guessing. This kid has, or had, long auburn hair.

With enough henna or dye it could look pretty red. Especially at a distance. Say from the office at the China Tapestry Motel."

"Son of a bitch," he said.

I spent what was left of the night in the living room, drinking milk to ease the persistent burning in my gut, listening to the wind through the open French doors to the balcony. I chewed over what Sharon Scovill had told us. Without the written confirmation of the file it meant nothing: double hearsay, one confidential source quoting another, who just happened to be an unnamed dead junkie snitch. Defense lawyers for convicted murderers do not receive the same fine understanding treatment from the courts about confidential sources that the state does when it is getting search warrants rubber-stamped.

I still couldn't piece together why Leach sabotaged the investigation. Was he protecting himself, Lawrence Poole, or a customer of Poole's who had murdered the three victims? Poole's sending Rogers to find Beasely's john book even after Polhaus had been convicted suggested a customer. But which one? There were thirty-seven men listed in Beasely's book. Questioning them and checking each of their stories would take a month, even with the money and lawyer time that the Lisle, Day firm could throw at the case. Unless I could convince Ahlberg or Merritt that Leach was directly involved, Leach could destroy any evidence that hadn't already been found. Persuading Ahlberg that his investigation of the motel-room murders had been tampered with would be hard. Persuading Merritt to reopen his trophy conviction six months before the September primary in the attorney general's race was a joke. It couldn't be done. Not on the word of a dead junkie snitch.

And why had Bolger killed himself?

At midnight I gave in to my aching head and took three aspirin with a shot of Irish whiskey. The only thing I could do now was go back to Jack Elgot, try to make peace with him, plead with him to open up the case and give me the kind of blank check it would take to pursue the tenuous leads I had found.

I needn't have wasted the time. I had Elgot's answer before asking, when his process server showed up at my door at seven in the morning to serve me with papers to take me off the case.

* * *

The Lisle, Day firm was known for practicing what lawyers call "scorched earth" litigation. Armies of young associate lawyers are dispatched to dig up every ugly fact about an opponent, no matter how irrelevant to the issues in the case. The opposing party is buried in motions, discovery demands, show-cause orders. The goal is to raise the stakes and the costs so high that the other side gives up before trial.

Elgot's army had done a thorough job on me. They painted my voluntary decision to stop practicing law as a failed practice that I was forced to quit. They pointed out that I had taken Polhaus's case only because of my friendship with Liz Kleinfeldt, and implied that it was charity on her part. They dug up every embarrassing problem in my life as a practicing lawyer, from a dismissed DWI charge to two bar association complaints filed by clients that I had sued for fees, and an assault charge that had once been brought against me in Kittitas County. The conclusion was etched in acid: "We do not seek to condemn Mr. Riordan either as a citizen or as a lawyer. But the plain facts are that he has been discharged, does not have the resources or the ability to pursue this case on his own, and is far too emotionally involved in the case, due to his personal relationship with our late associate, Elizabeth Kleinfeldt, to continue as Mr. Polhaus's counsel under the relevant ethical rules."

It was all I could do not to tear the papers up in a rage. I did the next best thing. I showed them to a sympathetic reporter.

"The sons of bitches," Terry Lasker said, crushing out his after-breakfast cigarette at his regular table at Firenze. "They even dragged Liz into this."

"They did. The question is, how do I respond?"

"Fight. Fight dirty. They've got what, five important clients on that list of Beasely's johns? Tell the court that they are trying to obstruct justice by inhibiting the investigation into Polhaus's guilt." His eyes gleamed. Lasker loved a good public pissing match.

"They've got an affidavit from Polhaus saying he wants to fire me."

"I'll bet. If I was on death row five weeks from my hanging and this big important law firm came to me and said they were going to drop my case if I stuck with you, I'd fire you. I'd be desperate."

I shook my head. "You're probably right. But this isn't

about me, it's about what best serves Polhaus's interests. I have to be careful."

"To hell with careful. Liz brought you into this because she had doubts about Polhaus's guilt. Everything you've turned up so far, even though it's not much, raises questions. I'm going to do a number on these bastards in the paper."

"They've got the list, Terry. They know you're on it. You haven't got many enemies, but somebody at the *Post* or the *Weekly* is going to print it."

"Not a problem," Lasker replied, "if I do it myself."

"It's going to be tough on you. The paper might drop your column."

"I doubt it. I'm not married. Nobody expects me to be an angel. I'm going to have lots of company. When's the hearing on this motion?"

"Next Monday. They shortened time on me. I could probably get it extended."

"Don't," Terry replied. "Let's put the heat back on them. I'll plan to run the column in the ten A.M. edition on Monday. It won't hurt to have the judge thinking a little bit when he hears this with me sitting in the courtroom." Lasker left the table to get himself another cup of coffee. When he returned he said, "Did you find out anything about the Ritter woman's missing sister?"

"Some. I've hired a private detective to look for her. If I'm right, she witnessed the last murder. Leach found her. He either killed her or forced her out of town so she couldn't testify. I don't know why. He must be protecting somebody, on Poole's orders. Don't ask me who." I rubbed my temples, trying to ease the tension headache that had returned when the process server appeared at my door.

Lasker finished his coffee. "By the way," he said, "there's something else on Sean Tyner. An ethics charge was filed against him a couple of years ago, just before he went up to the court of appeals. Something to do with the way he'd handled some of the juvenile prostitution cases, out-of-court contacts with the kids appearing in front of him. It got dismissed and the records were sealed. Got the story several years back from a caseworker down at Twelfth and Alder. Doesn't like Tyner worth a damn. A guy named Ted Ricks."

I looked up, startled. "I know that name. I've had it on a list of people I still need to talk to."

"Why?"

"Ted Ricks was Sharee Klimka's juvenile court caseworker."

"Jesus Christ," Terry Lasker said.

CHAPTER 27

Ted Ricks found me waiting outside the county youth facility at four-thirty.

"You're Riordan?" he asked, offering his hand.

I shook hands, nodding. Ricks was thickly built, with black hair pulled back into a short ponytail and a thick Zapata-style mustache spread bushily across his broad face. He wore engineer boots, jeans, a faded blue denim work shirt, and a brown sheepskin-lined bomber jacket so old that the leather was dried and cracked. At first I thought he was about thirty-five but the creases in the weathered skin around his eyes said mid-forties. That, and the fact that he was the very model of male style for 1972.

He looked me over while he stuck an unfiltered Camel in his mouth and lit it with an old-fashioned liquid-fueled Zippo. He exhaled smoke and sighed. "There are days," he said, "when I need a drink when I get out of this place."

I looked back at the youth facility, a 1960s red brick institutional school block with narrow windows. It housed four juvenile courtrooms, much of the county's youth services bureaucracy, and the jail for young offenders. It was flanked by several temporary overflow trailers surrounded by razor wire that glinted like bright spun silver in the cold edgy sunlight. On the other side of the building a new detention center was being built of gray concrete, with the cell-block architecture of a full-scale prison. "It looks like a cross between a grade school and a concentration camp," I said.

Ricks didn't laugh. "That's a fairly accurate description of what we do here," he said. "The last couple years, we've been getting them as young as nine years old. I was a cop for six years, between sixty-nine and seventy-five, before I got my social-work degree. I busted some pretty scary people. But I'd match 'em up, even money, against the fifteen-year-olds we get now." He shook his head. "I'm supposed to meet my wife. What was it you wanted to talk about?"

"Sean Tyner," I replied.

He smiled grimly. "Come along, then. Sheila'll have a few things to say, too."

We got in my car and drove down the Yesler Avenue Hill to Pioneer Square. Yesler cuts through the heart of the public housing projects, ramshackle Victorian houses, and potholed streets of the Central District.

"You know what I like about the CD?" Ricks asked, using the shorthand nickname for the neighborhood.

"What?"

"It still looks like Seattle to me. That," he added, gesturing down Yesler toward the proud glass-and-steel downtown skyline, backlit by the sun, "looks like Oz. This used to be a good town, relaxed and cheap, a working man's town. Now it's full of accountants and executives and real estate slobs with phones in their cars. And too many damned lawyers. No offense, I'm married to one."

"None taken. But I'm part of the problem. I moved here twelve years ago."

"Hell, you're practically a native. We've had two real estate booms since then."

I laughed. He said his wife was meeting him at the J&M Tavern, a dark rough-cut Pioneer Square bar not unlike those in my home state of Montana. Ricks's wife, a public defender named Sheila Murphy, was waiting for us at a back table. She was a stocky, darkly pretty woman dressed in a black business suit. I flagged down a waitress and ordered a pitcher of ale.

"I'm defending Robert Polhaus," I told them. "I was working with Liz Kleinfeldt before she was killed."

Murphy nodded. "I know. You're the subject of considerable courthouse gossip at the moment."

"None of it good," I said.

"No," she replied, "it's not. Kleinfeldt's firm did a public hatchet job on you. I'd like to know why. And what it has to do with Judge Tyner."

"Sean Tyner's name showed up in the john book of Melody Beasely, one of the motel-room murder victims," I replied.

Ricks had gone to the bar for a shot of bourbon. "I'm not surprised," he said, downing the shot and putting the glass on the table. "That son of a bitch has a thing for young girls. I'm surprised they haven't found him hanging around the school-yards, offering candy."

"What have you got to back that up?"

"Enough," he said bitterly. "Ask Sheila."

"Tyner spent a lot of time on the juvenile bench," she explained. "I've worked with juveniles for the last five years, as has Ted. You know how it is. Most judges will fight like hell to stay away from juvenile work. Tyner was different. He went after the juvenile assignments. Five years ago he was spending almost all of his time up on the hill."

"Was he a bad judge?"

"No, he was actually very fair, visibly concerned with reha-bilitation and treatment, as well as punishment. Tyner didn't al-ways take the cops' word as gospel; he listened and actually dismissed some cases where the evidence didn't support the charge. It took me a long time to spot the pattern."

"What pattern?"

"The out-of-court contacts, the little pats and hugs, the os-tentatious concern that the kids see him as a friend. Especially the girls, the ones up for prostitution busts."

"He takes them," Ricks said nastily, "under his wing. And if they're very good they get to see the Tyner family jewels."

"If that's true," I said dubiously, "how in hell could he stay on the bench?"

"No problem with the correct friends," Murphy replied. "I'm not saying that they know what's going on and condone it. I don't think they do. Tyner was good at hiding it. But the rumors about him inside the judiciary got so frequent that he was pulled off the juvenile bench by the presiding judge, as-signed to the complex trial docket. They put him on big civil cases with as much sex in them as the *Christian Science Mon-itor*."

"What about the Judicial Conduct Commission?" I asked, naming the state's judicial watchdog agency.

"It has a staff of two," Murphy replied. "The commissioners are mostly male lawyers from big downtown firms. The one time a complaint about Tyner was filed, it sank without a trace. It was dismissed by the executive director of the commission without the filing of formal charges, because of a lack of credible evidence. Meaning that the only people they talked to were social-service lowlifes like me and Ted, and a sixteen-year-old hooker and her mother, who was on welfare and made it plenty obvious she was looking for a big payoff. When Tyner was appointed to the appeals court I think the commission figured that solved the problem, if there was one."

I was still skeptical. "How could he get appointed to the appeals court? You'd think somebody from the governor's office would check his file with the commission."

"There is no file. When complaints are dismissed without the filing of formal charges against a judge, the paperwork is sealed, then destroyed." Murphy poured herself a half-glass of beer, then continued. "The commission doesn't investigate anything, it waits for cases to be brought to it. Hundreds of complaints are brought against judges every year, almost all of them groundless. With no real staff, the commission just ends up processing the garbage."

I shook my head. The beer was gone and I signaled for a second pitcher. "This is swell rumor," I said, "but it's nothing I can use. Are there any incidents that are documented, that I can hit him with?"

"Nothing you're going to be able to prove," Rick said. "A little over five years ago I had a seventeen-year-old hooker who came through his court who got assigned to the prostitution prevention program. That's okay, the program's good, we recommend it. But Tyner went after her. The kid was drop-dead gorgeous, by the way. Tyner was involved in the program, raised money for it, spent a lot of time there talking to the kids. I was the girl's probation officer—she had a pretty hefty juvenile record, mostly theft offenses, rolling johns and such. I thought she needed youth-farm time, she could use the structure, but Tyner just gave her the program. I got along pretty well with the girl despite recommending detention. She stayed in touch with me after she entered the program. She told me she'd balled Tyner. She thought she had the system wired, the next time she came through they couldn't touch her. She said Tyner told her that she ought to get off the street, work for a friend of his."

"Who was the friend?"

"Larry Poole," he said angrily. "The local prince of topless bars."

Ricks had been drinking shots steadily, chasing them with

beer. He was flushed and the words were coming much too fast.

"I want to question her," I said. "All of the victims in the motel-room murders worked for Poole."

"I know. I'm talking about Sharee Klimka."

I sat back in my chair, stunned. I hadn't seen the theft offenses in Klimka's record. They must have been sealed. "Why," I asked, "didn't you bring this up when Polhaus was on trial?"

"That was a year later," Ricks said. "Tyner had gotten off the juvenile bench, at least temporarily. Nobody asked. Who would I talk to, anyway? Polhaus's lawyer? Polhaus is a sexual psychopath. I don't doubt that he killed Klimka and the others."

"I used to think the same way," I said. "But I'm not so sure anymore."

"Meaning what?" Sheila Murphy asked.

"Meaning that this thing ties back into Lawrence Poole in the worst way. And Tyner along with him, if you're right." I frowned. Law enforcement in any major metropolitan area is split among so many different jurisdictions and agencies that investigators have coined a term for the resulting failures to communicate knowledge. They call it "jurisdiction interference." Each of the motel-room victims had touched a number of different police forces and social service programs, leaving a piece of information along the way. But no one had put all of the information together. Liz knew the problem, and from the start the Polhaus case had touched off her sixth sense that the investigation had not gone deep enough.

Ted Ricks knocked back another whiskey, his third in half an hour. He was sprawled loosely in his chair but his eyes were bright, ready to hit another bar or two on the way home. "I don't buy it," Ricks finally said. "God knows I'd love to. The murders stopped after Polhaus was arrested. That may not be evidence but it sure makes sense."

"You might be right, but they could have stopped for a lot of reasons. By the way," I added, trying to cover as many subjects as I could before Ricks drank himself past reliability, "did either of you know a psychologist, Martin Bolger?"

"Sure," Murphy said. "But he's been dead for quite a while, hasn't he? He testified in court a lot, usually as a defense expert witness. He treated a lot of cops and public defenders who couldn't handle the job-related stress. He killed himself, I think. He was a good man."

"Bolger treated all the motel-room victims. And he died one day after the last murder."

Murphy leaned forward intently in her chair. "Do you think there's a connection?"

"I don't know. I think Bolger was trying to find out who killed them. And that someone murdered him to make sure he didn't find out."

"You know what you're saying?" Murphy asked. "You're practically accusing a sitting court of appeals judge of serial murder, and of committing more crimes, directly or indirectly, to cover it up."

"I'm not there yet," I replied, seized by frustration. "The victims all were connected to Bolger and Tyner and Poole. And if Ted's right, Tyner's tied in to Poole, too. That's not enough. I can't go public, be wrong and destroy a judge's reputation. But if I can't get Polhaus's execution stayed, I'm going to have to."

Sheila Murphy shook her head in amazement. "No wonder you're an endangered species," she said.

CHAPTER 28

I had to spend the next two days in the cloistered silence of the courthouse law library, preparing my defense to Jack Elgot's petition to disqualify me as Polhaus's counsel. The legal attack was simple: under the Rules of Professional Conduct, a lawyer must withdraw from a case if his physical or mental condition impairs his ability to represent the client, or if the client has discharged the lawyer. Elgot argued both grounds, saying that my personal relationship with Liz, and grief at her death, impaired my judgment; Polhaus, told these facts, fired me. I worked my way through the Rules, the old Canons of Professional Responsibility, and the cases decided by courts and ethics committees. On the first point I found no cases that applied. Most of them, including those Elgot had cited, involved lawyers with drug, alcohol, or mental illness, particularly clinical depression, so common in the bar that research psychologists built careers studying why lawyers blew their lives apart. I was reminded of the old joke: psychologists had started using lawyers rather than laboratory rats in experiments because there were more lawyers, they'd do anything for money, and nobody cared what happened to them once the experiments were over.

The second issue was harder. A client's right to discharge a lawyer is absolute. The client need only say, "Be gone," and the lawyer must comply. But the client's decision had to be personally made and adequately informed. If the client was pressured into firing his or her lawyer, the lawyer had standing to object. I traced the point through the ethics cases, then followed the same trail through the related torts of wrongful discharge and contractual interference with the attorney-client relationship. There was no shortage of cases; lawyers had been stealing clients since the founding of the Republic. It took the better part of two days but I came up with enough law to be persuasive, if I could show that Elgot pressured Polhaus to fire me.

Polhaus refused to take my telephone calls and on Friday morning I flew to Walla Walla to see him. The guards brought him to the same interview room in 5 wing where we had met before. He was sullen, his eyes glued to the floor.

"Bobby," I said, "what the hell's going on here?" I threw his affidavit across the table to him. He picked it up and leafed through it, smoke rising in curled tendrils from the cigarette stuck in the corner of his mouth. Pale winter sun leaked into the room through the two narrow windows to the outside world.

"I'm sorry about this, man," he said dully.

"Who talked to you? And what did he tell you?"

"A lawyer came over from Seattle to see me. He said he was from Ms. Kleinfeldt's firm, that she was dead and that you weren't getting the job done." He squinted his right eye closed against the smoke. "He seemed kind of nervous about it. He didn't want to look at me."

"What else did he say?"

"That you weren't very smart. That you had some crazy ideas about the case. That if you kept doing what you were doing it might blow my chances."

"Did he tell you what happened to Liz?"

"No. Only that she'd been killed."

"Did he tell you what she was doing, Bobby? That she was murdered trying to find out whether the cops had withheld evidence that might have cleared you? That a cop might have gotten rid of the red-haired woman you saw at the China Tapestry?"

Polhaus was taken aback. He stubbed out the cigarette, a puzzled look on his face. "No. No, he didn't tell me that."

"What else did he say?"

"Only that they couldn't stay on the case as long as you were in it. That if I didn't fire you they'd quit. I'm sorry, man. But I need that big law firm behind me. I'm down to it, my last shot in court." His voice rose. "I've had three execution dates set. They're serious about this last one. That's like nothing you'll ever know, man. They give you that piece of paper with the date. And you spend the next two days heaving your guts out on the floor of your cell."

I was silent. I couldn't argue with him. It was his life and he was staring at the end of it, unless his luck turned in the cruel game of legal cat-and-mouse that ends every death-penalty case.

"I don't blame you," I said at last. "From where you sit I'd have done the same thing. But if I don't stay as your lawyer, I can't help you. I can't get subpoenas, can't force people to testify."

"What can you do that these other lawyers can't?"

"It's not a question of can't, it's whether they are going to pull out all the stops. The women who were killed had some powerful men as customers. They aren't happy to find their names dragged through a murder investigation."

Polhaus thought it over for a long time. His mouth worked as he struggled to make a decision. In his world there were few, if any, decisions to make. His life was a series of reactions, to prison rules, guards' orders, the threats and taunts of other inmates. He finally shook his head no. "I think you're a straight guy. But you're just one guy."

"I understand. Let me write out another affidavit for you to sign. Just tell the judge what they said to you."

He shook his head again, reaching for the cigarettes I had brought him. "I can't. They said that if I signed anything, or even talked to you, they'd pull out of the case. Sorry." He got up and motioned to the one-way mirror for the guard to take him back to his cell.

When he was gone I gathered up the papers strewn across the old, scarred table. I waited for the guards to take me back through the guts of the prison machine to the outside world. I was reasonably certain that I would be removed from the case. Polhaus had been pressured, all right. They had done such a good job that he'd deny it.

It was dark by the time I got back to my apartment in Seattle. I poured three fingers of Irish whiskey into an old-fashioned glass and took it to my study to draft a formal affidavit recounting what Polhaus told me. A Vivaldi concerto played softly in the darkened room. I was nearly finished when the telephone rang.

I snatched the receiver from its cradle. "Yes," I snapped, half expecting an outraged call from Jack Elgot about my interview with Polhaus.

"This is Jennifer DiGregorio," a husky voice replied. "You sound like you're ready to take somebody's head off, Riordan."

"Sorry. What's on your mind?"

"I've been thinking about what you said. And I saw in the paper that the lawyer you were working with got killed."

"So?"

"I think we should talk. There's something . . . but not on the phone."

"Where are you?"

"Working. I've arranged for somebody to take over for me at nine. Do you know the Owl Café, in Ballard?"

"Sure. It's a rhythm-and-blues joint."

"That's it. Be there about ten." She hung up. I put the phone down slowly, and thought. It was possible DiGregorio had some new fact she'd held out before. It was equally possible that she was setting me up. I looked at the clock on my desk. It was eight forty-five. I poured the half-finished glass of whiskey down the kitchen sink and made coffee, then changed into jeans, running shoes, and a sweater. I unlocked the top right hand drawer of my desk and took out a Walther PPK auto-

matic in a leather shoulder holster. I held it for a moment, then
shoved it back into the drawer. Anyone who wanted to shoot
me would have to bring their own damned gun.

CHAPTER 29

The Owl Café is on lower Ballard Avenue, south of Market
Street, in a neighborhood of boat brokers, fishermen's bars,
secondhand furniture stores, pawn shops, and warehouses. I
parked on a brick-paved side street near Shilshole Avenue and
walked the three blocks to the Owl in a light gathering mist.
The air was thick with the rich rank smells of the harbor—
seaweed and salt and diesel. I paid six dollars cover to the
doorman and paused in the doorway to let my eyes adjust to
the low lights and haze of smoke. Ballard is the last neighborhood in Seattle where you will not lose your teeth for lighting
a cigarette in public.

The Owl had a decent Friday-night crowd, enough to pay
the band, mostly couples or small groups of three or four men
and women. The Rhythm Hogs, a local band fronted by a
woman with blue punked hair and a sizable collection of tight
spandex dresses, was doing a cover of a slow Bonnie Raitt
dance tune. People shuffled and swayed on the dance floor,
holding close. Jennifer DiGregorio was not there. I ordered a
Red Hook Ale and waited.

The band finished the set and scattered to the bar, looking
for beer. The lead singer swayed slowly down from the stage
and stopped at the bar next to me. She gave me a sideways
look and held up a cigarette to be lit. I reached over with my
lighter.

"You're Riordan?" she asked.

"Yes."

"Jen's in the back, in our dressing room. If you can call it that. Come on." She led me into a back hallway, past a small kitchen turning out a stream of burgers, fish, and fries. She knocked once on an unmarked door and opened it. She paused in the doorway to look me over, then suddenly brushed her hand through my hair and smiled. "Jenny must be experimenting," she drawled, suppressing laughter. "You're a little more macho than I expected."

The dressing room was small and stuffy. Shoulder bags and instrument cases were scattered on the floor and a dirty Formica makeup counter. Jennifer DiGregorio sat on an ancient green mohair sofa, with a drink on the table in front of her and a cigarette smoldering in an ashtray. She wore a black cat suit with heavy gold jewelry that set off her slanting green eyes. She would have looked very good but she was nervous and pale. Her hands drummed the tabletop.

"Pretty dramatic," I said, taking a seat on the couch next to her. "The singer?"

"I own a piece of the band," she explained edgily. "After what happened to your partner I'm not feeling too good about any of this."

"I don't blame you. What's this about?"

"I lied to you. I didn't want you hassling my people." She stubbed out one cigarette and lit another. "Sharee had her own john book. I knew she had it and I warned her not to take anybody on who didn't come through the agency, or at least to tell me when she was going to so I'd know where she'd be."

"What happened to the book?"

"I don't know. She kept it at her place. After she was dead the cops searched her apartment. I was sweating like crazy because I knew if they found it they'd run down her customer list and try to make a case against me for promoting prostitution. But I never heard anything about it. It never turned up. Not that I heard, anyway."

"It's been buried. By one of the cops investigating the murders."

"Her private johns were all customers at Dreams. I knew some of them from there."

"You never told me that you worked for Larry Poole," I said.

She flashed a sardonic smile. "Everybody starts on the bottom in this business. In my case, literally."

"Is that how you knew about the parties that Poole had?"

"Yes. I never worked one. But they were out of town someplace. I don't know where. Poole had this place in the woods. Someplace east, in the foothills. Maybe you can find the property through the records."

"I'll check. Is there any way I can find out who went to these parties?"

"Maybe. Just before I left Dreams one of the other women told me that Poole taped them. Video cameras in the ceiling, that kind of crap. She said she saw the camera lens."

"Keep going."

"That's it. If he was pulling some kind of extortion, I never heard it. I think he just wanted his friends to stay his friends. And he liked that stuff. He taped all of us, when we went to work for him." She shrugged and gave me a sour grin. "I was there six months and I stayed as far away from Poole as possible. He never went after me because it's no secret that I'm gay. He's into the fantasy thing as bad as any of his johns. Life's just one big wet dream." She swallowed the rest of her drink. "I don't want to be seen with you. Give me some time to get out of here before you go."

"Okay." I got to my feet. "Thanks. I'm going to the bar for another beer. I'll stay half an hour. You should split before then."

I was halfway to the door when she said, "There's one other thing."

I turned. "What?"

"Here's your list. I've marked three names. I know she was still seeing those men when she was killed."

I opened the folded list.

The third name on the list was Sean Tyner. "Did you know Tyner?" I asked.

She nodded. "I knew of him. He was a judge. He's been hanging out with Larry Poole for a long time. Sharee was balling him ever since she was in his court."

"You're sure Klimka was still seeing him when she was killed?"

"Yes. But she was trying to break it off. She was afraid of him."

"Why? Did he hurt her?"

"Not physically. Not badly, anyway. He was into bondage, into near-asphyxiation stuff. Silk scarves, that whole trip. That scared her, especially after the other two women were killed. It was the way they were killed. The papers said they'd been strangled with a piece of cloth." She paused and lit her third cigarette in fifteen minutes, her hands shaking. "Oh shit," she sighed, blowing out a knife-thin plume of smoke.

"What's wrong?" I asked sharply.

"I'm just scared." She shuddered. "There's more. I saw Sharee's book the day before she died. She had a date the night she was killed. It was written in her book. Sean Tyner."

I felt a surging rush of adrenaline. "You're going to have to testify to this. You're going to have to go public."

DiGregorio looked up at me with defiance on her face. "Four women have been killed, including your partner. You bet your ass I'll testify."

"You've got half an hour," I said. "Stay safe until I can get in touch with you again. Thanks."

I waited through the band's second set to give DiGregorio more time to get away. I listened to retread John Coltrane with half an ear, trying to stay loose, stay slow. When I left I walked the wrong way down Ballard Avenue, away from my car, just to be sure I hadn't been followed. The street was quiet, not even a passing car. I could still hear the faint wail of a saxophone drifting from the club. The mist made halos around the cast-iron street lamps. I crossed to the other side and cut down the alley between Ballard and Shilshole Avenue, heading back to my car.

When I was halfway down the alley, lights came on behind me. I turned and heard a car engine accelerating. I started to run but I was still a hundred yards from the next street. The grinding of the car's engine grew closer. I saw a green garbage dumpster sitting in front of a small loading dock ten yards away. I cut across the alley and jumped, trying to hit the closed top of the dumpster with my hands so that I could tuck and roll over it. My hands slipped on the wet metal and I fell head-first into the gap between the loading dock and the dumpster. Warm blood trickled down my leg. I could feel something torn in the front of my right thigh. I crawled behind the dumpster. The car squealed into reverse and jolted back up the alley, shooting sparks as it bottomed hard on the brick pavement.

The car door slammed open and Raymond Leach rolled out. His eyes were bright in the harsh half-light of the alley and his breath thick and sour with whiskey. As I pushed the dumpster away and got up to face him he grabbed my shirtfront and slammed me back against the dumpster, then backhanded me hard enough to split my lip. Leach pulled me up by the collar of my jacket and propped me against the side of the dumpster.

Leach pulled a pint of Jim Beam from his jacket and took a deep swig. He pushed his face close to mine. "You listen to me, you fuck," he said, spraying spit in my face. "You're done with this case. Get out of it now, while you're still breathing. I've been a copper for twenty-two years and nobody is going to shut me down." He slapped me in the face, almost casually, a gesture of male dominance as old as the species.

I stared at him for ten long seconds. And as much as it hurt, I forced myself to laugh.

"God, you're dumb, Ray," I told him. "Nobody could prove the links between you and Poole. Not until now. I know you got rid of the witness, the woman at the China Tapestry. How far did you go, Ray? Did you kill Liz Kleinfeldt, too?"

He slowed, the whiskey courage draining out of him, replaced by creeping fear. "I didn't kill Kleinfeldt or anybody else. You can't prove a thing."

"Who is it, Ray? Who's Larry Poole protecting? Himself? Or is it Sean Tyner?"

He stared at me, his pouchy, slack face greenish in the half light of the alley. "You're crazy," he mumbled. "Just remember what I told you." He started to turn away.

"Larry Poole's errand boy," I said scornfully. "A dirty cop who takes bribes and extorts sex from teenagers. A baby raper. Everybody in your life is going to know it, Ray. Your wife, your kids, every con in the joint. And they're going to make your life one endless bleeding hell."

He turned in a fury and moved in close for the heavy work, battering my ribs and belly with short heavy blows. I could feel a rib crack but kept my arms up to protect my head and tried to move away. As I turned he threw a looping round-house left that landed like a piece of pipe under my right eye. I went down and rolled into a ball, too stunned to do anything but try to block the kicks that would be coming next.

I was saved by a car full of kids roaring down the alley, their oversized speakers pounding heavy metal music. They pulled up behind Leach's car and hammered their horn, shouting. Leach backed away to his car, his face white, all the whiskey courage gone. His car jerked away and raced down the alley, bottoming out in a shower of sparks when he hit the street.

I slumped against the brick wall. Two of the teenage boys stopped and helped me up. I declined their offer of a ride and limped out of the alley, headed for the emergency room at Harborview Hospital. My hands shook with cold and paranoia all the way across town.

I had the French doors to the balcony propped open to let the raw blustery morning air into my apartment. Vince Ahlberg and Nancy Karras sat on the sofa opposite me. They were drinking coffee but not liking it very much.

"You stupid bastard," Ahlberg said distinctly. He shoved the Sunday newspapers off the table in front of him. They fell to the floor. "You can't win this way. It's like calling in an air strike on your own position."

"More like staking a goat to draw them out," I replied.

"That's usually rough on the goat. Christ, I can't figure out why you didn't take him if you were going to pick a fight with him. You've got three inches in height and reach on him. But that won't help you if they decide to prosecute. Merritt's going to love this."

"You'd better talk to Dr. Friedman in the Harborview ER before you bust me," I said carefully.

"Why?"

"He's an expert trauma specialist. God knows he sees enough of it. He examined me Friday night. He found no evidence of skin under nails, abrasion marks, or any wounds or bruises other than defensive ones. He's already signed an affidavit stating that in his expert medical opinion I could not have assaulted another human being."

"You set Leach up," Ahlberg said. "You took a beating so you could prove that he tried to stop you from pursuing the case." There was a small note of grudging admiration in his voice.

"Correct."

"It won't help. We've already questioned him and Poole. We've spent four days trying to link them up. There's nothing but that old IIU complaint to tie them. It was dropped. IIU's head man says this snitch your source talked about never existed."

"Then you haven't gone far enough. Leach spiked the investigation into the motel-room murders, Vince. I think I know who he was protecting when he did it."

"Who?"

"Sean Tyner."

Ahlberg grunted in disbelief. "You've got evidence?"

"It's coming. Tyner was the sentencing judge for all three victims in juvenile court. He had out-of-court contacts with them. I have two witnesses who will say that he had an ongoing relationship with the third victim, Sharee Klimka, at the time of her death. And that he put her in touch with Larry Poole, got her to go to work for him. Right out of his own damned courtroom."

"That's not enough," Ahlberg said, thinking it over. "Not even close. You can't put Tyner at the murder scenes, you can't tie him in with any kind of physical evidence; you've got only hearsay. No court is going to buy it."

There was no answer to that and nothing left to say. I touched the stitches under my right eye. The spot was curiously numb, probably minor nerve damage. I couldn't stop touching it.

They got up to leave. When they were halfway to the door, Karras finally spoke.

"How much more of this do you think you can take?" she asked sharply.

"Enough," I told her. "It's about the only thing I'm good at."

CHAPTER 30

Terry Lasker's column ran in the 10 A.M. city edition of the *Tribune* on Monday. After briefly reviewing the facts of the motel-room murders and Polhaus's trial and pending execution, Lasker tossed his grenade.

The two-hundred-lawyer firm of Lisle, Day & Elgot [he wrote] has filed a motion in King County Superior Court to disqualify their co-counsel, sole practitioner Matthew Riordan, from further participation in the death-penalty appeal of Robert Polhaus. The motion was filed less than a week after the still-unsolved shooting death of Lisle, Day attorney Elizabeth Kleinfeldt, who retained Riordan to assist her on the case. SPD sources acknowledge that a link between Kleinfeldt's work on the Polhaus case and her murder has not been ruled out.

The battle over Riordan's handling of the case involves a newly discovered list of prostitution customers of murder victim Melody Beasely that was not found in the initial police investigation. Courthouse sources say that managing partner Jack Elgot filed the petition to prevent Riordan from examining the links between the three victims and their customers, who reportedly include a number of prominent civic, legal, media, and business leaders, some with ties to the Lisle, Day firm.

Terry went on to disclose his involvement. I could almost hear him swallow hard as he wrote:

Reporters love nothing better than having an excuse to expose the sexual lives of the people we cover. We tell ourselves that we're fighting hypocrisy, or we let the supermarket tabloids do the dirty work, and then piously report what they print. We repeat all the details and we're secretly glad that it didn't happen to us. This time it did.

I knew Melody Beasely. I paid her for sex on two occasions in the year before she was murdered. My name is in her book of customers.

I won't do a Betty Ford Clinic routine on this. I was sober; I don't drink anymore, and I don't use drugs. Like everyone else in this city, I have a dark side to my life. And that's all I'm going to say.

He finished by asking hard questions about Lisle, Day's role in the case.

Disputes between attorneys on how to handle a client's case are as old as the legal profession. They usually represent honestly held differences of opinion on how to serve a client best. Whether the same can be said here will be up to the courts to decide. But it seems peculiar, at least, that when a well-known and highly respected attorney like Elizabeth Kleinfeldt is murdered, possibly as a result of her work on the Polhaus case, her firm should go to court to fire the attorney she chose to assist her in the investigation. One wonders how the interests of Robert Polhaus, waiting for the hangman exactly four weeks and three days from today, are being served.

CHAPTER 31

At one-thirty I limped into the large, run-down presiding courtroom on the ninth floor of the King County Courthouse to wait for the assignment of a judge to hear Jack Elgot's motion to disqualify me. I nodded to Terry Lasker. He was chatting at the back of the courtroom with a *Tribune* photographer and a couple of other reporters from the *Post* and the *Seattle Weekly*. When he saw my bruised face he did a double-take and started to get up. I shook my head at him and waited in the first row of benches.

The presiding judge, David MacGregor, walked out to the bench a few minutes later. MacGregor was a diminutive Scotsman with carefully tended white hair and a matching, spade-shaped beard. He looked at me with hard-eyed disdain as his bailiff called the case, making no secret of his distaste for dog-fights between lawyers. I took my place at the bar beside a grim-faced Jack Elgot. The broken rib ached every time I took a breath. A trickle of sweat ran down my side. This had the makings of a very long afternoon.

"Counsel, Judge Stepanovitch finished a trial rather unexpectedly this morning," MacGregor said. His voice was sour. "I've sent him the papers and he is reviewing them now. He'll be ready for you at two o'clock." He glanced down at his docket sheet on the bench and whispered to his bailiff, then looked up again. "Step back. That's all."

I suppressed both a sigh of relief and a smile. Mike Stepanovitch was one of the better judges I could draw, a blunt, profane former public defender who started life as a welder at Boeing. He would have little sympathy for the rarefied concerns of a massive firm like Lisle, Day. As I passed Terry Lasker on the stairs at the tenth floor, I whispered, "At least I'll get a hearing."

He nodded. "Don't lead with your face. It looks like you've done that already."

Stepanovitch was a broad-faced, portly, thick-featured man in his early fifties with long, curling gray hair. He went on the bench in his small, modernized courtroom precisely at two o'clock.

"I've read the papers," he said shortly. "Everybody here?"

Jack Elgot spoke first, rising to stand before the bench with Wayne Porras at his side. "A preliminary, Your Honor. I see that the representatives of the press are here. Under the circumstances, I think this should be a closed hearing."

Stepanovitch leaned forward on the bench. "What for?"

"Some matters may come up, Your Honor, that could disclose either privileged communications with my client, or the attorney work product prepared in the course of the underlying appeal. We do not want to inadvertently waive any of those protections."

"Then why didn't you file your papers under seal?" Stepanovitch growled.

"An oversight, Your Honor." Elgot's voice was silky. "I have a motion to hand up to seal the proceedings."

Stepanovitch took Elgot's papers over the bench. "Mr. Riordan? What's your position?"

"I find it somewhat unusual, Your Honor, that Mr. Elgot and his firm just discovered this 'oversight' today. After, of course, publicly trashing my reputation. But I agree that there is a risk of inadvertent disclosure. That's why my papers *were* filed under seal. I stipulate to the motion."

I knew Lasker would be pissed off if the judge sealed the hearing but I hadn't counted on his bringing a lawyer. A short bustling man spoke up from the back of the courtroom. "Richard Wade, Your Honor, representing the *Tribune*. We object to closing this hearing. As a newspaper, we have statutory standing to challenge."

Stepanovitch waved him down. "I know, and I'm not going to seal this thing. What I am going to do is hear it in chambers, with a reporter. When we're done we're going to cut out anything that reveals privileged matter from the transcript. Then we'll release it. Come on back, Counsel. Not you, Mr. Wade."

I followed Jack Elgot and Wayne Porras back into chambers, pleased with Stepanovitch's ruling. It would protect Polhaus's legal position, but not provide cover for Lisle, Day. Elgot could still fuck me over, but he was going to have to do it in public.

Stepanovitch's chambers were as plain as his worn face: a county-issue black vinyl couch, a couple of straight-backed wooden chairs, a walnut judge's desk with the veneer starting to separate, a few plaques and diplomas. Case files were stacked on a credenza for review before the next day's motion calendar. There were no oriental rugs or expensive leather-bound legal treatises. The lack of show was a reminder of how strained the county's justice budget was, how hard the judges had to work to keep up with the endlessly growing caseload.

Stepanovitch settled behind his desk but kept his robe on. An elderly county court reporter was already seated to his left, his hands poised on the keys of his stenotype machine.

"We're off the record for now," he said. "What the fuck is going on here? Can't you guys settle your problems yourselves?"

"I got fired, Judge," I said. "But not by Robert Polhaus. Mr. Elgot decided to do it himself, days before Mr. Porras, his associate, thought to run it by the client." I paused to pull out two sets of sealed envelopes. One set contained a second affidavit that detailed the steps I had taken to continue the investigation, describing the new evidence uncovered. It was weak, with too many references to unidentified informants, suspects identified by number, not by name, and flat out rumor. The second set contained the sealed deposition transcript of the testimony of Jennifer DiGregorio, taken on Sunday afternoon in an Eastside motel room. It named Sean Tyner as the man Sharee Klimka was to see on the night she was murdered. I would hold it back until the last minute, wanting to gauge the drift of the argument before making a final decision on whether to use it.

"This petition," I continued, sensing that what the judge really wanted was an argument off the record, "is not premised on either my lack of resources or my unfitness. I was brought into this case by Mr. Elgot's firm, by Elizabeth Kleinfeldt. I was asked to investigate the facts. Ms. Kleinfeldt was not convinced that Robert Polhaus committed the crimes he was convicted of. Her strategy was to seek a new evidentiary hearing if the legal appeals failed, as she feared they would. I have continued to work on this case, and have spent over three hundred hours on it. No one has questioned my work or my ability. The only thing Mr. Elgot questions is the strategy that Ms. Kleinfeldt devised. As the court knows, she was murdered. I believe she was murdered because of her work on this case. That is why I am fighting to remain as counsel."

"Your Honor, if I may," Elgot said, clearly irritated by my speaking out of turn. Normally, the proponent of a motion goes first. "We've documented Mr. Riordan's deep emotional attachment to our late associate. We feel for his grief. But it is warping his judgment about what's best for the client. That last preposterous statement about Ms. Kleinfeldt's tragic death demonstrates the problem more clearly than I could put it into words. Mr. Riordan concedes that his interests are not those of the client, but in pursuing this strange . . . vendetta." Elgot cleared his throat and went on to his prepared argument. "Your Honor, when lawyers come together as a team, sometimes the chemistry fails. Their views on proper strategy are just too far apart. When that happens, the only thing to do is go to the client, explain the problem, and let the client decide. We did that. Mr. Polhaus chose to stay with us. It really is just that simple, Your Honor. Under the Rules of Professional Conduct, Mr. Riordan doesn't have a choice. He must withdraw. His refusal is utterly contrary to the ethical requirements, which the court should enforce."

"As I point out in my brief, Your Honor," I replied, "the client does have the final say—if that choice is informed, and made without outside pressures. Polhaus was put to a terrible choice for a man on death row facing imminent execution. He felt he had to fire me, a sole practitioner he'd met once. If he didn't, Mr. Elgot's firm, with all of its skilled lawyers and financial resources, was going to abandon him. Mr. Polhaus was told not to talk to me. I had to fly to Walla Walla to confront him and obtain an explanation. He refused to sign an affidavit detailing these pressures because he was told that if he did, mighty Lisle, Day was going to dump him. That is not informed, reasoned decision making. Mr. Elgot's conduct is perilously close to being tortious interference, as well as unethical."

Elgot began to respond but the judge cut him off. "You're making a hell of a charge here, Riordan. You say that Liz Kleinfeldt was murdered because of something she learned on this case, and that Elgot is obstructing further investigation. You'd better back that up, right now."

I handed the sealed envelope containing the evidence affidavit to the judge. "This is all work product, Your Honor. It's got to remain confidential, under seal." I handed a duplicate copy to Elgot. I waited while they read.

Elgot finished quickly, his face reddening. "Your Honor, this . . ." Stepanovitch raised a thick hand. "Not yet, Jack." He continued to read. When he looked up, he said, "What's in the other envelope?"

"This is a deposition transcript, Your Honor. It was taken yesterday afternoon. The witness who testified is at considerable personal risk. I will ask that you seal this document and review it *in camera*. Mr. Elgot has interfered with my investigation before and I do not want him publicly identifying or harassing this witness."

Elgot started to protest but Stepanovitch waved him down. He leafed through the deposition of Jennifer DiGregorio, slowly at first, then more quickly. His eyebrows went up, then stayed up, as he reached the page where she named Sean Tyner as the man Sharee Klimka had gone to meet on the night of her death. He finished the last page of the bound copy, then closed it thoughtfully.

"What's your position, Mr. Elgot?"

Elgot was waiting, red-faced with anger.

"Your Honor, this is utterly unfair. I demand to see what's in that document you've been handed."

"No, Mr. Elgot," Stepanovitch said softly. "I think Mr. Riordan's correct about the sensitive nature of this testimony. Address the affidavit."

Elgot picked up the affidavit, then pitched it on the judge's desk. "This isn't evidence," he said scornfully. "This is garbage. If this was an indictment it would be quashed in five minutes."

"It isn't offered as evidence of Polhaus's innocence," I responded. "It's offered to show that evidence may exist and that we should be working together toward a new evidentiary hearing. And to demonstrate that I have not, as counsel has so delicately suggested, taken leave of my senses."

Stepanovitch frowned, thinking it over, rereading a couple of paragraphs. I was betting on the latent public-defender instinct in him; he had fought his share of lost causes.

The bet was money-good. "I agree it's not much," Stepanovitch said slowly, "but it sure does tickle my sense of smell. Jack, why wouldn't you let him interrogate the dead girls' johns? Somebody should have, years ago."

"Your Honor," Elgot replied, "I don't see how we can harass these people simply because—"

"You're not harassing them, you're supposed to be questioning them." Stepanovitch's voice grew hard. "How many of these guys are your clients, Jack?"

"I don't know offhand," he said quickly.

"Five," I responded.

"Are any of them live suspects?"

I shrugged. "You can't rule them out until you've talked to them."

"True." The judge looked at Wayne Porras and tapped the affidavit with a finger. "You're the one who went to Walla Walla. Did you go over this information with Polhaus?"

Porras was sweating. He pushed his glasses back up on his nose. "No," he said, his voice small.

"Did you know any of it?"

"Some of it, Your Honor."

He turned back to me. "Anything else?"

"No, Your Honor."

He looked at me, curiosity twitching at the corners of his mouth. "Well, I've got a question. Who busted you in the face?"

"King County Sergeant Raymond Leach, the officer who investigated these murders. The officer who was under investigation himself for his ties to the owner of the escort service where the victims worked."

Stepanovitch said, "Jesus Christ, that tears it. I want Polhaus in here. I want to question him myself. If he's truly made up his own mind, Jack, I'll grant your motion. But I want to see him." He picked up his desk calendar and said, "Damn. I'm just chockablock busy for the next three weeks, and then there's the judicial conference. Let's set this over until April 10. I think you guys can live with each other for a month."

It was a gift. Stepanovitch could have ordered an evening or early morning hearing in a couple of days; he was giving me time. Elgot knew it.

"Your Honor, it may be difficult to wait. Perhaps an evening hearing, on shortened time, would put this matter behind us. As the court knows, most of our work will have to be done before April 20." A prim way to say that Polhaus might be dead after that.

Stepanovitch suppressed a grin. He was a decent judge but he was human and toying with lawyers is as much sport as most judges get. "No, Jack," he answered. "I want to take as much time with Polhaus as I need, a full day if I have to. This is a death case, after all."

Elgot stiffened with anger. "Then, Your Honor, I would request permission to withdraw."

"Denied," he snapped. "You're not going to walk away, Jack. I know it's a pro bono case but you took it, and you're stuck with it. And you'd better pursue it, Jack. I haven't ascended to heaven or the supreme court, but I do know that this thing stinks."

He turned to me. "Matthew, you're way out on a limb here. You're alleging a cover-up by a King County police officer, and possibly two murders, Liz's and this missing witness's, committed in the course of that cover-up." His voice hardened. He tapped the deposition transcript with a forefinger, then pointed at me. "If this witness's testimony leaks you are going to be crucified, and I'm gonna be there with the hammer and nails. I expect you to report to Jack and keep him informed. I suggest—I'm not ordering—that you show him this testimony. He might find it pretty persuasive." He straightened up in his chair, as if easing the kinks in his back. "I don't want you two back in here before April 10. I'm not going to baby-sit this damned thing." He turned to the court reporter and motioned him to get ready. "Now, gentlemen," he said. "Let's get this down. Make your arguments for the record and leave out any reference to the sealed documents' contents. I want a nice clean transcript with no possibility of waiver of the attorney-client privilege. We're on the record. Mr. Elgot."

CHAPTER 32

When I got home from the courthouse I started to pour myself a drink and then thought the better of it. I couldn't run with the broken rib but I thought a short walk would be okay. I was on my way out when the intercom squawked from the street. It was Wayne Porras. I buzzed him in without comment and waited for him at the top of the stairs.

Porras was sweating from the hike up three flights, and probably from nerves. He offered a tentative hand and I shook it.

"I'm puzzled," I said bluntly. "Is Jack sending you as his ambassador?"

"No," he replied. "I'm on my own. Jack doesn't know I'm here."

"Want a drink? I was going out for a walk but I'll join you."

"Scotch, thanks. Ice, no water."

I poured his drink in the kitchen, taking a bottle of beer for myself. When I returned to the living room, Porras was sitting on the sofa, uneasily perched on the front three inches of the seat.

"Relax," I said. "I'm not pissed off."

"I thought you'd throw me down the stairs," Porras said, taking the first gulp of his drink. He grimaced a little at the taste. It was good Scotch but Porras was not much of a drinker.

"Why would I do that?" I replied. "You're an associate, you're supposed to do what the lead lawyer on a case tells you. I didn't much like what Elgot did to me but I don't blame you." I paused to sip at the beer. "I don't know how

202

we're going to cooperate, but I suppose we'd better try. Should I call Elgot?"

"Not today," he said, grinning sourly. He pushed his glasses up on his nose. "Jack's still a little bit pissy after what happened in court."

"The judge gave me a gift," I acknowledged. "So what can I do for you?"

"Nothing. I thought I should fill you in on what we've been doing. We got these records," he said, pulling three thin files from his briefcase. "The victims' treatment records, from Dr. Bolger's clinic. I went to the families and got those consent forms signed. Just before . . . before Liz was killed."

I nodded. "Did you read them?"

"Yes, but I didn't see anything that meant much. Not to me, anyway. I thought you should see them." He handed the three file folders to me. I opened each folder and took a quick look. The records were relatively sketchy, each just a dozen pages of notes. I skimmed Klimka's file quickly, looking for references to Tyner or her other customers. I didn't find any.

"They don't mean much to me either," I said carefully. "I'll have to read them again. Thanks for bringing them."

"We still haven't heard from the clinic on the other stuff, but if we get anything I'll let you know."

"What other stuff?" I asked, surprised.

"The other records Liz asked me to get. We subpoenaed a list of all of the people Dr. Bolger treated. Of course, his clinic said they couldn't respond to the subpoena without getting permission. They're having a terrible time trying to contact everybody—it's been so long, and a lot of the addresses are no good. I guess some of these people are still—you know, on the street, involved in prostitution, so finding them and getting permission is going to take forever."

"Liz didn't mention this to me," I said, still puzzled. "Why did she want the names of his other patients?"

"I don't know." Porras shrugged. "I assumed this was something she talked over with you."

"She didn't," I replied.

"Well, I guess she was just being thorough. You know how she was, she always wanted to get everything in discovery she could. The clinic has billed us a thousand dollars so far for contacting the patients and asking for permission."

I frowned and leaned toward Porras. "When did Liz ask you to do this?"

"When she asked me to get the consent forms signed for Parker, Beasely and Klimka. About four or five days before she was killed. Why?"

"When did the clinic start contacting people?"

"The same day. I went over and screamed at them until they started."

"So the clinic would have been giving notice of the subpoena before Liz was killed?" I asked, my voice hollow.

He saw it as soon as I did. "Oh God," he said. "Do you think—"

"It's possible. I could never understand why the killer targeted Liz instead of me. I kept thinking it had to be tied into Leach's IIU file, that Scovill had told someone what she'd disclosed to Liz and the killer found out. Now I'm not so sure. The killer might have been reacting to the notice from the clinic. But how could we prove that?"

"There's Liz's notes," Porras replied. "She did have a couple of notations on Bolger and the prostitution prevention program, mostly just jotting down what you told her, I think. I've got them here." He opened a bulging soft-sided leather bag and rooted through it, finally pulling up a slim black three-ring notebook. "Here it is. I gave a copy to the police, but kept the original." He passed the open notebook to me.

The notes were written in black ink on yellow legal pad stock in Liz's small, distinctively neat hand. Liz filed each page in the notebook as her running log of the case. The key note read:

2/26 6:45 MR called. All 3 victims through PP program (says Sasser). MR wants victims' treatment records to see if customer names concur—assign Porras to get consents. MR says Shrink Boulger (Sp?) dead—suicide—day after Klimka murder. Why? Connect? Boulger involved/investigating? Maybe get records/names of all Shrink's patients in PP program? Group Therapy? Like T Case? Subpoena Names/Responses/Beasely Book/Ins. List/Question?

I put the book down and thought. Liz and I had talked briefly about whether there was a possible connection between the victims' participation in Sasser's program and the death of Martin Bolger. But why had she wanted to find out the names of his other patients? The statutory therapist-patient privilege was a strong one and the records would be presumptively privileged. Without signed consent forms her chances of obtaining the records through court action were between slim and none.

I looked up and saw Porras studying me. "Does it mean anything to you?" he asked.

"It's pretty cryptic. But Liz didn't do things without a reason. Did she say anything to you about this last phrase, 'Like T Case?' "

"No. I was pretty confused by it, actually. I thought it might be a name, Tom Case or Tim Case or something, but nobody with a name like that is involved in the Polhaus case."

"What about another case or file that she had at the office? Could she have been referring to a matter that was abbreviated as the 'T Case'?"

"Not that I know of. That's not the way we abbreviate file names."

"What about a court case? A well-known one."

"Tarasoff," he said suddenly. "Tarasoff was a woman killed by a psychiatric patient in California. The psychiatrist knew that his patient wanted to kill her, but he didn't warn her, thinking he'd be violating the therapist privilege. His patient murdered Tarasoff. Her family sued for wrongful death. They won."

I paused. "That's got to be it. When we talked about the victim's mental health records I told Liz that Bolger had killed himself just after Klimka was murdered, and that he'd possibly tried to investigate the murders himself. She must have been guessing that he knew something from one of his other patients that he couldn't reveal. Or that another patient of his was involved." I stopped, suddenly remembering what Karen Sasser had told me: "I don't want Marty's ghost haunting me. He was a real bear for doctor-patient confidentiality."

Porras was utterly confused. "I'm not following this," he said. "Liz was too good a lawyer not to know that we couldn't get the treatment records of any patient who didn't consent. The Tarasoff exception to the therapist-patient privilege requires that there be some kind of immediate danger to overcome the privilege. It doesn't apply to a case like this."

"Liz knew that there might have been another way to get the names of some of those patients she wanted," I said slowly.

"How?"

"You guys represent Pacific Health, don't you?" Pacific was the largest group medical insurance provider in the area, covering most of the public and private employees in King County. Like cops. And judges.

"Yes."

"Call an adjuster. Get a list of all the people insured by them who were treated by Bolger for the two years preceding his death. An adjuster could pull up a list of patient names from the computer by punching in Bolger's provider number."

He looked doubtful. "Wouldn't that violate some kind of privacy regulations?"

"Just about all of them."

"I don't know," he said slowly. "It could get sticky."

"Do it, Wayne. Please."

"What are you looking for?" he asked.

"Maybe the same thing Liz was," I said. "Liz could be devious, kid. She knew that Bolger's practice was mostly in criminal justice, victims and defendants and cops and lawyers. She knew that not everybody would consent to having their name disclosed. That's what she wanted. Take another look at her notes. She was going to get Bolger's patient lists from your insurance clients. Then she was going to find the names of Bolger's patients who *didn't* want their identities disclosed. And find out why."

CHAPTER 33

Sean Tyner lived in a low one-story house on the edge of a hill overlooking Puget Sound in the Innis Arden neighborhood in northwest Seattle. The house was shielded from the street by a dense line of evergreens. I drove between the carved cedar-log posts that marked the entrance to the driveway and cut my lights as I approached the house. The driveway was paved with brick and I slowed to muffle the noise of my tires. A ten-year-old Mercedes 450 SL convertible with a dent in one fender stood in the driveway. I got out of my car and walked around the left side of the house. The house had been built in the 1960s and expensively remodeled in a vaguely Japanese style. It was sheathed in gray cedar shakes. Light leaked through the blinds covering the front windows. The basement level opened onto a rear patio from two sets of French doors. The lights at the rear of the house were on. An uncovered hot tub steamed. I paused and listened. Faint music leaked through an open window. It took me a moment to recognize it. Madonna. Tyner had company. I didn't think he was a Madonna sort of guy.

I went back to the front of the house and stood under the entry trellis in front of a pair of carved double doors. There were Japanese lanterns on either side of the doors. The bell brought no response and I rapped on the door with my keys. It took another five minutes for the door to be opened.

"What?" Tyner asked sharply. He stood in the doorway in a short white robe made of thick cotton terry cloth. His face seemed slack with alcohol and I could smell the Scotch on his breath. The bright Kennedyesque charisma he affected in public was gone. He stared at me dumbly for a second before recognition set in.

"Oh, Christ, it's you," he said sullenly. "I've got nothing to talk to you about." He made no move to let me in.

"I'd have called you at the office," I said. "But we need to talk. In private." I looked past him into a cathedral-ceilinged living room dominated by a huge black granite fireplace. It was furnished with low couches and lacquered oriental furniture. A blond woman of no more than nineteen came into view, staring at us curiously. She was wearing a black silk robe embroidered with Chinese characters over a black leather Merry Widow corset.

Tyner gestured at the woman to go away. He closed the door behind him and said, "It's almost ten o'clock, for God's sake. I've got company."

"So I see. I'm freezing out here, Sean. Why don't you invite me in and pour me a drink?"

He laughed incredulously, a short barking sound. "Why the hell should I? I'm not going to talk to you."

"Yes, you are. I'm here because I respect what you've done with your public life and I respect the robe you wear. I don't want to embarrass you or wreck your career if I don't have the truth. But you knew Sharee Klimka, Sean. And you know more than you've told about the motel-room murders. You can talk to me now or talk to me on the public record. Your choice."

He closed the door and reopened it a few minutes later. He gave way silently and let me into the entry hall, then turned abruptly and walked down the three stairs to the sunken living room. Tyner opened a low cabinet set against the near wall and slopped more Scotch into his glass, then scooped a second glass into an ice bucket and poured it full of Scotch. I heard one of the back doors to the house on the lower level open and close. A minute later the Mercedes ground into life and backed out of the driveway, tires rasping on the brick pavement.

"Here," Tyner said sullenly, thrusting the glass at me. "Now tell me what the hell this is all about. I don't know this—what did you say her name was?"

"Klimka. Your name was in her john book, Sean. You were supposed to meet her on the night she was murdered. Surely you remember her? She was about the same age as that woman you just sent away. Looked a little like her, too." I took my drink and sat down on the edge of the sofa nearest the fireplace, stretching my legs out toward the warmth of the fire. Tyner paused where he was, then walked over and sat down facing me, curiosity overcoming fear.

"You've got brass balls, Riordan, I'll say that for you. I'm going to get you disbarred."

"It will be an interesting and very public hearing, Judge," I replied. I drank some of his Scotch and waited. It was bad Scotch.

"If you're threatening me, it won't work," he said loudly, alcohol in his voice.

Lawyers are notoriously lousy witnesses and I was listening for the sound of uncertainty when he spoke. I heard it, something out of place in the bluff, over-hearty voice of the fraternity boy grown older, but not necessarily up.

"You're the one making threats, Sean. I meant what I said. If you've got nothing to do with the motel-room murders, if you were just following your dick when you got involved with Sharee Klimka, if you stopped and you don't know anything about the murders, I'm going to leave you out of this. But if you don't talk to me I am going to have no choice. It's a different world out there, these days. Rich powerful white guys don't get to fuck the peasants anymore. When the press finds out what you've done they'll destroy you."

Tyner drained half his glass in one long swallow. "You haven't got any evidence," he finally said. His words slurred drunkenly now. He was still trying to brazen it out. "I'll deny everything," he added.

I shook my head, dismayed. "Sean, I'm giving you a chance to explain yourself," I pleaded. "Can't you see that?"

He stood up and finished his drink. "I haven't got time for this," he said with feigned scorn. "I haven't heard one word that implicates me in any crime. I think you'd better leave."

"Sit down," I said sharply. "In 1989, just before the motel-room murders were committed, you were removed from the juvenile bench by the presiding judge of the superior court for having unauthorized out-of-court contacts with female juveniles. A caseworker from Twelfth and Alder will testify that you started a sexual relationship with Sharee Klimka when she appeared in your court. Klimka told him that you sent her to work for Larry Poole's escort service, Dreams. Sharee Klimka came to this house on the morning of January 1, 1990, just three days before she was killed. Klimka's john book lists you as a customer, just like Beasely's. Klimka was supposed to meet you at the China Tapestry Motel on the night she was killed. She told a friend that she wanted to meet you at the motel with another woman, instead of her new apartment, because she was afraid that your sexual taste in bondage and asphyxiation games had gotten out of hand." I stopped, then added cruelly, "That enough for you, Your Honor?"

Tyner stood rock-still. His face suddenly lost its alcohol shine and was the color of gray paste.

"It's not true," he said at last. "I never . . . not like that."

"What's not true, Sean? That you picked up Sharee Klimka in your own courtroom and extorted sex from her? Or that you killed her?"

"I didn't kill her," he said dully. "I didn't see her that night. I never saw her after she came here on that New Year's Day."

I handed him the DiGregorio deposition, a copy with her name blacked out. "This deposition was given to Judge Stepanovitch this afternoon, Sean."

He read it slowly, painfully, his lips moving slightly as he read. When he finished he looked up with something like genuine confusion in his eyes. "I can't explain this," he said haltingly. "I didn't meet her. I didn't call her."

"Let's say I believed you, Sean. I'd like to. But all three motel room victims appeared in your courtroom. All three went to work for Larry Poole. Poole had a hook in Raymond Leach, one of the two cops on the motel-room case. He still does. Leach systematically destroyed the evidence about the victims' customers. Poole was trying to protect someone. I think he was trying to protect you, Sean. The question is, why?"

Tyner said nothing. He got himself another drink and stayed at the bar, his back toward me. My temper broke. I crossed the room in two strides and slapped the glass out of his hands, sending a spray of ice and whiskey across the room.

"What do you do for him, Sean?" I shouted, my face inches from his. "Feed him children out of the juvenile court? Launder them by referring them to the prostitution prevention program, then send them on to work for Poole?"

He said nothing. I hit him in the face once, then again. He rocked on his heels. "Tell me about Liz Kleinfeldt, Sean. Did you kill her, or did you have it done? Tell me now, Sean, or I'll kill you myself."

Tyner stumbled backward and fell heavily to the floor. He was a hollow man now, eyes dull and flat, the big shoulders and chest collapsing from within. He stood and straightened himself with an effort, trying to collect the shards of his dignity. "I would never do that," he said. His voice was a thick painful whisper. The aura of easy power he projected was gone now, peeled away like brittle old paint. It was astonishing how little of him there was left.

"I don't believe you, Sean. But it doesn't matter what I believe. You're a judge, you know about pen registers. They record the numbers you call. I've had your telephone records pulled for the last month, ever since I first talked to you about this case. You're a panicker, Sean. You've called Larry Poole half a dozen times last week. You made the last call on Friday, a couple of hours before Leach tried to rip my head off."

He looked at me and said nothing. But his eyes suddenly came alive, full of purpose. I took a cautious step backward.

"I know what you're thinking, Sean. That maybe one more death is going to end it, make the nightmare go away. It won't. I've talked to too many people. The chain is a little too clear. First Bolger, then Liz. They won't believe a suicide or a mugging gone wrong when it's my turn."

He looked puzzled again. "Bolger?" he asked. "Bolger wouldn't . . ." He stopped, confusion mixed with dread.

"Wouldn't what?"

He shook his head, groggy as a punch drunk boxer trying to shake off the one blow too many. His big hands clenched and let go spasmodically. He knew his ruin as a public man would be complete. I wondered if there was enough decency left in him to tell the truth.

"Sean, tell me this much. There was another woman, another prostitute. She might have witnessed both Beasely's and Klimka's murders. Was she working for Poole? Did Leach have her killed to keep her quiet?"

"He never found her . . . you still don't have it right," he finally said. He erupted in sudden, drunken laughter at some hidden irony only he understood. I slapped him, hard.

"Sean, for the love of God, tell me what you know." I reached out to him, trying to work past the denial of the sexual compulsion that had led him to sell his robe to Lawrence Poole. "You were a damned good lawyer once, a fair judge. Help me make the system work. Don't let Polhaus be executed for crimes he didn't commit. Don't let Liz's death be in vain."

He backed away from me, stumbling. "It doesn't matter," he said softly.

"Sean, it does. If you didn't kill them, was it Poole?"

"I don't know. We never knew. Isn't that just a fucking hoot?" He laughed again, emptily, on the edge of losing control now. "We had this . . . Oh God, the women, the parties, and then they were being killed, we didn't understand, each of us thought it might be the other, and then they stopped . . ." He bent forward suddenly and collapsed to his knees. He vomited sour alcoholic bile that ran down his chin and covered the front of his robe. "Jesus Christ . . . Jesus Christ . . ." he whispered, rocking forward and back on his knees, like a crazed penitent. "Clean . . . I've got to clean myself." He got to his feet slowly, covered with his own filth, and stumbled drunkenly out of the room.

I sat down heavily, adrenaline and overwhelming relief surging in me, breathing hard. Tyner would break, all the way now. For the first time since Liz had been murdered I felt as though the ground was solid under my feet.

I had just gotten up to follow him when I heard the shotgun explode through the empty house.

CHAPTER 34

Ahlberg kept me for twenty-six hours, more than long enough to have the lab tests confirm that my hands were free of gunpowder residue from the shotgun blast that had killed Sean Tyner. The rest was pure anger.

"You must like this," he said bitterly. We were standing in the deserted courtyard of the county building, next to a dozen scraggly dying trees that someone had imprisoned behind chain-linked fences and called public art. The midnight sky was milky with threatened rain. "You must like this fine. You get to tell the court that Tyner killed them and point to the empty chair." He dragged on a borrowed cigarette, the first I'd seen him smoke in five or six years.

"You don't get it," I replied. My voice sounded tinny, oddly distant. Exhaustion mixed with defeat filled every bone and joint, like a viral disease. "We've got the burden of proof in any hearing. With Tyner dead, Polhaus has got nothing. He'll hang on schedule." I threw the cold dregs of a paper cup of coffee into the street. "Did you find Poole?"

"No. He's gone to ground. We checked his banks. They've all filed cash transaction reports. He pulled out something like a quarter million dollars in green."

Ahlberg coughed once and flipped the cigarette butt into the street. "It still feels wrong to me. Even knowing that Tyner had a date with Klimka the night she was murdered."

"I'm just not sure," I said. "I always thought I could read somebody who was surprised. Tyner was too drunk to be in control of his reactions. And if he wasn't surprised when I told him that Klimka was supposed to see him on the night she was killed, he was one hell of an actor." I touched my cheekbone where Leach had smashed it. The nerves were still dead, the skin still numb. "Tyner kept saying they didn't know who was killing the women, they didn't know what had happened. As though he and Poole were as confused as anyone else." I stopped, frustrated. "Do you think Poole could have set Tyner up as a fall guy?"

Ahlberg grunted. "Too much theory. When you get past the suits and the Mercedes, Poole's just a pimp. They almost never kill the women who work for them. They see it as burning money."

"Maybe," I replied. "But I keep coming back to something that Liz said to me at the very beginning. That it smelled to her like a set-up."

He looked at me sharply, for just a moment, his face barely visible in the shadows cast by the street lights on Fourth Avenue. It was as though he had been seized by a sudden understanding, then just as quickly dismissed it.

"What?" I asked quickly.

"Nothing." He shook his head and started to turn away. "We'll know more when we get Poole. I think it's pretty simple. Polhaus killed the prostitutes. You and Liz just stumbled across Tyner's involvement with Poole. That's why Tyner killed Liz."

I seized his arm and jerked him back. "You'd like that a hell of a lot, wouldn't you, Vince? You can contain the scandal and bury IIU's obstruction of justice along with Polhaus. But it's too late for that. If I have to take the goddamn county apart I won't let it end that way."

Ahlberg peeled my fingers off his arm. "Get fucked," he said tiredly. "Get out of here." He limped away like an old man.

By the time I got back to my Capitol Hill apartment it was after 1 A.M. I hadn't eaten in two days and could barely stand in the kitchen long enough to cook. I soft-scrambled four eggs and made toast and strong Darjeeling tea. I managed to eat most of it. When I finished I picked up my mail. There was an unmarked manila envelope stuffed in my box. I tore it open and found a computer printout listing the names of every patient Martin Bolger had treated in the three years before his death. I checked quickly to see if Leach, Poole, or Tyner's names were on it, then checked every name from Melody Beasely's john book against the list.

When I finished I slumped down in my chair and put my head in my arms, defeated. There wasn't a single match. I saw other names that I knew, of cops and prosecutors, including Nancy Karras. That wasn't new. I'd already guessed that she'd been treated by him on the night I went to her apartment. I paced around my apartment, thinking. There were other insurance carriers that could have been providing coverage, but Tyner and Leach were both government employees covered by Pacific Health. If they hadn't known about the subpoena or about Scovill's statements, why had one of them killed Liz? I couldn't come up with an answer. I finally gave up at 3 A.M. and took a bottle of brandy from the kitchen cabinet to drink myself into a fitful sleep.

The kitchen phone rang. I snatched it from the wall. It was Carolyn Ritter. Her voice was soft, happy. She spoke the words I wanted to hear.

"She's coming home," she said. "Andrea's coming home. She's on the red-eye flight from Anchorage. She gets in at seven."

I put down the phone and slept like death until morning.

CHAPTER 35

Interstate 5 wound south through Tacoma and Olympia into the wide green valley formed by the rivers flowing down to the Columbia from the Cascade Mountains to the east and the Willapa Hills to the west. The rivers had names given them by the native peoples who once lived richly from the salmon harvest, Chehalis and Cowlitz and Toutle and Skookumchuck. I got off the freeway at Napavine and took Route 603 the last seven miles into Winlock through the older, quieter landscape of dairy farms, shake mills and sagging hay barns.

Carolyn Ritter's house was five blocks south of the main street of Winlock. The house was set in the trees on a ridge at the east end of the small deep valley that surrounded the old railroad town. It was solidly built, a two-story Craftsman bungalow with a wide front porch beneath the second-story eaves. The house needed paint and some of the posts supporting the porch rail were missing but the yard was green and neatly tended, with beds of early yellow tulips and pink climbing roses beginning to bloom.

I parked in the driveway. Carolyn was waiting when I got out of the car. "You're early," she said, smiling. "I thought you might be." We stood awkwardly for a moment before she led me into the house. "Andy's sleeping. She's been sick. Dick Bartke wants to talk to you, though."

Bartke was sitting in the living room, his feet up on an old leather hassock, reading a day-old Anchorage paper, a coffee mug on a table at his elbow. Sunlight streamed in the windows.

"Pretty good, huh?" He had a satisfied expression on his narrow, pointed face. "Took me a week. The kid was living in a shitty motel room in Fairbanks with nothing in it, just a bed and a bunch of boxes."

"She come willingly?"

He shrugged. "More like taking one of my kids to the doctor. She was too sick to decide anything. Her prescriptions look like she's got some kind of lung infection. So I got her in her clothes and dragged her to the airport. By the way, she's using coke. A lot of it, judging by the size of her stash. I dumped it before we left."

"Thanks for everything, Dick. I know you'll want to get home. I can take over."

"Not on your life. I want to know what she saw. I can help you question her. I've still got the layout of that damned China Tapestry Motel in my head, as well as all the information we got from the other people working there."

"Okay," I replied. "Let's talk to her." I found Carolyn in the kitchen. She agreed to wake her sister. "She'll want to shower and dress," she said. "We'll be down in a half hour. My son's in school," she added, "so we can talk freely. I don't want him to know all of this."

I went back and sat with Bartke. "What did you get out of her on the plane?" I asked. "Anything?"

"I didn't ask her about the motel-room murders. I was afraid I'd spook her if that's what she had run away from. She said she'd been in Fairbanks for the last three months or so. She's been in and out of Alaska over the past four years, but she says Alaska's where the best money is." Bartke shook his head sadly. "I got a daughter nearly her age. Anyway, I stuck to the story about her mother. We didn't find her in time, though. Her mother died last week."

"Damn. I'm sorry." I spent the next ten minutes telling Bartke what I'd been doing, then fell silent. He went back to his paper. I tried to read a magazine, then some of Martin Bolger's book. After a while I gave up. I kept reading the same sentences over and over. I had put too much hope into what Andrea Jacoby could tell me.

When she came down the stairs I thought with a sudden start that we must have found the wrong person. Andrea was supposed to be twenty-three. This woman looked perhaps fifteen, painfully thin in faded Levi's and a loose cotton shirt. Her hair was still wet, dark brown instead of auburn. Her cheeks had hollowed out with illness, her features now hawkish and striking. Her nose was long and slightly hooked, her eyes black, with dark circles beneath them. She walked shakily to a worn brown sofa facing us and sat down. All of her emotional defenses seemed gone after learning of her mother's death. Carolyn sat down beside her.

"This is Matthew Riordan," she said, gesturing at me. "He needs to ask you some questions, and I want you to answer him."

"Andrea," I said, "I'm a lawyer. I'm not a policeman, and what you tell me shouldn't hurt you. But you may have been a witness in a homicide case. I'm representing Robert Polhaus, the man who was convicted of killing Melody Beasely and Sharee Klimka. I think you know them. And him."

"I knew him," she said dully. "He was a security guard at a couple of motels in Seattle."

"That's right. I don't think Polhaus killed Melody or Sharee. I think you saw something relating to Sharee Klimka's murder. I need to know what happened, what you saw."

She looked down. "I don't know anything," she mumbled.

"Yes, you do. I want you to tell me what happened on the

night that Sharee was killed. Were you supposed to meet her at the China Tapestry Motel?"

"I can't talk about this. I mean . . . you know what I was doing."

"Yes. Everyone here is an adult. We all want to help you. But you must tell me the truth." I was questioning her as I would a child, gently but with a controlling hand.

"Sharee called me in the afternoon that day," she began, her eyes down. "She wanted to know if I would work a scene with her. She said she had a john who was into fantasy but he was maybe getting weird and she wanted a partner to work it. She said the john had lots of money and would pay for me, too."

"Did she say who the john was?"

She nodded, then coughed harshly. "Not his name. She said he was a judge."

"Was the date set up through Dreams?"

"No. I was still at Dreams, and I didn't want to get caught working for another service. Sharee said it was okay, she was on her own."

"Did Sharee say why the date was set up for the China Tapestry Motel, rather than her apartment?"

"No. I just assumed it was because of Bobby Polhaus. He'd make it cool to use the rooms at the places he worked if you took care of him." She shuddered a little, possibly from her fever, possibly out of self-disgust.

"Tell me about Polhaus. What was the deal?"

"You had to ball him in order to work his motel," she said simply. Her mouth twisted in disgust. "He was a creep."

"Why was he a creep?"

"Because . . . shit. He liked to hit, you know? And tie us up, for real, too hard, too rough. I stopped doing him. I told Sharee it was her date, if she wanted to use the motel she'd have to take care of him."

"When did you get to the motel?"

"A little after twelve. I was late, more than an hour, but I figured Sharee'd be okay. The john was supposed to be there at eleven, eleven-thirty, something like that."

"What happened when you got there?"

"I went up to the room. Sharee told me where she'd be, what room. She called me after she made the deal with Polhaus for the room. I knocked on the door and I didn't hear anything, you know, so I thought I must have had the wrong room. I tried the door. It was open, so I went in and I saw . . .

God, I can still see her. She was on the bed with no clothes on and her mouth was open and her face was blue. I knew she was dead. When I turned around to get the hell out of there I got hit from behind and it knocked me down. I must have blacked out for a little while because I felt sick when I got up, and had a big lump on the back of my head. When I came to I just ran the hell out of there."

"Where did you run? Toward the street, toward Aurora Avenue?"

"No," she said. "Why'd you think that?"

"Polhaus said he saw a woman running away from the motel, toward Aurora. He thought she had long red hair. Your hair would look red if you were using henna, or a red hair dye."

"It wasn't me. It couldn't have been. I was blond then, a total bleach job, even my eyebrows. And my hair was real short. I wasn't wearing any kind of wig."

I stopped, confused, suddenly fearful, feeling as if the floor had dropped beneath me. Oh, God, I thought, had Polhaus lied after all? "Where did you go?"

"There was a stairway in the middle of the hotel, at the corner where the two buildings meet. It's open to the outside but the building kind of hides it. I ran down the stairs and into the alley behind the motel where I'd parked a car that I'd borrowed to get up there."

"Are you sure? You were scared half to death. Are you sure you went out toward the back?"

"Yeah. I mean, all I could think about was getting to the car."

"What were you wearing?"

She shrugged. "God, I don't remember. Probably jeans and a sweater. I was going to change for the scene."

"So you carried other clothes in a bag?"

She nodded. "I had a big purse, a shoulder bag. I never dropped it, even when I got hit, because I fell on it. I know I had it when I ran away because the car keys were in it."

I swallowed hard and rubbed my face with both hands. Andrea Jacoby had been a witness, all right, but she couldn't have been the woman Polhaus claimed to have seen with long red hair, wearing the spandex tights of a streetwalker. Her testimony would do Polhaus no good. If anything, her story hurt his case. With Andrea Jacoby accounted for, Polhaus's story would be less plausible than ever.

"Let's go back over this." My voice sounded odd to me,

filled again with the endless failures of the weeks since Liz had been murdered. "When you went to the room, did you see anybody else in the motel?"

"No. I came up the same stairs I went down, the ones from behind the building, and I didn't see anybody standing around."

"When you were in the room, do you remember seeing anything of the man that hit you? Could you tell, for example, if he was black or white?"

"No. Nothing. I was just looking . . . at Sharee, for a second, and I turned around to get the hell out of there."

"After you were hit, and you got up to run, did you see anybody?"

"I don't remember. I don't think so. I was just so scared." She coughed again, her body shaking. "I'm real thirsty. I need to get some water."

Carolyn took her into the kitchen. I turned to Bartke. "What do you think?"

"She's got the layout of the motel right," he replied. "The alley in back widens out by the motel and cars do park there, alongside the building." He thought for a minute, as frustrated as I was. "I know a good hypnotist. We could try that."

I shook my head. "It'd taint her testimony. Hypnotic enhancement has been ruled out by the courts, completely."

When she returned I said, "Andrea, I know this is hard for you. I have some more questions, so just work with me, okay? First, why did you leave town?"

"I was scared."

"Yes, but why? If the killer was the one who knocked you down, he could have killed you right then. He let you get away. Why did you call up your sister for money, and then go to Karen Sasser?"

"I told you, I was scared. I'd heard . . ."

"What did you hear?"

"Sharee had worked for Larry Poole, and she'd had a thing with him. I thought maybe he knew she was working for someone else, and that he'd killed her."

"So you were afraid that Poole might find you?"

She nodded. "I thought he'd come looking for me."

"Tell me about Larry Poole. How long had you worked for him before Sharee Klimka was killed?"

"About six months."

"Did you have sex with him?"

She nodded, again. I was losing her. Her answers were becoming shorter, almost mechanical. But there was something in them that did not ring true.

"Let's try one more time," I said. "You told me that you ran away because you were afraid of Larry Poole. Why would you be afraid of Poole finding out that you were at the motel? Was Poole the man at the motel?"

She grew sullen. "You think I'm lying?"

"Yes. I think you're scared, and I think you're lying. Now tell me what really happened. I can help get you through this, but only if you tell me the truth."

Andrea turned to her sister but found no comfort. "Tell us the truth," Carolyn snapped. Her voice was harsh.

"I didn't see him at the motel," she finally said. "But when I was running away I thought I saw—somebody I'd seen before, with Larry. I thought he might be Sharee's judge. When I got back to my place, from the motel, I called Larry. I told him everything, about Sharee and the judge she was supposed to be meeting, and that I'd seen this guy. He said don't worry, he'd take care of it. The next thing I knew this other guy was in my room at home, slapping me. I knew he was a cop, a friend of Larry's. He told me that I'd better get the hell out of town or he would kill me."

"Do you know this cop's name?"

"No."

"Was he heavy, red-faced, with dark, maybe somewhat gray, hair?"

"Yeah. His hair looked funny, like he sprayed it with hair spray or something."

"Was he the man you saw at the motel?"

"No. I'm sure he wasn't."

I didn't have a picture of Raymond Leach, but from her description I thought she'd be able to identify him. I pushed on. "So you called your sister after he broke into your place?"

"Yeah."

"When did you call Karen Sasser?"

"The same morning, real early. A couple of hours later. Carolyn told me she couldn't help. I was scared." She sipped at the glass of water on the table in front of her.

"Did you talk to anybody else?"

"Some other girls I knew. I was trying to get some money."

"What were their names?"

"Annette. Sandy."

"Was one of them a junkie?"

She nodded. "Sandy shoots tar." Mexican heroin. IIU's dead junkie snitch.

I paused, and changed subjects. "You knew Melody Beasely, right? She called herself Jazz."

She nodded.

"You knew she was murdered?"

"Yeah. They told us."

"Who's 'they'?"

"Larry. He said that if we were questioned by the cops we shouldn't say anything."

"Were you with Jazz the night she was murdered?"

"No. I was in Vancouver, in Canada. Larry sent me there for this Japanese businessman. I didn't find out about Jazz until I got back."

"Were you scared?"

Her eyes widened like a child's. She nodded. "We were all scared," she whispered, coughing again.

I got up and got her another glass of water. "Let's talk about the China Tapestry one more time. Did you know who the man at the motel was?"

She shook her head. She was lying again, and I knew it.

"You'd seen him before, right? You just said you had seen him with Larry, that you thought he was the man Sharee Klimka referred to as a judge."

She didn't answer, but I thought I had a pretty good idea of where she had. "A couple of people have told me that Poole had parties for some of his customers," I said. "Did you know that?"

"Yeah." She looked away, kneading her hands together nervously.

"And you worked at some of those parties, didn't you?"

No answer. "Andrea, I need to know."

"Yeah." Sullen again.

"Where did Poole have them?"

"He had this place. It was like an old cabin, only bigger. On a lake, with a couple of little cabins off to the side."

"Where was this?"

"It was east of the city. I remember going across the floating bridges in his car to get there. We took the freeway and then turned off on a smaller road."

"Did you go over the mountain pass?"

"No. Not that far. It was only like an hour, maybe forty-five minutes from town."

"Could you find it again if you had to?"

"I don't know. I was only up there at night, and I was usually loaded the whole time."

"What happened at these parties?"

"What'd you think?" she asked angrily. "Usually four or five guys. That many women working. Sometimes people would pair off and sometimes everybody just got crazy."

"Did you take drugs at these parties?"

"Mostly coke, or X."

"Ecstasy?" Ecstasy is a mixture of amphetamine and a tranquilizer.

"Yeah. I got it from Larry. And we drank."

I stopped. She had given me something of worth, a possible club to beat Poole over the head with when he was found. Distribution of narcotics on the federal list wins you a mandatory ten-year sentence without possibility of parole under the new sentencing guidelines. The court has no discretion to lighten the sentence. I thought Poole would have a rough time with the food at Marion or Allenwood.

"Do you remember any of the men from these parties, besides Poole?"

She shook her head. "They were just faces. Bodies. Older, mostly older than Larry. They had money. Nice clothes. Manicured nails, big gold watches."

It was time. I took out a recent bar-association photo of Sean Tyner and half a dozen other lawyers in their mid-forties that I had cut and pasted into a photo montage. I put it in front of her. "Andrea, are any of these men the man you saw at the motel that night?"

"No."

"Are you sure? Look again."

She stared at the photographs, then pointed at Sean Tyner. "I've seen this one before. He was at some of Larry's parties. I think I screwed him." Her voice was flat, unemotional, then rose a little. "But I didn't see him at the motel when Sharee got killed. Honest. He wasn't there." I swallowed my disappointment and started again on a different tack.

"Andrea, did Poole take pictures at these parties at this old cabin or lodge? Videotape them?"

"I think so. I didn't dare ask him. But he always tried to keep things going in the one big room at the lodge."

I paused, unsure of how to get her to tell me who the man at the motel was. I looked at Bartke; he shrugged, nothing to add. I decided to get what I could from her before trying to break her story again.

"I asked you about a psychologist in the prostitution prevention program. His name was Bolger, Martin Bolger. I think he may have been trying to find out who killed Suzanne Parker and Melody Beasely and Sharee Klimka. Did you ever talk to him?"

"I don't think so. I was never in the program." She was hiding something again. She leaned forward, fighting nausea, her hands clasped together between her knees.

"He was a short, heavy man, balding. Between the night Sharee Klimka got killed, and the time you went away, did you talk to anyone like that?"

"No."

"Are you sure? I think I've got his picture here." I dug into my briefcase for the copy of Bolger's book. I turned it over, so that the picture on the back cover was visible to her.

"This is Bolger," I said.

She began to laugh, thinly, then hysterically. Carolyn put her arms around her and tried to stop her.

"That's him," she said, gasping for air. "That's who I saw at the motel."

The world pitched exactly one hundred eighty degrees. *"What?"* I nearly screamed.

The words rushed out of her. "He was there. He was at Larry Poole's parties, too. You didn't know? He worked in this fancy program to get kids off the streets. But sometimes, if the girls were good-looking enough, he'd get them off the streets, and straight to his friend Larry."

"Who told you that?"

"Jazz did. When we were up at Larry's place, a couple of months before she got killed. She said the judge had talked to her about working for Larry, and when she told her shrink about it he said okay."

Andrea suddenly gagged and slumped forward, her hands pressed to her stomach. "I'm going to be sick again," she said. She got to her feet unsteadily. Carolyn took her arm and led her up the stairs.

Dick Bartke whistled tunelessly. "I'll be damned," he said. "So good old Dr. Bolger was doing Poole's recruiting, right alongside Judge Tyner. And he was the man standing there, at the motel. Do you think he got into it more than that, and started killing them?"

"I don't know," I said grimly. Anger washed through me. "It looks like it, doesn't it? The son of a bitch knew all three victims, probably had sex with all of them. He killed himself, or was killed, right after the last murder. He didn't leave a note. Andrea said she saw him when she was running away. If she was knocked unconscious for five minutes or so, why was Bolger still standing there if he was the killer? I still think Tyner or Poole was killing them, and Bolger found out." Anger at the depth of his betrayal, a therapist who sold his patients, swept through me again. "That's what got him killed. But even if that's true, why was Liz killed? She was guessing that Bolger had learned something from or about one of his patients."

"To keep it quiet," Bartke replied. "Look at what you've got here. You've got Bolger and Tyner feeding young girls to Poole. Poole's got Leach, late of county vice, on his payroll, protecting him. If Tyner did the killings and got caught, the whole structure would come tumbling down. So Poole starts the cover-up. The part of the girl's story about Leach hustling her out of town makes sense, from that angle. It was the first step, maybe a not very well thought-out step, in the cover-up. The next day Leach has got Polhaus as the perfect patsy. He buries the evidence that could lead back to Poole, and puts together evidence that points at Polhaus. Once Polhaus was convicted, Poole had only two weak points. One was Leach, and Kleinfeldt was checking into him with IIU. The other is this kid. You're going to have to take care of her, not let anybody know that you've interviewed her until you're ready to make your case. Or she could wind up dead, and you with her."

"There's another weak link. The redheaded woman that Polhaus talked about. I asked Tyner about her, and his answer was weird. He said, 'We never found her.'" I grimaced in frustration. "Who the hell could she be?"

"I don't know. What's next?"

"I'm going to try to get Andrea to help me find this place Poole had. Where he had the parties. If she can't I'd like you to dig it up, from the county property records if you have to."

"Sure." Bartke got up from his chair. "I'm beat. I'm going to get in my car and see my family. I know a Lewis County deputy that owes me a favor. I'll see if he can put an unmarked car in front of the house. And take this." He took a .38 Smith &

Wesson police special, together with a belt-clip holster, from the small of his back. I took it and locked it in my briefcase.

I put out my hand. "Thanks, Dick."

He took it. "Too bad you don't practice law anymore," he said with bright irony. "You do get the damnedest cases."

CHAPTER 36

Sliding glass doors are a soft touch. A flat piece of spring steel slips the catch. I slid the lakeside door of the A-frame lodge open and stepped cautiously inside, searching for signs of a security system. No alarms sounded. I listened hard for the sound of a man breathing but heard nothing but the midnight stillness and the gentle lap of the lake touching the shore.

"Remember that the door was open," I said, turning back. "We came here looking for Poole, thought we heard someone, and found the door open," I said.

Terry Lasker nodded. "You picked up this little skill in law school, no doubt."

"Applied criminal procedure," I agreed. "But I'm dead serious. Breaking and entering is a felony. I'm giving us what's called the necessity defense."

"Even if we find something, won't it be inadmissible as evidence?"

"No. The exclusionary rule applies only to the police. Stolen evidence can be used in court if it comes from private citizens. Now shut up, Terry, and start looking."

"What is this place?" Lasker asked, still standing in the doorway. His breath plumed like smoke. The night was cold and there was no heat in the lodge.

"It's the party house," I replied. "Poole brought his friends up here, along with the women who worked for him."

"What are we after?"

"Anything we can find linking Poole, Leach, and Tyner. With Tyner dead, it's the only chance we've got of getting some evidence to get Polhaus a new hearing. Andrea Jacoby said that Poole made tapes of some of the parties. Look for those."

I waited a moment to let my eyes adjust to the pale ghostly light reflected from the lake. It had taken us seven hours to find the place, an old fishing lodge from the 1950s, crisscrossing the back roads in the east King County foothills with Andrea Jacoby. I knew with a cold sinking heart that the search had taken too long. Poole had two full days after Tyner's death to clean up any evidence and disappear.

The lodge walls were vintage knotty pine. A wide fieldstone fireplace filled a corner of the main room. Thick wall-to-wall carpeting had been laid on the floor. A large sectional sofa faced a projection TV with a big silver screen and a normal twenty-inch TV set in the corner. A wet bar, paneled in the same knotty pine as the walls, had been built out of what was once the grocery counter of the old lodge. Liquor bottles glinted in the light of my small pocket flash. The cabinet of the TV projector unit held a number of VHS cassettes. Most of them appeared to be commercially produced pornographic films. They had the usual double-entendre titles: *Debbie did Dallas* and a number of other cities.

I shined the light upward and scanned the ceiling in sections. One of the beams supporting the loft above was twice as thick as the others. I checked it carefully and finally found what I was looking for: a two-inch-diameter hole set over the center of the room. I got up on the sectional sofa and played the beam into the hole but didn't see the flash of a lens. "Might have been a camera here," I said. "Let's see what we can find upstairs."

I led Lasker to the upstairs loft. It had been cut into two bedrooms. There was a slight musty smell, not surprising since the foothills received almost twice as much rain as Seattle. The bedding was clean but damp and wrinkled. Terry searched the beds and nightstands. I stood in the front bedroom and estimated the location of the oversized beam below the floor. I guessed that it lined up with the wall dividing the loft into two bedrooms. I felt the carpeting where it met the wall, found a loose spot, and pulled the carpeting back from the tack strip. The wooden floor below had been cut. I pulled out a section of floor about two feet by eight inches. The false beam created an empty box. Camera brackets had been set into the bottom of the box around the two-inch hole.

"The video camera was mounted in there but it's gone now. Let's try downstairs again. There's a kitchen and bathroom we haven't gone through."

We searched the kitchen and the bathroom and again came up empty. The only room left was a small utility room with shelves of canned food, a nearly empty freezer, and a steel floor cabinet about four feet high. The cabinet was padlocked shut.

"It isn't for the booze," Lasker said. "The liquor's in the main room, out in the open."

"No," I agreed. I opened the waist-belt hiking pouch I was wearing and took out a small hacksaw with a steel cutting blade.

"You're demonstrating all kinds of interesting skills here tonight," Lasker said dryly.

"If you don't want to be a party to this, go outside. Don't smoke. Someone might see the glow of a cigarette."

He shook his head and watched, curiosity winning over caution. I worked quickly. The blade was diamond coated and the padlock steel cheap and soft.

It took less than ten minutes. I opened the cabinet. There was a small strongbox fitted with a combination lock, too small to hold what I was looking for. I shook it. It was empty.

I swore. "Poole's cleaned it out. Look." I pointed the beam of the pocket flash at the empty shelves. There was a fine, barely visible layer of dust inside the cabinet, but no dust on the part of the shelves where something the size of videocassette boxes had once been stored. Poole had been in too much of a hurry to wipe the shelves clean.

"One last chance," I said. "Let's check the cassettes in with the TV. Maybe Poole overlooked something."

Lasker switched on the small television and got the VCR working while I drew the heavy draperies over the glass sliding doors. I rifled quickly through the videocassettes, opening the boxes and setting aside tapes that had commercial labels pasted on the cassettes. I found three unmarked boxes with what appeared to be blank tapes. I handed the first one to Terry. He plugged it in and set the machine on fast forward.

We watched snow for about ten seconds but the tape was not blank. Terry slowed it to normal running speed.

It was Lawrence Poole. He was sitting on the sectional sofa while a black woman of perhaps nineteen slowly removed her clothes. He had her pirouette for the camera. Then he pointed down, to the front of his robe. She shook her head. He stood up and slapped her, hard. She swallowed the blow and complied.

"Now you know why county vice has never been able to put an undercover officer inside Poole's operation," I said dryly, pointing to the screen. "That's the employment interview."

I switched the VCR to a fast-forward setting with the images still visible. There were six encounters on the first tape, all similar to the first one. neither of us recognized any of Poole's sex partners. I took the second tape from its box and put it in the VCR. There was a piece of masking tape on the cassette. It said, "1989."

"What are you looking for?"

"A peculiar notion, a very long shot," I replied. I kept watching the tape. About halfway through, my heart nearly stopped.

"Wait," I said quickly. "Back it up. There. Now forward, normally."

"What?"

"There." I pointed to a woman on the tape. She took off her clothes and stood nude. She was older than the other women, slightly heavier, but her muscle tone was very good, legs firm, arms strong, breasts high.

She had long dark red hair.

"My God," Lasker said.

"Maybe. I can't see her face. The camera angle is too vertical."

I slowed the tape. The woman put a condom on Poole's erect penis as he fondled her breasts. Poole got down from the sofa, to his knees. He said something to her and took a cushion from the sectional and slid it under the woman's hips. She lay back as Poole entered her. The camera showed her face squarely now. The woman grimaced slightly and then her finely featured, determined face went slack. Her eyes were two dark disks, flat and empty.

"Oh, no," I breathed. "Oh my God, no."

It was Nancy Karras.

Lasker knew her too. He stared at the screen, slack-jawed. I felt a sour nausea in the pit of my stomach.

"I don't understand," he said. "What does it mean?"

"I'm afraid I do." I took out the list of Bolger's patients and found Nancy Karras's name. I handed it to Terry Lasker. "I think it means she killed all of them."

CHAPTER 37

I found a pay phone outside a motel in Fall City at six the next morning and called Vince Ahlberg at his home.

"What the hell is this?" he growled.

"I know what happened," I said. "I want you to meet me as soon as possible. And bring Karras with you."

"Where are you?"

I gave him the directions to Poole's lodge. "I'll look for you in an hour and a half," I added, then hung up.

I stood at the outside pay phone for a moment. My fingers ached with the cold and my head pounded. I had spent most of the night with Lasker in our motel room, piecing together what had happened. Lasker had gone off the wagon and I'd helped him through the better part of a fifth of Larry Poole's bourbon.

I found Terry sitting in the motel restaurant, eating scrambled eggs and working at a Bloody Mary. His color was bad but he looked as though he would live.

"Just like old times," Lasker said grimly. "Or Early Times," he added, naming the bourbon that had bit him. "I'd forgotten why I quit drinking. There may be truth in wine, but whiskey has even more snakes than I'd remembered."

"Go easy on that," I said, pointing to his Bloody Mary. "I may need you today."

"Don't worry, it's just the juice. Did Ahlberg go for it?"

I nodded. "They'll meet us there at eight-thirty."

"What are you hoping for?"

"I'm hoping to God that I'm wrong," I said.

I heard them before I saw them, the crunching sound of
Ahlberg's tires on the gravel of the drive. I stood on the deck
in front of the lodge, listening to the soft lap of water on the
lakeshore. Lasker waited inside.

They came down the hill from the parking area on the narrow path, slipping a little in the muddy places. Ahlberg was
dressed for duty, a suit beneath his customary black trench
coat. Karras wore a tan coat of waxed cotton with a green corduroy collar over a turtleneck sweater and jeans. They approached silently, with no wave or word of greeting. I waited
until they were standing on the deck, facing me.

"You'd better have a damned good explanation for this,"
Ahlberg said tightly.

"I have an explanation. One I don't like worth a damn. With
too much amateur psychology in it for my taste."

Ahlberg's long square face twisted into the tight half-smile
that he used to suppress anger. "You're fucking with me again.
What is this place?"

I gestured at the old lodge, sheltered beneath hundred-foot
Douglas firs. "This is the party house. It belongs to Larry
Poole. But Detective Karras knows that."

"I don't know what you're talking about," she said. Her face
was suddenly flushed. She had spoken much too quickly, and
she knew it. "I haven't worked vice in years," she added.

I looked at her sadly. "I don't want to do this," I said.

Ahlberg was ignoring me. "What the hell did you do here?
Break in?"

"I came up here to look for Poole," I said, rehearsing my
cover story. "I thought I heard him inside. The door was unlocked, but he wasn't here."

"We're still looking for him. If you know where he is you'd
better give him up, now."

I ignored Ahlberg. "Poole is at the center of this," I began.
"He cultivates his important customers, giving them women,
having parties up here"—I gestured at the lodge—"where they
can let their hair down, get drunk, and get laid. He collected
Leach, Sean Tyner, and Martin Bolger. They recruited young
women out of the juvenile court and the prostitution prevention

program to work for Poole, a little network always making sure that Poole had fresh talent and plenty of warning if the cops were coming."

I paused, then added, "I've got a witness to this. You should know that. Come on out, Terry."

Lasker emerged on the deck, carrying a Styrofoam coffee cup. He fished a cigarette out of his pocket and lit it, saying nothing.

"What do you need him for?" Ahlberg demanded.

"He's insurance."

His long square face reddened with anger. "What the fuck are you talking about?"

"Listen to me, damn it. Bolger was corrupt but he wasn't stupid. He saw the pattern in the motel-room murders: the victims were his own patients, the ones he and Tyner had gotten to work for Poole. Karen Sasser said he was obsessed with the murders, deeply depressed for weeks before his death. He knew who was killing them."

I stopped and looked at Karras. There was no expression on her face but her hands were moving, the same oddly compulsive wringing and pulling at her hands I had seen before.

"Poole wasn't sure who was killing them but he was afraid the investigation would break up his business. A prostitute who worked for Poole told him that she went to the China Tapestry to work a fantasy scene with Klimka. Tyner was supposed to be the john. Poole told Leach to get rid of her. Leach didn't have the stomach to kill her. He told her to get the hell out, but the girl didn't have the money to go. She called her friends and her sister in a panic. One of them was a junkie and a snitch for a detective with the county IIU. The snitch told IIU what Leach had done. She OD'd a few weeks later. By then Polhaus had been charged. IIU kept it quiet, destroyed that part of their file, to make sure the case against Polhaus wasn't damaged."

I stopped. The world seemed oddly still. The sky was like a pearl, the forest bursting with the new green of the spring. The only sound my own ragged breathing.

Ahlberg began to look queasy, unsure of himself. "Leach was the one who checked out the escort services," he said.

"Right. And he destroyed Parker's and Klimka's john books. He couldn't find Beasely's. We did. It led us to Tyner."

"Two days ago you said you weren't sure Tyner killed them," Karras said. Her voice was skeptical, cool, distant. I wondered how much longer she could keep the mask in place.

"I don't think he did."

"Then that leaves Poole," she said firmly.

"Not quite, Detective." I looked at her for a long time. She was watching me carefully now. I dragged the wet morning air into my lungs and looked out at the lake. Rain began to fall, dotting the placid water. Fog shrouded the far shore. I felt infinitely weary. I had already destroyed one life trying to get at the truth. Now I would add two more.

"There was another person involved. The red-haired woman who was with Melody Beasely at the King's Inn, who ran away from the China Tapestry. The woman Sean Tyner said they couldn't find."

I paused. "What do you say, Detective? Do you want to take it from there?"

She ignored me, a slight, scornful smile on her lips. Her eyes had taken on the same disassociative glaze that I had seen on the videotape.

"Her hands," Terry Lasker said urgently. "Look at her hands."

Karras had raked her nails into her own skin, suddenly bright with blood. She stared at her own hands, transfixed. Ahlberg stood rock-still, shocked at Karras's self-mutilation. The anger had gone out of him. He was starting to understand.

"Think of a woman, Vince, a cop. A good cop, hard-nosed, smart, ambitious, sensitive. She takes on the dirty jobs that women cops get in vice, working decoy, working with victims. She gets dumped out of her marriage in Portland, badly hurt, suppressing a volcanic anger. She leaves that life behind and gets a job on the SPD, ready to make a new start. But they assign her to juvenile and vice, deep in the same garbage. Half the time the kids she helps turn on her. She feels the sting of their ingratitude. It keeps the anger fresh.

"You were hurting in ways you couldn't control. You cracked and you nightsticked a john and a fourteen-year-old girl. You needed help and you got it. From Martin Bolger." I handed Ahlberg the insurance company's patient list. He took it hesitantly, not wanting to read it. "Her insurance records show that Martin Bolger was her therapist since October 1988. He treated her; she grew dependent on him, fell in love with him. It's common between patient and therapist. But Karras couldn't stop being a cop. She hears that kids who have been through the prostitution program were working for Lawrence Poole. Her suspicions start to grow. She went undercover, went to work for Lawrence Poole, turned herself into a prostitute to find out how Poole was recruiting them. And finds Bolger and Tyner and Leach."

Karras's eyes suddenly filled with aching desolation. "Rage piled on rage," I said softly, only to her. "I know that anger, Nancy. I felt it sweep through me again when I learned what Bolger did. The betrayal, not just of you, but of everything he was, every ethical and moral rule that the healing professions have."

I swallowed, hard. "Here's where I have to guess, Nancy. I think you turned that anger inside, plunged it into yourself like a knife. You got it wrong, got it twisted, saw yourself as somehow inferior to the women Bolger had sex with. You thought you were too old, too plain, too rigid, not sexual enough—whatever doubts you had about yourself became knife-edge accusations. The rage shifted away from Bolger to these kids you saw as whores, seducers. That's when you started to kill them."

It seemed like a long time before Ahlberg broke the silence. "Did she ... what about Bolger?" he rasped. He had gone from anger to doubt to rising anguish. His life's work was in the balance. I wondered, briefly, sadly, if he had loved her.

"Bolger tracked her," I replied. "He knew he had to stop the killings. He left Karras a suicide note. But not a note on paper. He hanged himself in a motel, mimicking her method of execution. He was telling her that he was the final victim. And that she must stop."

I took a deep breath, nearly finished now, filled with an anguish I would never admit. "You got the message, Nancy. You took five days personal leave after Bolger killed himself. I can only imagine the kind of horror you went through trying to pull yourself back together."

The rain began to fall harder now. Karras brushed at her wet hair with her hands, smearing blood across her face.

"When you found out Liz Kleinfeldt was checking on Bolger's patients you faked a simple robbery/shooting. But you picked a place I would never believe. You didn't know that Liz had been raped in a parking garage. She would never go into one alone. But she would go into one to meet a cop who offered her information—especially if the cop was a woman."

I turned to Ahlberg and handed him a cassette. "This is a videotape of Karras having sex here, with Lawrence Poole. She had to in order to get hired. It's dated about three months before the murders started. Karras is wearing the same red wig she used when she killed Melody Beasely and Sharee Klimka."

I saw pain twist Ahlberg's face. His ordered world was broken and he did not know what to do, perhaps for the first time in years. He turned to Karras, pleading wordlessly, searching for something that would make what I had said wrong, a joke, a ghastly error. She had nothing for him. Her eyes found his and started to fill with tears, then her whole face went slack, as empty as a stroke victim's. She turned and walked away, up the hill toward the car. Ahlberg stayed where he was. We heard the sound of the car starting, then the grinding of tires on gravel, fading as she drove away.

"For God's sake," I said, with quiet urgency, "get to a phone. She has to be found, stopped. She's insane, some kind of massive disassociative disorder. If she pulls the pieces back together she may kill herself."

"I wonder," he said, his voice anguished, "if that isn't what she wants. And needs."

APRIL

CHAPTER 38

The windows were open but a fire burned on the stone hearth, a perverse combination that drove the musty winter smells of damp and mold and absence from my house. The early-April day was cold but clear, with the edgy brightness of false spring.

I was building the loft stairs by hand. The geometry of staircases is complex and I worked slowly, measuring each cut twice before sawing, savoring the clean smell of sawed wood. There was comfort in the work. A three-foot tread, properly measured, is three feet. Nothing more, nothing less.

I switched off the table saw after cutting a tread and pushed the protective work glasses up on my forehead to wipe away a bead of sweat. When I turned to look for my bandanna I saw Vincent Ahlberg standing in the center of the open living room. He was looking at the half-finished house like a foreman, nodding as he checked the work.

I took off the glasses and sighed. "I don't remember the knock at the door," I said tightly.

"You didn't hear it over the saw motor," he replied. "Look, I know you don't want to see me. I got things to say. Can I get a cup of coffee?"

I went into the kitchen to get him some coffee. I returned with the blue-enameled pot, a bottle of whiskey, and a mug. I put them on the raised stone hearth of the fireplace. "Fix your own," I said. I got my own coffee cup off the temporary workbench in the back of the room and waited.

He poured coffee for himself but ignored the whiskey. "Too early," he explained. He paced the room.

"What's this about, Vince? Any talking we do is going to be in court. The supreme court stayed Polhaus's execution last week. His restraint petition gets heard in June. We're going to be pointing at your detective as the killer."

"I know that," he said. He hesitated, having more trouble finding words than I had ever seen in him before. "I want you to know we questioned her," he finally said. "About Liz Kleinfeldt. Served a search warrant for her apartment, too. I don't know yet if we can make a case. We haven't come up with any physical evidence that places her in Kleinfeldt's car."

"Don't bullshit me," I said angrily. "You're not going to make a case. To do that you'd have to accept that she committed the motel-room murders. Merritt's going to fight like hell to keep Polhaus's conviction from being overturned. He'll be goddamned if he's going to admit that he got an innocent man sentenced to death. Not with the primary election coming up." I poured more coffee for myself. "Where is Karras now? I'll bet she's not even been suspended."

"She's on temporary disability leave. Hospitalized. Overwork and exhaustion. The stress of the unfounded accusations you've made. So we've been told."

"Really," I said sarcastically. "I smell a defense lawyer somewhere in the woodwork. A good one."

He nodded, not happily. "She's got Sam Kemper."

"Smart choice. But it doesn't matter. Even if Merritt put her on trial, no jury would ever convict her. You've figured out what she was doing, haven't you? She was setting up Sean Tyner as the murderer, making it look like a serial killing. It would have worked if Leach hadn't gotten to the evidence first. Kemper can create a reasonable doubt by pointing the finger at Polhaus, or at Tyner's empty chair."

I had nothing more to say. Ahlberg fidgeted with his cup, his big shoulders slumped. He finally said, "They got Poole in California. Leach and his lawyer are doing some plea bargaining. Leach will take down Poole for promoting prostitution and racketeering when he goes. That kid you located, Andrea Jacoby, has quite a story to tell about Poole. He'll do some serious time."

"Swell. Always glad to help the county clean up its mess. Anything else going on?"

"Yeah," he said, "there is. I quit."

My face fell. Ahlberg had run Seattle Homicide for fifteen years. He was, if not brilliant, a skilled craftsman, on balance the finest cop on the SPD. Ahlberg was a complex and secretive man. I couldn't claim to understand him. He had gone through three marriages. He'd never had children. His friends were the people who worked for him, and he held them at a safe distance. The only thing I could be sure of was that he was, far more than most people, the sum of the work that he did.

"Why?" I asked, already knowing the answer.

"I had to," he said slowly. "I thought about it for a couple of days, worked through the whole case, from the beginning. It fits. She committed four murders under my command."

I sat down on the stone hearth. "Vince, I'm not going to say anything about your relationship with her. I don't see what you could have done differently. I don't blame you for this. I blame myself. I put pressure on Karras without knowing it, to the point that she killed Liz when she thought we were focusing on Bolger's patients. I should have seen it coming, made Liz take precautions. I should have done something. Anything."

I dumped my coffee and poured an inch of whiskey into my cup. I knocked it back and felt it burn my throat.

Ahlberg shook his head. "You couldn't have stopped it," he said slowly. "She would have taken you out next, set Leach up for it maybe." He finished his coffee, put the cup on the hearth, and turned to go. I reached out an arm and stopped him.

"Tell me one thing. Were you in love with her?"

He paused, his back still turned, struggling again for words. "Maybe," he said thickly, forcing the word out. "You're getting old enough now, you know how it is. You start to think about how the rest of your life is going to be. You find someone who knows what you do, understands it. I wasn't making anything up when I said she was a good cop. I respected her. She seemed . . ." His voice failed him.

"I talked to her a lot," I mused. "I'd like to think she was trying to warn me back from the place where she had gone."

I got up and tossed another log on the fire. "When it gets to where you can't stand it anymore," I said, facing the flames, "think of the way she was. The good she did. Before any of this happened."

Ahlberg didn't move. His face was carved in stone. In time, I hoped, he would find his own understanding.

"So what are you going to do?" I asked. Ahlberg had family money and had made more over the years, speculating in real

estate. He could go anywhere he chose, do anything he
wanted. If there was any place, or anything, left for him.

His face was grim. "I'm going to help you prove that she
committed these murders."

I slept that night wrapped in warm down against the raw
night air, sleep so deep that my dreams dissolved the line between memory and reality. I dreamed of Liz, of course, in the
early part of our time together. We had gone to Mexico when
Hugh Prokop's case was finally over. I spent a good deal of
time there walking the beach, trying to piece together the
things I could have done that might have saved him, with little
success.

"Did you get everything straightened out?" Liz had asked
one morning as I returned from my walk.

"Not completely," I had told her. "I don't think I ever will."

"Life's like that," Liz had said. "Full of loose ends, unhappy
endings, unfinished business. It's something you are going to
have to learn to accept."

JUNE

CHAPTER 39

The Washington Supreme Court sits at the Temple of Justice in Olympia, a turn-of-the-century beaux arts structure built of fine gray limestone, a color as soft as light on a pearl. The court's nine men and women are the state's final interpreters of law and, hopefully, justice. On the warm June Tuesday when Robert Polhaus's petition was to be heard, I waited in the hallway on the first floor, just outside the courtroom, pacing nervously. Jack Elgot, Gretel Anderson, and Wayne Porras waited in the corridor with me.

"Are you ready?" I asked Elgot. For the past month we had worked together uneasily to prepare the briefs and oral argument, each doing several mock presentations to be critiqued by the other, sharpening the arguments for the oldest, and rarest, ground for reversal of a criminal conviction: the actual innocence of the accused.

"I'm not going to argue this case," Elgot replied softly, the tone of his Southern drawl polite but still distant. "You are."

"I can't. I'm a witness. I've already filed a notice of withdrawal."

"Which I pulled back. I have a two-minute oral motion on that point. You will have to withdraw once the court remands for a new trial and you'll be called to testify. But not here, not today. This is your case. You should argue it."

I stared at him. "I truly do not understand. I thought you hated my guts."

He smiled, the irony of the situation plain on his face. "You and I aren't going to be friends, that's for sure. But this is Liz's day, and yours. Give me credit for that much. I started out as a public defender in Mobile, Alabama, twenty-eight years ago. I understand the importance of what you did. And what Elizabeth did. That's as much of an apology as you're going to get."

He stuck out his hand and I shook it. "I'm looking forward to your getting back into practice," he added.

"I don't think I'll go back."

"You will," he replied. "Liz said you would. She knew you pretty well. Let me know when you're ready. We'll send you some cases." The slight feral smile reappeared. "All the hopeless ones." He checked his watch. "We'll be called in about fifteen minutes now."

There were footsteps at the other end of the marble corridor. Two corrections deputies emerged from the elevators. Robert Polhaus walked between them, his hands manacled, his legs chained.

"I need to talk to Polhaus," I said urgently. "Let's find an empty office, but I need to see him. Alone."

Elgot looked at me for a moment, his eyes sharp and questioning, then silently led the way to the guards, who released Polhaus to us, and to an empty room in the clerk's office. He waited until we were seated, side by side, in front of a bare, unused desk. Then he pulled the door shut behind him.

Polhaus waited. He had been a convict for so many years that he waited until he was spoken to.

"Bobby," I said, "I don't know how much you know of what has happened."

"You got a cigarette?" he demanded.

I lit a cigarette and gave it to him, along with the rest of the pack. He smoked with both hands chained together.

"You know what we're going to argue here," I said.

"Uh-huh. That the cop killed Jazz and Sharee and the other woman."

"That's right," I replied. "That's the way we think it happened. We're going to try to get you a new trial."

I was taking it slowly, trying to make him understand. He thought I was patronizing me. "So what do you want from me?" he asked, irritated.

I took a deep breath, trying to control my temper. "A little understanding. About Elizabeth Kleinfeldt. She didn't have to do this for you, you know. She didn't have to take your case, or follow up on her doubts, or do any of this. If she had done what any other lawyer would have done, she would be alive today."

His face was a mask. "It was her job."

"No, it wasn't, Bobby. Not to go all that distance for you."

"Hey, when I'm out, we'll get her a medal. Okay?" He stood up and dropped his cigarette on the vinyl floor and stamped it out. "Don't we get into court soon?" he asked. There was a whining edge to his voice.

I shoved him back into his chair. "Listen to me, you little shit," I told him. "I want you to understand something, really understand it. Elizabeth Kleinfeldt was the best lawyer you could ever hope to have. She took your case because she believed in a principle. That everyone, no matter what their crime is, has a right to a lawyer and a full, complete defense. She believed in it so much that she helped you, even though she knew your record. What you did, to those women you beat up, those women you raped, those women you extorted sex from, made her sick. She hated you. But she put her beliefs above her feelings. And it got her killed."

He looked away trying to hide a scornful grin. I was boring him. He had no life outside himself.

"I'm not as good a lawyer as she was, Bobby. I cannot separate what I feel from what I do." I took a deep breath. "I think you're going back out. They'll give you a new trial and you'll be acquitted. That scares me, Bobby, because I don't understand you. I don't think anyone knows what makes people like you derive pleasure from inflicting pain. But when you're on the street, if you ever assault, ever rape, ever hurt another woman, I'll be there. I'll do everything I can to get you committed as a sexual psychopath. You'll be locked in a hospital room that looks every bit like a prison cell. Every time you come up for release I'll be there. And you won't get out until you are very old. Do you understand that?"

He was silent. His eyes had the same flat emptiness I had first seen in the Walla Walla interrogation room. Polhaus had learned nothing. Perhaps he never would.

There was a knock at the door. I heard Jack Elgot saying, "Riordan, it's time."

I turned back to Polhaus, filled with disgust. I stood up and put a hand around his thick neck, under his chin, raising his head to look at me. He tried to shake me off, but I gripped his throat so hard that he was forced to look at me. "I may also break your head with a baseball bat. Do you understand that? Now get up."

I dragged Polhaus to his feet. I took him by the arm and guided him out of the office and handed him back to the guards, chagrined by the threat made in anger. But I meant every word.

I waited at counsel table in the restored supreme court chamber, with its fine oak-paneled walls and rich green carpeting, an elegant, imposing place. There was an expectant hum from the press and spectators in the back pews.

The court took the bench. Jack Elgot made a brief argument that I should be temporarily excused from the ethical rules and allowed to present oral argument in favor of the petitioner, Robert Polhaus, for a new trial.

The court granted the motion. I stepped to the podium without notes, the words clear and precise in my mind.

"May it please the court," I began.